THE ARCHERS

VICTORY AT AMBRIDGE

Also by Catherine Miller

The Archers: Ambridge at War
The Archers: Home Fires at Ambridge

THE ARCHERS

VICTORY AT AMBRIDGE

Catherine Miller

SIMON & SCHUSTER

London · New York · Sydney · Toronto · New Delhi

First published in Great Britain by Simon & Schuster UK Ltd, 2024

1 3 5 7 9 10 8 6 4 2

Simon & Schuster UK Ltd
1st Floor
222 Gray's Inn Road
London WC1X 8HB

Simon & Schuster: Celebrating 100 Years of Publishing in 2024

www.simonandschuster.co.uk
www.simonandschuster.com.au
www.simonandschuster.co.in

Simon & Schuster Australia, Sydney
Simon & Schuster India, New Delhi

A CIP catalogue record for this book
is available from the British Library

Hardback ISBN: 978-1-4711-9555-6
eBook ISBN: 978-1-4711-9556-3
Audio ISBN: 978-1-3985-1280-1

Typeset in Palatino by M Rules
Printed and Bound in the UK using 100% Renewable
Electricity at CPI Group (UK) Ltd

This book is for
Winifred Davis
1916–2013
With love

Brookfield

Doris Archer	*Farming matriarch*
Dan Archer	*Her husband*
Christine Archer	*Their young daughter*
Phil Archer	*Their young son*
Jack Archer	*Their oldest, happy-go-lucky and at war*
Peggy Archer	*His new wife*
Wanda Lafromboise	*Land Girl*

Lower Loxley

Alec Pargetter	*Blue-blood*
Pamela Pargetter	*His haughty wife*
Gerald Pargetter	*Their well-meaning son*
Squadron Leader Reginald 'Dodgy' Dodge	*A convalescing old buffer*
Flying Officer 'Cad' Cadwallader	*A convalescing rotter*
Hildegard	*Impertinent Ladies' Maid*

The Store

Frank Brown	*Genial shopkeeper*

The Bull

Jim Little	*Taciturn landlord*
Ruby Bonnet	*Enigmatic refugee*
Michele and Evie	*Her young daughters*

Turnpike

Agnes Kaye	*Village gossip*
Denholm Kaye	*Her sleepy husband*

Holmleigh

Dr Morgan Seed	*Beloved village GP*
Nance Morgan	*His capable wife*
Tudor Morgan	*Their baby son*
Magsy Furneaux	*Meddling sister of Morgan's first wife*

The Cherries

Emmeline 'Mrs E' Endicott	*Genteel and thrice widowed*

Broom Corner

Stan Horrobin	*Lout*
Connie Horrobin	*His beleagured wife*
Vic	*Their brutish son*
Bert and Maisie	*Their younger children*

Woodbine Cottage

Grayson Lemmon	*Visiting historian*

Honeysuckle Cottage

Group Captain Max Gilpin	*Newcomer and war hero*

Grange Farm

Joe Grundy	*Exempted from military service*
Susan Grundy	*His lively wife*

The Vicarage

Rev. Henry Bissett	*Devout and aloof*
Frances Bissett	*His sanctimonious wife*

Noon Cottage

Cliff Horrobin	*Soft-spoken schoolteacher*
Lorna Horrobin	*Mild-mannered and bright librarian*

No 9 Platoon, 15th Battalion of the Borsetshire Home Guard

Walter Gabriel	*Friend to all, father to young Nelson*
Whitey White	*Postman*
Arthur Sweet	*Older gentleman*
Mick Lister	*Another older gentleman*
Chas Westenra	*Lens grinder*

P.C. Jenkins	*Gung-ho local police constable*
Valerie Micklewood	*Scarlet woman*

THE ARCHERS

VICTORY AT AMBRIDGE

SUMMER

1944

She had pagan eyes,
full of nocturnal mysteries.

THOMAS HARDY
Return of the Native

June

He walked through the small hours, out of May and into June.

Arriving just as the mauves of night lifted, he passed a square Norman church and crossed a stone bridge.

So this is the village, he thought, doubting the straggly thoroughfare deserved the title. Ambridge was small. A store, still shuttered. A chorus line of cottages, each stubbornly individual. A substantial inn. The buildings slumbered, but stirred as he passed, like eyelids trembling ahead of the dawn.

Group Captain Max Gilpin was looking for Honeysuckle Cottage, and it seemed that he would find it on the far side of the triangular Green that sat like a grassy heart in the centre of the village.

Strictly speaking, he was no longer a group captain; some other chap had already taken his desk at Bentley Priory, to drink unspeakable RAF tea, and trace a finger along the duck-egg blue sky maps. Locked inside Max was information about the next few days that he would share with nobody. Secret plans, at last coming good, which would transform the war.

The fighting must trundle on without Max; he was damaged goods.

Tall, slender, he was shot through with steel, but the long journey had tested him. He spotted Honeysuckle Cottage across the Green. The sky grew pinkish, and promised another glorious day.

The thought gave him no needle-prick of joy; one day was much like another since . . . Max wouldn't name it, even now.

'Get a move on, slowcoach!' The voice in his ear was his wife's and she was right, as usual. He was dawdling.

The day moved into gear, sun striking stone with a flourish. The sudden noise behind him was loud and wrong, reminding him of the capital city he had left behind.

Max wheeled to see a riderless horse. Its eyes rolled and its iron hooves smacked the hard ground as it hurtled towards Max like a steam train.

He dropped his case. Stepped in its path. Steel, you see. He waved his right arm.

'Stop him!' A valkyrie raced out of the sun. It felt like the moment when the light hits the stained glass and the choir bursts into song.

The shop spat out a shopkeeper. 'Watch yourself, sir!' he called.

'Whoa.' Max snatched the rein with his right arm. His only arm. He spun as the horse resisted. He stood firm. The horse halted and glowered, its nostrils flaring.

The valkyrie – a land girl, he realised, nothing supernatural about her – caught up. 'He always throws me! Nothing personal, must be *awful* being a horse, people jumping on you. Thanks ever so, whoever you are!'

She leapt onto the chestnut's bare back, grabbed its mane, and was off at a gallop. They jumped over the tub of begonias outside The Bull as if it was Beecher's Brook.

The moment shimmers.

Ambridge turns in its sleep, accepts the inevitable: it must get up.

Faces are splashed, yawns are quelled (if you are polite) or blast like foghorns (if you are Walter Gabriel). Beds creak. Cats curl round legs. Fat spits in pans.

Another day in Borsetshire, cocooned by velvet hills. But even the hills can't keep out war. We know, but the Ambridgians do not, that they are over the worst. They are hostages to time, so can see only the road behind them. That road is littered with lost loved ones, and shattered notions about how life should be.

As they do up shirt studs and push toes into boots, they can't know what is just around the corner. Momentous events that will bring good news and terrible news, both abroad and right under their noses.

Widower, father, grandfather and shopkeeper – Frank Brown was all of these. That morning he whistled as he dismantled the shutters and laid out knobbly Maris Pipers.

For once, Frank had one up on his lady customers. He was possessed of a priceless artefact – *gossip that nobody else had heard.*

He whistled smugly as Doris Archer browsed the custard powder, and Agnes Kaye eyed his onions. Only when Mrs Endicott came in, smelling of Parma Violets and wearing the layers of poplin and linen that were fashionable in her youth, did he unleash it.

'Something you don't often see,' he began, conversationally. *'A runaway horse.'*

'Runaway horse?' Agnes, five foot nothing of bad temper held together by hairpins, asked hopefully, 'Anyone hurt?'

'No. The creature was caught by ...' Frank was doing splendidly; the ladies were rapt. 'A *stranger*.'

'Him what rented Honeysuckle, probably,' said Agnes, and they all looked away.

Crestfallen, Frank embroidered his story. Beast and man grappled! The horse almost threw Brookfield's land girl, Wanda! He had to keep breaking off to open the till, or stamp a ration book.

'You're rushed off your feet.' Doris was sympathetic, waiting in line with her string bag.

'He keeps sacking his assistants.' Agnes was not sympathetic. 'Frank's too fussy.'

Old Mrs Endicott was benign, as ever. 'He has *standards*.'

Frank licked the end of a pencil stub. 'They either nick stuff or they're gormless.'

'Who's this fellow at Honeysuckle, then?' Doris nudged Agnes.

'Well ...' Agnes knew everything about everybody. 'Decorated hero, so I've heard. Lost his wife in the Blitz.'

Mrs Endicott tutted. 'That Hitler . . .'

'Booted out of the RAF. Trouble with his *nerves.*' Agnes waited for the kind clucking to subside, and lobbed her last titbit. 'Lost an arm in France.'

There was a respectful silence for the arm. So many men came home different, lacking.

One of them rushed in now, asking for Spam. Grayson Lemmon was easy to love, with his wire-rimmed glasses and the lop-sided gait of the one-legged. He took a tin and cradled it like a baby. 'Ah, Spam. Food of the gods.'

Silently, Doris thanked heaven for Brookfield's munificence. The Archer family farm gave so much, and saved them from Spam.

Such a pet was Grayson that the ladies allowed him to 'push in', usually a hanging offence.

'I do hope you're all coming along to my lecture in the village hall,' he said, without guile, like a child who expects to be indulged.

'Well . . .' said Doris, once again astounded by men's ignorance of just how much women had to *do.*

'Of course we are,' beamed Mrs Endicott, sentencing everyone present to attend.

'Excellent.' Grayson pushed a pile of coins across the counter. 'My research in Ambridge is very important to the British Museum, and I want the whole village to feel involved.'

'Ooh,' said Mrs Endicott. 'The *British Museum.*'

'You've given me too much, son.' Anyone under thirty was 'son' to Frank. He held out a tuppence.

'That's for yesterday's eggs,' said Grayson. 'I underpaid and it's been on my conscience ever since.'

'Heartwarming to see such honesty.' Frank glared at Agnes, who was implicated in a missing Oxo Cube.

It was standing room only in the darkened church hall, testament to Grayson's popularity. The village was flattered, and a little puzzled, that a London academic should consider Ambridge worthy of study.

Manning the slide projector at the back of the hall, Wanda straightened up as Grayson stomped onto the low stage, his tin leg unnaturally straight.

He coughed, shuffled papers on a lectern last seen in an am-dram Gilbert and Sullivan, and began.

'The British Museum have funded me to come here and study a woman well known to you all, but obscure to the rest of the world. A woman of wisdom and talent, foresight and fortitude.'

'That's you, love,' said Dan Archer to his Doris, who shushed him.

Still puzzled, his audience raised their collective eyebrows when Grayson nodded at Wanda and the screen beside him lit up with the words 'Mother Molly'.

Some tittering, and a few subdued tuts, sounded before Walter Gabriel stood up, in his workaday corduroy, and bellowed, 'You're bonkers, me old pal. Mother Molly's an old wives' tale, a humpbacked hag with a warty nose! What you interested in her for?'

'She's very much more than that, I assure you.' Grayson seemed hurt.

Beside Doris, her teenaged daughter Christine asked, 'Mum, is that the same Mother Molly you used to say would nip my toes if I didn't go straight to bed?'

'That's her,' whispered Doris. 'My old mum told me she spirited away naughty children who wouldn't finish their greens.' She put up her hand, and said, 'Mother Molly didn't really exist, though! How can you study her?'

Another nod, and the screen showed them an oil painting of a woman in what Christine would call olden days clothes. 'Mother Molly was very real indeed, Doris. Molly Hunstanton was a herbalist and a healer and, like me, a scholar, except she was interested in the medicinal properties of nature.'

'She was a witch!' shouted someone.

Mrs Endicott crossed herself, and Christine shrank in her seat.

Grayson smiled. 'It was all too easy to be accused of witchcraft in the seventeenth century. Mother Molly cured maladies with the herbal concoctions she brewed in her dark kitchen, but soon rumours swirled that she cast spells and had visions. But why would her neighbours call her a witch?'

''Cos she was a witch,' said Walter, arms crossed, with confident logic.

'Or,' said Grayson, warming to his theme, 'because she was daring, progressive and intelligent at a time when impoverished women were expected to know their place.'

'She stole children,' said Walter, as his audience shuddered. 'And ate 'em.'

'That,' said Grayson, 'seems unlikely'.

The next slide showed an old image of a grand house they all knew.

'Lower Loxley, home of the Pargetter family for over two hundred years. When Mother Molly's community grew restless, and murmured about hounding her out – or worse – Edward Pargetter offered her sanctuary in the grounds of Lower Loxley. It was fashionable, believe it or not, for the gentry to invite picturesque hermits to live on their land. In Mother Molly's case, the Pargetters built her a quaint stone grotto to shelter in.'

The next slide, slightly wonky – Wanda was chatting up an RAF officer – showed a stone building, conical, like an igloo.

'Old Molly wasn't picturesque.' Doris was sure of her facts. 'She was scary-looking.'

Mrs Endicott stood up. Unused to raising her voice in public, she quavered as she said, 'Did she not claim to see the future? We're all flattered that you should be interested in Ambridge, but should you stir up such darkness, Grayson, dear?'

Grayson leaned on the lecturn. 'Please don't worry, Mrs E. Nobody can truly prophesy the future. No doubt Mother Molly claimed such a gift in order to frighten her neighbours and stop them harassing her. I'm a professor of history not black magic!'

They were ill-chosen words. The hint of satanic sorcery made his audience shuffle in their seats.

Troubled, Grayson said, 'My assignment here is to put

Mother Molly on the historical map, to tell the world about one of your daughters. The British Museum will add anything I uncover to their permanent collection. I aim to excavate the foundations of her grotto and hopefully some of these infamous prophesies will turn up too.'

His audience were divided at this – some found it thrilling; more found it unsettling.

'You already know about the prophecy that's kept under glass at Lower Loxley.' Grayson pointed to the slide of a slip of rough paper covered with sprawling handwriting. He read it out. *'Your bewhiskered ally lies without breath, without spark, and melancholy seizes the noble house.* That was presumed to refer to the Pargetters – *your noble house* – and their dog, or *bewhiskered ally.*'

There were mutterings. The villagers all knew their lore; that prediction came true: the dog died.

'Mother Molly's so-called powers don't stand up to scrutiny, dear friends. All pet owners know that dogs, sadly, are outlived by their masters. Now, if the prophecy was *dated,* and the doggie died on that day, it'd be a different matter.'

'So she's a con artist?' asked Walter.

'No, no . . .' Grayson floundered. 'She was a woman of her time and of *our* time.' He waved his hands at the spluttering. 'Mother Molly was a scientist, a medic, a truly learned individual. But she was also living in peril, using her wits to protect herself, and trying to anticipate a future where things would be different. Rather like . . .' Grayson shrugged. 'Us?'

As the assembly broke up and scattered into the warm night, Agnes said huffily, 'I for one don't believe in such nonsense, but all the same . . .'

Doris nodded. 'Leave those prophecies in the ground, say I. The future's not our business. It's in God's hands.'

'Daresay Grayson won't find a thing,' said Dan. 'I tell you, if he grew up hearing stories of the old girl with her hunchback and her wicked ways, he wouldn't be so keen to get digging.'

The current crop of Pargetters at Lower Loxley had no picturesque hermit in the grounds. They had, instead, convalescent RAF officers billetted in every bedroom.

Pamela Pargetter regarded herself in her boudoir looking glass. She would join the chaps for the sacred cocktail hour, but before that she must do something with her hair.

Or, rather, her new lady's maid must. Hildegard looked the part in her black frock and white headpiece, as she plied a comb through Pamela's glossy cap of dark hair.

On Pamela's lap sat a Pekinese, regarding its own extravagant hairdo in the mirror.

The door banged back on its hinges, and gave them Gerald. He slammed down a salver – 'Post, Mater!' – and launched himself at a chaise longue. He was in khaki; as tradition demanded, he had joined his father's regiment.

'It's not your place to bring me the post, Gerald.' Pamela was brisk. 'Let the staff do their jobs.'

Gerald lolled on eau-de-nil satin. He had lolled a great deal as a child, and Pamela had hoped that joining the army would put an end to his lolling, but apparently not.

'When do you return to barracks, darling?'

'Getting rid of me, Ma?' Gerald was dog-like. Lumpily made. Grey eyes that were sad if you looked close enough. 'I'm expected back in Bridlington on the eighth.'

'I have a job for you on your way there.' Pamela searched her reflection with an unsparing gaze. She checked in on her beauty, found it tolerable. Her nose, her nails, her manner – all were sharp.

Gerald cowered. A job from his mother never brought anything good.

'You can represent the family at a funeral in Wilsthorpe, on the seventh. Distant cousin of your father's.'

Gerald scowled.

'It'll be fun, darling. Well, maybe not *fun*. I don't ask much of you, and the *strings* I had to pull for the petrol. Take darling Dodgy for company.'

They both knew that Squadron Leader Reginald Dodge's function would be to keep Gerald out of trouble.

Comb in mid-air, Hildegard found her mistress's eye in the glass. Her accent was local, her figure outrageous. 'Is Madam sure she wants her fringe pinned back? In't it a little young for Madam?'

'Crikey!' spluttered Gerald. 'Duck! Incoming!'

Pamela didn't speak for a moment. 'Hildegard, do remember to keep personal remarks to yourself. I know you're new to this position, and you're coming along nicely, but such comments are unwelcome.'

Gerald's eyebrows raised at such restraint.

Hildegard pouted.

That was not welcome either, but Pamela had noticed the blue envelope on the salver and wanted to be alone. 'I'll finish, Hildegard, thank you. And Gerald – out.'

Sloping out – he really did slope – Gerald asked the dog on his mother's lap, 'How come you're allowed to loaf about all day, Minko, but I have to be *useful*?'

A small sound erupted from the dog's fluffy back end.

'Oh *Minko*!' Pamela wrinkled her nose and deposited the creature on the rug. Withstanding the sudden perfume, she tore open the letter.

The chatelaine of Lower Loxley scanned, spiked and discarded a great deal of post; the blue aerogrammes from her husband were lingered over. Pamela read with one eye on the door, as if such sentimentality was a vice.

War had wrought changes in her marriage, a union of ancient genes and new money. Pamela's people were in trade; not a stick of inherited furniture stood in her father's Mayfair mansion. Marrying Alec Pargetter had catapulted her into society, and paid for indoor plumbing at Lower Loxley.

She felt closer to the man in the letters than the flesh and blood version; she imagined him drifting through the gore and debris of warfare, far from waxed parquet and the ticking clock on the landing. She heard his hesitant drawl in the handwriting.

Another long letter from you today. I wonder if you know how much they mean? How they provide a pinprick of light for me to wade towards? Hearing news of Ambridge is like sinking into a warm bath — and baths here are few and far between, I can tell you.

'Even so,' said Pamela to herself, 'I'd bet good money that moustache of yours is groomed and perfect.'

Exhilarating times here.

Pamela missed when life was dull and un-exhilarating; the war was one long pivotal moment.

Bothered by my stomach.

Familiar with her husband's stomach, Pamela knew this meant he was anxious. Suddenly, like a twin in a Gothic tale, so was Pamela. She put a hand to her throat, where it touched the cool hardness of Pargetter diamonds.

When things went so wrong between us, the thought that I would die on a battlefield brought me caustic comfort. Not anymore. I intend to live, and come home to you. Cruel timing, what? Separated just as we fell into step, old girl.

Years of training had failed to educate Alec out of calling his wife 'old girl'.

Their staid marriage had withstood the fireworks of two

affairs. Pamela had not thought either of them capable of infidelity, but she had been proved wrong. He had strayed, and then she, glacial vestal virgin, had stepped down from her pedestal for a tit-for-tat liaison.

The digressions had forced them to talk, but only a little. Enough to admit they were both guilty of neglect. Bruised, Pamela and Alec surprised themselves by turning to each other after a history of turning away.

She noticed a miniscule PS.

I adore you.

Taken aback, she told Minko, 'Goodness, he adores me,' as she placed the letter with the others in an enamelled box.

The dog panted like an idling double-decker, watching with little interest as Pamela stepped into the gown required for dinner. She turned, giving herself a businesslike once-over.

I am adored, she thought, taking up a chiffon stole, and heading downstairs. Pamela's part in the war effort involved sourcing sufficient vodka to keep martinis flowing. Her irritation at having her home invaded by recuperating pilots had long faded; she catered diligently to their comfort in the hiatus before they would be thrown into the air again, like so many doomed doves.

As she greeted and air-kissed, she composed a reply to Alec in her head. She'd gripe wittily about Hildegard, and describe Grayson's fascination with Mother Molly. She knew

Alec would sardonically agree that it's terribly easy to predict a death if you don't affix a date.

Dodgy suggested a martini. 'Why not?' she said.

I am adored.

'Are them the mess tins I ordered?' Peggy asked the pimply boy lugging in a crate. Queen bee of the Warpole End Manor ATS stores, she swung her hips to the wireless as she snatched the chit he held out. 'Says here there's *two* crates.'

'All right, blimey . . .' The boy schlepped out.

Nineteen now, Peggy joined up the moment she could. Her ten shillings a week went a long way. Some to her savings, some to her mother, and the rest on fun. Dances ended after lights out, but if you palmed a girl a sixpence, they'd leave a dorm window open. Her year in the Hertfordshire barracks had made a woman of her. Independence, responsibility, pressure – Peggy Perkins took them all in her stride.

Peggy Archer, she reminded herself. The name still felt new. Trekking up and down to Ambridge from her home in London to check on her evacuee brothers had given her a distaste for the countryside – *All that green!* – but had introduced her to the Archer family, and their soldier son, Jack.

She followed the boy out to the cobbles. A light-headedness made her stop in the doorway. Peggy ignored it, the way she ignored anything she didn't like.

'There's a hop tonight, if you're in the mood.' The

boy jumped down from his truck. 'You're my type, I reckon.'

The head of stores appeared, hearty in ATS khaki. 'Hand over the mess tins and hop it,' she said. 'Peggy's an old married woman now.' As they carried in the second crate together, Peggy's boss asked after Jack. 'So romantic, him getting that sudden leave back in April. When you starting a family?'

'Give us a chance! We're being, you know, careful.' Peggy's voice wavered then. She remembered that one snatched night in the hotel. She frowned, and almost dropped the box.

'You all right?'

'Yes. Fine.'

Peggy needed to be alone. To do some very important arithmetic.

Doris Archer rinsed an enamel basin under the pump in the yard.

She ran her fingernail over a new dent in the bowl. There were dents in everything. *Including me.* Doris groaned as she straightened up, sounding just like her old dad used to when he rose from his favourite armchair.

The world turned beneath her feet. Slow, steady, predictable. Doris squinted up at the sky and felt very small. She turned to Brookfield, which at times seemed like one greedy open mouth; she felt less small. She felt necessary.

One more groan and she followed the dog inside. Glen was another hungry mouth. 'Come on, my bewhiskered ally, let's see what I can rustle up for you,' she said.

June was extravagant.

Her hedgerows burst with wild chamomile and fat hen, and gypsy roses looped through hawthorn branches. Within the iron gates of Lower Loxley, lawns behaved and sweet peas lined up like soldiers.

The dutiful sun shone on tables offering sandwiches and scones and clotted cream with dishes of gem-like jam. Gilt chairs stood about the terrace. Round tables dotted the grass. Pamela did a quick inventory. 'It'll do.' She tweaked a platter.

'Darling lady,' said the tubby gent tailing her, Minko in his arms. 'Where are the *girls*?'

'Don't panic, Dodgy, they'll be here.' Every 'gel' for miles was on a three-line whip. The RAF chaps perked up when exposed to chatty young women; Pamela's catering guaranteed a take-up on her invitations.

'May I?' Dodgy's hand hovered over the sandwiches.

'Just one.' Pamela indulged Dodgy the way she indulged her dog, and felt a similar fondness. Reliable, sweet, always *there,* his rotund shadow on the stairs, his jolly smile dependable. Surely long recuperated, Dodgy seemed to have been forgotten by the RAF; *perhaps,* she thought, *we'll keep him when the war's over.*

That fantastical eventuality had reared its head. A corner

had been turned; Ambridge gulped in the incredible news like pure oxygen. Western Allies had landed in France – D-Day, they called it. After three years of Soviet pressure on the Nazi war machine, a push was underway.

Even the most pessimistic – those who call themselves realists – felt encouraged after the long muddy slog of the past few years.

Chaps gathered and raised full glasses to Pamela, their sexless matron despite the beautiful cut of her lace day dress. They petted the black Labrador, Hero, who was a shadow of his former self. The creature pined for Alec. Pamela did her best but knew she was no substitute.

'Gerald!' Pamela's tone was sharp, as it so often was when she said her son's name.

'You let Dodgy take one.' Gerald spat crumbs. Leaden footed, he had none of his parents' elegance. 'Cheers, Hildegard!' he said as the maid proffered a tray of drinks.

'Is she . . .' Pamela stared after the retreating Hildegard. *She is! She's wearing scarlet lipstick.* If Pamela had noticed, she could be sure the chaps noticed too.

'I see you've already dragooned Max whats-his-name,' said Gerald, mouth now full of both sandwich and Pimms.

'Handsome fella, ain't he?' said Dodgy, as the guest made his way towards the terrace.

'Very.' Pamela approved of good looks, and Max was finely drawn, fair and blue-eyed, in crumpled linen, with the the kind of aloof beauty the English are good at. *Although,* she thought, regarding the weak chins and sloping shoulders around her, *the English can get it very wrong, too.* 'Max is reserved. I like that in a man. Better than a braying donkey.'

As she said this, a chap honked with laughter. Nothing is *that* funny, but Flying Officer Cadwallader – Cad to his friends – was a live wire.

'Max's old guvnor is a chum of mine,' said Dodgy. 'Good man, he told me. A solid head and a solid heart, but he began to falter. Lost weight, couldn't sleep. War asks a lot of a fellow.'

'And a lass,' suggested Pamela.

'After some persuading, Max conceded he should get back to Civvy Street.'

Gerald ambled off to introduce himself to the fresh meat, and Pamela said, 'Dodgy, you'll keep my boy out of trouble at the funeral, won't you? Get him to his regiment in Bridlington in one piece?'

'Don't worry about old Gerald. He made a hash of school, but school don't suit everybody. He's grown up a lot since then.'

'I'm not so sure. He lacks common sense.'

'So do I!' laughed Dodgy. 'And I do all right.' He kissed the dog's nose. 'Don't I, Minko?'

'Mr Gilpin!' called Pamela, and waved.

Max dutifully approached, and Cad muttered, 'Careful, old chap, you're about to be stuck like a butterfly on a pin.'

*

It's hard on the bottom to ride on handlebars.

Lorna Horrobin bounced and giggled, feeling every bump in the lane.

'Nearly there!' said Wanda, with what little puff she had left.

Not obvious friends, the girls loved each other. One bookish and born in a two-room cottage, the other cheerfully ignorant and raised in bourgeois comfort. Quiet Lorna was a trusted confidante for Wanda, and she, in turn, relied on Wanda to twirl her round until she was dizzy.

'Hurry up!' Wanda dinged the bicycle bell at a gaggle of girls, arms linked, turning into Lower Loxley's drive. 'Or we'll scoff all the scones!'

Max Gilpin put a different spin on his story. No mention of insomnia or nervous exhaustion or stepping down. 'I grew up not far from here. When a position came up at Modder and de Beer, in Borchester, it seemed like fate.'

'I know the de Beers.' Pamela knew everyone. 'And I know your people.' The Gilpins were an Ambridge institution; Max was the only son of the wealthy Dorset branch. 'Prepare to fend me off! I'll invite you to *everything*. Let me introduce you to my fliers.'

She steered Max to where a knot of pilots gathered around Hildegard. She was serving Pimms and flirting, better at the latter than the former. Hildegard winked at Gerald, who, thrilled to bits, whispered, 'Don't let the mater see you. Oh Lord, she's coming our way.'

Hildegard's scarlet lips pursed. Below stairs had the same

rigid rules as above: a lady's maid shouldn't be expected to waitress. 'We must all pitch in,' her mistress had said, but Hildegard didn't notice Pamela breaking a nail for the war effort. She set her pointed chin and offered her tray to Cad, asking, 'See anything you fancy, sir?'

'Oh *Hildy*,' he murmured, just as Pamela bore down on them, a firm grip on Max's one arm.

'I hear the 4th American Infantry are taking Montebourg,' she began. 'Some real impetus at last.'

War talk took over. Max noticed how the men condescended to Pamela, even though she was better informed than any of them. Suddenly, Pamela reminded him of his wife, who was cut from a far softer template, but had always been fascinating company.

There was no voice in his ear that day; she was allowing Max to negotiate this particular battlefield on his own.

'Invalided out, eh?' Cad slapped Max on the back. 'Cuckoo, are you?'

When Max didn't respond, Dodgy stepped in. 'Poor chap needs a rest, that's all. Been through a hell of a lot.' Dodgy was sensitive beneath the walrus moustache. 'These landings might be the beginning of the end, what?'

Cautious agreement from the men was drowned by one of them saying, 'About time we spilled some German blood! I'd like to grind every one of them into the muck.'

'They're opponents, not monsters,' said Max. His voice was deep, fluid, unhurried. 'We'd have a great deal in common were it not for Hitler.'

'Ah, look!' Pamela wheeled. 'Here come the girls!'

Max turned and saw a phalanx of frocks approach, one laughing woman in the lead. *That's her,* he thought. *The valkyrie.* The flowers seemed to turn up their scent.

'Hel-*lo*!' said Cad, and the ladies were lionised.

Lorna knew the attention wasn't for her; her new husband, Cliff Horrobin, considered her a beauty but Lorna was realistic and was happy to be the homely counterpoint to Wanda's glamour. There was something piratical about Wanda, with her brownish curls, oval face and flushed cheeks. Lorna watched Gerald fawn, and Cad make goo-goo eyes, knowing they had not a hope in hell of getting anywhere with her canny friend.

A cheer went up for another arrival. Grayson was a favourite with the men; impromptu impersonations of his lurching walk broke out. That was how the chaps showed affection.

'Hey, Max,' said Gerald. 'Meet our brainbox.'

'Grayson's a fellow reject, Gilpin!' yelled Cad.

'Gilpin?' Grayson jerked his head, intrigued. 'Anything to do with Blanche Gilpin from the village? She's an old friend of my mother. She lent me her home, Woodbine Cottage, while she's in London.'

'We're cousins, of sorts, although I call her Aunt Blanche.'

'The Gilpin sisters!' Gerald had grown up around them. 'Blanche and Jane, a right pair of old biddies.' He looked around furtively; he would never be too old to receive a clip round the ear for speaking ill of village elders. 'The Gilpins matter in Ambridge, Max, old boy.'

'Aunt Blanche is, well, um, a bit of a character.'

'Could say that!' laughed Gerald. 'Bullied her poor sister into the grave, they say.'

Grayson seemed sentimental about his benefactress. 'Blanche is seeing out the war in high style, gently pickled from noon each day in her Mayfair apartment.'

'You'd better behave yourself, Max.' Gerald poked his lapel. 'Your surname carries a lot of weight in these parts.'

'It's just a name.' Max was diffident.

Gerald rolled his eyes. 'You have much to learn about village life. You're a *Gilpin*, man. You represent the family. And you're being *watched*.'

The buffet astonished Wanda. She hadn't given much thought to food before the war; now it was an obsession; rationing will do that to a person. The hand that reached for the egg and cress was blistered, the nails short; her mother had deplored them on her last visit home. 'How does Pamela pull off this kind of spread when *everything* is in short supply?'

'She has her ways.' Lorna quoted Thomas Hardy, knowing Wanda wouldn't catch on. 'She is the stuff of which great men's mothers are made, feared at tea parties, hated in shops, and loved at crises.'

Wanda wasn't listening. She had seen her White Knight. 'C'mon, let's mingle.'

*

Slopped beer seeped through the newspaper as Bob Little leaned on The Bull's counter and read the tightly packed column inches. Pleas for ale went unheard. He licked his finger and turned a page.

Absent-mindedly folding his purple stole, the vicar of St Stephen's read the headlines in the vestry. They proved that, as the Reverend Henry Bissett constantly reminded his flock, *God is on our side*.

There were gravy stains on the Brookfield copy of the *Daily Express*. Doris leaned over her Dan's shoulder – she knew he hated that – and her heart leapt. Good news meant the possibility of their Jack coming home. War had taught Doris to be wary, though; she understood little about the big picture, but she did know that all victories were paid for in blood.

Wanda kissed Grayson's cheek and nicked his drink. He blushed, and lost his thread for a moment, before carrying on. 'You asked how I lost my leg, Max. Tunisia. Forty-three. Battle of Mareth.'

'Bad luck.' The men rarely professed anything more sympathetic than this bald phrase. 'So you came home to academia?'

'I'm attached to the British Museum.'

Lorna said, 'Grayson oversaw the relocation of the treasures to the tunnels in Aberystwyth.'

'Well, I *helped*. It's a historical figure, Mother Molly, who brings me here, to Ambridge.'

If someone was taking notice, they would have spotted

that Wanda did not look at Max throughout, and Max did not look at Wanda. None of the airmen noticed.

Lorna did.

'Strange to think Lower Loxley was the height of fashion when Edward Pargetter took in Mother Molly back in the 1700s,' said Grayson, looking up at the high windows. 'The current lady of the house kindly lets me spend half my days in the house's library, and the rest poking about the grounds. Mother Molly's grotto is out there somewhere.'

'May I help?' said Max. 'My new duties aren't taxing.'

'That's jolly decent of you.' The light of hero worship already shone in Grayson's eyes; Max inspired strong reactions despite his detached demeanour. 'Mother Molly was a seer. Load of old you-know-what, but it's fascinating to see how women of her sort got by. The legend goes that she buried prophecies in the ground, and the family has one in the house . . . Look here, why don't I show you?'

The little band broke away from the terrace and followed Grayson indoors, trooping across the cool, panelled hall, and up to the library, a room the Pargetters didn't trouble much. It was ornately panelled, with a smattering of stained glass.

Grayson tapped a display cabinet. 'In here, see, a prediction, written on parchment, and then folded up and placed in that rather bashed-about leather pouch.'

'Red ink!' said Wanda.

From the back of the room, Pamela said, 'If one believes the stories, it's mouse's blood. A clever little rodent took dictation and used his own blood to write the prophecies'.

'Ooh,' gasped a land girl. 'Read it out, Grayson!'

'Glad to.' Grayson lifted the lid off and extracted, with exaggerated care, the scrap of paper. *'Your bewhiskered ally lies without breath, without spark, and melancholy seizes the noble house.'*

'There's more.' Wanda bent nearer. 'In tiny writing.' She made out the blood-red postscript. *'All is you.'* She lifted her head. 'Odd. Doesn't seem to go with the rest of the riddle.'

'I've never noticed that.' Pamela sounded like someone trying to care when she asked Grayson what it meant.

'I'm working on it. I have a theory it's a code. One more layer of mystery. One I can't break, sadly.'

Timid as a schoolchild, Lorna ventured to say, 'I'm the librarian at Borchester Library. I could research the Pargetters and Mother Molly in the history section. If you like.'

'Gosh, that's kind.' Grayson blinked his thanks behind round glasses. 'I've had a good browse but I daresay you know the place like the back of your hand.'

A portrait gazed over their heads. 'So that's the legendary Molly?' Wanda wandered over and touched the grand gilt surround. 'It's framed like a painting of a noblewoman.' Mother Molly was stout, plainly dressed, with grave and direct eyes that held Wanda's gaze through the centuries. Surrounded by greenery, she wielded a dripping pen. 'She doesn't look dangerous.'

'Admit it, Grayson,' said Cad. 'You believe the prophecies.'

'I'm a historian.' Grayson seemed amused by the accusation. 'I'm interested in her life, her impact on society.'

'Yet you empathise with Mother Molly.' Wanda leaned in. 'Why?'

Max, pretending to examine a crumbling atlas, went still, intent on Grayson's answer.

'Because ... she was an outsider. They told stories about her being different, about her being hunched over, physically deformed, *marked*. Like me.'

'But you're such a handsome chap!' smiled Wanda.

Grayson lifted his messy fringe to show her a splash of purple birthmark. He let it drop and Wanda lifted it again, to examine him.

He suspected mockery, but she said, 'That's why you cover your forehead. You have a constellation hidden there.' She took away her hand. 'I think it's pretty.'

She danced off, careless, to pluck a book out of Lorna's hands and whisk her down the stairs.

Seeing Grayson gape after her, Pamela patted him on the shoulder. 'Wanda has that effect,' she said. 'But you have competition ...'

Max had taken off after the girls. He passed them on the oak stairway, hurrying as if he had a train to catch.

'He could jolly well wait for us,' said Wanda. 'Not very gallant.'

'He was gallant when he saved you.'

'I didn't need saving.' Wanda laughed at the idea. 'He just caught a horse's reins.'

'I find him romantic. Suffering is transformative – Thomas Hardy knew that.'

'You and your old Hardy.'

They stepped out into the sunshine, as the romantic myth Ambridge wove for Max Gilpin began to harden about him like a coffin.

'Maybe,' said Wanda, 'just to be polite, I should thank him for catching the reins.'

Astute Lorna saw through this, and watched Wanda walk oh-so-casually over to where Max rejoined the men in air-force blue. Without Wanda, Lorna felt exposed; she was a Horrobin by marriage, another name that meant something in Ambridge, and none of it good.

Her Cliff was the exception that proved the Horrobin rule. He was decent, reserved, and he waited for her at Bluebell Cottage, a house, which, despite its shortcomings – they woke up to ice inside the windowpanes in winter – was full of love, and books.

Touching Max's arm, Wanda opened her mouth to speak, then shut it again as he moved away from her.

'Don't waste your time, beautiful.' Cad's mouth was against her ear. 'He's married to a ghost.'

She pushed him. Wanda had experience pushing men and was good at it; he staggered backwards and the men cheered as she followed Max across the lawn.

God, he's infuriating, thought Wanda, breaking into a skip, finally cornering him on grass so pampered it felt like carpet.

'I wanted to thank you,' she began.

'No need.' Max's blue gaze was rudely direct.

She swung her arms, stumped for something to say as this man clearly felt no obligation to keep their conversation going. 'Marvellous grub at these do's. All those *teddibly* thin sandwiches.' When he still didn't speak, she said, 'Your arm. How? If you don't mind.'

'I do mind, rather. My life ended that day.'

'Gosh, *one* life, surely?'

'You don't know what you're talking about, and I'm glad. I hope you'll always be happily ignorant of loss.'

'You take a lot for granted. You know nothing about me.'

'You're right,' said Max. 'I don't.' He bowed his head and moved away.

It was awkward pedalling so slowly, but Wanda's bike kept pace with Doris's broad feet as they crossed the bridge.

Wanda persevered because she needed to confide in Doris; it felt as life hadn't happened until Wanda filtered it through the Boss. 'So, turns out,' she said, wiggling on her saddle, 'this hero everyone idolises is a frightful prig.'

'For a prig,' said Doris, with a magnificent side-eye, 'he turns up a lot in your conversation. Handsome, is he?'

Wanda circled Doris.

'I'd better get back to Brookfield or Dan'll have my guts for garters.'

'Yes, my husband, the ogre,' said Doris. The shop beckoned, with its smorgasbord of chit-chat, but Doris tarried by the bus stop to watch an elaborate leave-taking.

A bus idled as Connie Horrobin waved at her son, and he yelled goodbyes and farewells.

Odd, thought Doris. Vic was generally surly and monosyllabic.

Unlike his brother Cliff, Vic was pedigree Horrobin, bred for villainy. Smart in his army gear, Doris knew that underneath, the lad was still a housebreaker, a poacher, a bruiser.

'Take care, Ma!' he bellowed, possibly the only kind words he'd ever spoken to Connie, who was a handful of twigs in faded cotton. 'I'll miss you, Doris!'

Doris waved feebly, bewildered.

'The dear boy,' said Mrs Endicott, from the shop doorway. Her kind heart took everything at face value.

'Hmm.' Doris could pack a lot into a 'Hmm'.

'*Do* you mind?' The Rev. Henry Bissett and his wife, laden with luggage, struggled off the bus, impeded by Vic's extravagant farewell.

Frances left her husband to deal with the suitcases and trotted to the shop. 'You'll never guess!'

'Probably not,' said Frank from the counter. 'So why not just tell us, Mrs Bisset.'

'Henry's been offered a wonderful new living!' A purser of lips, Frances was rarely animated, but that morning she was kittenish. 'A *modern* rectory! A, how can I put this, *high-quality congregation*.'

Doris and Frank exchanged a speaking look.

'Frances, please.' Henry was keen to be away, his expression sheepish; he often had to tidy up after Frances's rudeness.

'And ...' Frances had a parting shot, 'there's a *selection* of emporiums on the doorstep! Oh.' She jumped back as a small girl barged past.

'Are you Mr Frank?' Dressed immaculately, with a starched Peter Pan collar, the child had a puzzlingly deep voice.

'I am,' said Frank.

The woman hurtling after the girl apologised. 'Sorry, sorry, she got away from me.' She held a taller girl by the hand, and dumped a heavy bag with relief.

'You must be Mrs Bonnet,' said Frank.

'Bon-nay. I married a Frenchman.'

Nobody asked after him; men were an endangered species.

'*Nous sommes francaises*,' said the smaller girl belligerently.

'What a poppet,' said Mrs Endicott. She sounded unsure as the poppet stood, legs apart, hands on hip, staring them all down. 'And she can speak English!'

'Of course I can.' Evie Bonnet seemed insulted. 'I can even swear.' She opened her mouth wide.

'Evie, *non*.' Her mother got there before the word escaped.

'You didn't mention children.' Frank was troubled.

'Didn't I?' The woman was no good at dissembling. 'This is Michele.' A brunette of about ten, demure Michele gave little away.

Poor kid's nervous, thought Doris.

'I'm Evie. I'm seven.' Her hair a yellow supernova, Evie was not demure.

'Oh well, the more the merrier.' Frank had recovered with

great speed; perhaps this had something to do with Mrs Bonnet's smile. 'You do know I'm only offering a trial period, Mrs Bonnet?'

'Call me Ruby.'

She looked capable to Doris. Sturdily built, with auburn hair and a serene face that outshone her tired but well-cut dress.

'You're lodging at the vicarage to begin with, I understand,' said Frank.

'Well . . .' Ruby swallowed while Evie made a swaggering tour of the shop, poking and prodding. 'We met the vicar on the bus, and his wife said they can't accommodate children because they might be wild.'

Saintly Michele heaved a sigh at this.

Doris slapped her shopping list on the counter. 'Frank, I'll be back for this, and don't you worry, Ruby, I have lodgings in mind for you.' She left, bristling with purpose.

'When do I start?' asked Ruby.

'As soon as you're settled,' said Frank, shoulders drooping as the door delivered three women, all of them vying to get to him first.

Ruby took an apron down from a hook. There was a name embroidered on the pocket: *Nance*. 'Girls, play outside.' She turned to Mrs Endicott. 'How can I help?'

The Bull was smoky that evening, vibrating with the rumble of male voices. It was sanctuary, holier than St Stephen's for those who worshipped the twin gods of ale and ferrets.

Fuming, Bob pulled Stan Horrobin's pint with bad grace.

Doris had no right! When Dan Archer came in, he'd tell him to sort out his wife.

'To my Vic!' Stan raised his glass. 'Gone to serve his country, even though it's never done nowt for him!' He supped, wiped his thin mouth on his sleeve, pointed past Bob, and said, 'You've got an intruder'.

It was little Evie Bonnet, a clean smudge on The Bull's tobacco browns.

'Oi, you! Get!'

Evie scampered back up the stairs.

'You running an orphanage, Bob?' The bar was full of wags.

'Don't get me started.'

Dan Archer pushed his way to the bar. 'Evening, gents.' As Bob opened his mouth to fulminate, Dan said, with the geniality typical of him, 'Doris tells me she boarded that French family with you. Well done, mate. You know her husband was with the French Resistance? Dead now, and poor woman had to flee. Can't imagine what she's been through, just to get here. Kind of you to give 'em your Jimmy's room. It's been a while since he, well, *went*.'

Yet another euphemism for blown to bits; Bob's son Jimmy 'went' right at the beginning of the war.

Above their heads, giggles sounded like thrown silver.

The wind was taken from Bob's sails. 'Doing me bit, I s'pose.' He recalled Doris's insistence that he stop treating Jimmy's room as a temple. She was right; perhaps that was why he'd been so furious.

'T'aint right. Children in a pub,' sulked Stan. Badboy, his

young Jack Russell, danced on his hind legs. One eye scarred shut as if winking at his master's criminality, he sniffed Stan's coat. Stan delved into the pocket. 'Nice bit of pork 'ere, a shilling. Who'll have it?'

'So *that*,' winced Dan, 'is the smell.'

Like Baby Bear's porridge, Honeysuckle Cottage was not too big, not too small, but just right for Max's needs.

The whitewash and thatch were sufficiently different to Queen Anne's Mansions to stir no memories. There was no view of London plane trees. No chiding when he smoked late at night. No gentle rebuke if he mashed the tea in the pot.

Max scanned the road as he leaned on his gate. Now that petrol was more precious than gold, colleagues shared the drive into work. He rather dreaded the small talk on the way; his boss was a 'character'.

The local policeman cycled by.

Jenkins? Yes, Jenkins, that was it. Max was getting to know the names of his neighbours. Whitey White was the postman. Frank ran the shop. Doris Archer loomed large. This was his new community, his new life, and he must make that life, inch by inch, day by day.

Without her.

Dearest Pamela,

By now you know what we've been up to here in [redacted].

The latest letter from Alec was a mosaic of censored phrases, but Pamela deduced he was part of Operation Epsom, the Allies' drive to retake the Normandy city of Caen.

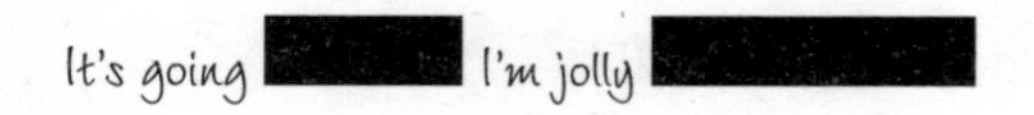
It's going [redacted] I'm jolly [redacted]

It was going slowly? He was frustrated? So was Pamela, groping her way through the pages. The euphoria of D-Day had clearly dissipated, to be replaced by the drudgery of battle.

She imagined Alec, tensed, that lean frame ready. At home, he was languid, legs sticking out from ancient armchairs to trip maids. Pamela bent to stroke Hero. 'He asked after you, boy. Nothing about adoring me, now he's out of imminent danger.'

A half-written reply sat on her blotter. Not the stuff of war memoirs.

Our new eccentric, Grayson, is getting stuck into his studies. The library light burns all night – he's a proper swot. You'd like him, I think. Sincere, clever. And of course fascinated, for some reason, with your precious Mother Molly. I recall you telling me about her and I realised that, even in adulthood, you still retained a fearful respect for the old battleaxe. But O! I almost forgot! The big news is that Henry Bisset is leaving us. Such a bore. New vicars take an age to bed in. What if the new one's all fire and brimstone?

That wasn't what Alec wanted to hear. He wanted an answer to the question in his letter. She rifled, found the page and pinned down the paragraph with one glossy red nail.

Pamela, fighting a war brings one's life into focus. I see what I am proud of, and what stains my conscience. Now I must write a name I know you do not want to hear.

Kitty.

Not a cat, but a woman. A penniless widow, Kitty had been pitied by the village and desired by Alec. The Pargetters discussed the affair before he left for war, and put it to bed.

Pamela raised an eyebrow at her unfortunate metaphor.

The period before he left held the glitter of a honeymoon in her memory. No, it was better than that – their actual honeymoon had been stilted and dull – this time around they discovered that compassion diluted their problems. Understanding the whys of their transgressions, they forgave, they began again. Or so Pamela had believed; now he disinterred their painful past.

I hope I don't need to repeat that K has gone from my life absolutely. There is room only for you, and I rarely think of her. Another name, however, is not so easy to evict. Caroline will be about six years old now. As you know, I had no idea that she was my daughter until she left Ambridge, after the wretched end of my shameful relationship with her mother. Pamela, Caroline is my blood. She's a Pargetter. I want to find her, and contribute financially and emotionally to her upbringing.

Darling, I want to be Caroline's father. Won't you give me your blessing?

July

AMBRIDGE WOMEN'S INSTITUTE MEETING MINUTES

Date: 7th July 1944
At: St Stephen's Vicarage
Chairwoman: Pamela Pargetter
Present: Doris Archer, Agnes Kaye, Emmeline Endicott, Magsy Furneaux, Lorna Horrobin, Nance Seed, Ruby Bonnet
Minutes: Frances Bissett

1. Pamela opened by welcoming Mrs Ruby Bonnet (who is most fussy about how to pronounce her surname).
2. Doris said it's a shame Connie Horrobin doesn't attend our meetings. (Note to self: ask Henry to have a word with

Doris about the limits of Christian charity i.e. the Horrobins.)

3. Pamela said could we stay on track today please. She congratulated us on the Queen of the May procession. All agreed that the Queen vomiting all over the float barely mattered in the end. Pamela said 'Full steam ahead for the Flower and Produce Show on 19th August.'

4. I apologised for the smell of vicarage drains. Doris said 'You would hardly notice it.' Agnes said 'Does anybody have a peg for my nose?' All were fascinated to hear about the new rectory Henry and I are moving to, its CARPETED BEDROOMS (four) and LARGE MANGLE.

5. Pamela said 'Can we please get on?'

6. Doris said 'I have an idea.' She said she feels helpless in the face of global catastrophe. She said the earth is rattled and shook and nothing can be relied upon to still be there in the morning, with maps changing constantly.

7. Pamela enquired where this was going.

8. Doris apologised for rambling. She said sewing can be soothing. The needle going in and out. She said there are images everywhere of refugees.

9. Agnes said 'I have the dentist in two hours, you know.'

10. Doris said 'Let's make a quilt for refugees. Something good in the face of wickedness. Each of us sews a square and we pass it on.'

11. I myself pointed out there is a shortage of fabric as it is, never mind giving it away to Johnny Foreigner.

12. Doris said could we vote on it.

13. Pamela said 'We are not socialists Doris' and told me to sew the first square and pass it onto Lorna or Nance.

14. Ruby said 'Oh you're Nance, I wear an apron with your name on it at the shop.' Nance said 'Yes Frank is my dad and I worked with him before I got married to Dr Seed and had my baby.'

15. Pamela asked could we get on.

16. Mrs Endicott asked Ruby how her English is so good and Ruby said 'Bless you – I am from Birmingham.' She said she married Onry (spelling?) and they were both artists (!!!) and he joined the Free French Force and then the Resistance. He died in October 1942 in the second battle of El Alamein.

17. Mrs Endicott blew her nose and said

Ruby was a poor poor girl. She said she loves the floppy satin bows in the little girls' hair it's so very French.

18. I said 'Yes but they are English girls now and must behave like it.'

19. Pamela said last time she checked, the Women's Committee was not designed to discuss children's hairstyles.

20. Magsy asked that we all take a moment to remember our menfolk pushing for liberty in France.

21. Agnes said 'You haven't got no menfolk.'

22. Doris said her Jack is in France and he drives an A27 Cromwell with a Rolls-Royce engine, which means his new wife Peggy can boast her husband drives a Rolls.

23. Magsy said she heard of a grenade dropping right down the turret of a tank and the whole thing was blown to smithereens.

24. Doris said nothing.

25. The vicar waved through the window. (Note to self: have word with Henry about interrupting vital parish business.) I myself said 'He is on his way to his stupid hives.'

26. Nance asked will there be honey to sell for the Women's Committee and I myself

said 'I do not know and I do not care - I detest those bees. There will be no bees at our new vicarage but there is a TWO-CAR GARAGE.'

27. Pamela said perhaps we should adjourn.

'Gerald, it's a terrible line.' Pamela had to bellow into the receiver. 'Did the funeral go well?'

'The old cove's buried if that's what you mean. Dodgy got squiffy. Mother, listen, I have news.'

Pamela gripped the Bakelite telephone.

'I've been accepted for the RAF.'

'I don't understand.'

'Ma, don't make a fuss. The army's not for me. I applied and the RAF want me! I'm going straight to London to start training.'

How like Gerald to deviate from the path. How like him to leave her to explain it all to Alec. 'Darling, *generations* of Pargetters have served in—'

'Don't be stuffy, Mother. Be glad! I'm going to *fly*. Oh, and there's more.'

'Oh Lord, what?'

'It's so exciting, I'm—'

The pips intruded. The line went dead.

* * *

Ruby stubbed out her cigarette and regarded herself in the sliver of mirror propped up on the chest of drawers.

She was grateful for the rigmarole of raising two daughters; a busy mind cannot be sad. Today, though, they were at school, shoehorned into Arkwright Hall by the redoubtable Doris.

Just you and me, Henri, she told the photograph propped up on a beam.

An artist's wife gets accustomed to rackety set-ups; after the endless – and perilous – train/boat/train/cart/bus exodus from France, Ruby was content with the mattress on the floorboards, while her girls slept top-to-tail in the bed beneath the sweet-smelling thatch.

She rubbed at a mark on her collar. The dress was threadbare, but it leaked colour into a utility world where clothes, furniture, vehicles must all be grey.

Gypsophila picked – nicked? – by Evie was lolling in a jug. Ruby tucked some into her hair. Yes, she had come to Ambridge on a quest, but there was room for beauty too.

On a whim, she pulled out Henri's paints. The smell was *him,* an oily whiff of life. Their house in Sceaux, beneath the cathedral that rose like froth above the town, was full of his work. Posters and shop signs to pay their bills. Surrealist images for his own pleasure.

Just one canvas made it out of France. Her most treasured possession, it would baffle the good ladies of the committee. Disembodied eyes – *my eyes,* thought Ruby – hovered over a table; a hand reclined in a chair.

Her dress felt superfluous; Henri had painted her nude so often that she felt clothed by her body. It was androgynous, strong, *sportif*. She wouldn't buckle, even though her mission was daunting.

Another cigarette. It helped with the hunger, she found. And the anxiety about what she must soon face.

The sun blessed the village for the umpteenth day in a row.

Nance positioned the pram in the shade of the wisteria by Holmleigh's front door. Tudor was fast asleep, eyelashes resting on sugar-paste cheeks. She smiled at his ripe completeness. Her boy. So small. She tiptoed away.

'I'll keep an eye.' Magsy Furneaux plonked her bulk into the rustic bench in the porch. 'He likes to know his aunty Magsy is nearby.'

'Aunty' was an honorific title that did not fully explain Magsy's complex relationship to the baby boy.

Magsy's sister had married Morgan back when they were all young, before Nance had been born. The bride had lived long enough to present Morgan with two fine sons, before a brief illness cruelly stole her from her little family.

The loss devastated Morgan; his sister-in-law stepped into the breach. A stout-hearted bossyboots, Magsy sacrificed any marital ambitions to bring up the boys and keep house for Morgan, who was, then as now, the village GP.

After the grown sons left home, Magsy stayed put as housekeeper, general scold and – so it was whispered – presumptive second wife. This was before Morgan astonished Ambridge by marrying quiet young Nance, whose father ran the village store.

Nance and Magsy had circled one another, each feeling the other encroached on their territory. An amicable peace had broken out, tested sometimes by Magsy's comparison of Nance's ways to her 'dear dead sister's', or Nance's difficult-to-conceal wish that Magsy might pop in less often.

One thing they agreed on was the perfection of baby Tudor.

'Right.' Nance rolled up her sleeves. There were rugs to beat. Floors to wax. Her gold and pink colouring belied her strength.

On hands and knees, she heard Magsy say, from the porch, 'Can I help you?' The imperious tone was one she knew well, the one Magsy reserved for tinkers, or drunks sloping home from The Bull.

Lifting her head, Nance peered through the open hall door, and saw it was, in fact, a well-dressed man. The tone was to do with the fact that he was standing on their patch of lawn, bowler hat in hand, peering into Tudor's pram. Inspecting the baby, as if he was a museum exhibit. Nance hurried out, dropping the tin of wax.

Apron still on, Nance plucked Tudor from his bedding, and held him against her, where he breathed sleepy huffs into her neck.

'I heard about him from the hospital,' said the stranger. 'Wanted to see him for myself.'

Nance backed away.

'We don't know your name, sir,' barked Magsy from her bench.

'Ah! Look at his face!' The man pointed at Tudor, who, woken by the noise, had turned to beam on the visitor. 'It's said they smile all the time!'

'They?' spat Nance and Magsy together.

Morgan joined them from his surgery in Holmleigh's front room. The small garden was full.

Their consternation didn't register with the stranger, who cordially introduced himself. 'I'm opening an establishment nearby. You could be my first patrons.'

'Apologies, but we don't buy at the door.' Morgan made to turn away.

'You misunderstand me, Doctor Seed. Take my card. I'm starting a home for idiots. I'd be happy to take this young fellow off your hands.'

Nance held Tudor tighter, her body charged as if struck by lightning. The boy felt the change in her. His teardrop-shaped eyes clouded, and he put a chubby hand on her cheek.

It was shock, they decided later, that meant they had allowed the man to witter on.

'You can visit, although it's not advised. His every need will be met by trained staff. We'd have no expectation of progress, of course. Think of the problems it would solve! No social ignominy, no despair about the future, no—'

'There's no despair in this house, sir.' Morgan, portly in linen, lifted his chin. 'My son is not an idiot. That language is offensive. He is healthy, intelligent, and he grows and thrives every day.' He took a step closer, barely able to keep his voice even. 'As for ignominy, there can be none for one who brightens our lives so much. We only hope he doesn't grow up to become the kind of brute who pushes into people's houses and insults their children. Good day.'

They bustled indoors, Nance and Magsy tripping over one another in their haste.

Nothing was said for a while. The clang of the letterbox sounded.

'The bounder's put his card through the door!' Morgan was red in the face.

'Dear, don't . . .' One side-effect of marrying a much older man was the careful watch Nance must keep on his blood pressure.

Magsy recalled a family she knew – 'comfortably off, *nice* people!' – who 'put away' their daughter. 'Just imagine . . .' She stroked Tudor's fair head. 'Impossible.'

A commotion in the yard.

Doris went to the window to see the new draught horse refusing the cart. Again.

Dan was so proud of his canny business sense the day he brought that animal home. Full of how he had checked out its bloodline and haggled with the Grundys.

A meaty creature with shaggy socks and an arrogant head, Stalwart was strategically deaf and endlessly contrary; the name was, apparently, ironic.

Wanda came up behind Doris. 'That one needs to be bribed with a sour apple.'

'The horse or Dan?'

The kitchen smelled of butter. Rich, slightly off. The farm's symphony drifted in through the window: Dan's oaths; a moo or two; some bleating.

Not so much bleating these days. Pasture had been turned over to the plough; Dan took his War Ag duties seriously.

The regional War Agricultural Executive Committees strove to maximise the production of food for the home front. Since the 1930s the nation had become dependent on imports of wheat, flour, and much else; now that such trade was impossible, the farmers had a real responsibility to stave off starvation.

Brookfield was a small component in a huge apparatus that Doris knew was no sleek machine. It gasped and hiccupped and seemed eternally on the brink of collapse.

In came Dan. 'Blast that horse!' He dumped a filthy harness on Doris's newly scrubbed table and it took all her self-control not to yelp.

'Letter from Peggy.' Doris handed it over, knowing he wouldn't read it. 'Girl's a grand correspondent, I'll give her that.'

Doris waited for Wanda to tug on her wellies and leave before she said, discreetly, as if Mother Cat might be earwigging, 'What if Jack's marriage is a rebound jobby, Dan? Years on end, Peggy wasn't interested, then suddenly they're wed.'

'It's young love.' Dan was filling his pipe. 'Remember young love?'

'That's the problem. I *do* remember.'

Beneath her pinny, Doris was still the giddy girl who stared at the back of Dan Archer's head in church.

'The speed of the courtship . . .'

'That's war for you.' Dan, ever-ready to believe the best of people, never joined in when Doris dissected motives.

'What about that GI boyfriend? One minute Jack has a rival, the next, wedding bells.'

Dan looked stern. Or, as stern as Dan could look. 'You're telling yourself tales, Doris. This isn't some Hollywood melodrama. Jack and his Peggy are married, and that's that. Just leave 'em be.'

Doris said nothing, too busy wondering how a man could live with a woman for decades and never notice that leaving things be was not her way.

Since Jimmy died, Bob Little only truly came to life when his inn opened its doors.

He would haul himself out of bed and waddle about unkempt, only making himself presentable for his first customer.

These mornings, he shaved early. Clean shirts were plucked from the wardrobe. Didn't seem proper to be unkempt around little girls. Whistling in the kitchen, he recalled growling at Doris, 'Can't be doing with kiddies in the house!'

Now, he said 'Bon mat-ann' to Evie, when she emerged

with sleep in her eyes. 'Ready for one of my horrible breakfasts, lovey?'

Evie giggled. She giggled at most things. It was a charming sound, and Bob felt she did a public service with it. If every household had an Evie who giggled at every daft joke, the war wouldn't seem so terrible.

Ruby followed Evie in.

It had taken Bob a fortnight to notice how beautiful she was. It ambushed him, kicking him in the knackers and rolling him in the sawdust. Now he noticed it afresh every morning, when she came downstairs smelling of girly smells, and bright. Always bright.

'Two horrible Bob breakfasts coming up.' Eggs blackened in the pan.

At first, Evie had been horrified – ''Orrible,' she'd pronounced, in her candid way – but she was becoming accustomed to English food.

Bob poured the first cuppas of the day, holding the pot high and letting the tea cascade.

'Such little cups!' Michele took her seat. She was ladylike beside her swashbuckling sister. 'At home we have bowls to drink from.'

'Come here, *mon tresor.*' Ruby tweaked the bow in Michele's hair and settled the gingham smock she had sewn in a French orchard. Every day her daughters walked to Arkwright Hall in clean, pressed, colourful outfits. It was a small triumph, but it mattered. 'Evie, sit up straight.'

Evie was lost in daydreams. *Les aventures d'Evie* unscrolled behind her eyes, the adventures more vivid since they abandoned their little house in the middle of the night. She might look as if she was at the breakfast table, but she was actually leaping from castle ramparts, about to save, um, *bunnies*, that was it. Those bunnies needed saving from the evil *comte*, and Evie was just the girl to do it.

The hectic pan spat. Ruby said, 'I'll cook *dîner* tonight. I see you, snatching a bite of bread and cheese. No way for a fine man to eat.'

Bob's red face was partly to do with the heat from the incinerated sausages, but more to do with being described as 'fine'.

Susan Grundy, four months pregnant and already a ship in full sail, bandied her green ration book. 'I gets first pick of the fruit, Frank.'

The ration system was the bane of Frank's life. 'Plus a pint of milk a day, and double eggs. I've saved you some Brasso. Your mother-in-law was asking.'

The day was softening, levelling out into another balmy evening. There was usually a rush in this last hour, as folk remembered they needed this or that.

Ruby packaged up Susan's goods – lusting a little; she, like everyone else, was preoccupied with food – and glanced through the open door at her daughters, poking about the Green. 'You should stock cornichons, Frank,' she said, placing the eggs with great care in Susan's basket.

'I might if I knew what they were.'

A jeep roared to a halt outside the store and two men leapt out with great urgency.

'Military Police,' yelled one, his red cap confirming it. 'We're looking for a fella named Vic Horrobin – you seen him?'

'We saw him make a hullabaloo of leaving for his regiment,' said Frank.

'Never reached them.' The officer was a man of few words, all of them loud. 'Bugger's gone AWOL.'

'Ooh,' said Susan, thrilled.

PC Jenkins careered up on his bike, crashing into a crate outside the shop. He dashed in, clearly desperate to be part of the drama. 'Have you seen Vic Horrobin?' he panted.

'He just asked us that,' said Susan.

Out on the Green, the other officer bent to speak to Evie. Ruby bit her lip. She kept an eye.

'It's a crime to shelter a deserter.' The officer in the shop regarded them all suspiciously.

'Yes,' said Jenkins, straightening up with difficulty. 'It's a crime.'

'He just said that, an'all.' Susan frowned. 'We wouldn't hide Vic. Them Horrobins are riff-raff.' The Horrobins were one of the few families the Grundys felt able to look down on.

Grayson hobbled in. 'You're welcome to search my cottage, gentlemen. You'll find only books, and, well, books.'

The other military policeman came in from the Green, his bulk seeming to fill the shop. 'Let's check his folks' place. Broom Corner, innit?' He and his companion clattered out.

He turned back and asked Ruby, ''Ere miss, your little tot out there told me I'm a cacker boodan. What's it mean in English?'

'It means brave hero,' said Ruby.

There was silence after the jeep drove off, until Frank said, 'What's it really mean?'

'*Caca boudin?*' Ruby rolled her eyes. 'Poopoo sausage.'

'Little tykes!' laughed Susan.

Ruby smiled, but froze when the next customer came in.

Agnes looked her up and down. 'How long'll this one last, Frank?' She turned to Ruby. 'I'm Mrs Agnes Kaye, of Turnpike.'

It still gave Agnes a boost to introduce herself, and remind everyone that she was now a well-heeled married woman.

'Cat got your tongue?' She frowned at the stock-still assistant. 'Chop chop!'

Agnes's order was 'out back', that hallowed realm beyond the swing door. Ruby leaned against the shelving until Frank followed her.

He reached for the box marked 'Kaye', and whispered, 'Don't let Agnes put the wind up you, lass. Her bark's worse than her bite.'

Agnes called out, 'No, it's not!'

He lowered his voice further. 'She doesn't like folk to know she was in service most of her life. It makes her hard on shopgirls and the like. You see, Agnes was maid to the Gilpin sisters, them as are related to that Max Gilpin. One day, out of the blue, she upped and married dozy old Denholm Kaye. That came as a surprise, I can tell you. We all thought one of the sisters would nab him, but no, the maid got there first!

Denholm lived with his mum until she passed away; most respectable and worth a bob or two, but . . . let's just say he's no Romeo. Then, suddenly, he's wed the most cantankerous woman in the village. Don't let her get to you, Ruby.'

Out in the shop, Agnes poked Grayson in the ribs. 'You found your grotty yet?'

'Grotto,' smiled Grayson. 'Not yet. Soon. And then I'll find the prophecies.'

Susan was cynical. 'There's no prophecies! How would they stay hidden for two hundred years?'

'Predictions scare people,' said Grayson. 'They let sleeping dogs lie.'

'You should, too,' said Susan. 'Maybe they'll foretell, like, *bad* things.'

'What could be worse', asked Grayson, 'than war?'

'It's all tommy rot,' said Agnes. 'Mother Molly was a chancer.'

A shriek sounded outside. *Les Aventures d'Evie* often involved Michele being rugby tackled.

Agnes pulled a face. 'Kids. I thank the lord every day I never had none. Now, listen you.' She eyed Frank as he and Ruby emerged from the back room. 'Chops?'

Ruby admitted she'd bought the last one. 'I'm cooking it for Bob, with apple sauce and some brandy from behind the bar.'

Frank harrumphed at this.

Agnes narrowed her eyes. 'You Brylcreeming your hair these days, Frank?'

He ignored her.

*

Meanwhile, north of the village, Doris braved the welcome of snarling dogs to drop in at Broom Corner.

She told Connie Horrobin the good news that had arrived by post that morning – 'I'm going to be a grandmother!' – and moved on to the real reason for her visit. 'Why not, Connie?' Doris politely accepted a cup of tea that looked like petrol. 'Joining the women's committee'd take you out of yourself.'

'Who says I need taking out of meself?' snapped Connie.

The fierce pride was in direct correlation to her hapless situation. Thin as a needle, wracked with an endless cough, there was no need for Connie to talk about life with Stan; her body told the story when she showed up to church with a black eye, or a tooth missing.

Head down, Connie stirred something unmentionable on the stove. Her youngest, Bert, picked his nose and studied Doris.

'The ladies are a decent bunch.'

'To you, maybe.' Connie poured in salt. A lot of salt.

Doris saw a woman in distress when she looked at Connie, but the world at large saw a foul-mouthed, fists-up slattern. 'At least, think about it.' Doris stood. She would return. She would persevere. Kindness is never small; Doris believed that compassion was mighty, and never more important than during war.

She took one last look around. The room had a topsy-turvy air. Nothing seemed to be in its proper place. An armchair faced the wall. And what was a wardrobe doing in the kitchen?

Shouts filtered through from the front yard.

Stan's curses preceded two uniformed men bursting in.

'Is he here?' thundered one.

'Horrobin!' hollered the other, and shouldered the door to a pitiful bedroom.

Badboy the Jack Russell snarled and lunged around their ankles. Stan swung punches, careful, Doris noticed, not to land any on the burly military policemen.

'Now look here!' Doris was incensed. A bed was turned over. The stew went flying.

'Stay out of this, missus.'

'He ain't here,' said Stan.

'Who ain't here?' Connie shrank, and shielded Bert.

'Our Vic's gone AWOL. Fair play to him, says I.'

'If you see him,' said one of the men, 'tell him to turn himself in. It'll go badly for him, otherwise.'

'If you hurt him . . .' Connie's face was wild.

She and Stan – and Badboy – tailed the police to the jeep, all of them snapping and threatening.

Doris remained behind. She and Bert regarded each other. They both looked at the wardrobe, inexplicably neglected in the whirlwind. They both saw how it rocked.

Doris took a deep breath, and put her hand on the catch.

Nose to nose with the choppy surface of the oil paint, Grayson communed with the portrait of Mother Molly.

From the far side of the library, Pamela peered through a shroud of cigarette smoke. She was trying – truly, she was – to find Mother Molly interesting, but the painting was just another of Lower Loxley's dull antiquaries. She would fill the place with chrome if she could. If Alec were home, he would be sunk deep in Grayson's research; the class she married into was obsessed with forebears. 'Shouldn't you be out in the sunshine chasing real live women, like the RAF fellows?'

'I don't have their chutzpah.' Grayson seemed embarrassed by Pamela's question. He tapped his tin leg. It made a brutal, hollow sound. 'Not much of a catch.'

Pamela was not the sort to offer platitudes. 'Must be hard,' she said.

'I wasn't cut out to be a soldier. I tried, though. And failed, as you can see.' Grayson didn't allow Pamela space to demur. 'Came home all bashed up, an utter failure who couldn't help protect his own country. My work on Mother Molly might seem small, *niche*, but history is something I *can* excel at, something I can offer, and I think that illuminating the past is significant.'

'I see.' Pamela hadn't expected an outpouring. She took another long drag on her cigarette.

'My boss at the museum was packing me off to Northumberland. They've discovered a fine bronze-age haul. But Blanche, Max's aunt, had told me about Mother Molly, and how she haunted the nightmares of Ambridge children through the generations. Definitely more compelling than objects in the mud! If I can resuscitate her, clear her name, establish Mother Molly as a wise woman and not a witch, and then shuffle her into the British Museum, well, I'll have done something positive.'

'You'll redeem yourself.'

'Exactly.' Grayson smiled at her understanding. 'And I'll have done something for Ambridge, a place that welcomed me with open arms, despite my shortcomings, and showed me nothing but kindness.'

'Goodness, you make it sound like a little Eden.' Pamela felt the atmosphere had got a touch heavy. She waved her cigarette at the portrait. 'What's the old dear pointing at with her pen?'

'The future?' Grayson took a small bottle and soft cloth from his pocket. 'May I?' He rubbed gently at the painted pen, and the ink that dripped from its nib.

'Why did Alec's forebears believe her silly riddles?'

'Belief in the unseen was commonplace in the 1700s. Electric light chased away many of the old fears. War, however, has a way of dimming the light, so . . .' Grayson took a sudden step back. 'That's not a pen, Pamela. It's a dagger. And that's not ink dripping from it. It's blood.'

Doris had a rapt audience in Brookfield's kitchen.

'So, the Military Police fellas are just gone, no sign of Vic anywhere but the wardrobe's shaking and jumping, and I pull open its door and . . .'

'And?' said young Christine and Phil together, the siblings' eyes like dinner plates.

'And *ferrets.* The wardrobe was full of 'em.' Ferrets were

Stan's accomplices, sent down warrens to sink their sharp little teeth into the tenants. 'Vic could be anywhere on Broom Corner, that place is full of hidey-holes.'

'Them Horrobins'll never cooperate,' said Dan.

A most unpatriotic thought occurred to Doris. *If our Jack deserted, I'd hide him*. Not that Jack would ask her to hide him; he'd gone as cheerfully to war as he used to go to the hops in Penny Hassett.

Alone with Mother Molly, Grayson jumped when Lorna crept into the Lower Loxley library, a massive book in her arms.

'Plenty of juicy mentions in this history of the area,' she said. 'I found a letter from the bishop castigating Molly for avoiding church.'

'A major crime back then.'

'Still is in Ambridge!' said Lorna. 'The more I read, the more I believe the Pargetters let her live at Lower Loxley because they were frightened of her, not for charitable reasons. Any progress on the little phrase at the end of the prophecy?'

Grayson wrinkled his nose. *'All is you*. Nothing. No idea.'

'I have a theory.' Lorna was reticent.

'Let's hear it.'

Grayson's encouragement was balm; he didn't differentiate, as others did, on the basis of accent or status. To him, she was clever, bookish Lorna, and her dropped 'g's meant nothing. 'What if the words are coded *dates*? The Pargetters were so impressed by the prophecy about the dog's death, it *must* have been dated. If we can discover when the poor thing died, we can work backwards.'

'And crack the code!' Grayson's birthmark glowed. 'I need to do that, and find the grotto, or my project will run out of steam. I can't return to London with nothing. Not again ...' He noticed how Lorna had crept to the painting. 'What are you peering at?'

'Look, in this corner. A mouse. *The* mouse. Mother Molly's familiar, visiting from Hell.' On its hind legs, the tiny creature fixed them with red eyes. Lorna shivered. 'It's pointing.'

'In the same direction,' said Grayson, 'as Mother Molly's dagger.'

They shared a thought. 'Has the portrait always hung here, Grayson?'

A mezzotint on the opposite wall depicted the library in the 1700s. The portrait was in the same position.

'So,' said Grayson, 'Molly and her demonic chum have always pointed out of the window.'

They ran to the sash like children.

'That clump of trees,' said Grayson.

A small dip in the land was upholstered with beech and silver birch. They arrived, breathless, to find a dark, aquarium bowl despite the sunshine.

'Listen.' Lorna shivered. 'No birdsong.'

Grayson fell to his knees, and scraped at the earth where a shoulder of rock jutted out. 'This stone was cut by hand,' he said, as Lorna fell to her knees and scrabbled like a terrier.

There were more rocks. They formed an irregular ring.

Grayson kneeled back on his heels. 'We're in the grotto.'

The homily was especially twee that third Sunday in July.

In the vicar's eyeline, Doris did her damnedest to look attentive, and hid her relief when he turned to parish business.

'Thank you, our sterling Mrs E and redoubtable Magsy Furneaux for the, um, *enthusiastic* flower arrangement.'

The ladies simpered as all eyes went to the towering wigwam of hollyhocks, which rendered the vicar almost invisible.

'Congratulations to our new friend, Mr Lemmon, who has unearthed his grotto.' Heads turned to look for Grayson, but he was nowhere to be seen. 'But beware the glamour of the occult! The only real magic is in the miracles wrought by our saviour. Mother Molly was a charlatan!'

A bird flew into the stained glass and dropped like a stone.

Even Henry was disconcerted by the starling's timing. Collecting himself, he glanced at his wife who sat upright in the front pew. 'Lastly, I must quench a rumour. Frances and I have no plans to move away. We will remain in Ambridge, where my heart is.'

Frances seemed to radiate frost.

There'll be words in the vicarage tonight, thought Doris. She glanced at Pamela, surprised to see that lady on her knees.

Pamela had never prayed before, and would not blame

God if he ignored her. The blues and golds of the glassy St Stephen blurred, as she begged him to protect Alec.

Bring him home to me.

The terraced London house was steeped in a stale Sunday.

Peggy lay marooned on her mother's sofa, staying out of her way and listening to her father whittle something in the kitchenette.

Her ATS supervisor had been sharp. 'Three months gone? Take some iron tablets and go home, Archer. You can't rest on army time.'

Facts must be faced. Jack was *not* careful when they lay together on his last leave. His reaction to her predicament was to write, 'A baby! Hurrah! I know we planned to wait but first of six, what do you say, Peg?'

She said many things, none of them polite.

Returning home as a daughter, when Peggy was a married mother-to-be, was unbearable. Especially as her mother was restored to her pre-war, ebullient spirits.

'Anyone seen my knitting?' called Mrs Perkins from upstairs.

It was on the floor beside the sofa. Peggy kicked it deftly out of sight. Her mother had joined the Women's Voluntary Service – the uniform was a shocker – and was helping the war effort by combing the Perkins' German Shepherd to knit his fur into, presumably, the nastiest sweater some unfortunate soldier ever had to wear.

Like Alice in Wonderland, Peggy grew bigger and bigger

in this dolls house. Pregnancy enhanced her sense of smell, and each fried egg turned her stomach. The fear was unexpected, but surely labour is called that for a reason? The doctor was breezy – 'a rite of passage,' he said.

The invitation in the post was lukewarm. But it *was* an invitation; Doris offered her Jack's room, writing that 'clean air will do you good in your condition'. Peggy smiled at the Ambridgian distrust of 'that dirty London'.

Clean air. Space.

But also stinging nettles. Cow muck. Gossip.

The German Shepherd bounded into the room and took off with her shoe.

While the congregation sang the final hymn, momentous events took place in the churchyard.

Atop a tomb, Evie singlehandedly fended off the Nazi hordes. She flourished her weapon, her medals glinting in the sun.

A figure hurried out of St Stephen's, and Evie leapt down, *Les Aventures d'Evie* over for now, her chain mail transformed into pink cotton decorated with ribbon rosebuds. 'I miss baguettes,' she told the lady with the baby.

'Do you, dear?' Nance jiggled Tudor in her arms.

'English bread is *pfff*.' The rituals were so different here. No trotting to the bakery with a coin, and nibbling the tip of the baguette on the way back. 'Why is your baby crying?'

'Wish I knew.' Nance walked with him, whispered to him. Tudor sank his head into his mother's shoulder, making her sweat. *Come along, Morgan!*

The church porch delivered not Morgan, but the vicar's wife, still scowling at her husband's announcement. 'Honestly, Nance, will that baby *ever* let you sit through a whole service?'

Mild as ever, Nance said, 'He's only young, Frances. He doesn't understand.'

'Will he ever understand? You know, being the way he is.'

Nance wasn't built for battle. Frances's rudeness took her breath away.

Her son did the talking for her. He lifted his head and blew a fruity raspberry.

Others joined them, chattily relieved to be free of the stuffy church. Advice rained down on Nance.

'Tickle him!'

'A drop of gripe water!'

Susan Grundy patted her hillock of tummy. 'My turn next!'

Give the little scrap some space! would be Doris's advice. She wondered how Peggy's pregnancy was going; odd to have a grandchild cooking so far away.

'Let me.' Magsy persisted in believing she had a magic touch with Tudor. Over his redoubled bawls, she said, 'My dear late sister, Morgan's first wife, had a way with babies.'

As Nance reminded herself that Magsy meant well, her husband was waylaid by Frances, who told him discreetly, 'That cream you prescribed did the trick.'

A village GP must endure such blurring of boundaries. 'I suspect you have an allergy to something. Possibly milk.'

Doris butted in at such blasphemy. 'Allergic to *milk*?'

'Yes, according to the *Lancet*—' began Morgan.

'Wholesome milk straight from the cow never hurt anyone,' said Doris, on behalf of farmers' wives everywhere.

Except for a touch of TB, thought Morgan, conceding nonetheless.

The vicar joined them, his glance flickering over his wife with some nervousness; the flash of defiance hadn't lasted long. 'I see Connie's absent again. I never expect Stan, but I hope to save at least one soul from the Horrobin household.'

'She's . . .' Doris couldn't manufacture an excuse. Possibly, new bruises kept Connie at home, but such matters were not discussed in the churchyard.

Good tailoring made the most of Max's lean height. One sleeve fell slack. Buttonholed by Magsy, he endured a brisk interrogation.

'I can give you the name of an excellent daily woman, can't have you doing for yourself.'

'Nothing essentially feminine about housework, surely,' said Max. 'I can wash my own shirts.'

Magsy sniffed.

Behind her, listening in – *This isn't eavesdropping, it's difficult not to overhear* – Wanda silently cheered Max's deviation from Ambridge's expectations.

By a stone angel, Ruby hailed Agnes. 'Mrs Kaye! Lovely day, isn't it?'

'I suppose so.'

'Do you believe in fate?'

'What a question. I believe in what I can touch.' Agnes

looked pointedly at Evie, sucking her thumb. 'And I believe in good manners.'

'Evie does that since she lost her daddy.'

Agnes moved on, catching up with her husband, grateful that he had no more curiosity than a sentient chest of drawers, and never asked abrupt questions. Chiding him about the dandruff on his collar, she chivvied him through the lych gate. 'Mind out!' she said, as Grayson barrelled through.

'A prophecy!' He waved a leather pouch, staggering on his tin leg. 'A *prophecy*!'

St Stephen's flock gathered round to peer at the red scrawl on nibbled parchment.

'It was by the grotto, beneath the subsoil, I just—'

Walter interrupted. 'Read it out, man!'

All listened to a message that had taken two centuries to reach them. *'An Ambridge widowman, sad and sore, will take to his bed a lady he should not, all covered over in finest wool.'*

'A widowman!' laughed someone. 'Oi, Walter! Who you been taking to bed, eh?'

A sudden wash of scarlet swept over Walter's features.

'Then, underneath, again, in smaller writing, a short phrase.' Grayson squinted. '*Busy inn.*'

Dan said, 'Anybody could write that and bury it. You're being hoodwinked, son.'

'But why would . . . No. This parchment is ancient.' Panic-stricken, Grayson turned to Max. 'Am I being had?'

'Looks authentic, old chap.' Max was lively, engaged. 'What a find!'

Eyes sparkling, Wanda rounded on him. 'Authentic? Do you mean that Mother Molly wrote it, or that it'll come true?'

Max, stiff again, said without meeting her eye that we all need to believe in something bigger than ourselves.

'I believe in the here and now,' said Wanda. 'Perhaps I can convert you.'

Across the path, Doris put a restraining hand on Christine, who wanted to go to her idol, to Wanda. 'Hang on, love,' she whispered.

'How would you go about converting me?' asked Max.

'I'd show you all the beauty and life around you. A walk! I'll walk you around Ambridge after church next Sunday, and try to convince you there's more than enough going on in the here and now.'

Pamela leaned in. 'A walk, Max, and with such a lovely guide.' She pressed, 'What harm can it do?'

There was a battle on Max's face; he knew he was being managed. 'Thank you, I'd like that.'

Not the type to punch the air, Doris allowed herself to tighten her grip on her handbag.

The widowers of the parish found themselves discussed as Ambridgians filed home.

'Frank's a widower!' Mrs Endicott was distracted from contemplation of the odd pain in her eyebrow. 'Is dear Frank having a romance?'

'With someone wearing wool,' mused Magsy. 'In this weather.'

Others put Bob squarely in the frame, even when Susan Grundy asked, 'Who'd want to get into *his* bed?'

Then there was Max. Doris had a wool coat she could lend Wanda . . .

As the vicar waved them off with an admonition not to become the devil's playthings, Christine asked Wanda, 'Why d'you like that old Max? Don't you want someone who's *happy*?'

'Shush you,' said Doris. 'Max is deep.'

'Huh,' said Christine.

'Who said I like him?' Wanda went on ahead to hide the smile she couldn't shift.

Gerald's defection to the RAF was the subject of Pamela's next letter on blue aerogramme paper.

Alec,

Let's not lean on the boy. I spoke to his new C.O. and it appears Gerald's a natural in the air. His induction is at London Zoo of all places. He had his basic fitness test – you know, heart, lungs, pee, etc – in an empty cage!! Remember that night the zoo copped a hit in the Blitz and they apprehended a zebra headed for Camden? The carnivores have all been sent to the countryside in case they escape and eat a cabbie.

Her pen paused.

Did we damage our son with our high expectations? Did the affairs affect him?

She scribbled that out; Alec would not want to hear such fluffy nonsense.

Gerald has other exciting news, so he says. Can't be as bad as the RAF bombshell so let's not worry our pretty little heads.

'Come in.' Pamela answered a timid knock on the drawing-room door. She half turned in her Hepplewhite chair. 'Dodgy, darling man, why the long face?'

'My conscience is bothering me.' Dodgy sat on a dainty stool that almost groaned. 'I didn't tell you everything about Bridlington.'

'Spit it out.'

'As I said, Gerald did you proud at the funeral, but then . . .'

'Dodgy . . .' Pamela lowered her chin.

'The thing is, Gerald sort of slipped the leash. Came back walking on air. Met a girl, the prettiest, loveliest, sweetest etcetera etcetera at the theatre.'

'Was she *at* the theatre?' Pamela framed a question she didn't want answered. 'Or on the stage?'

'On the stage,' said Dodgy, fearful.

To the naked eye, Pamela simply blotted her letter with a square of paper. Within, she seethed like a boiling kettle. Gerald must *not* plunge the Pargetter name down the social ladder. She herself had clawed her way up, rung by rung, each step papered with her father's *nouveau* fortune.

'Julia, she's called,' said Dodgy. 'Nice name.' Perhaps he saw how that comment went down. 'Daresay it'll blow over.'

'London to Bridlington is a long way for any Romeo,' said Pamela.

'Except . . .' Dodgy swallowed. 'This Julia is performing at the Stohl Theatre, on Portugal Street.'

'In London,' said Pamela.

'In London,' agreed Dodgy.

Gerald turned into Portugal Street.

Head to toe in air-force blue, new boots creaking, he saw the throng of stage-door Johnnies. Hanging back, he let the other chorus girls troop out, a mere aperitif for the beautiful Julia.

She emerged, and saw him. 'Sorry, Gerald,' she pouted. 'Not tonight. I'm spoken for.'

'But . . .' Gerald opened a large, beribboned box.

Out came the mink. Gerald saw the change in her eyes.

Julia read out the note tucked into the fur. 'To warm your heart as you have warmed mine.'

'Spot of supper?' he said.

'You bet!' She took his arm

* * *

That evening, Cliff Horrobin walked north out of the village, his usual route home from Arkwright Hall school. He passed his own front door and kept going.

He kept to the edge of the path, the left side of his face nearest the tangle of hazel and hawthorn, and fat wild strawberries. The left side of Cliff's face did not match the right. His right eye was a bright blue, but the other was a dead colour and made of glass.

War had gouged out a mass of Cliff's face and burned smooth grooves in his hands.

'Only me!' Cliff pushed at Broom Corner's broken front door, and was relieved when vicious little Badboy didn't greet him. *I'm in luck – Dad's out.*

'Son!' Connie lit up, a spent match somehow flaring.

Cliff laid a few coins on the table. 'Hide it, Ma.'

The two youngest Horrobins skulked. Stolid eight-year-old Bert had his eye on a cheese rind – survival of the fittest in that dank kitchen.

'This Vic situation . . .' Cliff put his hands on his mother's shoulders. 'He's in big trouble, Ma.'

Mulish, Connie shook off Cliff's hands. 'What if your brother's had an accident? Lying in a ditch somewhere. But no, just 'cos he's a Horrobin he must've deserted.'

'The village suspects Dad's hidden him.' Cliff hesitated. 'So do I.'

'Your dad'd never keep it from me. He knows how bad I get with my nerves.'

A voice from the porch, dark as charcoal. 'You and your

bleedin' nerves. I've put up with them nerves all me life.' Stan ignored Cliff just as he had done when the boy – the changeling boy with his love of literature and his refusal to bludgeon baby rabbits – lived at home.

Bert and little Maisie left the room like vapour; they were A+ students of their father's tone and demeanour.

'Your Lorna's coming up the lane. Checking up on her husband.'

'She doesn't need to check on me.' Cliff was calm, determined not to rise to his father's bait.

Badboy leapt onto the table and stole the cheese rind.

'Don't pester your dad, Cliffy.' Connie set out a frugal meal with haste. 'He's got a lot on his mind.'

Yeah, thought Cliff, *poaching and nicking and getting drunk.* 'I have a theory. I reckon Vic's in Wales. We used to daydream about it when we were kids, about how big and wild it was.'

Stan snorted.

'You know summat, don't you?' Cliff stepped nearer. 'Are you hiding him?'

Connie intervened. 'Ignore them villagers, son. Tell 'em you're proud of our Vic.' She bridled at Cliff's look of repugnance. 'Well, ain't you? Why should he go through what you went through?'

Cliff put a hand to his disfigured cheek. His father had not looked him full in the face since Dunkirk. 'I don't believe men should be sent to war, but not because of what happened to me. I've always felt that way. Vic could be an objector, he could *help.* Deserting makes him an outsider for life!'

'We're already outsiders,' said Connie, flatly.

The broken door opened again. 'How do, all,' said Lorna.

Stan wiped his mouth on his sleeve. 'Take your husband home, missus. Lad's spouting his usual garbage. Learnin' made a fool of him.'

'I brought some cherries.' Lorna laid her bounty on the table. 'From Mrs E's famous trees, Connie.'

Connie loved cherries. Her eyes thanked her daughter-in-law.

'Go on, Cliff, *get*.' Stan stood and his chair fell back. 'Telling me to snitch on my own blood. The government left one of my lads good for nothing. Why would I offer them another?'

Lorna's voice trembled. 'Good for nothing? My Cliff's perfect.'

Stan guffawed. 'D'you think he'd settle for *you* if he still had his looks?'

Lorna placed her small hand flat on Cliff's chest as her husband bucked. 'Love, don't.' He never gave into what he called his 'Horrobin side'; she had never seen him raise a hand in anger.

'He ain't got the bottle,' was Stan's predictable verdict.

'We should go,' said Lorna, but Cliff pulled away from her.

The physicality was sudden and surprising from a man who lived in his head. Cliff shoved his father, and Stan staggered back, falling to the flagstones.

Badboy joined in, joyous and mean, as Cliff grabbed Stan's collar and lifted his fist.

He glanced at his wife. Both of them came from homes

where men used their hands to communicate. He let his father drop. His chest rising and falling like a bellows, he said, 'I'm not coming back, Dad. You don't deserve to know Lorna.'

Connie saw them to the road.

Cliff wore a circle in the dust. 'Ma, enough's enough. Bring the babies and come with us right now.'

That shocked a laugh out of his mother.

'We're family,' said Lorna. 'Let us help.'

'When he's hittin' me,' said Connie, 'he's not hittin' the little'uns. If I last until they're grown, I'll have done me job.'

'Can you hear yourself, Connie?' Lorna wanted to shake her.

'Don't you judge me!' Connie's anger always landed on the wrong target. 'Stan loves me. In his own way. If you're going to talk low about my man, I don't want nothing to do with the pair of you.'

She turned and left them.

Lorna took Cliff's hand, and watched the jagged journey of his tears down the left side of his face.

No 9 Platoon, 15th Battalion of the Borsetshire Home Guard, marched through the fleecy dusk.

'Marching', perhaps, does not describe exactly what they were doing.

New Platoon Commander Max Gilpin hid his horror at their straggly, slow stomp, just as he had hidden it when shown their 'ammunition': a handful of Lee Enfield rifles from the first war, some spigot mortars and a handful of grenades. On closer inspection, the grenades were home-made dummies.

Whitey White – postman by day, warrior by night – pointed his gun at the village pump as it reared up out of the twilight.

Max bellowed, 'Never point your weapon, man!'

They passed The Bull; Max felt the whole platoon yearn. 'Left, right, left, right,' he said, as they minced behind him. 'Who's smoking?' he barked.

'Nobody,' coughed old Mick Lister.

Some Whitehall pen-pushers suspected this last phase of the war – *Dear God, let it be the last*, thought Max – was the moment the Nazis would step up their fifth column work and crumble the Brits from within.

This paranoia infected the Home Guard, especially Whitey White, who jogged to catch up with Max.

'We should change the password, Max, I mean, sir.'

Max sighed. Whitey imagined spies lurking in the dahlias. '*Please* point that rifle at the ground.'

'Anyone we meet, we challenge them to say the password.'

'Anyone? Even old Mrs E?'

'*Anyone*. She could be held hostage and forced to, um . . .' Whitey couldn't think of any way in which Mrs Endicott might be useful to a foreign power. 'The new password is . . . wash my windows.'

'Wash my windows?'

'Wash my windows. It's common knowledge that your

Nazi can't pronounce his double-yous. He'd say vosh my vindows. And we'd 'ave him!'

Later, yearning for his bed as he walked santa-bearded Arthur Sweet home, Max strained in the special quiet of night to hear a voice.

Perhaps I can only hear her in London. As if his wife broadcast on a delicate radio frequency that didn't stretch this far.

'Goodnight, Arthur,' he said at a cottage door. 'Oh, and next time – perhaps not carpet slippers, eh?'

Minko trotted into St Stephen's behind Pamela.

'You sure dogs are allowed in church?' asked Frank, as woman and peke passed his pew.

'Minko's not a dog,' said Pamela, and that was an end to the matter. 'Hup.' Minko hopped leadenly up beside her.

A finger poked Pamela in the back. 'The panting,' said a brave woman, 'is off-putting.'

'So is Walter's snoring,' said Pamela.

Hymnals open, the congregation gossiped about the prophecy. Harmless fun, they decided, but it wouldn't come true.

Frank heard his name bandied as a likely 'widower'.

Bob muttered, 'Chance'd be a fine thing' at the suggestion he had a lady in his bed.

Walter? He basked in the attention. 'Life in the old dog yet,' he said.

A new topic passed like forest fire through the church.

'One thing the Germans get right,' someone was saying. 'They shoot deserters.'

Lorna, leaning against Cliff, shrank as she heard someone say, 'Vic's in Connie's shed, mark my words.'

The vicar's wife appeared at Lorna's side, and handed her a small package. 'Your turn next.'

Inside the package was a neatly hemmed quilt square. She showed it to Cliff, whose face was something of a quilt, with its sewn-together textures and colours.

'Black?' Cliff raised an eyebrow. 'Bit sombre for a quilt.'

'All Things Bright and Beautiful' brought the congregation to its feet. The singing was loud; there was an element of showing off. As Henry processed up the aisle in his black cassock, the singing tapered off until he bowed towards the altar to silence, even the organ giving up with a surprised burp.

The vicar turned, bemused, to see everyone staring at him. He turned, like a dog chasing its tail, to see a large square cut out of the back of his cassock, displaying a snapshot of milk-white leg and long undershorts.

Evie and Michele snorted helplessly. Walter stamped his feet. Doris covered her face with her bible.

The vicar fled, and Frances followed at an amble. 'Oh dear,' she said laconically as she passed Lorna's pew, where the black fabric square lay in Cliff's lap.

It would go down in Ambridge lore as the Sunday they saw the vicar's knickers.

It held a different significance for Wanda. After the service, she smoothed down her dress – her best dress – and picked her way around the graves, looking for Max.

Her hair was washed, their route was planned. Walking alone with a man she barely knew was generally something sensible Wanda avoided, but she sensed she was safe with Max.

Doris had agreed, adding, 'But is *Max* safe with *you*, my dear?'

She prowled. She searched faces. None of them were fair and fine and his.

The RAF contingent loitered until Pamela and Minko joined them. 'Our theory,' said Dodgy, 'is that the widowman in the prophecy is good old Max.'

'The woman in the bed'll be your maid.' Cad was cheerful in his spite. 'Hildegard's a cheap tart, anyone's for half a shandy.'

Pamela fixed him a hard look, nostrils flaring, until Cad looked away. 'Where *is* Max Gilpin?'

'Yes,' said Wanda, a little too loudly as she joined them. 'Where *is* he?'

'Been gone a couple of days,' said Grayson. 'Didn't say where.'

Max's no-show meant Christine had Wanda to herself on the walk back to Brookfield. 'Are you peeved?' Christine had learned this word in the pages of *The Twins at St Clare's*. 'Because you look peeved.'

'Not really.'

Wanda was extremely peeved. Even though it wasn't a *date*. Just a walk.

'You *are* peeved,' said Christine. 'And if you're peeved, I'm peeved.'

My darling Pamela

Don't forget to clip Hero's nails.

Pamela tutted – *You'd think he was married to the bloody Labrador* – and turned the page. Ah. There it was. The meat and potatoes of the matter.

I'm saddened that you didn't mention my request regarding my daughter.

I beg you, Pamela, do not be cold, not like you were before. I parcel up our marriage as before and after. Before we were polite and distant. After — after our entanglements — we worked desperately hard and found common ground.

We <u>must</u> discuss my daughter. I need not just your blessing but your help.

'And me?' Pamela asked the mute Minko. 'What do *I* need?'

AUGUST

Wanda had been loaned out, like a library book, to help with the barley harvest at a neighbour's farm.

On her way in the Brookfield cart, she soon saw the coarse spears of meadow foxtail and dense tufts of cocksfoot give way to the comparative order of the village.

The work would be hot and hypnotic, following the lumbering reaper binder up and down the fields as it spat out sheaves. Land girls were not obliged to keep going until the work was finished, as farmers must, but Wanda was a team player, and never downed tools before Dan. '*No*, Stalwart.' A flick of the reins brought the horse into line.

If only Mother could be managed so easily.

More than miles separated Wanda from her family in Bath. Her mother looked forward to the resumption of 'normal life'. This would entail Wanda's marriage to a local fellow. Blonde children would ensue. The war would be reduced to a hiccup. What Wanda's mother didn't know was that independence and hard work had changed her daughter; Wanda was loathe to give up either.

Lorna stood waving on the edge of the Green. As the cart slowed, she said, 'You're getting all sun-tanned.' Lorna could never wear the halter-neck and dungarees that constituted Wanda's summer plumage, but thanks to Wanda's infectious *joie de vivre* she now wore lipstick, even on days when it was just her and the library cat in the cold stockroom. 'It's your turn to sew a square.'

Still only two squares big, the quilt was dormouse-sized. 'Your contribution is prettier than Frances's,' laughed Wanda. Alongside the original black square sat one of white crepe, covered with daisies. 'Is it cut from a party dress?'

'Nope.' No need to tell people it was one of Cliff's old facial bandages, washed, ironed, embroidered. Transformed.

'How's the code-breaking coming along?'

'Me and Grayson're doing our best, but without a solid date to work backwards from, it's difficult.'

'You'll get there. Oh, Stalwart's decided we've chatted long enough.' The horse took off at a trot.

Later, Wanda would swear the evil horse purposely headed straight for the rut in the road outside Woodbine Cottage. The cart jolted sideways. Wanda flew out like a rag doll.

Emerging from Woodbine Cottage at the sound of land girl hitting dirt, Grayson dusted her down. They put their shoulders to the cart, his birthmark swelling with the effort, but had to admit defeat.

'Let me.' Max was there suddenly, taking off his jacket.

Wanda folded her arms. Women's magazines advised huffiness when meeting a man who has slighted you.

The men grunted and pushed, until the cavalry arrived, in the form of Walter and Bob. 'One with one leg,' hooted Walter, rolling up his sleeves. 'The other with one arm!'

When the cart was righted, Max held out his hand to help Wanda up into the seat. Not committed to the huffiness, she let him, even though they both knew she could spring up, unaided, like a monkey. 'You and horses again,' he said.

Wanda did not wish to show her hand by asking him where he had been. 'Where've you been?' she said with her next breath.

'Visiting an old friend, a renowned palaeography expert. I showed him the prophecy.' Max turned to Grayson, triumph in his face. 'The parchment's genuine, old boy. Without doubt it's from the 1700s. What's more, that isn't ink. It's blood.'

As Grayson did a stiff jig of joy, Walter scratched his head. 'You posh folk are so well connected. The only people I know are renowned experts on cows' arses.'

'Can I give you a lift?' Wanda had never met an impulse she didn't act on. 'It's too hot to walk.'

'Only if it's on your way,' said Max. 'I'm headed to Lower Loxley.'

'That's where I'm going!' lied Wanda.

Ruby nodded along politely at her matronly customer's theory about the unearthed prophecy. 'The widower might find a woman in a *flower* bed.'

Frances, tetchily waiting her turn, rapped on the counter. 'Apples!'

Ruby slipped out to the yard to bring in a box of sweet, juicy Sturmer Pippins. 'Morning, Walter!' she said, finding him by the lean-to greenhouse.

He shushed her, but Frank was out in a flash. 'I know your game, Walter Gabriel! Step away from my marrow.'

Walter pointed at the vegetable, reclining grandly on its own leaves. 'Not your best effort, Frank. You should see *my* marrow. A family of four could live in it.'

Michele and Evie materialised to watch the stand-off, looking from one man to another as if watching a tennis match. 'I measure a man by his marrow,' said Frank. 'And mine's twice the marrow yours'll ever be.'

'We'll let the judges at the Flower and Produce Show decide that, me old pal, me old darlin'.' His rival discombobulated, Walter sauntered away.

'Your marrow, Frank,' said Ruby, straight-faced, 'is magnificent.'

'Qu'est que c'est un marrow?' When her mother pointed to the striped vegetable under glass, Michele let out a Gallic, 'Huh.'

Ruby kissed her daughter's shiny hair. 'Be kind. You know the way I feel about you two? That's how Frank feels about his marrow.' Hearing a new voice in the shop, Ruby went back indoors and elbowed Frank out of the way so she could serve Agnes.

Watching the care Ruby took with wrapping the butter,

Agnes seemed suspicious. She sniffed. 'Your girls run wild. Drinking from the village pump, the other day.'

'They're only children,' said Ruby, even-tempered.

Frances, picking over the apples, froze when Agnes said, 'So, you're staying put in Ambridge after all?'

'Unfortunately.' Frances tossed down an apple, bruising it. 'This place has nothing going for it.'

Frank hung his shopkeeper's head.

'I think it's paradise,' said Ruby.

'Hmm.' Frances stalked out.

Eyes narrow, Agnes said, 'I hear the vicar's giving Frances the cold shoulder.'

'How long have you lived here, Agnes?'

Ruby's directness startled Frank: *nobody's brave enough to ask Agnes questions.* He had assumed nobody could replace his beloved Nance, but his new assistant had reorganised the shelves, brought the delivery men to heel, and she gently removed the pencil from Frank's hands when he sat down for the weekly ordeal of totting up ration coupons.

Agnes didn't answer Ruby, sending her out to the back-room for powdered egg. Doris joined her at the counter, and Agnes hissed, 'That girl's up to something. Asking questions! Speaking French! What if she's a spy?'

'You're right, Agnes.' Doris flattened out her shopping list. 'Ruby has a direct line to Hitler, telling him all about your doings. Bet he's *fascinated*.'

*

A few false starts lay crumpled in Pamela's wastepaper basket. 'How much more can Alec ask of me?' she said to Minko, who only understood the word 'biscuit'. 'I mean, *really*! I'm to help him find his bastard daughter? The little girl's innocent of course, but she's a reminder of a dreadful time. Little Caroline's mother whisked her away; she doesn't *want* Alec's help.'

Snatching up her pen, she told Alec she wouldn't stand in his way. Pushing herself, she added the hope that he would find Caroline, and forge a loving relationship. A Pamela can't change its spots, however, so she was unable to resist adding a little sermon.

Your approaches may not be welcome. Kitty raised the child to believe she's the daughter of her dead husband.

It was disloyal, but Pamela hoped the chaos of war would keep Alec and Caroline apart. A postscript occurred to her.

The village might construe this as meddling!

She knew Alec had a great fear of meddling in Ambridge's affairs.

Pamela had no such fear.

Stalwart took his time.

Perhaps he was enjoying the poppies and wild fuchsia showing off in the hedgerows. He can't have been enjoying

Max and Wanda's conversation because they were both mute. Nothing had been said once Max apologised for missing their walk. 'Unforgivable,' he said, and Wanda agreed.

He did not suggest another walk.

The horse's harness jingled. Wanda wanted to ask why Max had gone to such lengths to verify the parchment. Instead she mirrored him, and stayed quiet.

Accustomed to fending off men, Wanda found herself in no danger. *Max isn't remotely interested in little ole me.* He was not, as Lorna would put it, one of her scalps.

The gates of Lower Loxley were just ahead. She had gone miles out of her way for nothing, and the farmer who was expecting her would carp to the Boss about her timekeeping.

She sneaked a look at Max's impassive profile. Teutonically clean and straight – ironic how German and English archetypes were so similar.

As if he sensed her scrutiny, he turned. He looked not at her eyes but at her cheek. He put up a forefinger and touched her face.

Wanda blinked.

'Your face.' His touch was warm on her skin.

'My face?' said Wanda stupidly.

'There was a scratch. When the horse threw you.' He seemed to notice his finger and pulled abruptly away. 'It's healed.'

'Yes,' said Wanda, still stupid.

'Good.' Max's smile was tentative, like an old habit resurrected. 'We're here,' he said.

'What? Oh, yes.' Wanda halted the cart.

A polite thank-you. A cursory goodbye. Why, then, did she feel so elated?

Hildegard passed Max, bobbing a curtsey. As was the practice, she jumped onto the cart; offering a lift to a neighbour on foot was mandatory.

'Got to post this.' Hildegard brandished a blue envelope. 'It's not me job. Lady Muck's got a cheek.'

'I'll drop you as near as I can, but I'm not going to the village.'

'A looker, innee?' Hildegard wiggled in her seat to watch Max disappear. 'Went a bit nutty, I heard.'

'It's hardly nutty to feel low after you lose both your arm and your wife.'

'S'pose.' Hildegard faced front again. 'Shame about the arm. Looking at him you'd never think he was less than a man.'

'He is *not*.' It came out far more hotly than Wanda would have liked.

'Only saying!'

'Well, don't,' said Wanda, and giddied up Stalwart.

The horse ignored her.

Doris rapped on the door at the top of the stairs. Trouble with a public house was the smell of beer that seeped into the fabric of the building.

Ruby welcomed Doris to '*Chez moi*', whatever that might

be, and handed over the jersey she had knitted, as requested/ commanded by the Women's Committee.

'Lovely. This'll keep some sailor boy warm on a cold night at sea.' Doris tarried. There was something unsaid about Ruby. Something she couldn't put her finger on, but Doris had learned to trust her intuition. 'Lodging at The Bull is working out, is it?'

'We feel safe.'

The sincerity touched Doris. 'I'm glad, after all you've been through.'

The newcomer was so capable it was easy to forget she was a displaced person. *She lost everything,* thought Doris, taking in the room's warm clutter. Crochet blankets on the bed. A small canvas propped up on the sill. *Lips in mid-air! Well I never!* Doris was not a connoisseur of modern art.

On her way out, Doris bade goodbye to Bob, who was pushing dirt around a window pane with a cloth. 'Remember, you were dead against taking in Ruby and I said it'd be good for you and I was . . .' She looked at the ceiling, as if thinking hard. 'Ooh, what's the word I'm looking for? I was . . . opposite of left.'

Bob gave in. 'You were right, Doris.'

'Wait, Doris!' Ruby danced down the stairs in a dress the colour of daffodils. 'You can walk me to work.'

Oh dear. Doris clocked Bob's expression. *Perhaps I was a little* too *right.*

* * *

True, a little girl who looked like Evie Bonnet, and wore the same spotless smock, sat in St Stephen's listening to Henry's interminable sermon, but the real Evie, heroine of *Les Aventures*, leapt from pew to pew, fencing with a Nazi.

'Bees!' The vicar changed tack.

'Not this again,' hissed Joe Grundy to his wife.

'The industrious bee has much to teach us.'

Industrious Doris's mind wandered to the crab apples waiting at home, soon to reach their apotheosis as a clear and jolly jelly.

Beside her, Dan yawned. Sick of bees, eager for a pre-lunch pint, he was tired after a late night sifting through War Ag paperwork.

'But enough about bees.'

The relief was tangible.

'Some good news for Ambridge!'

All sat forward.

'Your humble parson has been chosen to speak at the Church of England conference on the Preservation of Historic Religious Buildings.'

All sat back.

Evie knocked out the Nazi with Mrs E's handbag.

'His Most Reverend Excellency, the Bishop of Felpersham, Governor of the Lords Spiritual, will entrust the care of his delightful dog, Hannibal, to my wife while we are away.'

Frances's face could turn milk.

'All in all, a great honour, but I do it in your name.'

'Not in my name, boyo.' Walter led the charge to The

Bull. 'I don't give a pig's ear for his reverend bloomin' excellency.'

Over his first beer – very much not his last – Walter took his companions to task for doubting Mother Molly's messages from the grave. 'Me own missus had the gift. Mock her at your peril.'

Evie ran up the back stairs of The Bull, to her room. Where, wouldn't you know it, yet another Nazi lay in wait. She was forced to tie his shoelaces together and push him out of the window.

Peggy Archer used to have big plans.

A smart cookie, she had dressed as chicly as her budget would allow. Clearly, the young woman was going places.

The place she was going that sticky day in August was Hollerton Junction. The gods had twanged the length of elastic that brought her back, again and again, to Ambridge.

I wonder if Doris's heart sank when I accepted her offer to stay?

There was no room for another woman in Doris's kitchen, but the smell of the railway behind the Perkinses' house had made up Peggy's mind. Her heightened sensitivity to smell – *Thanks, baby* – meant the pong of London knocked her off her feet.

Train doors banged open. Peggy alighted, rubbing the small of her back. Borsetshire smelled better than town. Sweet and real.

It's still Nowheresville, though.

Wanda bounced by the truck. 'Welcome back!'

Peggy's waistband dug into her midriff. Soon she must resort to those marquee dresses. 'I'm only here 'til baby comes,' she said, as Wanda crunched the truck into gear.

'We'll see! War makes all plans provisional.' Wanda's bare shoulders were tanned. She gabbled like one of Doris's hens while Peggy withstood her heartburn. 'Of course, the prophecy's just a bit of fun.' She put on a spine-chillling voice. 'An Ambridge widowman, sad and sore, will take to his bed a lady he should not, all covered over in finest wool.' She scrabbled in the glove compartment as she took a bend at too many miles per hour. 'Oh, and take this.'

'What is it?' Peggy unfolded three mismatched patches sewn together.

'Our quilt.' Wanda explained the philanthropic plan. 'The apricot silk's from a bag my mother made to store my delicates. She doesn't grasp that I sleep in my dungarees.' She winked. 'You've arrived just in time for the Flower and Produce Show!'

'Hurrah,' said Peggy.

The rafters creaked above Evie and Michele, chatting in their single bed.

'Sleep, girls!' admonished Ruby from the lumpy mattress on the floorboards. 'Shush!'

In truth, she enjoyed their muted conversations. She heard Michele whisper, 'You *are* afraid of the dark!'

'Shut your mouth,' said Evie.

'Hey now!' That quietened them.

Every night, Michele would slowly wind down and drift away, whereas Evie suddenly switched off, like a wireless.

Ruby tried to settle, but memories came, unbidden. France. Him. Her knuckles went to her eyes.

Thank heavens for the secret assignment that drew her to Ambridge. It stopped her dwelling on the cat-green of Henri's eyes. The slap of his bare feet on the stone slabs of their kitchen. She turned, and dived into sleep like a trapeze artist.

Her little wireless, Evie, had not been switched off.

The girl tiptoed to a chest and took out a candle. Carefully, she lit it and took it back to bed. A flame capered, purifying the dark. She would wake first, as usual, and put away the candle before the others saw.

Wasn't it common sense to be afraid of the dark?

It had been dark, after all, when Papa dragged them out of bed, kissed them roughly, and set her hat on the back of her head.

'Allez-y, ma petite chaton,' he said.

Evie was his *petite chaton*. Papa's little kitten. He was out there in the dark. Without a candle in the window, how would he find them?

A few miles away, as the crow flies, Lower Loxley was bright behind its blackout blinds. No shushing here; cocktail glasses chinked, and the war was the hot topic.

There was concern about the Japanese capture of Hangyang.

'Where is that?' asked Mrs Endicott, her face anxious over a small sweet sherry.

'China, dear lady,' said Dodgy.

'But we *are* doing well in France?' she asked the men.

A pessimist shrugged. 'Yes, but the 8th Army's Italian campaign isn't catching fire.'

Cad turned to Pamela, and asked after Gerald.

'He's training in Stratford-upon-Avon. Hasn't so much as *seen* an aircraft.' Pamela was droll. 'It's all ground planes and blackboards.'

When the chaps laughed, Pamela felt grotty about the sardonic mask engraved on her face, and felt obliged to add, 'The boy's keen as mustard.'

There had been no recent mention of the chorus girl. *For once Gerald listened to me.* Pamela had made it clear no Pargetter could 'get serious' with a member of the theatrical profession.

Mrs Endicott treated the airmen to an inventory of her health. She was 'a martyr' to her tummy, her knee was 'a constant worry', and she feared 'dear Morgan is keeping the truth from me about my big toe'. Despite all this, the delicate lady was the last to retire.

'My earring!' Mrs Endicott's hand went to her earlobe as Pamela helped her on with her coat. An heirloom, she remembered having it when petting Minko out on the terrace.

'We'll find it.' Armed with a flashlight, Pamela led her out into the lush night.

They both heard the noise from the shadows.

'A parachutist!' The only exercise Mrs Endicott got was jumping to conclusions.

'Probably a fox.'

They both knew it wasn't a fox.

'A spy!' Mrs Endicott pointed. 'Look! A flash of white on the ground! It's an enemy message.'

'It's a message all right.' Pamela swiped the white scrap into her pocket.

The earring was discovered in Mrs Endicott's pocket, and Pamela closed the French windows with a click.

If that nocturnal crow took off again and flew over Brookfield, it would see Peggy lying alone in Jack's narrow bed.

Farmers turn in so early!

Sleep wouldn't come; in the oppressive quiet she wondered if she had made a terrible mistake. City flowers don't thrive in the country. She recalled Christine's disbelief at the unsuitability of her shoes.

Made out I was Marie-Antoinette because I don't own wellies.

Doris was inscrutable. The women were mannered, both of them trying a little too hard.

Complicated choreography around the stove meant they trod, literally and figuratively, on each other's toes. Peggy winced, remembering how she had covered a pan of potatoes with water from the noisy old tap.

'You salting them?' Doris frowned. 'Wait until they boil.'

'This is how we do it in London.'

'Hmm. London . . .' Doris's tone insinuated the city was twinned with Sodom and Gomorrah.

Romantic Christine begged for details of the proposal. Peggy made something up, knowing Jack's 'wanna get wed?' wouldn't satisfy her young sister-in-law.

Don't know who was more shocked when I said yes – me or Jack.

With only forty-eight hours before he left for overseas, the wedding was an improvised wartime affair. She wore her blue two-piece. Jack was in uniform. The bouquet took Peggy aback; Jack sweet-talked a florist out of a month's supply of red roses.

Eighteen to Jack's nineteen, Peggy was a virgin. Jack? She wasn't sure. By the time he hurried back to his regiment, Peggy had crossed that Rubicon.

The baby cartwheeled within her. The roses sat on a shelf. Dessicated, no scent left.

Peggy remembered the village quilt. Rifling the wardrobe, she looked for something that held no sentimental value.

Perfect! She reached for the hanger, and crept downstairs in the dark to find Doris's dressmaking shears.

Outside Max's window the village was busy.

A striped marquee staggered to its feet. The Flower and Produce Show was set up, with shouts and yells and much 'Mind your 'ead!' Yet, inside Honeysuckle Cottage, Max slept later than usual.

As the day nudged at him, Max had a feeling of

well-being, something rare and almost forgotten. His bed was warm, difficult to leave. Then his hand found something on the pillow and he let out a shriek far too high-pitched for a gent.

Banging a nail into a sign that read 'FLOWER TENT' in sloping capitals, Frank cocked an ear. Max appeared at the door of Honeysuckle, in paisley pyjamas.

People ran towards him. Suddenly acutely aware of his state of undress, Max managed to say, 'A sheep!'

A lamb hurtled out, straight into Wanda's arms. She held it as it bucked and baa-ed. 'So this is your ladyfriend, all covered over in finest wool.'

'Mother Molly's prophecy!' Susan Grundy blessed herself.

'It came true,' said someone.

'Well, I'll be . . .' said another.

'I should, um . . .' Max looked down at his rumpled pyjamas. His lean face split into a smile. He caught Wanda's eye. He faltered, retreated.

She kissed the lamb's nose. 'Oh, *behave*,' she told it.

'How'd it get in?' Frank scratched his head. 'Surely a farmer would notice a lamb gone missing?'

'Black magic!' Agnes held a cake doomed to come second to Doris's Battenburg in the Baking Section. 'Black,' she repeated, eyes narrowed, 'magic.'

The battered cathedral of the beer tent was up. Trestle tables were invisible beneath competing entries in Flowers, Vegetables, Miscellaneous. A painted Aunt Sally balanced on its stick. Pamela cut the ribbon and declared the 1944 Ambridge Flower and Produce Show open.

Hope was in the air, alongside the scent of strawberries and the green fog of mown grass. Heady, it lent the day sparkle.

'D'you hear about Paris?' villagers asked as they meandered.

'Liberated!' said Wanda. 'What a wonderful word.'

Ruby held her daughters and wept over them. They were unable to tease the jubilation from the sadness. 'They did it!' Ruby's voice was snotty. 'General de Gaulle led the Free French into Paris!'

Michele was silent, contained. Evie, wrenched from her *aventures*, asked, 'Might Papa be with them?'

Michele flared up. 'We told you! Papa is—'

Ruby quietened Michele with a kiss on her pink cheek. 'Papa helped bring this day about.' She clapped her hands. 'Let's go and celebrate!'

Whitey White and Dan toasted each other at the beer tent.

'Grand drop,' said Dan.

'The Bull's not what it was.'

This was sacrilege. 'How'd you mean, Whitey?'

'It's *clean*.' Whitey was scandalised. 'Old Bob's clean, an'all.'

They glanced at the meaty landlord and, yes, he did seem pinker, more polished than of old.

'He smells of *soap*.' Whitey shuddered. 'His fingernails is spotless.'

The reason for Bob's new grooming habits was easily guessed. 'You got eyes for your French lodger, Bob?' laughed Dan.

Bob didn't laugh. 'Where'd you hear such piffle?'

'Only teasing.' Dan tamped down his pipe. 'Just as well,' he said between puffs.

'Oh aye?' Bob did a poor job of looking uninterested.

'You'd have competition. Frank's soft on her.'

'Frank?' Bob banged down the tankard he was wiping. 'That old fool prancing about in an overall? What would she see in him?'

What would she see in you? thought Dan.

A cabbage as big as your head won the brassica class. Walter applauded politely as Pamela awarded the rosette, but kept to his post by his marrow. Pamela's hat stumped him; chiffon spun away from her brow like whipped cream.

Opposite Walter, Frank guarded his own marrow, presented at a witty angle on its bed of hay.

Both carefully nonchalant, they kept a lookout for last-minute dirty tricks.

Barely noticing the impressive vegetables, Grayson wandered, dazed, with nothing to offer the villagers who asked, 'So the prophecies are *real?*' A man of reason had been wrong-footed by a witch.

As he passed Susan Grundy she murmured, 'Old Blanche Gilpin would never've lent him Woodbine Cottage if she'd known he was going to put the wind up Ambridge like this.'

'It's hardly Grayson's fault!' Pamela was a non-believer, in this as in much else. 'Without a date the prophecy is mere coincidence.'

Arm-in-arm with Lorna, Wanda tailed Max at a sufficient

distance to fool him that she was not tailing him. She did not fool Lorna, who waved at her husband as they passed the Arkwright House swingboats, and fervently hoped Cliff had tightened the wingnuts.

Max searched for a very different lady. He found her trying to Guess the Weight of a tortoise named Jeremy.

The Handbell Association chose that moment to launch into something that may have been 'Greensleeves', so Max had to bellow at little Mrs Endicott.

'Could you possibly lend the Home Guard a hand?'

Breathless with the honour, Mrs Endicott listened to Max explain he had pulled strings and appropriated a cache of rifles.

'They're somewhat greasy. Could you oversee the cleaning of them?' Max knew there were not one but two charwomen at The Cherries.

'I'm overjoyed to do this for the war effort.' Mrs Endicott put down the bulky Jeremy. 'Even though I am fatally allergic to some metals.'

'You're too kind.'

Mrs Endicott went a bit silly at his bow.

A brouhaha by the hoopla.

Stan stood accused of cheating, and defended himself. Loudly.

Steering clear, Doris looked out for Christine, and spotted her with the other girls, all in Sunday best, all bent on dancing, giggling, whispering secrets.

Those same girls would be husband-hunting in a few years; Doris imagined the pickings would be slim. War plucked men like dandelions.

She browsed the Fancy Item class, and was astonished by a peach. Rounded, furry, perfect as a baby's bottom, it posed on a velvet cushion. Grown in a Lower Loxley hothouse, the peach made the other Fancy Items look decidely un-fancy.

Magsy's 'Pebble That Resembles Mr Churchill' doesn't stand a chance, thought Doris, just as she bumped into a baby carriage.

'Good morning, Tudor!' Doris bent over the boy, laying like the Sun King against his pillows.

Nance was conflicted about Mother Molly. 'Surely she can't really have foretold that lamb turning up in Max Gilpin's bed?'

Doris did not care to admit she was chilled to the bone. 'Ooh, there's Peggy.' She waved her handbag.

Hurrying over from where Dan was losing badly at the Skittle Alley, Peggy handed Nance the embryonic quilt, now four squares big.

'What a cheerful blue.' Nance held the fabric away from Tudor's jammy fingers.

'It's from a suit I don't care for.'

Doris said, 'You wore it to get wed!'

'There was no need to do that.' Nance was shocked. 'What a sacrifice!'

'It wasn't a proper wedding.'

Doris swallowed hard. *Imagine my Jack hearing his wife*

say that! 'You have a proper husband, girlie, and a proper baby on the way.' It was sharp, but Doris could not regret saying it.

'Excuse me!' Pamela pushed past the trio, giving Peggy a chance to flee. 'Hildegard!' she called.

The girl swivelled. 'I'm off duty.' She added a 'Ma'am' somewhat late, as Minko snuffled around her peep-toe sandals.

'Enjoying the show?' Pamela's manner was as correct as her elegant outfit. 'I have something of yours.' She produced a floaty white item from her bag. 'I believe you dropped it the other night on the terrace.'

Hildegard said immediately, 'They're not mine.'

'Really?' Pamela unfurled the camiknickers. 'Yet they're embroidered, with "Hildegard". An uncanny coincidence, some other Hildegard dropping her drawers on my flagstones.'

Hildegard snatched the knickers and balled them up. 'It's not what you think. The staff are all against me.'

'I'm not a fool, Hildegard. You know fraternising with the chaps is forbidden. Don't let it happen again.'

'You can hang me by my thumbs, ma'am, but I'll *never* divulge the name of my beloved!'

'Gracious, Hildegard, I'm far too busy to hang maids today.' Pamela sighed. 'If your beloved is who I think it is, he's not worth your loyalty.'

'Yes, ma'am. Sorry, ma'am. You're so right, ma'am.'

The frothy insincerity was insulting, and Pamela moved on.

*

'I'm just a gooseberry,' laughed Wanda. 'Cliff, take Lorna's hand and whisk her away.'

Cliff watched Wanda walk away and said anxiously, 'Have we upset her?'

Lorna smiled at his naivety. 'Wanda might look as if she's dawdling through the fair but she's making a beeline for—'

Wanda snatched a wooden ball out of Max's hand just as he took aim at the Aunt Sally.

'Hey!' He saw who had robbed him. His annoyance melted. 'Think you can do better?'

She hurled the ball overarm. The painted head flew off its post. Her prize was a yoyo, and she unfurled it, up and down, as they strolled.

They both spoke at the same time.

'You first,' said Max, just as Wanda said the same thing.

'You, I insist.' Max was in cream linen, one sleeve tucked into his blazer pocket.

'I know why you went to all that trouble to test the prophecy's parchment.'

'I wouldn't call it "all that trouble".'

Wanda caught the yoyo. They both knew the difficulties of wartime travel; Max had gone to considerable effort.

'Enlighten me,' said Max.

'You *need* the paper to be genuine. You *need* the prophecies to be real.'

'Do I?' Max didn't smile.

Wanda feared she had taken the wrong path, meeting

nettles instead of daisies. 'You need there to be something beyond this.' She waved an arm, taking in the fiddler beneath a tree, the children playing Ring-a-Rosy around the pump, the women partnering each other in lazy waltzes.

'That's what you think?' Still no smile.

'If I lost someone special, I'd like to feel there was something left of them. Some afterlife.'

The straight line of his mouth could have warned her to stop. Wanda chose to carry on.

'You've been through something terrible. That's what you meant when you said you were glad I'm ignorant. That's why you believe in Mother Molly. You need another world, one you might even . . .' Wanda slowly lifted her finger until it brushed against his lapel. 'Touch.'

Max jumped as if she had branded him. 'All rather dramatic. Mine's a commonplace heartache.'

'Oh Max, there's no such thing.'

As if Max was a prize trout, Pamela came between the pair and hooked him with her arm. 'Let's eat!'

Max turned back and saw Wanda staring after him. He closed his eyes as if dismissing a headache, and Pamela deposited him at the Women's Committee Dessert Buffet.

She advanced on a nearby table of fliers, who sat up a little straighter. 'Who can I tempt to blackberry pie?' Pamela laid her hands firmly – clamped them, you could say – on Cad's shoulders, and bent to speak into his ear. 'I know you're partial to a tart, despite turning up your nose at them in public. Or did you have your fill the other night?'

His blush was Pamela's reward.

Hildegard doesn't realise I'm on her side.

The Vegetable Tent was tense.

Joe Grundy primped his beetroot, feeling PC Jenkins' eyes upon them. The way Joe saw it, he had already won; *Jenkins doesn't know I bagged a brace of pheasant on Lower Loxley land last night.*

The marrow corner fizzed with testosterone.

'May as well go 'ome now, me old pal,' Walter told Frank.

'Time will tell.' Inscrutable, Frank hoped the judges would overlook the bruise his marrow had somehow collected.

On the Green, jitterbugging broke out.

Jitterbugger-in-chief Wanda went through the motions with a farmhand, the curls she had carefully bunched over her forehead flopping into her eyes.

She had danced with many men. None had stirred her. Wanda was a thing in transition. A pupa. What manner of butterfly would emerge, she didn't know.

She spun, her dress wild.

Independence was potent. Sleepy Ambridge might be a trap for Peggy, but it was a springboard for Wanda. She would leap in a crazy arc and land ... *somewhere.*

The fliers whooped and clapped when she knocked into their table.

Max sat back. He did not whoop, but she knew he had noticed how her dress described her body. She knew he had caught the rose scent of her eau de toilette.

She also knew he could take her or leave her.

So I must do the same.

Not like Wanda to get her nylons in a twist about a fellow. Particularly one so uptight. She yanked Cad Cadwallader up and drew him into the dance.

Tapping her toes on the sideline, Peggy wondered if it would be wrong to join in? Would it jar her womb? The baby seemed to be both enormous and miniscule. It didn't just belong to Peggy and Jack; it was already an Ambridgian.

What would Doris think?

Peggy knew her mother-in-law suspected hoity-toity Peggy was too sophisticated for farm life; only that morning Wanda had laughed at Peggy's revulsion upon learning that land girls nipped behind a bush to spend a penny.

'What's more,' Wanda had added, with a nudge, 'we wipe our bums with a dock leaf.'

The heat seeped out of the day. The light grew gauzy. Final rosettes were presented, to final rounds of applause.

'Oh dear,' said Pamela from the dais. 'I must award the next prize to myself!'

The peach had trounced all pretenders to the Fancy Item crown.

'Fix!' Agnes tried to throw her voice.

'And next,' said Pamela, unperturbed, 'the Dog with the Waggiest Tail.'

Glen from Brookfield would have preferred a pig's ear, but he accepted the ribbon on his collar with good grace.

The vicar was wistful. 'If there were a prize for the dog who misses his master the most, poor old Hero would win paws down.'

The black Labrador kept to the edge of the marquee, turning away when he felt eyes upon him.

'Henry has such a soft heart.' Frances took her husband's arm, but was shrugged off. She knew it had been noticed. She knew she would be hammered on the anvil of village gossip.

'Get on with it!' Stan always heckled when he was drunk. Stan was always drunk.

'Pipe down, you.' Walter waved his fist; marrows were last on the list.

'Hoping to win, Walter? Ain't no prize for fattest belly!' Stan shook off Connie's restraining hand, and she toppled backwards.

Righted by outraged onlookers, she waved them away as if they, and not her husband, had knocked her down.

With a look of condescension, Walter took the moral high ground – not territory he was familiar with – and turned around to hear Pamela say, 'And now for the hotly contested Marrow class!'

'Ooh,' said Mrs Endicott.

'This'll be good,' said Agnes.

'What'll be good?' asked Denholm.

Walter puffed out his chest.

Frank smoothed down what there was of his hair.

'First prize goes to—'

'Mother!'

Pamela turned to a man outlined in the opening of the marquee. She shaded her eyes. The hazy figure looked like – in fact, *was* – her son.

'Carry on, missus!' shouted Walter.

A woman stood beside Gerald, her arm through his. He pushed through the crowd, accepting patriotic slaps on his uniformed back.

'Ma!' He grinned up at her on the dais. 'This is Julia.'

She's beautiful. Alarm bells clanged beneath Pamela's chiffon hat.

'First things first,' called Frank hopefully. 'The marrow . . . ?'

'Mrs Pargetter, I've heard so much about you.' Julia's teeth were white, even. Her chin was determined. She had the lithe lines of a racehorse.

'You have the advantage, um, *Julia,*' said Pamela. 'I've heard almost nothing about you.'

'Can she stay, Ma?' Gerald bounced on his heels, his triangular RAF hat set back on his head like a short order cook's.

'Stay?'

'I'm off to Brize Norton, then Manchester ACDC, then it's probably Rhodesia. Can't leave my wife in horrid digs.'

The word galvanised the villagers and made Pamela bite the inside of her cheek. 'Wife, Gerald?'

'Lordy, did I not tell you?'

'You did not.' Pamela crushed the card with the marrow champion's name on it in her glove.

*

In her quiet sitting room, the lamps lit, Mrs Endicott opined that, after such drama, one teeny weeny sherry might be appropriate.

She poured two whoppers for herself and Magsy.

'Fancy young Gerald turning up with a *wife*,' said Magsy.

'And fancy someone taking a bite out of Pamela's prize-winning peach!'

Back in the beer tent, the diehards drank among the debris of the day.

Hildegard clinked glasses with a farmhand who thought she didn't know he was married.

Frank and Walter commiserated. An outsider had won; their marrows were also-rans.

'Every cloud has a silver whatsit.' The other side of too many pints, Walter gave a sly wink. 'Now that the Flower and Produce Show's finished, I can concentrate on the top-secret weapon I'm developin'.'

He waited for Frank to ask what this weapon might be, but Frank was asleep.

'Come on, layabouts!' Bob slapped the counter with a tea towel. 'Don't you have no 'omes to go to?'

The farmhand took Hildegard's arm. He pointed to a stain on her dress and bent to sniff it.

'You smell like a peach,' he said.

AUTUMN

1944

I won't be a slave to the past –
I'll love where I choose.

THOMAS HARDY
The Mayor of Casterbridge

September

Before that lamb clambered into Max's bed, Grayson toiled alone at the grotto.

Now he was inundated with volunteers, all keen for the glory of unearthing the next prophecy. Bending and scraping, they uncovered the foundations of a rock igloo. No mod cons for Mother Molly, hers was a barren home even by the standards of her time. The contrast with the many-chimneyed luxury of Lower Loxley was stark.

'Keep going troops!' Grayson winced when nobody was looking; that metal leg made bending painful. 'Isn't this the last day of your school holiday?' he asked Evie and Michele.

'I hate school.' Evie knelt in a corduroy tunic, intent on her work. 'Hope I find the next profi-thingy.'

'No, that will be me!' Fabio was an Italian prisoner of war from nearby Quartershot Camp. POWs had been given permission to help at the grotto before the year moved on and the ground became too hard to dig.

The news from Italy was discouraging: the German army

were pushing back, hard. Fabio was from Riccione, near the Coriano Ridge, venue for recent bloodshed. 'Is up and down.' His hand described his hilly homeland. 'Hard country for fighting.'

Nimble as a rat, Fabio crossed himself at every mention of Mother Molly. 'She and wife are only women who frighten me. Wife is big, like man.' He lapsed into a reverie. 'That is how I like women'.

'Um, *lovely*,' said Grayson.

'Do you have a ladylove, Grayson?' asked Evie.

'Evie!' Michele was appalled. 'That's rude.'

'Who'd want *me*?' smiled Grayson.

'I'll marry you,' said Evie. 'If you like.'

Grayson's eyes went soft. 'Gosh,' he said.

Evie was already distracted. Her trowel was a lance, her corduroy armour. Plunging into the grotto, she put paid to the dragon within. It was quiet in the circle of rocks, a peculiarly autumnal calm. She lowered her lance.

Her mother said Papa had 'passed'.

Words had more than one meaning, especially when you flipped between two languages like a deer leaping a fence.

Passed, thought Evie.

She imagined Papa sitting patiently in a waiting room, between here and there. Between alive and not alive.

Barely two when war broke out, Evie had scant memories of her father, so she built a personal Papa who was always just beyond her line of vision. Behind a door. Outside in the sunshine.

The lance was just a trowel again, and she threw it.

'Lowna!' Fabio mangled the name. He took off his cap. *'Ciao.'*

'Chow yourself!' beamed Lorna. 'Guess what? I've only gone and cracked the bloomin' code!'

Talking entirely in exclamation marks, she told the little band how she had sought out a packet of historic Pargetter correspondence at the library. 'I'd already looked through them, and found nothing. But this time, oddly, something fell out.'

'And?' Grayson looked as if he wanted to pull the information out of Lorna with his hands.

The girls gathered to listen. The Italians downed tools.

'It was a letter, well, a *note,* from Edward Pargetter, to his wife. She was away, visiting family.' Lorna knew it by heart. *'Dear Lady, I have a sorrowful report to make. The hound departed this life not one hour since.'* She stared at Grayson.

He said, 'Please tell me it's dated.'

'It was written on Christmas Day 1757!' shrieked Lorna.

'So?' Fabio was confused.

'Don't you see?' Grayson walked in tight, excited circles. 'If the phrases in tiny writing under the prophecies is actually code for the date, that means the phrase under the first prophecy – *All is you* – must equal 25th December 1757. We might be able to work backwards and decipher the other two.'

Lorna squealed, 'I've already done it! I've cracked the code!'

'But . . . how?' Grayson was impressed.

'I wrote down the date, the way they wrote dates in the

1750s – month, then day, then the year, so 12/25/1757. I drove myself crazy, trying all sorts of complicated codes, but it was pretty simple in the end. I just harnessed the number three.'

'A holy number,' said Fabio. 'God the father, God the son, and God the holy ghost.'

'But also,' said Grayson, 'a powerful occult number.'

'Exactly,' said Lorna. 'The number of time itself. Past present future. Birth life death. So I wrote out the alphabet three times, then numbered each letter one to zero, starting at one for "A" and starting at one again each time I reached zero. It gave me this.' She fished out a lined page, covered with a neat grid of letters and numbers. 'Each number has at least eight letters attached to it. I set down all the letters attached to the numbers 12/25/1757, and lo and behold, I was able to spell out "All is you". *I had the key to the code.*'

'Did you test it on Mother Molly's prophecy about the lamb in Max's bed?' Grayson hardly dared to ask. 'What was that phrase again?'

'It was *Busy inn.*' Lorna nodded so hard her little straw hat fell off. 'It worked out as nineteenth August 1944, the day of the Flower and Produce Show. She was *exactly* right, Grayson. Heaven knows how, but Mother Molly saw into the present day. She saw *us.*'

Fabio mumbled, 'May God help us.'

Evie looked into the black mouth of the grotto. 'I want to go home,' she said.

* * *

Peggy had escaped.

That's how it felt. Brookfield's walls crept inwards an inch every night. Peggy pulled a twig from a tree and whipped at the sedge.

Damn rabbit.

Dan had brought it home, and Doris frowned – 'Full of pellets!' – and shoved the furry corpse towards Peggy.

'What?' Peggy had recoiled.

'Finish gutting it, love,' said Doris.

'I *can't*.'

The connection between fluffy bunnies and dinner could be ignored in London, where meat came in greaseproof paper. Peggy knew that the Archers treated animals with respect, but her heart, which was wayward since she fell pregnant, saw only a poor dead cottontail.

Doris's silence was loud as she took back the rabbit.

Hence Peggy's need to escape.

Summer lingered right into September. Arkwright Hall was further than Peggy thought. She got up onto a five-bar gate to rest, wobbling with her new centre of gravity.

She was failing all Ambridge's tests. Alongside the capable, common-sensical Archers, Peggy felt foolishly ornamental, a hothouse bloom in a vegetable patch.

Something bright winked from the grass. Toadstools, red-capped with white polka dots; so perfect they seemed fake. Peggy hopped down and gathered them. Tonight, at least, she would contribute something to dinner.

Arkwright Hall revealed itself through trees still dense

with summer leaves. Cliff was up a ladder, painting a window sill.

'Thought you were the boss around here!' Peggy shaded her eyes to look up at him.

He climbed down, wiped his hands. 'I'm everything around here. Can't get the staff. There's a war on, apparently.' He smiled, and his good eye creased.

Teaching, caretaking, social work – Cliff did everything, scribbling all the while in notebooks. Short poems about the way shadows decorated the classroom walls, or even shorter ones about the Bosch hell of Dunkirk.

'Let me help.' Peggy's new, fuller face shone. 'I'm going bonkers at home, Cliff. I'll do *anything*.'

'You'd be doing me a favour if you took on the admin. It can be a pain; kids come and go. Nothing's permanent in war.'

'When can I start?'

They sat in his cubby hole of an office. She told him she had visited his mother. 'I've a lot of respect for Connie. She did her level best for my little brothers when they were billeted with her.' *Even if their language did deteriorate.*

'We're not on speaking terms,' said Cliff. 'Dad makes everything difficult.' He asked how Connie seemed.

'About the same,' sighed Peggy.

Dan loved beer. Beer loved him right back.

Suffused with this love, he entertained The Bull with the

story of his daughter-in-law frying up Fly Agaric toadstools for dinner.

Walter slammed down his pint. 'Everybody knows Fly Agaric gives you hallucinations.'

'Townies know nowt,' growled Stan.

'Peggy's a good girl,' said Dan loyally. He lowered his pint slowly when Bob appeared behind the bar. Wondering if he had eaten some Fly Agaric by accident and was, in fact, hallucinating, he asked, 'That you, Bob?'

The landlord was what Dan would call 'spiffed up', in his best suit. His only suit.

'You've combed your hair,' marvelled Stan.

'Put your eyes back in your sockets.' Bob was tetchy as he pulled a shandy for Joe Grundy and took the fourpence.

'Here's another fop!' Walter pointed to the doorway, where Frank stood holding a posy of Maiden Pinks and wearing a suit similar in age and style to Bob's.

'Ruby about?' Frank's chin was high, his tummy in.

When Ruby was called down, she seemed flustered. 'Oh, Frank, you were serious when you suggested a Sunday stroll . . .' She was polite, surprised and reluctant, but this last didn't register with Frank. He presented the flowers with a courtly bow that tested the men's resolve not to snigger.

'I'll just pop upstairs and settle the girls.'

Frank waited, rocking on his heels, withstanding the bemusement in the bar.

Stan muttered, 'Somebody's in love.'

Bob snapped, 'It's only a walk!'

Dan and Stan shared a rare moment of mutual amusement as the rival swains glared at each other like dinosaurs across a primeval swamp.

'Let's go!' Ruby, pulling on white gloves, had plastered on a brave face. She took Frank's arm.

Bob came out from behind the bar.

The men were awed. They rarely saw him this side of the counter.

'You're right, Frank,' he said. 'It's a sin to waste this sunny day. I'll join you.' Bob chucked his tea towel to Walter. 'Man the pumps.'

The men were in a brave new world; just touching the pump could get a chap barred.

Frank gawped. 'But, Bob, I didn't mean *you*!'

'Ruby?' Bob held out his arm and off they went, their pretty hostage sandwiched between them.

The Cherries was idyllic, the trees that gave the house its name circling it like a band of trusted friends.

Mrs Endicott's world had shrunk to a pile of rifles.

It was a solemn duty that Max had entrusted to her. Even more patriotic than she was hypochondriac, Mrs Endicott did not involve her maids; she used her own crabbed, arthritic hands to scour and polish the Home Guard guns. Each was a work of art by the time she finished, but she felt as if she had been dipped in grease herself.

She lugged the latest to the porch, and her shoulders sank at the pile still awaiting her attention.

'Hallo there!' Nobody passed The Cherries without being hailed by Mrs Endicott. She waved her duster at the odd trio. *Frank, Bob and Ruby?* How stiff they were, looking neither left nor right, and the dear girl's head down, a pose Mrs Endicott remembered from interminable nature rambles with her governess.

I may as well not be here, thought Ruby, as the men sparred above her head.

They were solicitous – 'Are you too warm, Ruby?', 'Mind that pothole, Ruby' – as they made their slow way around the Green, but she knew she was only a bone for them to fight over.

'Ruby makes me a grand dinner every night.' Bob was smug when Frank's face fell. 'A smashing cook. Some queer Frenchified ways of course. Olive oil on lettuce, would you believe?'

'This has been lovely but—' began Ruby at the corner of the Green, but the men turned left, making for St Stephen's. Straitjacketed by courtesy, their prisoner went with them.

'Them Slovak resistance fighters are going great guns,' said Frank. 'Two airports recaptured, they say. The Soviets are flying in equipment.'

'Giving the Germans what for,' nodded Bob.

When Ruby spoke, her suitors seemed surprised she was still there. 'Never underestimate Nazis. They'll fight to the last man.'

After a respectful pause for her hard-won knowledge, Frank said, 'Too warm, Ruby?'

'I'm exactly as warm as I was the last time you asked, two minutes ago.'

'Stop pestering the girl,' said Bob.

They stood aside as a cart crammed with grumbling ewes bumped past.

'Remember that time you had one too many, Frank?' Bob was sly. 'When you toppled into the pigsty at the coronation fete?'

Frank's cheeks went up in flames.

'Can't hold his drink.' Bob nudged Ruby, and she staggered.

'The ladies don't admire a hard-drinking man.' Frank was pious.

'The ladies want a rough diamond!' Bob puffed out his chest.

'Depends how rough,' murmured Frank.

Ruby thought of her cosy room, her daughters' chatter, the sewing lain on the arm of her chair. When they finally turned for home, she smothered her groan of rude relief.

'What's all that commotion?' she said, as they neared the inn.

Raucous singing shattered the Sunday calm. The door of The Bull flew open and out tottered Arthur Sweet. The noise of glass shattering and wild cheering propelled Bob into a trot.

'Oh dear, Bob, oh dear oh dear,' grinned Frank as they walked in on Walter pulling pints with a magnanimous hand. All around, men lay felled like warriors on a battlefield.

The till was empty.

*

Not for Pamela a leap between flannelette sheets in a cambric nightie; going to bed was as much a performance as going to the opera.

Oyster-coloured silk nightgown. Lace bedjacket. Satin eye mask resting on pinned hair. Parisian face cream on breadknife cheekbones. Spritz of lavender water on her pillowcase.

And, naturally, Minko snoring on the eiderdown, stuffed to his doggy gills with violet cremes.

Pamela settled back with Alec's latest letter.

His regiment was pinning down the Fifth Panzer Army around an area the British press called the Falaise Pocket, in Calvados.

The newspapers had been frank about the nightmare conditions, publishing details the censors would not allow Alec to share.

'Are you sure you want to read this?' Dodgy had asked, reluctant to hand over *The Times*.

'Quite sure.'

And so she had read about the officer who walked for hundreds of yards on bodies, his feet sinking into dead flesh. She read about the gassy corpses – husbands, sons, brothers – being shot before they were burned.

And all of this was happening as Pamela awarded the prize for Ugliest Vegetable to a demonic carrot.

Thank you for the socks, dearest P. I don't believe for one second that your elegant white hands knitted them. Was it Mrs E? How she used to bore me with her ailments but what I wouldn't give to see her hove into view with that coquettish Edwardian smile.

He told Pamela he was privileged to lead his men, that he prayed he was worthy of them, and she envied his faith.

Once she had mocked its simplicity, but war had changed Pamela. She didn't always look backwards with pride at the woman she used to be.

His PS was so rushed she could hardly decipher the scrawl.

I am touched by your blessing for my quest to find little Caroline. What a woman you are. A labyrinth I am happy to be lost in. Thank you, old girl, from the bottom of this tired Englishman's heart.

She kissed the envelope, glad that Minko wasn't awake to see such schoolgirl soppiness.

Across dark fields, over woods so sunk in shadow they seemed blank, two people lay themselves down in a very different bedroom.

No satins and frills at Brookfield. Doris's doughty nightdress was buttoned to the neck, and out of its collar rose a face red with annoyance, anointed with Ponds cold cream and framed by curlers. 'It's all your fault, Dan Archer.'

He quailed. She had broken out his surname.

'It was you planted that seed, telling daft Bob he had a *love rival*, as if he and Frank are Cary Grant and Clark flippin' Grable.'

'Gable, love. Not Grable.'

Only a skinful of beer would prompt Dan to correct his wife in full flow. He sensed tomorrow's hangover whistling to itself and polishing its shoes, ready to jump on his head at dawn.

'Bob would *never've* left The Bull in Walter's hands if it wasn't for your meddling. Thanks to you, half of Ambridge is blind drunk. They found Whitey White under a cow, and poor Arthur Sweet doesn't know his own name. You didn't hold back neither, going by the way you careered into the hayrick in the yard.

Dan pulled hay from his hair. He reached for Doris. 'C'mere, you,' he whispered.

Doris sprang up, like Dracula rising from the tomb. 'You cannot', she said, 'be serious, Dan Archer!'

The Cherries was low-ceilinged. Max's presence turned it into a doll house. He examined a rifle. 'You've done a fine job, Mrs Endicott.' He couldn't bring himself to call her Mrs E; perhaps in a year or so he would feel entitled.

'My pleasure.' Mrs Endicott had cursed the filthy guns. 'Tea?'

Trained by his aunts, Max knew this was a rhetorical question. He was expected back in the office, but sat patiently as a brass kettle boiled and doilies were arranged.

'Who are these lovely folk?' Max crossed to the piano and took up a photograph in an ugly frame. Grainy faces beamed out at him from a sepia garden. 'Can this be you?'

'I was only a girl,' simpered Mrs Endicott beneath her steel grey curls. 'That's my parents, God rest their souls, and of course you recognise the two other notables?'

'Of course,' busked Max. The man and woman bookending the homely family were unfamiliar to him. A different species to their hosts, vibrant and accustomed to being photographed. 'Heavens!' said Max. 'The lady's dressed as a man.'

'That was her stage act. They are, but you know this, The Burtons. Bathsheba wore a suit and sang droll songs, and Donald . . .' She put her head on one side. 'Donald Burton gave us thrilling monologues.'

'The Burtons, yes.' Max had never heard of them. 'Very daring for the time, for Bathsheba to wear trousers.'

'This was 1900, so yes, she was rather scandalous. My mother was keen on the theatre, and had them to stay when they performed in Borchester.'

Max tapped the famous Donald, whose fingers were hooked into a waistcoat. 'He's a dandy.'

'He was the most attractive man I ever met. I still have a souvenir of that day.' Mrs Endicott gestured to a frame above the fireplace. Pinned flat behind glass, was a chequered waistcoat. 'It was,' she said, 'quite a summer.'

The kettle boiled. Mrs Endicott jumped.

Sometimes, alone in her bedroom at Lower Loxley, the newly wed Julia danced.

The space, the sensuous comforts, the windows that gave onto the garden's strict beauty all inspired her to break out her high kicks. A true showgirl, she used the approved Folies Bergère tactic of turning her head slightly as she kicked, as if afraid of hurting herself with such a bravura move.

Settling into the great house meant acclimatising to ease. No more 'accidentally' using her sister's coupons for stockings. No more café snacks. No wonder Julia can-canned around the four-poster.

Hard to imagine Gerald as a boy marooned in such a bed. She had listened to his stories of childhood with rapt attention. 'Nobody,' he had said, squeezing her hard, 'ever listens to me the way you do, my darling. Papa is Victorian, aloof. High expectations, short on cuddles. And Mother? Glamorous but untouchable, with handbrake turns into neediness. Sometimes I feel guilty about how I snarled at her and shook her off. I knew too much, you see, about their *liaisons,* and it weighed me down.'

Julia was an excellent listener, her eyes never strayed from his face. Who was to know it was because she didn't take other people's interior lives particularly seriously?

Perhaps, thought Julia now, flinging herself on the chaise longue with a copy of *Vogue, that's what wives do for husbands. We carry their sadness, and, in return, they carry our bags.*

Being a wife was her most demanding role yet. It required a new wardrobe, new postures. Julia hadn't set out to marry Gerald – he was sweet, but somewhat unseasoned compared to her other lovers – until he showed her a snapshot of the family seat. That was when Julia made up her mind to fall in love.

Now that she was inside the photograph, Julia wore jewels instead of paste, and danced for free when the spirit moved her. She opened the magazine at a picture of Princess Margaret Rose, whose complexion she greatly admired.

Footsteps on the stairs.

Julia recognised that drumbeat. She sat up as Pamela marched in and clapped her hands at her as if she was one of the slower household hounds.

'Chop chop! Life isn't all chaise longues. Pargetters need to show their faces in the village. Off you pop to the grotto. Give Grayson a hand digging up his old witch.'

Morgan walked Peggy to the door, as if she had come for luncheon and not a check-up.

'Your job at Arkwright Hall is good for you. We can't have a strong young lady like you sitting around twiddling her thumbs.'

'It gets me out of the house, as they say.' Peggy would have liked to sit a while more in Holmleigh. The doctor was so gentle and understanding, with no talk of female rites of passage. The caterpillaring of his brows when she confided her fear of childbirth soothed her as much as his exhortation not to worry, and to remember that he would be with her all the way.

Peggy did worry, though. She wished, not for the first time, that her husband had kept the only promise he ever made her. To be 'careful'.

The vision in crepe de chine nonplussed Grayson. 'You want to help?'

Julia waved a spotless trowel. 'I'm here to do my bit.' Her diction was diamond-clear, her delivery designed to reach the back of the stalls. 'Consider me your slave.'

'Crikey.' Grayson collected his wits and showed her an untouched corner of the grotto, one square foot of unpromising ground beneath the canopy of beech trees.

'Like this?' Julia tapped the earth as if breaking a boiled egg.

'Perhaps a *touch* more vim.' Grayson seemed reluctant to criticise his exotic new assistant. Besides anything else, she had interrupted a rebuke from the vicar on Grayson's unfortunate habit of leaving Woodbine's curtains open during blackout.

'I do hope,' called the vicar, on his knees to her left, 'you don't believe in Mother Molly, Mrs Pargetter?'

'Do call me Julia.' She turned the full wattage of her professional-strength charm on Henry. 'The old sausage sounds rather a scream to me.'

'Superstition can worm its way into the naive mind.' The vicar straightened up. 'I support Grayson in his academic endeavours but finding another prophecy would only unsettle the village.'

Julia scratched aimlessly at the earth. 'Isn't Mother Molly a diversion from the silly war? A bit of fun?'

'Fun?' Henry Bisset leaned back, in a stance known and feared as his sermon stance. 'If one wants fun,' he began, in a lofty tone of voice, 'one need look no further than the bee.'

'Which bee?' asked Grayson.

'*The* bee.' Henry was severe. 'The no-nonsense lives of my hives are a buffer against the devil.'

'I disagree.' Tap-tap-tap went Julia's listless trowel. 'There's all sorts of spooky traditions about bees. When my grandfather died, Granny had to go and whisper the news to the hive.'

Grayson backed her up. 'The bee is everywhere in folklore. From Aphrodite's high priestesses reincarnated as honeybees, to the ancient Celts trusting bees with messages for the dead.'

'Bingo!' cried Julia, holding up a leather pouch covered in muck.

Grayson was speechless.

The vicar held up one hand. 'Please,' he said, suddenly pale. 'Leave it in the earth.'

Too late. Grayson grabbed the pouch and took out the parchment. He opened it with both care and greed, and read out the spidery writing.

'Farces in the north chuse to sink a gentleperson known to all in the river of Lethe.'

'Farces?' giggled Julia. 'Surely old Molly meant forces?'

'Lethe,' breathed Henry, troubled.

'I did panto there in thirty-nine,' asserted Julia. 'Babes in the wood. There were bedbugs in my digs.'

'Different spelling.' Grayson's birthmark blazed red. 'This

Lethe is the river that transported ancient Greeks to the afterlife.'

'It's a death sentence!' Julia put her hand to the throat.

'It's a childish joke.' Reluctantly, the vicar asked, 'Can you decode the date, Grayson?'

Holding the parchment closer to read the all-important coded tag, Grayson gulped before reading out, *'I die ill.'*

'Mother Molly really wants to scare the pants off us this time,' laughed Julia.

Grayson whipped out the decryption key Lorna had given him. 'Ninth of October.' He hesitated, but went on. 'Nineteen forty-four.'

'That's next month.' Julia's gaiety faltered. 'Some poor soul doesn't have long left.'

News travels fast in a village.

If that village includes Walter Gabriel and Frances Bissett and Agnes Kaye, it travels at the speed of light.

Nursing a cider outside The Bull, Wanda wondered if she qualified as a 'gentleperson known to all'. It's hard to spook a valkyrie; she was more concerned with her aching foot. A ghostly scar complained every now and then. Wanda was a conscientious objector's only victim; sent to help with apple picking, he rammed the spike ladder down on her foot. It tore through welly, sock and flesh, but once Doris had bound the wound, Wanda was back to the orchard.

See? A valkyrie.

A strange shadow, like conjoined twins, fell across her. She squinted up into the light and saw Grayson and Max. 'You know, you two could be brothers.'

'Are you crazy?' spluttered Grayson. 'We may be the same approximate size and shape but only one of us is a golden Gilpin boy.' He pressed Max to sit, saying he'd get the beers in. In an aside only Wanda heard, he added that he might be some time.

Earthy, muddy beside Max, so pressed and clean in his suit, Wanda made light conversation. *Mustn't trample over his boundaries again.*

Polite prompting meant he told her about his new job and his family home near Shaftesbury, in 'Thomas Hardy country'. From mentions of the ornamental lake and the attached farms, Wanda ascertained that the Gilpins were wealthy, even by the standards of her own, comfortably off, clan.

It pained her that this mattered. It pained her that her mother would label Max a 'good catch'. The war had rattled society's game of Snakes and Ladders; Wanda hoped the notion of class might soon be a quaint relic.

Surely I'm classless now; no 'proper' young gel had red raw hands or knew how to sheave corn.

Neither Max nor Wanda seemed to mind that Grayson was taking so long to bring out the drinks.

'The sun makes everything better.' Wanda lifted her face to its attentions.

She didn't see how Max studied her – closely, as if Wanda was a map of somewhere he longed to visit.

'Harder to feel guilty when the sun shines,' he agreed.

'No need for you to feel guilty. You almost gave your life for your country.'

'I'm guilty about living . . .' Max spoke like a man picking stones from between his teeth. '. . . when my wife did not.'

That sounded like a Keep Out sign. If Max knew Wanda better, he would know she routinely ignored such signs; she swam in private streams and sunbathed naked in farmers' meadows. Accustomed to trespassing, she stole into Max's territory.

'Max, it's no sin to survive.' The air turned thick, a private storm. Together they generated electricity.

Wanda felt the prickle of it. She never expected life to be simple; she assumed love would be the same.

She put down her glass. She took Max's chin in her hand and kissed his lips.

He was shocked. So shocked he laughed. He didn't move away. Instead he reached for her as if he was drowning, and kissed her, hard and expertly.

Kissing was nothing new to Wanda. The war was all kissing, when it wasn't callouses and shovelling dung. Wanda attached zero significance to kisses – they were no contract – but she felt history wake up in this embrace.

This man is not to be toyed with.

She felt his power, and her own. She felt how it squared when it met his.

We could really hurt each other.

Wanda leapt up. She staggered into Grayson, standing

open-mouthed with a tin tray of glasses. She mounted her bike like a murderer fleeing the scene of the crime.

Pamela found women to be diverse; a pick'n'mix of personality. Men she found samey, like overbred pedigree dogs.

Dear Pamela,

So much going on! Dashing through days, like ants across the pantry floor. The enemy's on the run!!!

Take care of Hero.

And yourself.

The lack of soft language disappointed Pamela. When men were busy, their brains became mechanical.

Lying back on scented silk, she idly stroked Minko's fur, noticing it was gummy. The dog had once again rolled in something unmentionable. Pamela closed her eyes. Unaccustomed to missing things or people, she missed her husband. She had expected to miss him the way she missed those Ferragamo shoes Hildegard had thrown out by mistake, but this was more keen.

She missed feeling happy.

She almost overlooked what was written over the page.

Sad news. Caroline's mother has passed on.

Pamela sat up. Minko squeaked.

Details are obscure. Little Caroline was handed over to Kitty's people as far as I can make out. Ireland is an easy place in which to disappear.

Ignoble relief coursed through Pamela.

Therefore I now have a different ambition. Not just to be financially responsible for Caroline, but to bring her to live at Lower Loxley.

When Minko heard Pamela's loud 'No!' he threw himself off the bed like a lemming.

The child believes herself an orphan but she has a father — me.

Pamela sat up and hugged her bony knees.

AMBRIDGE WOMEN'S INSTITUTE
MEETING MINUTES

Date: 22nd September 1944
At: St Stephen's Vicarage
Chairwoman: Pamela Pargetter
Present: Doris Archer, Agnes Kaye, Emmeline Endicott, Magsy Furneaux, Lorna Horrobin, Nance Seed, Ruby Bonnet, Susan Grundy, Julia Pargetter
Minutes: Frances Bissett

1. Pamela welcomed Julia to the committee and asked could we please stick to the agenda for once.

2. Mrs E said 'I always stick to the agenda.' She said to Magsy 'Don't I always stick to the agenda, dear?'

3. Magsy said 'I have never known anyone so punctilious about sticking to the agenda except perhaps myself.'

4. Nance apologised for keeping the quilt so long.

5. Pamela said 'It is a shame the squares aren't all the same size.'

6. Doris said 'The quilt is sewn with love.'

7. Agnes said 'It looks as if it is sewn with boxing gloves.'

8. All present heard the front door shut. Susan said 'Ooh the vicar never said goodbye. Is hubby still cheesed off with you Frances?'

9. I myself maintained a dignified silence.

10. Pamela passed along Max Gilpin's gratitude for Mrs E's work on the rifles.

11. Mrs E said 'Max asked me about the time I met Donald and Bathsheba Burton. Did I ever tell you all about that?'

12. Everybody said 'Yes' very emphatically.

13. Pamela said 'Who will volunteer to iron bunting for the Lower Loxley croquet match?'

14. Agnes said nobody warned her how much of the Women's Committee would be taken up with (crude word deleted) bunting.

15. Ruby tittered. Note to self: ask Henry to have a word with Ruby re: encouraging bad language.

16. Mrs E asked Nance if dear Tudor is over his sniffles and Pamela said 'Agenda!' and I as an interested neighbour asked if Tudor is slower at learning than a normal child.

17. Pamela said 'Everyone is normal, Frances.' Note to self: ask Henry to have a word with Pamela re: snappy tone with the wife of a clergyman.

18. Nance took no further part in the meeting which at least one observer found very rude.

19. Pamela suggested an Ambridge Christmas show. She asked for ideas for a title. She said 'Winter Tonic' and then she said 'Excellent' and wrote it down. She said 'Julia, as resident thespian you can be in charge.'

20. Julia said 'Oh' or similar. Note to self: ask Henry to have a word with Julia re: beauty does not come from outward adornment, especially <u>lipstick during the day.</u>

21. Susan said 'I will sing "White Cliffs of Dover".'

22. Doris said 'I will help backstage.'

23. Ruby volunteered to sing a song in French, which I myself found HIGHLY dubious.

24. Magsy said 'The ninth of October is a fortnight away. I do not believe in Mother Molly's prophecies so I am not worried, not in the least, not even a tiny bit.'

25. Ruby said 'Agnes, are you scared of Mother Molly?'

26. Agnes said 'Mind your own.'

27. Lorna said 'My head says the prophecy is bunk but my heart says what if somebody we know dies.'

28. Mrs E said 'I cheat death every day simply by getting dressed.'

29. Pamela said 'Agenda.'

30. Lorna said 'Surely farces in the north is a mistake and it means forces in the north. Perhaps Scotland.'

31. Magsy said 'Or north Borsetshire. I

have never quite trusted the strange folk of north Borsetshire.'

32. Doris said she is too busy with the harvest to worry about Mother Molly.

33. Pamela said 'Cliff Horrobin has asked for donations of books to Arkwright Hall's library.'

34. Mrs E said 'Ah the darling kiddies.'

35. Agnes asked what is so darling about kiddies, they are just smaller adults, and thanked heaven she was spared the curse of childbirth.

36. Ruby let out a (very European) gasp.

37. Mrs E said 'Dear Agnes doesn't mean that.'

38. Agnes said 'Dear Agnes ruddy well does.'

39. Pamela said 'Yes well anyway' and Susan said 'Lorna, tell the truth and shame the devil. You know where Vic is, don't you?'

40. Lorna went red, which <u>some</u> might say is proof that she <u>does</u> know the whereabouts of her AWOL brother-in-law.

41. Ruby said 'Is that all, only I have to get back to the shop.'

42. Mrs E said 'Back to your beau? One cannot help but notice that Frank and Bob are sweet on you. I do love romance.'

```
  43. Agnes said 'Those two jowly so-and-
so's and should know better at their age.'
  44. Pamela said 'That seems as good a
place as any to finish.'
```

Pamela took off like a whippet, nimbly sidestepping Mrs E's naked need to talk shingles. There were errands to run, servants to chastise, but when she got back to Lower Loxley, Pamela made straight for her writing desk.

'Dear Alec,' she wrote, before starting over with 'My love.'

Doris Archer tells me she prays for you, so I feel confident you'll make it home without a scratch. That lady has a simple faith in God, and an equally simple faith in YOU. Like the rest of Ambridge, she looks up to you. Introduce a child out of wedlock and where will Doris be?

Where will the village be? Hasn't there been enough disorder?

Pamela knew she sounded like a prig. What she really wanted to say was 'I don't want Kitty's child in my house!' Six-year-old Caroline would be a permanent memento of Pamela's shortcomings, of the frigidity that forced her husband to look elsewhere for softness and sensuality.

She carried on.

By all means give the girl the life she deserves. She has Irish relatives to supply the love; you can supply the financial support and protection from afar.

But bring her here? Really? Haven't you told me countless times that our behaviour affects the whole village?

Time to show her hand.

Alec, what about me? I would be thrust into the eye of a storm. Fingers would point, the gossip would be thunderous.

Think of me and reconsider.

Believing herself to be working-class blood royal, Hildegard was amused by the upper-class habits of Lower Loxley: changing clothes to eat dinner; mangling words – 'vair' for 'very'; a love of croquet.

Keeping to the shadows lest she be pressed into duty, she watched soft-handed toffs bang hoops into the lawn, as instructed by Pamela.

She adores cracking the whip. The pilots emasculated themselves in front of Pamela, but showed their true selves to Hildegard. *And I love it.*

'Hiding?' Wanda winked. 'Don't blame you.' She was early, eager to spot Max before he saw her. She turned to Hildegard but the maid was gone, and Wanda was freed from the duty of conversation. It had been a tough week, riddling potatoes through a wheezing machine and packing the smallest off to a factory that made what passed for jam in wartime.

The futile game began. The terrace filled up. The thwack of mallets competed with chit-chat.

Julia's fan club gathered around her, enjoying the girlish questions she asked about the war. 'Where on earth *is* Banska Bystrica?' Her eyes widened. 'Gosh! Slovakia? And those *marvellous* resistance fellows have wrested it back from the ghastly Nazis?'

A hand took her elbow, and Pamela suggested Julia bestow herself on the other guests.

'Is it true what Cad told me?' whispered Julia. 'The RAF only expects fliers to survive six missions?'

'Let's not bother our heads with that today.' Pamela palmed off her daughter-in-law to the vicar and his wife, standing in barren matrimonial silence. *Would Julia weep if my son caught it?* Pamela couldn't be sure.

Heels vandalised the velvet grass, and wilting ladies were given first dibs on the wrought-iron chairs. Gossip flowed with the lemonade.

'Heard Nelson Gabriel was caught filching tuppence from the poor box,' laughed Susan Grundy.

'Youthful folly.' Doris was forgiving. 'Remember when Nelson fell in the Am on that Sunday School picnic?'

Susan guffawed, and called to Frances, 'You saved his life, remember? Swam like an eel, you did.'

'I'm an excellent swimmer,' preened the vicar's wife.

'Daresay you regret your heroism, seeing how the tyke turned out.'

Country doctors must show their faces at every get-together. Morgan watched his sister-in-law swing a mallet. *Magsy's competitive,* he thought. Her father, old Aubrey Furneax, would gloat for days when he beat Morgan's own father at tennis. It was a sort of entitlement, the sense that the Furneaux clan was better at everything: tennis, croquet, soothing babies. Not that it dented the two families' friendship; Aubrey and Morgan's father had shared the gamut of Edwardian interests: botany, science, but above all, tennis.

'Lemonade, sir?' Hildegard's breath smelled of Players no.5.

'Please!' Nance plonked Tudor in Morgan's arms and took a goblet.

'You keep that little'un indoors on the ninth.' Hildegard slid a nail across her throat. 'Someone's gonna get it.'

'Hildy, you're a menace.' Julia took a cup, and coochy-cooed over Tudor, who lay serenely against Morgan's tweed lapel. 'Beautiful eyes . . . Oh! Is he, what do they call it?'

'Yes, he is.' Nance grew taut, but Julia only said, 'What a little dreamboat!' and moved on.

Introducing Tudor could be tricky. The world didn't always allow Nance to show the intense pride she felt in her boy. She heard sniggers on the bus, or in cafés; almost worse were the tongues tied by pity.

Tudor had been whisked away the moment he was born. Nurses were cagey, avoiding her bed. Nance had no idea if she had delivered a boy or a girl, until he was returned to her washed and dressed – *I never saw him uncivilised!* – with glittery, hard smiles.

When Morgan arrived, he picked up the baby and she saw in his face fierce and tender love but also concern. 'Our boy,' he told her, 'he's not quite like the other babies here. There'll be challenges, and he'll grow up a little differently.'

Nance had wanted to know why, what had she done? The medical profession's answer? 'It simply happens.'

All babies simply happen, thought Nance. *And they're all perfect*.

Although none, of course, as perfect as Tudor.

No other word for it – Wanda was *skulking*. She kept her eye on Max in the milieu, but hung back.

Another woman eyeing Max made her way towards him as he chatted to Grayson. *Can't he ever smile?* thought Pamela, even though she appreciated Max's habit of keeping his troubles to himself. 'You've made yourself unpopular,' she said to him, interrupting. 'Your Aunt Blanche would *not* approve of a Gilpin requisitioning the Sawyers' land like that.'

'I know, but needs must.' Max had appropriated a neglected corner scattered with roofless barns; both of them knew his narcissistic Aunt Blanche wouldn't give a fig. 'It's essential for Home Guard manoeuvres. Even though there's less threat in Ambridge than, say, a dockyard, we're not playing games.'

'Dodgy's playing games!' smiled Grayson, and pointed at him, blindfolded and bumbling after the village children.

The little ones evaded him and Dodgy caught, instead, Cliff.

Wanda headed to a pergola, feeling she'd be safe there from bumping into Max. 'You're avoiding me,' said a voice from the shadows.

'Clearly I'm not doing it very well.' Wanda turned to leave.

'Wait,' he said.

Recalcitrant, don't-tell-me-what-to-do Wanda waited.

'Well, face me,' said Max. 'Do you need an apology? Am I a rotter? Because you ruddy well kissed me first, you know.'

'Apologise? Don't be silly. I just don't know what to do next,' admitted Wanda. 'It was intense.'

'Kisses are supposed to be intense. You didn't like it?'

'What a question!'

'I liked it,' said Max. 'I want to do it again.'

She laughed. 'That's handy, because I want you to do it again.'

He didn't move, and Wanda suppressed a tut.

'There's a but,' said Max. 'I'm married. My wife has gone but it's still true that I'm married. I love her, Wanda. I was faithful to her when she was alive, and I find I can't change the habit. Even with . . . someone like you.'

'I'm not someone like me, I *am* me. If I was dead, I wouldn't expect the world to stop turning.' Wanda put her hand to her mouth. 'That sounded callous. It's hard to find words for this. Especially with you being so close.'

'I used to hear her talk to me. Go on, call the doc and have me locked up, but she'd comment on my breakfast, tell me I looked wretched after a late night. Then I met you.' Pain dragged Max's lean face still tighter. 'And she went silent on me.'

'What do I do with this information?' Wanda was pained, too. 'What are you *saying*, Max?'

'I'm saying . . .'

Dodgy blundered in, on the run from a blindfolded Cliff, and Wanda was glad of the intrusion.

Her thoughts were sticky, confused, like a tangled ball of string. She left the two men in the pergola and resolved to put Max out of her mind. She had kissed many a chap and forgotten them all.

She grabbed a mallet from Cad's hands and hammered a ball through a hoop.

The moment shimmers.

Ambridge is a-bed. Well, *most* of Ambridge is a-bed.

Stan is plunging through a misty wood, whistling. To himself. To someone else? He staggers a little; he spent the evening in The Bull.

Another whisky is a bad idea, but Max has one anyway.

At The Cherries, Mrs Endicott makes herself some cocoa. She pads past the photographs on the piano, and raises her mug to the Burtons.

Nance tries to put Mother Molly out of her head. She imagines a bullseye on her back; what if Nance is the 'gentleperson' who will topple into the Lethe on the ninth of October? Nance has no time to die – who would look after Tudor? Nance has to live, well, *forever.*

Peggy roves the farmhouse. She has heartburn, and the moon shining on the stove has no sympathy. She thinks of Jack; he doesn't make her heart burn.

Alone, Frances stands in her bedroom, ear cocked. Out in the passage, Henry approaches, and then continues on his way. She hears the spare bed give. It will be October tomorrow; the year is turning, and Henry is turning too, away from her.

Dumb animals don't know autumn is at the door. They all sleep and snore. Stalwart in his stall, Glen and Mother Cat by the Aga, Minko on a coverlet. Badboy turns on an abandoned blanket. The ancient budgerigar in Mrs Endicott's scullery sneezes. They know nothing of the wireless's optimism, they just know they are well fed, and tomorrow is another day.

October

Only a fool expects regular letters from servicemen.

Pamela put the lack of communication down to a mail ship sunk or a pen mislaid, and not to Alec's disgust at her refusal to have Caroline come to live with them.

Filling a page with Ambridge news, Pamela characterised her reluctance to broach the topic as tact, and not a backsliding into their old habit of avoiding the important issues.

My dear,

Mother Molly has the village in a tizzy. A hundred theories about the next victim, but nobody thinks it's them, of course! Some wish Grayson would stop digging for such dark magic.

Me? I say tosh, and I say it very loudly.

Many others said the same.

At the shop Hildegard put a bar of ration chocolate on the Pargetters' tab, and said, 'The prophecy's bunk! River of Lethe? What've we got to do with ancient Greeks?' She sniffed. 'What's that smell? Summat gone off?'

Frank quietly binned his cologne.

Counting his change, Joe Grundy opined that he wasn't a 'gentleperson known to all' so he felt perfectly safe. 'And you, Ruby, you're new in the village, so no need to worry. A shopkeeper, though . . . might be you, Frankie boy, dying an 'orrible death on the ninth of October.'

The Italian POWs playing football in Quartershot Camp agreed they were outsiders and had no fear of the prophecy. Tots at Arkwright Hall knew nothing of it as they laboured over their alphabet; the Home Guard told each other it was a load of bilge, but told their wives something different.

Back at the shop, the queue jumped at the loud toot of a passing car's horn.

'There goes the vicar.' Ruby peered over the display of, well, very little, in the window. 'Must be the bishop's car, there's a big crest on the front.'

Should vicars show off? Doris was always dismayed by Henry's feet of clay.

A wild yapping announced Frances, dragged in by what appeared to be a doormat but turned out to be Hannibal, the bishop's beloved dog. 'I have two nights with this maniac while Henry lives it up with gourmet dinners and fine wines. Nothing ascetic about the bishop's wartime table, I can tell you.'

'Get him off the Lux!' yelled Frank.

The dog bit open a precious box of soap flakes.

'Stop it!' Frances was ineffectual; Hannibal moved on to

harass the doorstop. 'What was Henry thinking, volunteering me to look after this creature? *And* his blasted bees!'

Hannibal pulled her into the street, where he barked at a passing cart as if it was his nemesis.

The unseasonal warmth meant bees were still on duty. Cliff saw one flagging on an Arkwright Hall windowsill, and offered it sugar water. His new General Administrative Officer brought him a brew, and they watched the bee pull itself together.

'Don't stay late tonight,' Cliff told Peggy.

'I'm sorting out your so-called filing system.' Peggy's take-home pay was more than the ATS. *But there's nothing to spend it on.*

'You need your rest.' Cliff gestured to her tummy with his cup.

'Who can sleep,' said Peggy, 'with Mother Molly on the rampage?'

Cliff knew she was joking. He also knew she stayed late to avoid going home. Before Lorna, he used to feel the same.

The bee took off through the open window.

Brampton Green barracks was jumping to the beat of 'Chattanooga Choo Choo'.

Toes tapping, Wanda was desperate to get back to the dance floor, but she did her duty by the young ATS girl crying her eyes out in the dingy lavatory.

'He hasn't asked me up *all night*,' the girl wailed.

'There, there.' Wanda was distracted, realising she

suddenly understood why girls cried in the ladies' loos. Max had got under her skin, the first man ever to do so. He was intrigued by her, yet made no move to pursue her. All the behaviour that would deter another woman made Wanda want him more ardently. Lorna had quoted Donne, saying that poet never rhymed 'dove' with 'love'; he saw every affair as idiosyncratic: 'I am peculiar and intricate.'

I'll never cry over Max! Despite his fine eyes, his straight nose, the way he kissed ... 'Come on!' She blotted the damsel's tears. 'Make the rotter jealous!'

They ran back to the noise and heat. Wanda grabbed a spotty lieutenant and jitterbugged so peculiarly and intricately that she wore him out.

Max wound his alarm clock, yawning, ready for sleep.

Sleeping through the night was commonplace now. He wondered why the tide had turned, why he was able to sleep. And then he wondered why he was wondering, as the answer was obvious.

Her.

Nocturnal creatures went about their business as the village drifted off. Young owls tested their wings in the trees around Lower Loxley, and Hildegard let herself out of a side door. Her assignation was outdoors, but they would keep each other warm.

* * *

The smell and noise of the barn surprised Peggy, as she handed over Wanda's lunch. The calves were being bucket-fed, and their din as they scrambled to get to the milk created a Piccadilly Circus hubbub of its own.

'Was she hungry?' asked Doris, as Peggy came back to Brookfield and took her seat at the table.

Wanda had fallen on the sandwiches, shocking Peggy by first spitting in her hands to clean them. 'Said she was *ravenous*.'

Phil asked what that meant as he dived into the parsnip soup. 'Wanda speaks so posh.'

'Our Wanda's a lady,' said Doris.

And yet you're so close to her. Peggy didn't dress up her envy. Comparing her own stuttering stop-start relationship with Doris to Wanda's easy familiarity left her confused. The land girl was born into wealth, she had *options*, yet she and the farmer's wife were thick as thieves.

'Out 'til all hours at a dance,' said Doris indulgently. 'Then fresh as a daisy at cock's crow. See if you can keep this down, Peggy.'

Peggy took the soup. Talk of dancing triggered a sudden memory of winning the spot prize at the Hercules Ballroom, back when her cumbersome body was light as air.

Dan plonked himself down between Christine and Phil. 'Look at this!' He showed them a War Ag brochure of the equipment that promised to change his life. 'Tractors.' He leered at them the way other men might at saucy postcards, as he dipped bread into his soup.

'Can't wait for Monday,' said his son, mouth full. 'When we see who drops dead.'

'Phillip Archer!' Doris was appalled.

'Glad I'm not a "gentleperson".' Dan winked at Phil. 'Else I'd be making out a new will.'

'Leave the farm to Mother Cat, Dad,' suggested Christine.

'Feels blasphemous to even half-believe in Mother Molly.' Doris doled out seconds; the pot was bottomless in her kitchen. To change the subject, she asked Peggy, 'Any word from Jack?'

'What?' Peggy was wrenched back from Bassingbourne. 'Nah.'

There had been little since D-Day. Strange to think of common-or-garden Jack taking part in history.

'Was it romantic the last time you saw Jack?' Christine neglected her soup; she was not at home to parsnips.

'He was drunk,' said Peggy, immediately regretting it as she felt Doris bristle.

'It's a self-confidence thing,' said Doris.

'It's a getting drunk thing,' said Dan.

As if Mother Nature was wary of Mother Molly, the morning of the ninth of October dawned dim and grey, with a speaking breeze that whispered to the village.

'You ladies are in a hurry,' called Frances from the gate of the vicarage, where she was polishing the brass nameplate.

Magsy and Mrs Endicott were out of breath.

'I can hardly keep up!' puffed Magsy. 'We're rushing back to The Cherries; she left the cloth draped over the budgie cage.'

'I don't like to upset dear Twinkle Toes,' panted Mrs Endicott. 'He gets rather pecky if everything isn't just so.'

'You're not rushing home because of the prophecy?' Frances was shrewd. 'If any demons come knocking, I'll see them off. Nothing frightens me.' *Except wondering how long my husband can hold a grudge.*

Magsy paused, to lean on the gatepost and catch her breath. 'Your house guest is quiet at last. That silly dog howled through the night.'

'If Hannibal wasn't the bishop's dog, I'd have turfed him out. Chewed up a cassock and did his business on a pouffe. I locked him in the coal shed.'

'Do liberate him!' Mrs E was stricken.

'Suppose I must,' grumbled Frances.

'It's quiet today.' Ruby had tidied the shelves twice. 'Surely it's not because of Mother Molly?'

'Folk can be very namby-pamby,' said Frank. 'Bob, for example. That man's scared of his own shadow.'

The door banged open and Frank jumped a foot in the air.

'Is he here?' Frances was distracted, her hat askew, a lead dangling from bony fingers. 'The dog, Frank, *the dog!*'

Hannibal, the bishop's bewhiskered ally, had found a way out of the shed.

'Henry', gibbered Frances as she took off again, 'will kill me!'

At her Arkwright Hall desk, Evie Bonnet attempted to divide twelve by three, in the hope of impressing Cliff. The view distracted her – trees shivering in the sudden cold snap. The groggy clouds cast shadows that rippled and moved.

Mama told her they were lucky. They escaped. France, however, was held hostage by evil. If Evie asked how to recognise evil, her mother would say it was intolerance, violence, the absence of liberty. *Nobody,* thought Evie, getting back to her sums, *has the right to hold me captive.*

Not even Mother Molly, the witch who held Ambridge hostage on that horrible day.

The requisitioned corner of Sawyers Farm stood eerie and silent in the darkness. Angled roofs loomed over the Home Guard as they defended it against Nazi phantasms.

'Eyes peeled for the missing dog!' said Max. Behind him, the men were in surprisingly neat formation; the new guns had inspired them. 'Now, scatter.'

They scattered, some of them rather slowly, at least two of them in the wrong direction.

Max squatted by a gutted barn. He heard Whitey White hiss, 'What was that?'

'Silence!' said Max.

'Laughter!' Whitey dashed out from cover. 'Ghostly laughter!'

'It's 'er,' gasped Walter, emerging from shadow. 'Mother Molly's come for us.'

'Our enemy is flesh and blood.' Max's face seemed to shape-shift in the intermittent moonlight.

'There it is again!' squealed Whitey.

'I heard it that time,' said Denholm.

'Don't be damned silly,' snapped Max.

But he had heard it too.

Ruby sat on the stairs, sewing. She could hear the men in the bar chakking like the fieldfares that woke her every morning. Her daughters were quiet, asleep, safe.

The noise in the bar changed. Surprised shouts. And crying? Ruby sprinted downstairs to see, incredibly, Evie and Michele sobbing in their best coats, surrounded by the Home Guard platoon. The children's faces were blacked, and . . . was that a gun in Evie's belt?

'Mrs Bonnet,' began Max gently, but Denholm butted in.

'My fallen arches', he began, 'are agony, yet I came out to do my duty, only for manoeuvres to be ruined by these two fifth columnists!'

Evie ran and hid her face in Ruby's skirt. Michele blubbered where she stood, quaking and mortified.

'They ruined nothing.' Max had protected the children from Denholm's ire on the cold march back from Sawyers Farm. 'But I've explained to them how dangerous a game they were playing. Evie's gun is wooden, but my men have live ammo.' He could have added that 'his men' were trigger-happy and frightened half to death by Mother Molly.

Ruby knelt to Evie, and the girl stuttered out, 'I . . . wanted to . . . get a Nazi because . . . they took Papa.'

Male hearts melted.

'Let 'em get to bed, poor mites,' said Walter.

'Where they should be already!' Denholm's heart was not so easily melted.

'Goodnight, young ladies,' said Max, and saluted. Like his platoon, he was glad to finish this eerie day in the warm fug of the bar.

The shop was Ambridge's nerve centre; all news passed through it.

'We'd have heard by now if anything untoward happened yesterday,' said Frank. 'All village personnel are accounted for.'

'Yah boo sucks, Mother Molly,' said Ruby, weighing out suet for Doris.

The sun shone, crisp and optimistic. All days are a fresh start, but this one felt especially so.

'Give us a hand!' Susan struggled in, Hannibal the dog bucking in her arms.

As Frank took the animal, Doris said, 'Where'd you find him?'

'Sitting in the vicar's rowboat, large as life,' said Susan. 'Stuck in the mud by the bridge. Barking its head off, of course.'

'Frances'll be relieved,' said Ruby.

Hannibal leapt out of Frank's grasp, and would have made a break for it if Max hadn't been in the doorway. 'Hey, fella,' he said, and grabbed the dog's collar.

'Well done, son,' said Frank. 'National Loaf?'

Max nodded, and Doris felt a twinge of pity. Brookfield was saved from the dreaded grey and crumbly wartime bread by Doris's yeast-free wheaten bread, made with best buttermilk.

Max asked after Evie and Michele. 'They were crying so hard. I felt terrible.'

'You made little girls *cry*?' asked Doris.

As Hannibal decimated the stock room, the story came out. 'It really wasn't Max's fault,' said Ruby. 'He was kind.'

Doris felt differently. 'You need to make it up to those kiddies. And this is how you do it.'

Doris reached the vicarage in double-quick time, pulled along by Hannibal on a length of rope. 'You get along home, love,' she said to Susan.

'I want to see the reunion,' laughed Susan. 'And Frances might give me a bob or two for finding the little bugger.'

Going round to the back, as was the country way, Doris pushed at the open kitchen door. Her fluting 'Fran-*ces*' echoed dully in the house.

'Must be in the garden,' said Susan. She was blithe, but Doris, shutting Hannibal in the coat cupboard, had an itchy sense of apprehension.

'How'd the boat just drift off?' she mused, as they picked their way down the stepping stone path to the bank of the Am.

Susan pointed down-river. The vicar's precious beehive was on its side. 'Summat's not right, Doris.'

They sped up, Doris puffing into a lead. A shoe lay on the grass. 'Stay back, Susan!' It wouldn't be right for a pregnant girl to see what Doris could see.

Frances was face up in the river, shackled by reeds. She bobbed and swayed, her eyes staring up through the water at the sky.

'Get help!' shouted Doris. She heaved the body – Frances Bisset was already *the body* – out of the Am, her feet slithering in the mud. She took off her coat and tucked it around Frances.

Gently closing the dead woman's eyes, Doris wondered if the last thing they ever saw was Mother Molly.

Death is not an infrequent visitor to any community, especially in wartime, but sudden death in middle age, a woman alive at dawn and gone by sunset, is shocking.

Pamela, preoccupied with Frances's fate, didn't join in with the Lower Loxley breakfast table conversation.

The chaps were gloomy, theorising about the Italian campaign. 'Ammo's low, and you know why!' said Cad. 'We've decreased production in anticipation of the Germans giving up.'

'The Soviets are standing firm in Norway,' said a newly

arrived air commodore. 'Dashed odd, but they use deer to pull their munitions.'

Pamela had too much on her plate to worry overmuch about what reindeer might be up in Kirkenes. The vicar had been recalled from his conference, and it was her duty to pay her respects. She didn't relish such visits at the best of times; the vicar was such an odd fish, there was no way of knowing how he would take the dreadful news.

'Frances!' Dodgy threw down his *Times*. He had scribbled across an advert for Wincarnis nerve tonic. 'The prophecy *included* the poor lady's name.' He was an inveterate crossword-solver. 'Farces in the north is an anagram. Muddle up the letters of "farces" and add an N for "north", and what do you get?'

Pamela wouldn't answer.

'You get *Frances*!' Dodgy almost popped with excitement. 'Mother what's-her-name was spot on from a distance of two hundred years!'

'Poppycock,' said Pamela.

'Is this coffee pot poppycock?' Dodgy waggled the silver pot. 'No, it's in front of your face, dear lady. Just like the prophecy.'

In the shop little else was spoken of.

Frances was deified, her good deeds – scant though they were – recounted and embellished. All lamented the gap she would leave, and wondered how the vicar would cope alone. And then, without fail, all turned to the occult aspect of Frances's death.

It couldn't be ignored. Agnes was opening her mouth to hold forth when Henry entered, and she coughed instead.

'Um, eggs?' asked the vicar hopefully. 'They're on a list Frances left by the sink so I must fetch them, I suppose.'

He wavered, and Frank whisked a chair beneath him. As Henry rubbed his glasses with his cuff, the customers gathered round. Doris offered to cook something hearty and leave it on his doorstep. Frank said he'd deliver the eggs and anything else necessary. Walter gruffly offered to see the vicar home: 'You look half done-in, me old pal.'

Refusing all help, the vicar wandered out again, without the eggs.

There was a reverent silence for his pain, until Agnes said, 'D'you think he had anything to do with it?' She rolled her eyes at the gasps, certain she was only saying what they all thought. Frances was not an easy woman to live with. Her current sainthood wouldn't last; the whitewashing would peter out and they would remember her more accurately, as what Agnes would deem 'a right old bag'.

'The reverend was miles away, but there *is* something peculiar about how Frances went,' muttered Frank.

Doris said, 'What bothers me is how did the dog get in the boat and float off?'

'Who knocked over the bees?' asked Agnes.

'The big question is,' said Walter, tapping his nose, 'how did such a strong swimmer drown in that quiet stretch of the river?'

* * *

Black coats were buttoned up and black hats adjusted in subdued houses. Stepping out, villagers converged on St Stephen's, its tower pointing up at an appropriately miserable sky.

The world took no notice of one paltry death; since Frances passed, the German army had retreated from Greece, and that country now teetered on the verge of civil war. Ambridge, however, felt the solemnity of the funeral keenly.

'I hate funerals,' whispered Julia to Pamela as they walked towards the church door.

Who doesn't? thought her mother-in-law.

'But then again,' Julia added, 'I do look good in black.'

Grayson's fringe lifted and his birthmark was lurid. He spoke to nobody; his shoulders were around his ears.

In whispers, Susan and Peggy compared pregnancy aches and pains. Joe Grundy, father-to-be, contributed nothing to this 'women's business', turning to Bob and enquiring, ''Ere, Bob, you growing a 'tash?'

Florid-faced, Bob would not reply.

'Ma!' Cliff sprang over to Connie, holding her to him, feeling her feather-weight bones. Then he sprang away, as Stan and brazen little Badboy came through the lychgate.

The dog pranced into church alongside the mourners, and was the only one not stopped in his tracks by the coffin.

Wreathed in velvet and surmounted with waxy lilies, the wooden box contained what remained of Frances. Everything but her essence. She was both present and absent at her special service.

Morgan nodded respectfully as he passed. He had examined Frances, and discovered that she didn't drown. By the time she went into the water, her throat had closed up from anaphylactic shock. Her cold body was punctured over and over with bee stings. Respiratory arrest would have been swiftly followed by cardiac arrest. It was quick, merciless. A horrible series of coincidences.

All Doris could think of as she filed past was that one sensible shoe left in the mud.

Still a Johnny-come-lately, Max didn't have a designated seat. He sat alone, near the back, and steeled himself. The last funeral he attended was his wife's. Her life was now bound up with her death, an injustice he couldn't accept.

Don't listen, he counselled himself.

The beautiful old words of the service for the dead would drag him down again into contemplation of the meaning of, well, *everything.* He recalled how his sensitivity about planes going down, of men being lost, was cited by the RAF as proof of his 'nervous problems'. He had been told to toughen up, but Max treated death with exaggerated respect.

Officiating, Henry was monotone. The congregation strained to hear. 'We die unto the Lord,' he said, or so his flock guessed.

'The little girls are a credit to you,' whispered Agnes to Ruby, shocked into a compliment by Evie and Michele's demeanour.

'That's nice of you to say,' Ruby whispered back. 'Perhaps you'd like to get to know them. We could come to tea?'

'In this country, we wait to be asked.' Agnes enjoyed being reproving. She glanced at her husband, fighting sleep beside her. 'My Denholm doesn't want to be bothered with kiddies.'

The Archers had their own pew, and bang in the middle of it sat Wanda. She was glad of their comforting bulk, their uncomplicated equilibrium. Despite her determination to stay away from Max – for what good could come of kissing such a man? – she had almost sat by him when she saw the pain in his eyes.

He had refused to look up, even when she lingered, so she had slotted in beside Peggy, and now concentrated on singing 'The Day Thou Gavest Lord is Ended'. Behind her own back, she listened for Max's voice in the chorus.

Oh God, is this what love is like? After all her anticipation, love was turning out to be dreary and full of longing. *Who wants a dead woman as a rival?*

Studying her, Peggy knew Wanda would make a far more suitable daughter-in-law for Doris. She rubbed her bump, straining the dreadful sack of a dress which was now the only thing that fitted. Her bump was company when she found herself adrift; she thought of it as hers, nothing to do with Jack.

The congregation sat, boots scuffling on stone. Badboy chased a mouse around the font. Mrs Endicott dabbed her eyes. Ruby passed her a handkerchief; *I won't cry,* she told herself.

There had been no funeral for Henri, dropped in battle.

She dreamed about him now and then. Hide-and-seek in the garden in Sceaux. It was amusing at first that she couldn't find him, but she always woke up desperate. Hide-and-seek without an end is no fun. Ruby swallowed hard, regretting the loss of her hanky.

The sermon was about Frances's death, but not about Frances. It was about Mother Molly, and the vicar became jerkily energetic. 'I will tolerate no godless talk of magic.'

Lorna squeezed Cliff's hand. They agreed on most matters – that they could live on love if they had to, that Cliff could survive estrangement from his family so long as he had Lorna, that good bread and good cheese made an excellent supper – but they had disagreed that morning.

Death, Cliff insisted, was banal and terrible. No point in trying to make sense of it. Mother Molly, he had said, foreshadowing the vicar, was just a woman and had no powers.

Lorna's world was fragile; when push came to shove, it contained only Cliff. A haphazard universe was far more frightening than one governed by folklore and religion.

The vicar leaned over the pulpit. Ten minutes into his homily, and still no real mention of his dead wife's qualities. 'Molly did not foresee the accident. It was a random act. If I hadn't kept those hives . . .' Henry gathered himself. 'God has a plan for each of us, and it pleased him to gather Frances to his bosom.'

'Bosom!' sniggered little Nelson Gabriel.

* * *

Pitching in. That's what Dan called it. 'Could you pitch in with the muck spreading, Peggy love?' And now here was Peggy, heading to the field that abutted Walter Gabriel's land. 'But don't go near Walter's shed,' Dan warned. 'You'll disturb his work on his top-secret weapon.'

He had laughed then, and Peggy had tried to do the same, but she didn't always get countrypeople's jokes. She wasn't laughing now, as she led a cart piled with ripe manure.

'All you have to do,' he had said, waving Peggy off, 'is keep hold of Stalwart. He knows the way.'

Wanda, coming into the kitchen for Doris to rub grease on her cracked fingertips – harvesting sugar beet was brutal work – was incredulous. 'You lousy lot, giving her Stalwart to handle. Took me months to get the better of that horse.'

'Have you gone deaf?' Peggy asked the horse as he bent to nibble the sparse grass by the side of the track. 'Come *on*.' Her wellies were stuck fast in doughy mud. She pulled at the rein, and the creature moved.

He moved as far as a pond, the manure wobbling and swaying as the wheels bumped in the pitted earth.

'I was just about to send a search party,' said Dan, when Peggy got back to the farmhouse.

'What's that pong?' Phil sniffed the air. 'Oh, it's *you*.'

Not only did Peggy smell, she was red in the face and covered in mud. She hoped it was mud.

A little late, she got the joke. She'd been pranked. After a moment's hesitation, Peggy did a very un-Peggyish thing. She ran out.

'I'll go,' said Wanda, when Doris and Dan looked at each other, startled, repentant.

It was warm in the barn, with the calves.

'Come here,' said Wanda, and Peggy came there, glad to be embraced, finding her new neediness most alien.

'They hate me,' said Peggy.

'It's just farm life.' Wanda held Peggy away from her, and pushed her hair out of her eyes. 'It's rough and ready, but a trick like that means you're one of the team, that's all.' She took Peggy's arm. 'Bet you're ready for supper. If I know the Boss, she'll chuck you an extra sausage.'

Peggy took her meal in her room.

'Take those off, Hildegard,' said Pamela, when her maid came up to brush her hair for dinner.

'Me 'orns?' Hildegard was sulky as she removed the red papier-maché devil horns. 'Just a bit of Halloween fun, ma'am.' She took up the brush.

'Ow,' said Pamela. 'Gently!'

The hiatus in Alec's letters had begun to worry her. Surely heaven wouldn't take him just when they had found their rhythm? But then again, wasn't that exactly how heaven operated? 'That'll do, thank you.' She took the brush from Hildegard's hand. 'Pull the curtains tighter, I see a chink.'

Halloween must be kept out.

Pamela took up her rings and slipped them on. They twinkled like the envy in Hildegard's eyes.

It would be too cruel if the last exchange Pamela ever had with her husband was her refusal to take in his daughter.

The Home Guard tramped through the village.

'Nobody about, sir,' said young Chas Westenra, an able lad exempted from service due to his job as a lens grinder.

'There's no taste for Halloween this year,' said Max. He should have chided the boy for chatting, but he didn't. He was glad of the sound of a human voice as they passed the churchyard, and its new humped grave.

'He's up,' said Walter sadly.

The men knew who he meant. A lone light glowed in the vicarage.

'Up,' said Max, 'and all alone.'

November

Grass didn't grow in November, and livestock gravitated into outbuildings, except for the hardy sheep who stuck it out on the land. Male calves, unaware they would be castrated before the first frost, kept each other cosy in the barns' companionable fug.

Similarly, human livestock migrated to The Bull, a bright spot in the autumn mist.

There were crumbs in Bob's new moustache. He knew the punters tittered about it behind his back, but Ruby declared it 'distinguished' so the tash stayed.

'You must admit, Dan,' he was saying, as he pulled a golden pint, 'dairy farmers get fed up with your War Ag interfering with their milk production.'

'First, it's not *my* War Ag,' said Dan, who never got to his second point because Joe Grundy cut in.

'Our herd at Grange Farm never have so much as a cough. It's the herbs in the pasture, keeps 'em bright-eyed.'

'Mebbe,' said Dan, glad when Max appeared to distract the company.

Upright in full Home Guard rig, Max saluted and asked if his 'new number nine platoon volunteers' were ready.

'They've been ready for ages,' beamed Bob. The saloon bar erupted into cheers as Evie and Michele came down in chic khaki jumpsuits, camouflage ivy threaded through their shiny hair.

Max bent down to them. 'Remember the deal? You come out for one night, lead the way, and after that you do as your mama tells you and stay tucked up in your beds?'

Evie waved her fake pistol, to another ribald ovation.

'Thank the Lord you're both available. We desperately need young soldiers with great courage.' Max winked at Ruby; he had promised her zero danger. 'Here.' He got out a tin of blacking and rubbed it on their pink cheeks.

Michele had the look of a soldier who would rather be reading, but Evie gave off sparks of excitement.

'Bye, *Maman*!' she called as she marched out. 'I'll bring you back a Nazi!'

Like bookends, Peggy and Wanda sat either side of the fire. Wanda dozed while Peggy flicked through a magazine she had already read twice.

'Ooh!' Peggy sat up, remembering something. Yes, there it was, at the bottom of her bag.

'Drinking chocolate!' Wanda gaped, as if Peggy had produced the Koh-i-noor diamond.

'Only a scrape left.' Peggy shared the tasty loot with Wanda, Christine and Phil. 'A chum gave it me.' She didn't mention the chum's name: US servicemen, queuing to dance with ATS girls, had been surrounded with a sweet air of plenty.

'Mam'll get blown to bits in this wind.' Phil had a chocolate moustache.

A rota had been set up and it was Doris's turn to 'do' the vicar – air his mattress, wash his crocks, whatever he needed.

'She says,' said Wanda, 'that Henry Bissett barely notices her. Without the Ambridge ladies nagging him, he'd wear the same underpants for a week and dine on the mould in the jam jar.'

The Home Guard were on their bellies, crawling around the ruins of Sawyers Farm. Arthur Sweet was allowed to merely crouch. 'So windy,' he said mildly, as he followed the others.

A pincer movement of Max and Evie crept stealthily around the perimeter. Michele was in the care of Chas Westenra, who was flummoxed by his diminutive, reluctant corporal.

Evie's keen young eyes spotted movement beyond a crumbling wall. She threw a dummy grenade overarm.

'Ow!' said Whitey White from the darkness.

'I killed you all!' exulted Evie, doing a war dance in her khaki.

'That's true,' said Max. 'But they're on our side.'

With that, the 'enemy' closed in, Arthur apologising before saying 'Hands up.'

The girl's enthusiasm, even when misplaced, put a spring in the platoon's step. The evening flew past, with many a pseudo-Jerry captured.

The little ones are good for morale, thought Max, watching Evie tiptoe in Whitey White's borrowed jacket, far too long and trailing behind her.

The atmosphere changed abruptly when Max heard Denholm croak, 'Halt! Who goes there?'

Standing sentry by a rusting pump – not because he was observant but because he irritated the men with his constant grumbling – Denholm said it again, this time with real fear in his voice.

The unhelpful moon hid, and Max ran through the dark, hissing, 'Stay here!' at Evie.

'Password!' bleated Denholm.

Max rounded a corner to see him pointing his rifle into a ramshackle shed.

'Password! Password, I say!'

Chas rocketed to his side. Others followed. It was not the slick reaction Max would want, but it was immediate and heartfelt.

Torchlight lit up the shed's crumbling interior. 'Movement!' said Whitey. 'Some bugger's in there all right.' The torch shone on a wireless.

''E's a spy!' said someone.

The men danced from foot to foot, weapons cocked.

'Password!' yelled Chas.

'Nazi swine!' yelled Whitey.

Michele put her fingers in her ears, blocking out the night which had suddenly filled up with familiar terrors.

Her sister – disobedient to her marrow – crept nearer. Perhaps this was the Nazi who had made Papa pass? Ramming her hands into the pockets of the borrowed jacket, her small fingers encountered something.

The Nazi spoke. 'Calm down, me old pals.'

Denholm threw down his weapon. 'You buffoon!' he said, as Walter Gabriel bumbled out.

The fake grenade had already left Evie's fingertips. It curved gracefully through the air before diving into the empty shed.

The shed exploded and knocked the 9th Platoon off their feet.

With the curtains drawn, nobody at Brookfield saw the fire-works over Sawyers Farm way.

Bed beckoned. Peggy knelt by hers as if to pray, but she was searching for something under the mattress. A bumpy manilla envelope, ATS issue.

She spread out the contents on the coverlet. Tiny black and white photos. Peggy and her pal on their bikes. Peggy in her ATS uniform, blurry – Mum was no good at taking snaps. A ticket for the Saturday Spectacular at the Hercules Ballroom. A flower from a GI admirer, pressed, its scent quite gone.

They were modest treasures, but treasures all the same. A portal to a life that had changed out of all recognition. Peggy picked up the flower, careful not to crush it.

Downstairs was a-bustle. Doris was home, the kettle was on, Phil was being told off for some boyish crime. Suddenly, Doris put her head around Peggy's bedroom door.

Peggy jumped and crumpled the envelope under the mattress. 'Can't you knock?'

Doris pulled in her chin.

'Sorry, I just . . .' said Peggy.

'I came up to say there's a brew on if you fancy it.'

Doris withdrew with dignity and Peggy lay flat on the rag-rug, furious with herself.

Evie was amazed by the destruction she had caused.

The shed was flattened. The postie Whitey White had no eyebrows. Denholm slumped against the pump, mouthing *password, password*.

Speechless at how close the men in his charge had come to disaster, Max shook himself and said, 'Home, girls.'

'Do we have to?' For once, Evie's real life had trumped *Les Aventures*.

'We have to,' said Max, wondering how on earth he would to explain to Ruby that her daughter had been given a live grenade.

The costumes packed away under the stage in the village hall had served many times.

They're knackered, thought Doris, rifling through wilting ostrich feathers, moth-eaten velvet and damp pompoms.

'Welcome, welcome.' Julia nodded at her troupe as they filed in for the first Winter Tonic rehearsal. 'So grateful to have a gentleman among us,' she said to Walter as he lurched past, scratching his behind through tatty trousers.

From the piano, Mrs Endicott gently reproved him. 'Heard you almost blew up the village last night, Walter.'

'I was drunk, missus! Off me 'ead! *Pie-eyed*.' Walter was not apologetic. 'I was working on me secret weapon – Wompo!'

'Womp-what?' queried Julia.

'That's what Walter calls his home-brew hooch,' coughed Doris as dust rose from a long-dead Pargetter's frock coat.

'What's the best way to defeat them Nazis?' Walter answered his own question. 'By being happy, of course! And by gum I was happy last night.'

As the women chose their costumes for the opening number, Agnes reported on the vicar. 'Eating hard cheese he was, like a glum little mouse.' She tied a feather boa around Peggy's neck. '*I* wouldn't miss Frances. Mother Molly did him a favour.'

'Gracious.' The very shockable Mrs Endicott dropped the dog-eared sheet music for *Run Rabbit Run*.

'No sequins?' asked Julia, surveying the trunk.

'Ambridge,' said Doris, 'isn't a sequin sort of village.'

'We'll soon change that.' Julia regarded her ensemble, all of them in bobble hats and mittens. The grieving vicar had denied permission to light the boiler. Doris's nose was red; Agnes had the look of a woman who would not take direction, and Walter . . . well, Walter was Walter. Shoulders back, chin up, she said, 'I know it's cold, gang, but you're in show business now, and the show must go on! Are we all here?'

'All except Nance,' said Wanda, just as Nance hurried in.

She was beaming. 'There's a new soul in Ambridge! Morgan just got back from delivering Susan Grundy's baby boy.'

'Monday's child is full of grace,' said Mrs Endicott.

Clamping down on baby chatter, Julia put them through their paces. Her pep was inspiring, but exhausting.

'One-two, one-two, heel toe!' Julia marked time with a walking stick as her chorus line mooched across the stage. Wanda had a magnificent high-kick – *that girl's wasted harvesting mangolds* – but Doris moved like a grand piano sliding downhill. As for Nance: *two left feet.* Julia saw a slight figure creep into the back of the hall, and waved. 'Hellooo! Come to join in?'

Connie snorted. 'Me?' She was delivering a square for the village quilt. 'Only I don't know who's next, like.'

'Give it here.' Doris bent from the stage and her corset creaked.

'Pretty fabric,' said Wanda.

'It was a dress. Me best dress.' Connie looked into the middle distance. 'Wore it the day I first clapped eyes on my Romeo.'

Agnes, a tutu over her coat, opened her mouth to pour scorn on such misguided mush, but Doris's warning frown made her reconsider.

Doris turned the yellow and green cotton over in her hands, noting the tiny, careful, woeful stitches. *Maybe thinking of Stan as her Romeo is how Connie gets by.*

Before Doris had time to thank her, Connie hurried off, like a whipped dog that knows it shouldn't be indoors.

'Take your places. Once more from the top.' Julia's command couldn't compete with the catarrh noise of a jeep drawing up outside. Her soubrettes ran to the window.

'Look who it is!' laughed Wanda.

Gerald jumped down from the wheel, and barged through the hall doors to sweep Julia off her feet. Their kiss was passionate and turned Mrs Endicott scarlet.

'I've got forty hours, darling, and then it's back to Rhodesia.' Gerald threw his RAF cap in the air. 'Ladies, tell your other halves the drinks are on me tonight!'

Still no letter from Alec.

Pamela carried on regardless, writing informal bulletins every other day.

Gerald turned up out of the blue! He'll drive from here to Liverpool, thence to Cape Town to board a train to Bulawayo, where he'll join the Elementary Flying Training School.

She didn't write the words she wanted to write. Some version of *Please write back! I need you.* Pamela would save the soppiness for when they were together again. She would hold his hand and stare at him; she would do all the foolish in-love things they had avoided doing for years, for reasons Pamela could no longer fathom.

Unmentioned, Caroline drifted, ghost-like, between the lines. Their basic disagreement about who should take responsibility for the motherless lamb was driving a wedge deep into their new rapport. Relentlessly just and logical, Pamela baulked at what he asked of her; she would not write the child's name; she would not give Alec's argument any oxygen.

Bizarre, isn't it, that war has been the making of Gerald? One of his great pals went down, I'm afraid. His instructor told them to think of it as their friend catching an earlier train, but they are all headed for the same destination. Please, darling, don't catch that wretched train.

Free beer is a powerful lure.

The Bull was so packed Ruby was dragooned into pulling pints. She had abandoned the pierrot costumes she was sewing for Winter Tonic, using the last of her good petticoats and a row of home-made pompoms.

Grayson took his pint greedily.

'You've been digging at the grotto in this weather?' asked Ruby.

'I half hope I won't find another prophecy. Not after . . .'

'Poor Frances.' Dan Archer shook his head.

'I've brought nothing but sadness to Ambridge.'

Slapping Grayson's back, the men assured him it was all that old witch's fault, and then looked around furtively, as if Mother Molly might hear them.

'All the same,' said Dan, 'if you do dig up another prediction, none of us'll get much sleep until the date passes.'

'More beer!' shouted Gerald, and superstitious fears were drowned by Bob's fine ale. 'Wet the baby's head, eh?' Gerald clasped new father Joe Grundy in a manly hug, and then Julia in a gentler one.

There were – whisper it – *women* in the bar. Not just Julia, in diamonds, but Wanda in her corduroy britches. Lorna held Cliff's hand and sipped her ginger beer. A kiss-curl fell over Hildegard's eye. Peggy reckoned the atmosphere was worth Doris's displeasure at going to The Bull 'in your condition'.

'My condition', Peggy had muttered, 'is bored stiff.'

'Farmhands', Wanda was saying, 'are *rascals.* One threw a nest of mice at my hair.'

Cad insinuated himself alongside her. 'And you have such lovely hair,' he murmured.

'Flatterer.' Wanda dutifully flirted back; it was part of the war effort to flirt with serviceman, and meant nothing to her.

It seemed to mean something to Max, watching them over the rim of his glass.

She stepped outside, 'for air'. A moment later – *surely preplanned,* thought Max – Cad wiped his mouth on his sleeve and followed, something vulpine in his expression.

Stan made the most of Gerald's generosity. He held out his glass to Ruby, and said, over her head to Bob, 'Nice-looking lass. Bet she does more than cook for you.'

Frank, at Stan's elbow, was gruff. 'Don't you talk about a lady like that, Horrobin.'

'Ooh, have I touched a nerve, shop boy?' Stan looked groggily from Frank to Bob, and back again. 'Love rivals, eh?'

Frank leapt forward, but was restrained by Walter and Dan, who knew he was no match for Stan's sneaky moves.

Bob pointed at the door. 'You're barred, Stan! Out, you little rat!'

The little rat knew the crowd was against him, and out he sauntered, Badboy at his heels. He was too inebriated to hear the scuffle going on by the porch as he turned for home.

Neither did he hear the slap, nor Cad's heartfelt 'Ouch!'

'Don't you take liberties with me.' Wanda kicked him for good measure.

'You led me on.'

'Rubbish. You're an entitled fool who expects every woman to swoon over his – let's be honest – second-rate lines. *Never* pounce on a woman like that again. Got it?'

Without answering, Cad shouldered his way back into The Bull. Livid stripes on his cheek began to sting.

'What happened out there?' Hildegard hobbled after him on her heels, but jumped back when Max took Cad by one of his air-force blue lapels.

'What did you do to her?' barked Max.

'It's not what I did, matey, it's what she won't do!' Cad felt himself hoisted lopsidedly into the air, nose to nose with the taller man. 'Hey!' His voice went up an octave.

'Now now.' Bob was on it. 'This isn't like you, Mr Gilpin.'

Wriggling free, Cad did his best to return Max's adamantine glare.

'I'll make sure she's all right.' Max turned away.

'You're just what every girl needs, aren't you?' Cad's courage returned when Max was at the door. He shook off Hildegard. 'A conquering hero with one arm.'

'Out!' bellowed Bob for the second time that night, and Cad slunk out the back way.

Max caught his reflection in the door's glazing. Sometimes he forgot. And then he would notice his empty sleeve. He caught Peggy's eye. 'Would you check on Wanda?'

'Sure thing.' Peggy instinctively knew that Max had been a different man before the war stole his arm. She also instinctively knew there was no need to check on Wanda; *that girl's a Sherman tank.*

Delighted with the shenanigans, Gerald entertained his tipsy guests with tales of the next phase of his training, 'EFTS'.

'How you boys love your abbreviations.' Julia barely listened. His war talk bored her. A sudden panic pounced and she interrupted to say, 'You *will* come back, won't you?'

'Oh my sweet girl!' So hungry was Gerald for love that the semi-circle of faces fell away and he saw only his bobby-dazzler of a wife. 'I love you, Julia.'

'And I love *you*, darling.'

He watched her walk to the bar, a path opening up, all eyes upon her. A voice in his ear – Hildegard was the exact height to whisper in ears – said, 'Funny thing about actresses, you can never be quite sure they mean what they say.'

'Look who we found outside!' Wanda and Peggy frog-marched the vicar in between them.

The hubbub dimmed; Bob scowled. A holy man in the house meant a drop in drinking. Still, he poured a tot of whisky and asked, 'How you getting along, Reverend?'

'Fine, thank you.' Henry looked at the whisky, and asked it urgently, 'Did I do wrong by my wife? I was so cold those last months, when I could have guided her out of her judgemental ways. Was I a good husband?'

Nobody said a word. Soul-searching was never on the menu at The Bull. When Henry pushed his drink away untouched and left, his parishioners were profoundly moved, and profoundly relieved. The jingle-jangle of saloon talk revved up again.

Pulling on her jacket, Hildegard announced she was off to meet her beau. 'He's promised to get me out of this dump. The man's crazy about me.' She saw the glance exchanged between Lorna and Wanda. 'It's a secret for now, but not 'cos he's ashamed of me!'

Where another might sneer, Lorna was gentle. 'Cad's not the marrying kind, Hildegard.'

'Shows how much *you* know,' said Hildegard, and braved the night.

*

A lone candle flickered.

Stan snored in his chair. He had dragged Connie out of bed to make him something to eat on his return from The Bull. Somehow she had conjured a plateful from the bare cupboard, and now she sat by the table, watching him, and rubbing the mark on her arm his fingers had made.

The newspaper on his lap was pilfered from the pub. Connie reached over carefully, slid it across his lap. Stan twitched in his sleep. She froze, waiting until he settled again, and then she took the paper, and spread it out beneath the candle.

Newsprint was just pattern to Connie. Written words were doormen denying her entry to a club even her youngest child had joined. The pictures were another matter.

Cursing the bluntness of her scissors, Connie carefully snipped around a photograph of David Niven. He was a bona fide hero; ignoring his celebrity status he had insisted on joining up. How dashing he looked in his uniform and beret. What a smile. And what a gent. Was it a thousand years since she had first seen him in *The Charge of the Light Brigade*? Connie had worn her yellow and green dress, her best dress, to meet Stan outside the Roxy. She was slender then, not yet scrawny, and her head of dark hair came up lovely after a good brushing.

She felt like a million dollars, even though Stan made her climb over a fence to get in the side door for free. The dress tore on a nail.

'Come *on*,' snarled Stan.

She forgot all about her torn dress when the velvet curtains swished back and the big screen jumped to life.

Errol Flynn was nice enough, and Olivia de Havilland was as pretty as a picture, but David Niven outshone them all.

Connie put the snipped photograph to her lips and kissed it, eyes closed, the way they do in the movies.

My Romeo, she thought.

WINTER

1944–5

Why didn't you tell me there was danger?
Why didn't you warn me?

THOMAS HARDY
Tess of the D'Urbervilles

DECEMBER

Last day of term was topsy-turvy and delicious.

Arkwright Hall smelled of mince pies, and the children were given leeway to whoop and rough-house to their heart's desire.

Peggy didn't share Cliff's relief at the thought of a break. She would miss the sticky hands and the squeak of shoes on the stairs, the cool corners she could always find. She clapped extravagantly at the end of Cliff's speech, and the little ones followed suit, even though none of them understood the literary allusions. *Such a bashful man.* Cliff's shyness made her momentarily grateful for her Jack's chipper nature.

'Come here, you two!' Peggy looked out for Maisie and Bert Horrobin in the melee spilling out onto the drive. She wiped Bert's face and neatened the bow on Maisie's plaits. 'Tell your mum Merry Christmas from me,' said Peggy, knowing they'd forget.

'Au revoir, miss.' Evie curtseyed, then ran after her sister, both of them keen to get home to Ruby.

Everyone was avid to shake off Arkwright Hall, except for Peggy. Now it was just her and Doris and the claustrophobic haze of Brookfield's kitchen until the baby came.

A girl? A boy? An ally? All Peggy knew was that it would hurt.

'No you don't!' Ruby whipped the whisky out of Bob's hand and replaced it with a cup of warm milk.

'But . . .' Bob surrendered. 'I know.' He quoted Ruby back at herself. 'This is better for me.' His annoyance was play-acting; he relished being bossed about by Ruby. Looked forward to the hearty sandwiches she left out for him after he closed up at night. It made him feel cared about.

He sipped. 'What's in this?'

'Honey.'

'Sweet,' said Bob, watching her as she went back upstairs.

Christmas bore down on Ambridge.

With ten days to go, presents – modest, utilitarian presents – were squirrelled away, and black market goose changed hands. There were those who held their breath, hoping no new prophecy would spoil the season.

Washing day at Brookfield would not be derailed, Christmas or no.

An appointment with the doctor meant Peggy was excused the rumpus of stripping the beds and dragging out the copper dolly. Dan waited outside Holmleigh with the cart while she, wincing, told Morgan about the constipation that prune juice couldn't cure.

'Babies cause mothers so many indignities,' said Morgan, scribbling on his prescription pad. 'Not long to go now.' He looked sideways at her, his wise eyes warm underneath their canopy of grey brow. 'We're not anxious, are we? About labour?'

'No,' fibbed Peggy.

'Good. We'll get through it, my dear.' He patted her hand, and Peggy almost cried.

As she left the house, she heard Tudor chirrup in a back room, and felt serene.

The feeling didn't last long.

Back at Brookfield, Christine grated soap into the dolly. She was, naturally, grumbling about it, wondering aloud why Phil never had to do such boring chores. 'I should be practising my tap dance. I'm one of Santa's Little Helpers in Winter Tonic.' In her head, Christine was the lead Little Helper.

'Oh lordy,' said Peggy, taking off her hat. 'I forgot to strip my bed.'

'Mum did it for you.'

Peggy tensed. Coat still on, she went upstairs to find that Doris hadn't stopped at taking off the bedclothes. The room was rigorously tidied.

Everything's changed around!

The book left by the bed was now on a shelf. Her writing

pad was neatly stowed in a drawer. And the manila envelope was propped up, centre-stage, on the mantelpiece.

December days were short.

While the brittle sunlight did its best, Mrs Endicott hurried to the shop, and took her place behind Nance.

'Can't you take that poster down, Dad?' said Nance to Frank. She gestured at a cartoon Father Christmas exhorting, 'Make it a War Savings Christmas!' She argued that 'after five wartime Christmases we know what's what.'

'There's some,' said Frank, 'as need reminding.'

Mrs Endicott dug in her coat pocket. 'Something for your girls, Ruby!'

'They'll love them!' Ruby studied the chestnuts, still in their spiky overcoats, and felt Frank study her. She bent lower over the chestnuts. *I'm here on a mission! Why must men trip women up?*

'And before I forget . . .' Mrs Endicott handed the quilt – growing now, no longer a rag – to Susan Grundy. 'How's our newest Ambridgian?'

Little Alfred – Alf to his friends – was at home with his granny, Susan told her. 'She dotes on him.'

'How nice.' Mrs Endicott knew that Ma Grundy told anyone who'd listen that the baby was 'a horror'.

The new square was satin, chequered ivory and black. 'Ooh, top quality,' said Susan.

'It felt proper to use something precious, when so many have sacrificed so much.' Mrs Endicott was earnest. 'I'm snug and safe and surrounded by good neighbours, so I donated a fragment of my heart.'

'Righty-ho.' Frank was brisk. 'You here for your butter ration, Mrs E?'

She was not to be so easily deflected. Her powdered face was coy. 'I lost my heart to the wearer of this fabric, even though our closeness lasted only one day.'

A penny dropped. Nance said, 'It's from the waistcoat framed over your fireplace! The brother and sister music hall stars!' She couldn't remember the moustachioed man's name.

'We stole a kiss.' Mrs Endicott went pink.

Donald Burton. That was it. Nance swayed with the romance of it all.

Closing her eyes, Mrs Endicott went on. 'How I remember being held against that waistcoat, the pearl buttons digging into me, and my breath taken away by the sudden nearness of that dear face.' She tittered. 'It was so very naughty. My pardon was begged. I asked "Will you remember me?" and the answer was "Forever". I believe it, for I have never forgotten . . .'

The little widow petered out, back in a long-gone summer, a contraband kiss on her lips.

'So do you want your butter or not?' asked Frank.

Hairy Bittercress grew low to the ground, valiantly surviving the cruelty of December.

Peggy stepped over a circle of it, placing her feet carefully.

If she slipped out here in the pasture, she may never get up – she was as round as a beetle.

She saw Dan tapping a crusty stone into place in a damaged wall. 'Luncheon is served.' She laughed at how greedily he took the waxed paper parcel. 'Hard work for a cold day.'

'I'm getting there.' Dan waved his sandwich at Peggy's tum, protruding from her coat. 'So are you, love. Shouldn't be out here in the weather.'

'I try to help.'

Dan chewed thoughtfully. 'You and the missus . . . me and the kids don't like it when you have words.'

'She meddled with my room, Dan.'

'She was making your bed, love. Finding something *hidden* . . . it brought her up short. There are no secrets at Brookfield.'

'That's not true of any house. Another word for "secret" is "private". Doris had no right.'

'It's her house, Peggy.'

'But it's *my* room.'

This was a carbon copy of the 'words' so both of them gave up.

'Don't fret,' said Peggy, who was deeply fond of her gentle father-in-law. 'Peace will break out soon enough.'

Dan sighed. 'But are you here for good, Peg? Are you one of us now?

She didn't answer. She went back to Brookfield, boots crunching on the iced earth.

* * *

Village women wandered through Lower Loxley in belted tablecloths, tea towels on their heads.

Biblical shepherds for the nativity, I presume, thought Pamela, regretting her permission for Winter Tonic rehearsals to be held in her great hall.

Christmas was stomping up the drive and its imminent knock on the door could not be ignored. Pamela wished it would pass her by this year, but she was leader of the revels and must put on her gayest gowns and arrange diamond pins in her hair.

Accustomed to her body doing her bidding, Pamela hated the waves of nausea she felt as she waited, waited, *waited* for a letter from the front. When Julia began to conduct the ladies in 'Away in a Manger', Pamela darted upstairs, bumping into Hildegard on the landing.

'Ma'am.' Much irreverence was crammed into the word. She held out a salver.

Pamela took the envelope calmly. She did not run. Only when she was in her bedroom did she tear at it the way she had seen red-eyed goshawks do with squirrels.

Pamela

My fingers are frozen — forgive the rotten handwriting.

Speeding through the tightly spaced lines, Pamela found no explanation for the intermission in communication, and precious little personal detail, but, she thought ruefully, *Alec is, to say the least, a busy man, playing his part in opening up the Allied invasion route to Germany.*

Let me tell you about Private Joe E. Mann. With his injured arms bandaged to his sides, this young man saw an incoming grenade and threw himself onto it. Saved lives by forfeiting his own. I think of him every day. As for your husband, he's a tad bashed about. Shot in the hand! Strapped up and no bloody use, but it's only my left hand so I can still smoke. And stroke dear Hero.

That hand, thought Pamela, *is the one I long to hold.* She recognised Alec's habit of understatement and worried about his injury. Holding hands was new to this long-wed couple, and they had been cautious about it, as if dabbling in something illicit.

She regarded her own left hand, cool and perfect, and turned the page to read the last paragraph.

I'm saddened by your refusal to have Caroline live with us, but I understand. It's a silly fantasy that brightened the gloom of battle but it was wrong, and as ever I must thank you for putting me right, my darling. I will find Caroline and provide for her, but it will be at arm's length. I'll do my best for her, but I'll also do my duty to Gerald.

And you.

'Bob, d'you know anything about this?' Ruby found him in The Bull's scullery, and held up a small box, covered in brittle utility wrapping paper and finished with an awkward bow. 'It was outside my door when I got up.'

Bob cleared his throat. 'Open it,' he said.

'Mon dieu.' Ruby held up a sparkling brooch.

'It's nowt,' said Bob, both embarrassed and bold. 'Found it in me wife's things. I've nobody to leave it to, so I thought why not make someone happy? Couldn't wait until Christmas.'

'But Bob . . .' began Ruby.

He interrupted her before she could carry on. 'If you wear it on Sunday, to Midnight Mass, that would let me know that, well, I have cause to hope.'

She was gentle but thorough. 'This is beautiful, Bob. Thank you. But I'm a widow and I came to Ambridge not to find a husband, but for quite another reason. I can't be distracted by you, or anything else. Please, take a step back. I'm so grateful for your kindness to me and the girls, and I value you enormously, but there can be no misunderstandings.'

Bob went puce. He turned the scullery tap on and off. He said, 'Just what are you insinuating, missy? Can't a fellow give his lodger a present without all these wild claims? If you're going to slander a pillar of the community perhaps you should find somewhere else to live. I'm giving you a week's notice. Be out for new year.'

Ruby felt as if he had struck her. She placed the brooch gently on the draining board and left.

Doris was headed for the postbox, but slowed down when she spotted Pamela approaching from the opposite direction. Still smarting from what amounted to a ticking-off from Dan, Doris was in no mood to chat, especially with haughty Pamela.

'This isn't like you, Doris!' Dan had said, pointing his pipe at her, as close to violence as the man ever got. 'All this frostiness between you and Peggy. Isn't right.'

She had been tart with him, but they knew he had a point. Doris never let her feelings overcome her basic decency. *But* . . . Doris smiled to herself; when Christine or Phil began defending themselves like that, she would say, 'But me no buts, young'un.'

But, she insisted, *Jack's so far away and what if his wife isn't playing fair with him?*

The stack of photographs under the mattress, Peggy's distaste for the nuts and bolts of farm life, the horrible suspicion that Ambridge was just a pit-stop in her daughter-in-law's life – Doris could no longer tell intuition from paranoia. Jack and Peggy's new marriage was not built on solid ground; a separation in the family was too terrible to consider. *And what if Jack never comes home?*

Doris stopped, winded; she worked hard to keep that thought out. She took a deep breath. It hurt to suspect her daughter-in-law, but the girl had such airs and graces, and seemed to just about put up with their hospitality, constantly wishing herself elsewhere.

At the postbox, Pamela seemed frozen, her fingers still on the envelope she held at the slot.

With no option but to greet her, Doris rallied. 'Morning! Looking forward to the show?'

'The what?' Pamela let the letter go. 'Oh. Winter Tonic. Very much.' She gestured vaguely. 'I must . . . you know . . . get on.'

She got on, in her pixie hood and soft-lined boots, thinking only of what her letter didn't say. She couldn't mention Caroline's name to Alec, even though now, as flakes of icing sugar snow began to drift from the sky, Pamela wondered what sort of Christmas the little girl would have.

She shook her head. *She'll be fine. She's with family. I endured many a lonely Christmas as a child and it did me no harm . . .*

So lost in thought she almost bumped into Ruby, Pamela's 'excuse me' seemed to go unheard, as Ruby strode, head down, towards the shop.

Ruby had barely noticed Pamela, nor the new snow. She needed to set things in order. 'Frank!' she called as she reached the shop. 'I need a word.'

Hanging up her coat, Ruby marvelled at the delusion of old duffers who assumed that all available women in a hundred-mile radius would lust after them given half the chance. *As if I'm a beggar! As if I can't survive without them!*

Frank turned away from Mrs Endicott's possibly endless anecdote about her cataracts, but was hijacked by Nance, who said, 'Do you mind if I speak to Dad first, Ruby? Won't take a minute.'

Taking Tudor into her arms, Ruby attended to Mrs Endicott as Nance shut the door to the back room and began, in a gentle voice, to tell Frank that she'd been watching him with Ruby.

'Dad, I can see you like her. Oh! Don't blush!' Nance laid her hand on Frank's cheek. 'I don't want to embarrass you, truly, but sometimes men don't realise how fragile life can be for women. Ruby needs this job, and your attentions make her feel insecure.'

'I admire her,' protested Frank. 'What's so wrong with that?'

'Face facts.' Nance was mock-stern. 'You're a lovely man but you're too old for her. Or she's too young for you. However you want to put it. Where's this going, Dad? You seriously going to take on two little girls? The same Frank Brown who won't get a dog 'cos it'd need walking?'

'I'm lonely, love,' said Frank. 'Not for family, or friends, but for a lady by my hearth. A lady I can spoil. When your very own lady hugs you, you feel like a teenager, like you can do anything. I know you think I'm bowled over by her youth but it's her *heart* that draws me in. Yesterday I overslept – well might you gasp, girl, happens once a century – and when I came down, Ruby had opened up, left me out a bite of breakfast.' Frank shook his head. 'Nobody ever does me little kindnesses like that no more.' He sighed. 'I got carried away, love, didn't I?'

'Just a bit, Dad.'

At the counter, Ruby had ceded Tudor to Mrs Endicott, who was whispering in his ear that he must never go near stinging nettles. As she totted up purchases, Ruby almost asked if the old lady had any room at The Cherries. Nobody in Ambridge saw refugee Ruby as the woman with the wonderful old house in Sceaux, who kept chickens and baked for her neighbours.

I have to stay here. I am bound here with an iron hoop until I get what I came for.

A hand on her arm, and Nance was saying, 'I've just had a, um, *chat* with Dad, regarding his ideas about a certain lady getting a little out of hand. There's no harm in him, quite the opposite, but just so you know, Ruby, you've nothing to worry about.'

Ruby could have cried. 'And my job is safe?'

'He couldn't do without you!'

The door banged open. Peggy came in and stamped her feet. 'Perishing snow!'

'But it makes the village look so pretty,' said Mrs Endicott.

'In London it melts the moment it lands.' Peggy was nostalgic for the dirty streets, so easy to navigate.

'Be with you in a tic,' said Ruby, giving Nance's hand a grateful squeeze.

'No hurry.' Peggy was thankful for the shop's shelter from the weather, and from the atmosphere at Brookfield, which was almost as glacial.

Ever honest, Peggy admitted her own part in the conflict. It had been wrong to go off like a firework when Doris tidied a room in her own house; it was the sarcastic display of her private treasures that rankled.

The pressed flower was just dust now.

I feel guilty for missing being young! For having some sport!! Peggy had been true to Jack; she had kept her word. *More than I can say for him*. She recalled his last letter.

Hope you're not still fuming, Peg. I know I promised I'd be careful but it's your fault for being such a corker!!!

A newcomer, swathed in scarves, said to Peggy, 'You look as if you're about to pop!'

'I feel it, too,' smiled Peggy.

'Mind if I push in? I only want ciggies.'

'Now now,' said Frank. 'There's a queue, madam.' He was helping Mrs Endicott up from the chair, and Peggy put her arms out to take Tudor from her.

The queue jumper stage-whispered, 'Wouldn't touch 'im in your condition, might be catching.'

Peggy saw Nance stiffen, and knew it was up to her to answer. 'In that case, love,' she said, hoisting a giggling Tudor, 'your poor mother must've touched somebody with suet pudding for brains.'

The woman left without her cigarettes.

Ambridge flaunted its white winter furs.

A long way away, US forces pressed against the Japanese perimeter in the Pacific, but in the village hall all was safe and snug. Paper chains made from newspaper looped across the ceiling, and mistletoe sprigs were nailed to beams. Excitement hung in the air like talcum, as the audience for Winter Tonic found their seats, leaned across to greet old friends, and exclaimed at seeing family members' names in the programme. *A Happy Christmas to all friends at home and abroad* was emblazoned on the front page, prompting thoughts of dear ones fighting, and of what Christmas might look like for them.

Shaking hand after hand, Morgan suspected the revue would be more of a tonic than the medicines he prescribed.

The other side of the red curtains, Julia clapped her hands. 'Ladies and gentlemen of Winter Tonic, this is your fifteen-minute call!' She caught Joe Grundy as he passed. 'You know your cue?'

'Yes,' said Joe, who didn't. Exempted from active service because he was needed on the farm, Joe privately felt it would be less stressful to be in the Eindhoven-Nijmegen-Arnhem corridor right now.

Both Wanda and Doris wore gowns repurposed from a Lower Loxley bedspread, but the effect was quite different. Wanda looked like a movie star. Doris looked like a sofa. But she was a happy sofa, as she peeked out from the side of the stage and waved at her husband in the front row.

Disobeying Julia's command to 'preserve the magic of theatre', Doris nipped out to give Dan a twirl of the frock, and to have a word with Max.

Not a patient woman, Doris had witnessed quite enough of the Max and Wanda Show; she needed a happy ending. She poked Max in his good arm. 'Forgive me, Group Captain, but I'm about to meddle.'

Swallowing hard, he said, 'Go ahead.'

'We're grateful for your heroism. No need to look uncomfortable, Ambridge is proud of you! However.' Doris folded her arms. 'There's more than one form of courage, young man. When this war ends, you'll have a life to build. Be brave.

Find her. *Declare yourself.*' With a final harrumph, Doris went off, stately in her bedspread.

Backstage was hectic. 'S'cuse me.' She swept past Hildegard and Susan Grundy, both in ragged dinner jackets for Act 1's 'Burlington Bertie'.

'Acts like she owns the place, that Doris,' grumbled Hildegard, before returning to the topic at hand. 'Don't be daft, Susan, the next prophecy won't be about your baby.'

'They're getting *mean*. The one about the lamb in Max's bed was a bit of fun, but the vicar's wife . . .'

'Someone's for the chop,' agreed Hildegard.

'My Joe', said Susan, who quoted her husband as if he was a famous philosopher, 'is convinced they'll dig another one up at that blinkin' grotto before Christmas.'

Passing them with a cask of ale on his shoulder, Bob said, 'Don't you worry, ladies. Mother Molly's given up on us. Grayson's found nowt for weeks.'

Stepping out from a side door, Ruby blundered into Bob. 'Oh,' was all she said, unsure how to greet him. He had cold-shouldered her since their showdown. It hurt.

'You do realise,' said Bob, as he set down the cask, 'your notice is up tomorrow.'

'I'm unlikely to forget.' Ruby plastered herself against the wall as a pantomime horse cantered past.

'Where you going to live?' Bob was gruff.

The door behind Ruby swung open, and Evie emerged. 'This', she said, 'is our new house and it's *stupid*.'

'It's temporary,' said Ruby, her face hot. 'I'm saving for

somewhere proper. I just couldn't bring myself to ask for more charity.'

Bob took in the cupboard-like space, piled with boxes, and the mattress on the floor. 'Ain't my fault,' he said.

'Did I say it was?' Ruby laid down her bruised feelings; she was on the most important assignment of her life and had bigger fish to fry. 'Let's forget we ever knew each other, Bob.'

'*Maman*!' Evie was shocked.

'Into your costume, child. *Tout suite!*'

Pamela sat between Grayson and Dodgy, on a silk cushion she had brought with her. 'It's like a West End first night.'

'Better!' Grayson arranged his fringe over his birthmark. Long days digging the compacted earth of the grotto had left him drained. There was a cut across the bridge of his nose, leading to jokes about Mother Molly knocking him about. The more prosaic truth, he admitted, was that he slipped in the bathroom and bashed his face on the sink. 'My mother will be mad at me when she discovers I've spilt blood on her dear friend Blanche's rug.'

'The Blanche Gilpin I know wouldn't turn a hair.' Pamela scanned the programme, bored. 'I'm immune to music.'

Dodgy was not. 'I intend to cry the whole way through.'

Every seat taken, the hall crackled with anticipation. Max stood and slipped through the side of the red curtain like a wraith.

As luck would have it, she was right there, nervously

running through her lines. When Wanda saw him, she stopped, her mouth a perfect 'O'.

'You have a flower in your hair,' said Max, because he had to say something.

'Part of my costume.'

'It suits you.'

Wanda smiled a *what's-all-this-about?* Smile.

Their corner became sealed over, a bubble, cut off from vocal exercises and the clatter of tap shoes. Max put a hand on Wanda's shoulder. 'I'm so dreadfully, frightfully slow.'

'True.' Her teeth flashed white in the dusk of backstage.

'It's not that I don't admire you.'

'Say it then.'

'I admire you.' Max laughed at his own stammer. He, who had flown a Spitfire! 'You're sublime, Wanda.'

'You're not so bad yourself.'

'How can I . . . why would you . . .'

'I'm on in a minute, Max. Giddy up.' She smelled his clean, soapy smell. Enjoyed the up-and-down of his cupid's bow.

'This is pointless. You can't be lumbered with an old crock.'

When he took his hand from her shoulder, Wanda felt as if she was falling backwards through space. 'Surely that decision is mine to make?'

The only woman Max had truly spoken to was his wife; they had a shared language. Now that she was silent, so was he, and talking to Wanda felt like flying blind through night skies. 'What happens to you, Wanda . . . how you are . . . it matters to me.'

'And?' Wanda felt herself begin to open, petal by petal. '*And*, Max?'

He blurted, then. 'Plenty more fish in the sea, and most of them have two fins.'

She pulled him to her by his tie. 'It's not the lac of a *fin* that's the problem. It's the lack of another part of your anatomy, which, as a lady, I can't mention.'

Walter chose that moment to saunter past, juggling two balls.

Their bubble burst, they spluttered at Walter's unsuspecting metaphor, until Max leaned down, his face close to Wanda's, and whispered, '*That* part of me is unscathed.'

Wanda took the fake bloom from her hair, kissed it, and tucked it into Max's buttonhole. 'Flowers wilt if left unpicked.'

He stared. They were still.

It was the single most exciting moment of Wanda's life, overshadowing every passionate kiss or roll in the hay. He bent his head. She closed her eyes.

Julia pulled Wanda away. 'Smooch later, playmates. It's showtime!'

'*Les Enfants Charmant*' were first on the bill, singing an old French children's song. 'So long I've been loving you,' they warbled, stomping about in their Pierrot outfits, with white-painted faces and sad clown expressions. 'I'll never forget you.'

'Do shush, Dodgy, we can't hear the words.' Pamela handed him her handkerchief for the tears rolling down his red face.

Evie pirouetted. She was deep undercover, the double

act merely a front as she searched for her father, the intrepid Henri.

How skinny her little legs are, thought her mother, from the side of the stage.

A magic trick, next. Frank was billed as 'Ambridge's Very Own Houdini'.

Ruby, in tattered spangles, placed a hood over Frank's head and tied his hands behind his back. With many elegant gestures, she guided him into an upright coffin of a box he had made himself. The words 'Jacobs Crackers' were still visible through the paint; some wag called out, 'More like old Frank's crackers!'

Once the box was padlocked, the audience counted to a minute while Ruby arranged herself decoratively. She made a great flourish but the box remained shut. The count went up to two minutes, before Chas Westenra dashed on and took a hammer to the box.

Frank fell out, gasping and still tied up, to roll about the boards. The curtain fell.

Out strode Julia, and at the sight of her megawatt glamour, the audience forgot about poor Frank. 'Hit it!' she called, and the piano started up an approximation of 'Shoo-Shoo Baby', a racy number which called for racy choreography.

Pamela sat, stunned, as her daughter-in-law high-kicked and shimmied, and when everyone rose to their feet at the last note, she joined them.

When the cheering ended, Mrs Endicott crept out into the limelight. She cleared her throat and began to read 'Nature's

Questioning' by Thomas Hardy. A short poem, it felt long to the audience, and their applause when it ended was equal parts affection and relief.

'Such a diamond of a lady.' Dodgy mopped his eyes and Pamela rolled her own.

'Ballet?' scoffed Phil Archer, sinking in his seat as a row of ballerinas tiptoed out, arm in arm, their backs to the audiences, tutus wafting. They turned, one by one, and each lady was acclaimed as they showed their face. Hildegard's lipstick was visible from the back of the hall; Nance blushed like a beetroot; the last one provoked the loudest huzzah. Cliff, in a curly wig and some healthy chest hair, sent the hall wild.

Backstage, Doris heard the hoots and smiled. *It took a lot for Cliff to get out there in front of the village.*

The evening was long, but there was no let-up in the applause. The audience were giddy, as new snow fell to further insulate them from reality, and the village hall's coloured lights made a Hollywood of Ambridge.

No revue would be complete without a pantomime horse. Bob was already in the front half of the costume, but Julia saw that Frank – still recovering – was in no fit state to go on as the back end. Stan was found at the back of the hall, doling out bloody packs of black-market beef, and pushed and pulled into the costume, despite his stated aversion to 'sticking my nose up Bob's rear end'.

'If the punters laugh loud enough,' said Julia, shoving the wretched steed before the footlights, 'they won't hear the swearing.'

The finale brought Italian POWs shuffling onto the stage, to form two rows in their much-mended uniforms.

Fabio stepped forward. 'We sing for you a song called "Bella Ciao". An old song, Italians change the words when fascists take our country. This means much to us. Thank you.'

Dodgy was already bleary-eyed as the first sweet verse began. The men had melodic, crooning voices, and the song began slow and yearning.

'This is the flower of the partisan, who died for freedom.'

'Oh,' said Dodgy, his hand to his mouth.

'Bury me up in the mountain
In the shadow of a beautiful flower . . .'

The chorus was simple. It built and built, until the Italians were belting it out, and the villagers roared along.

'Bell-a-chow! Bell-a-chow!'

The last lines were sung solo in a quivering, slow falsetto by a dark-haired prisoner, his hand on his heart and his eyes tightly closed.

'This is the flower of the partisan
Who died for freedom.'

'*Viva Italia*!' yelled Grayson, as the last, defiant note died to tumultuous applause. For a few moments, Mrs Endicott, Doris, Walter *et al* were Italians, united by the injustice of war.

'Forgive me for weeping yet again.' Dodgy turned to Pamela, but she couldn't see him through her tears.

* * *

The knock woke Ruby.

Late to bed after Winter Tonic, she heaved herself up. Her last morning under The Bull's thatch; *Bob clearly wants me out early.*

She opened the door, but instead of Bob she saw a tray. All dainty, with a lace mat beneath a boiled egg in a stripy cup. An envelope – used, creased – was set against it.

'Pardonne-moi,' read Ruby.

They talked over the egg, down in the chilly kitchen.

'There's nothing to forgive,' she told the big man fussing with the teapot. 'Men and women often misunderstand each other.'

'I took a long hard look at meself,' said Bob, sitting with a thump. 'I saw a man who was prepared to turf out a woman and her children for the sake of pride.' He fidgeted with the doily. 'I like having you all here. Before youse I was lonely, like.'

'I know about pride, Bob. I know about loneliness, too.' *I was born lonely,* thought Ruby, remembering why she had come to Ambridge, and what she must do here. 'We'll stay, and we'll keep you company, and you'll cook the girls breakfast every morning, just like before.'

Bob coughed to disguise his gratitude. 'That Max Gilpin helped me with the French.'

'Most impressive. But Bob.' Ruby caught his arm as he stood. 'We are friends again, yes?'

'Wee-wee,' said Bob.

T'was the night before Christmas . . .

A goose sat stuffed and ready in Brookfield's pantry,

and the farmhouse was gilded with firelight. At the table, Christine wrapped a tie she had knitted for her brother in a hoarded scrap of patterned paper.

Phil realised, a little late, he should have got a present for his sister.

The quilt, bigger now, lay folded on a shelf. The dairyman's wife had added a brown rayon square. Several sprigged muslins had appeared. One lace panel stood out.

The sewing shears flashed as Doris cut up old clothes to make dishcloths. She picked up her mother's favourite scarf and held it to her nose, remembering her, transported by the scent of Lily of the Valley.

Mum would approve. The scarf would become part of the quilt, part of the embrace offered by Ambridge to some wretched soul adrift in war.

With customary neatness, Doris laid the dishcloths and the square side by side.

Pulling her weight, Peggy washed a pot at the sink. The frost between her and Doris persevered despite the furnace of Christmas. Putting down the pot, Peggy took a cloth to dry her hands.

Doris stopped dead as Peggy dropped the scrunched-up cloth to the draining board. 'Mother's scarf!' She snatched it, straightening the sodden creases. 'Why can't you be more careful?' Doris's voice caught in her throat.

Peggy didn't understand the sudden emotion. 'It was beside the pile of cloths.'

'Exactly. *Beside.*' It felt like an insult to Doris. She

remembered her befuddled ma, thin and vague in her last days, in this very kitchen. 'That was my mother's scarf.'

'How was I supposed to know?'

'You might know if you ever listened.'

'I might listen,' said Peggy, hands where her hips used to be, 'if you ever said anything that wasn't a complaint!'

The kids slunk out. Mother Cat followed them. Dan turned smartly in the doorway and smoked his pipe in the passage instead.

The sheepdog, Glen, sat between them, sad.

The argument wandered as it rose in volume. It took in Peggy's habit of leaving her bed unmade and Doris's s reluctance to have seconds when Peggy made roly-poly.

They paused, gasping. Peggy shouted, 'Doris, what the hell are we arguing about?'

Doris shouted, 'I don't know!'

The moment teetered. It could go either way. Peggy said, 'I'll heat the iron. Your mum's scarf'll come up good as new.'

'Look at poor Glen's face.'

The women petted the dog and he was reassured.

Peggy said, 'I'm sorry.'

Doris said, 'No, I'm sorry.'

Dan said from the hall, 'You're both sorry, now get the kettle on.'

Lily of the Valley rose in the air as Peggy ironed.

Dan walked his family to St Stephen's, then scurried to The Bull for one last pint before Midnight Mass.

The bar was packed with unusually tidy men, all after their own one last pint. Ruby helped out, avoiding the mistletoe and returning the slurred seasons' greetings as she cleared glasses.

'Where's that Stan Horrobin!' Walter burst in, lips thin. 'That beef he sold me. It's *horse*!'

Fisticuffs ensued.

'Was it pantomime horse?' asked Bob as he held the door open and the two men fell through it, still swinging punches.

Taking Max's empty glass, Ruby heard him ask Dan if Wanda would be at church.

Men, she thought.

In came Julia, wrapped in furs, hair up, *unescorted*.

The men melted into silence. Amused, Julia ordered a pink gin. On tour, she frequented all manner of dives without a male escort. 'Light?' She held up a Sobranie cigarette.

Max produced a gold lighter, and the men resumed their discourse with fewer cuss words.

'Did you see the box of goodies Gerald sent me?' Julia smiled through the smoke ring she blew. 'And in wartime too! Chocolate, liqueurs, *marshmallows*!'

Having met Gerald just once, Max wondered how a dim but decent chap could handcuff himself to someone as insubstantial as Julia. *If all he needs is beauty, I suppose it might work out just fine.*

Max wanted more. Once, he had had more.

Was it wrong to feel Christmassy? Nineteen forty-four

was his fifth Christmas since his wife died, and the first he hadn't ignored. Ambridge's festive cheer was infectious, and he succumbed without a fight.

And of course there was Wanda.

He listened, in the clamour of the bar, for his wife's voice, for some permission, but all he could hear was the bawdy song Joe Grundy was singing. 'Where's Cad?' he asked Julia. 'He said he'd come to The Bull tonight.'

'He's never where he says he'll be. We suspect a village *affaire de coeur.* Naughty boy's the only one who dares flirt with an old married matron like me. *You* won't flirt with me, will you?'

Max yelped a 'No' he hoped wasn't too impolite, and Julia turned to Grayson, whose eyes widened. 'Don't panic, darling, nobody's asking you to volunteer.'

All were shooed out at five to midnight. 'Can't have the vicar blaming me for you lot being late for mass,' said Bob, pulling the door to, and following them.

Dan pulled up his collar against the cold. 'Poor old vicar's too melancholy to care this year.'

Grayson peeled away from the straggling crocodile of beer-perfumed men. 'I'm off to the grotto. I have a funny feeling . . .'

'You're a man of learning!' teased Max. 'You don't have funny feelings.'

'I know.' Grayson seemed perplexed. 'And yet . . .' Like a man in love, Grayson was clearly pulling against the tug of Mother Molly, and couldn't quite resist.

Max knew how he felt, as he tailed the menfolk over the bridge.

The stained-glass windows were blacked out, so entering the church, with the candles lit and the altar festooned and the organ trilling, was an assault on the senses. Christmas was begun, in all its gilded glory.

Julia approached the Pargetter pew, her coat open, and the diamonds at her throat flinging off sparks.

'That necklace . . .' said Pamela.

'Is it too much for church, Mama-in-law? Thought I'd add a little Christmas gaiety. Gerald gave it to me over the entrée one evening.' Julia pulled off a glove and revealed a ring. 'Then handed me this with the main course!'

'Didn't they . . .' whispered Magsy to Pamela.

'Belong to Alec's mother? Yes.'

Of course, the heirlooms must pass to this girl at some stage, but Gerald had been wrong to dole them out like sweets.

A few pews back, Doris compared notes with other village stalwarts on Henry Bissett. They had all, it transpired, invited the vicar for Christmas lunch and all had been refused. Heads were shaken, and lips were pursed, and then the organ got going and they cleared their throats and stood.

Michele didn't follow the service. She stood and sat mechanically when her mother did so, and played with the bobbles on her hand-knitted mittens. She was remembering other Christmases, back in Sceaux.

She knew Papa was dead, even though she had given up contradicting Evie when she said he might come back. If his name came up, Michele was both cheery and downcast. It was quite a lesson for one so young, that it's possible to happy and sad at the same time.

'The vicar seems lost in the service,' whispered Agnes to Denholm.

'Eh?' said Denholm, his customary retort.

Agnes half turned and saw that Ruby's eyes on her. The little madam looked away. *Nosey so-and-so.* Agnes deplored her own faults when she found them in others.

Back outside, shoes crunching on new snow, the villagers emerged into the small hours of the great day.

Wanda had felt Max's presence as surely as he felt hers. She hung back, trusting his radar to find her around the side of the church.

They were one with the shadows. Wanda put her finger on his lips, and felt it burn.

On the path, a lady bent with age told Peggy her pregnancy was 'one in the eye for Hitler!'

Smiling, Peggy thought hotly that she wasn't having a baby for the war effort. *Let's hope this child never has to fight!* She reached out and took Doris's arm as her mother-in-law passed.

'Let me tell you,' she said, 'about that envelope I hid.'

Doris listened, and learned that the mementoes were not secret, and certainly did not hint at a love affair. 'They were all I had of the old me, the independent me who looked after herself and worked hard and had fun. I don't miss that me anymore, Doris. Not really.' Her past, she said, was a strain of old-fashioned music, limp bunting from a party long-over.

Gratified, Doris said, 'You're an Archer now, girl. You don't just have Jack, you have all of us. Remember that, if we ever lose our wits and come to blows again.'

A shout went up, a happy chorus of greeting for Grayson, stomping through the lychgate.

Max and Wanda did not hear the rowdy welcome. They were close by but on another planet.

Kissing Max, Wanda understood something basic for the first time. She understood the poetry and the urgency of sex. Its blindness. Not a transaction, it was sacred and pagan, and made them more than the sum of their parts.

But. Always there was a but.

She pulled away from his lips.

'I don't want to kiss you in the shadows, Max. You're opaque, you are beside me and then you're gone, and you leave me to connect the dots.'

'I can offer you so little.'

'You choose to offer me so little.'

A small voice intruded. 'Ooh, *kissing*!' Evie was thrilled; Wanda less so.

'Scram, minx,' she laughed, wanting to lasso Max to her until they had one more kiss, one more crumb of clarification.

But Ruby was suddenly there, with Mrs E behind, looking

for her little one, and Max and Wanda were property of the community once more, no longer a pair.

A crowd had gathered around Grayson, amused by his lack of puff.

Bent over, he wasn't laughing. He managed, 'I came as quick as I could. I found one. A prophecy.'

Mrs Endicott crossed herself. Magsy grasped Morgan's arm. Lorna stepped forward, ready to decode.

Grayson took the slip of paper they all dreaded out of his breast pocket. *'A beast will gild the sky,'* he read. 'And then the footnote.' He passed it to Lorna. *'To sirs.* Short and sweet this time.'

It took a moment, but clever Lorna deciphered the date in her head. 'Seventh of February, 1945,' she said.

Henry Bissett had a passenger as he drove to Evershot Camp in the early hours of Christmas Day. The goose, puckered and bald, sat wrapped in greaseproof paper. Henry's loss would be the POWs' gain; his parishioners were kind, but he barely ate since Frances's death, and the fowl was wasted on him.

The sky was the colour of cold milk. Not gilded, and the only beast the vicar passed on his journey was a crow croaking out season's greetings from a wych elm.

The prophecy was much discussed at the Brookfield lunch table.

'What if,' asked Christine, spearing a sprout, 'Hitler is

the beast and he's gonna drop bombs on us on the seventh of February?' The sparkle of Christmas was dimmed; her sleep had been troubled by bad dreams, and she had given her parents an extra-hard hug when she opened her presents.

'No, no, no!' Fabio, invited to lunch with his chum, a spotty Milanese by the name of Dino, waved his knife. 'Ambridge is heaven. No more trouble at Ambridge.' But he crossed himself all the same.

Dino said, 'More geese please, lady?' and Doris carved another slice, exchanging a look with Peggy; the guest's appetite tickled them both.

The women had worked in harness to bring the feast to the table. Rations increased a little at Christmas – Doris had stretched the extra pound and a half of sugar until it begged for mercy – but the meal was still a shadow of pre-war celebrations. She vowed to herself that she would never again refuse the children a sweetie when rationing finally ended. *They can make themselves sick on humbugs if they like!* 'More gravy, Peggy?'

'Don't mind if I do.'

Doris had never understood why, when folk clashed, others would say they were too alike to get on. Now she saw the truth in it. In a fit of self-aggrandisement that horrified her, Doris suddenly saw herself as an empress, powerful but ageing, knowing the young heir is getting stronger by the day and will one day seize her sceptre.

Although my sceptre is a rolling pin.

'Don't you fret about old Mother Molly,' said Dan, leaning over to his daughter and stealing a roast potato. 'We don't fret about anything today. Except perhaps . . .' He winked at his wife. 'How to fit in a bowl of your mother's famous pud.'

Before setting off for Magsy's house, Mrs Endicott permitted herself a medicinal sherry.

White curls set, muffler on, gloves ready, she toasted the family photographs in her drawing room. 'And you, of course.' She raised her glass to the black-and-white Burtons, her stage idols. She touched the face she carried in her heart. 'I think of you, dear, on all the high days and holidays.' She hesitated before confessing, 'Even my wedding days.'

Presiding over the crystal glassware, the Meissen dinner service and the steaming tureens of the Lower Loxley table, Pamela's word was law. 'All talk of the prophecy is *banned*. Nobody will die in February, or if they do it'll be nothing to do with Mother Molly. Frances's sad end was a coincidence.'

'Hmm,' said Dodgy, slipping Hero a chipolata.

The ruffled lace collar Ruby had laboured over and given, wrapped, to her younger daughter, was tied around a teddy's neck.

Typical! Thought Ruby. *She'll never wear it. Too girly for my Evie.* She had left the children downstairs with Bob, playing a rowdy game of Snap. She took up the teddy and held it as she lay down for a snatched moment of quiet.

Henri would smile at Evie's resistance to the ladylike collar. He encouraged the girl's quirks.

Closing her eyes, Ruby conjured him up. She remembered him in snatches, like a jigsaw. Today, she saw his forearms, strong and dusted with dark hair, the sleeves of his heavy shirt rolled up. Last time she saw him, he had ammo in his pocket, instead of the lemon pastilles he loved to suck.

He was complaining of toothache.

Ruby found herself worrying about that. Ridiculous, when Henri was beyond toothache.

The Horrobins sat down to rabbit. Connie had done her best with the scrawny bunny, and she smiled at Bert and Maisie's innocent excitement.

'What's these?' Stan, taking his seat, slammed down an envelope.

'Them?' The gravy jug shook in Connie's hand. 'Savings stamps. I found 'em.'

'Found them?' Stan didn't like that answer.

Bert sat lower on his chair. Badboy retired to a bundle of rags in a corner.

'Stroke of luck, eh?'

Stan sat back, scratching his chin. 'Let me get this right. You *saved up* for that wooden toy you gave the kids, and you *found* some savings stamps? What a resourceful and fortunate woman you are, Mrs H.'

She couldn't eat. She watched Stan polish off his plateful.

He dug and probed and nagged until Connie admitted that a 'nice lady' from the British War Relief society had been round. 'She gave me the stamps, and the toy.' Connie saw how Bert and Maisie's eyes flickered to the little red cart that was their new – their only – treasure.

'Charity!' Stan thumped the table and the cracked dishes danced.

Connie's voice arrived and she used it to shriek, 'Yes, charity, and I grabbed it with both hands, Stan Horrobin!'

Stan grabbed her hair. The children fled. Badboy hid his eyes under his paw.

'You must miss being with your family at this time of year, dear lady,' said Dodgy.

'We actresses are nomads,' said Julia. 'I'm used to being away from them.'

'And now,' said Dodgy, gracious despite the crumbs down his front, 'you are a Pargetter and have a new family.'

'We must meet your people some time,' said Pamela.

'Definitely.' *Imagine that.* Julia's mousy parents had christened her Joan, and had high hopes she would become a secretary. Her new husband had no idea – he was incurious – but Pamela was a different matter. She had, Julia knew, sniffed out her real origins.

Takes one to know one. Pamela's wealth was *nouveau* – Julia would swear to it. Money was bleach; it could erase history. She was starting afresh, just as her mother-in-law once did.

*

'Are we spoiling him?' Nance watched Tudor playing with his new balsa wood zoo.

'Probably.' Morgan, patting his pockets for his post-luncheon cigar, was in the opposite armchair. 'But how many boys have a birthday at Christmas?'

'Two years old,' said Nance. 'Our big boy!' She stood and fetched the silver cigar box. 'Here, take another. Magsy worries you're smoking too much, and picked your pockets.'

'Dear Magsy should know by now that I give advice, but rarely take it.' He chose carefully from the row of cigars as Nance read aloud the inscription on the lid.

'One good friend is all I need.'

'This box was a gift from Magsy's father to my papa, after their one and only disagreement.' Morgan's brow wrinkled as he puffed a cigar to life. 'Damned if I can remember what it was about. *I* never fall out with my best friend because she happens to be my wife.'

Nance's smile was short-lived. 'Morgan, remember I said I might, possibly . . .' She waited for him to catch on, and he did. 'I was wrong.'

'Ah.'

The red mess in her underwear had put a dampener on the day. Tudor was more than enough for her, and he was Morgan's third son, but Nance had a duty to bear another child.

The future for her boy would not entail his growing away. *He'll always need me.* Nance bent and handed Tudor the striped tiger he was searching for. One day she would disappear, and if no sibling was on hand to step in, what would happen? *I have to be immortal.*

Magsy was, at that moment, offering a cigar to one of her Christmas guests, from a similar silver box.

Sebastiano took one with glee. 'You are so generous,' he said, in his melodic accent. 'Lunch was magnificent.'

'My friend is an excellent cook.' Mrs Endicott was on the other side of the hearth. 'My appetite can't do her justice. I eat like a bird.'

The Italian wondered if his English was at fault. What bird could this nice old English lady mean? A vulture, perhaps?

'My friend is at another lovely home today,' he said. 'The Grrundees.'

'Oh dear,' said Magsy and Mrs Endicott together.

Stan was face down in the matchstick remains of the table. Snoring off his stupor, he didn't feel Badboy snuffle around him; the dog's wildest dreams had come true and he was gobbling up the entire Christmas meal.

In the bedroom, Connie sat and shivered. The children were under the covers, quiet, like pensioners.

Hunger was nothing new. It was the worry that felt like it might kill her. She thought of Vic, friendless and hunted. He could be in the next lane; he could be a hundred miles away.

But Cliff got out. She clung to that, like a string of rosary beads. *He got out!*

*

The boy who got out was just then exchanging gifts with his wife.

Cliff handed Lorna a book-shaped package, and she gave him a book-shaped package.

Neither of them had ever been happier.

The Brookfield Christmas pudding was, as ever, a triumph.

'Nobody guessed,' winked Doris as she filled Peggy's hot water bottle, 'that I bulked it out with breadcrumbs and grated carrot!'

'Wonder what Jack ate today,' said Peggy, and regretted it when Doris's face lost its cheer. They both worried about him, but Peggy's fear was broad, inchoate, not acute like Doris's.

Doris brightened, and packed Peggy off to bed. 'I'm ready for the land of nod meself,' she said. Letting Glen out, she gazed over the white fields, serene and severe in the moonlight. 'Come on, Glen, in, boy, in.' She shut the door on the snow, grateful for the comforts and security of Brookfield, comforts her son was fighting to protect. She thought of her neighbours in their homes, in their beds, all of them indoors on this sacred night, with no Bull to entice them out.

'Goodnight, everyone,' she whispered.

Not everyone was indoors. The grotto was a web of silver and shadow.

Hildegard blew on her hands. 'What a place to meet! Merry Chris—' She pushed against him and ducked away from his mouth. 'Gerroff, you wicked boy. Wait until you're asked!'

'If I'm wicked,' he said, 'what are you?'

'Freezing,' said Hildegard, creeping under his greatcoat.

The moment shimmers.

The earth breathes. The slow wheel turns. The year tumbles from old age to rebirth, new lives sleep deep below the snowy crust.

There is one such new life in Peggy's womb. Curled, it can feel the warmth from the hot water bottle supplied by its grandmother. The newbie doesn't know its mother nodded off tussling with a moral puzzle, doesn't know Peggy asks herself if she defrauded Jack by marrying him when she doesn't love him. 'Not in *that* way,' as she puts it.

A recently arrived new life screams the house down at the Grundy homestead. King Alf is displeased.

Fully clothed, the vicar slumps in a chair beside the marital bed. The sheets are cold and uninviting; they were never all that welcoming, but even an old sock will miss an old shoe. Henry trusts his saviour, and tries his best not to question His plan.

Walter doesn't question God's plan either. Walter is drunk. Walter dreams of ladies without the benefit of clothes and smiles in his sleep.

At one end of Pamela's bed, Minko wheezes like a sentient toupee. At the other end, Pamela removes her eye mask and wishes day would creep over the sill, with all its expectations and chores. Down in the great hall, Hero pads about and can't get comfortable. Their anxieties are strangely similar. They both involve Alec.

The Christmas baby is in his parents' bed. They often smuggle him in to sleep between them. He is safe and he is loved. There is no more confident creature in Borsetshire than Tudor Morgan.

January

'New year, same old turnips!' Susan Grundy eyed the vegetables on offer at Frank's shop.

'Have you seen Peggy about?' asked Ruby, taking ration coupons and scribbling figures on a pad. 'Maybe the baby's come.'

'Rather her than me,' said Susan, and launched into a report of her own recent labour that threatened to turn Frank's hair white. He scooted to the back room, to move crates about so he couldn't hear things he shouldn't, about mysterious feminine experiences.

He emerged only when Agnes turned up, who told both women she didn't care whether or not Peggy's baby had come but she *did* care whether her order was packed up and ready to take.

'Happy new year, Agnes,' said Ruby, heaving the box of goods marked 'Turnpike' onto the counter.

'Mrs Kaye to *you*.' Agnes prodded the quilt, folded on top of the Bisto and tinned pork brawn. 'What's this?'

'I believe you're next to sew a square,' said Ruby.

'I've opted out of all that.' Agnes reached out to push away the patchwork, but her hand stilled. She stared at the newest square. Rabbits on a pale blue background. She snatched up the box, quilt and all, and bustled out.

'Hang on!' Frank turned to Ruby. 'She was supposed to settle her bill!' It would take a braver man than Frank to chase down Agnes. 'Put it on her slate, Ruby.'

His assistant didn't move or speak.

I blame babies, thought Frank, seeking out the tick book. Talk of them sent women doolally-tap.

A short letter, but very 'Alec'.

> We hold on.
> We stand firm.
> Just as you do at home.

Pamela assumed that news of the Allied recapture of Barga would have reached him, and encouraged him. Army censorship meant she must guess this; Alec's own discreet censorship meant she must also guess at how he felt about Caroline.

It might have been wiser to wait until he came home to clamp down so definitively on bringing the girl to live at Lower Loxley. They had spoken of Alec's fatalist presentiment that he would die on the battlefield; *I mocked him about that.* So much of what Pamela said and did seemed to be controlled by some brusque spirit who would rather step on toes than show even a glimmer of emotion.

She wrote a speedy reply. No mention of the prophecy, which had sent the village quite cuckoo, and no mention of Caroline.

That done, she took another sheet of paper and began a very different letter to another individual. Not knowing quite how to express herself, she kept it short and to the point.

Turnpike was a neat, dignified cottage. It smelled of polish. It was Agnes's pride and joy, representing her leap from a maid's attic bed in a similar house to the master bedroom bed of this one.

The man who had facilitated her ascent up the slopes of Ambridge rarely looked at the clock; Denholm's tummy told him the time, and now it told him that dinner was late.

He mentioned this to his wife and she snapped at him.

'This isn't a restaurant, Denholm Kaye.'

Denholm went into an immediate and deep huff. *Mother never snapped,* he thought. Taking himself off, he tripped over a canvas bag by the stairs. 'What *is* this?'

'Nothing. Leave it.' She was still snapping.

He opened the bag. 'Ah, the famous quilt.'

'Give it here.' The bag was exiled to the cold back step. After dinner, Agnes didn't join Denholm for their customary hour with the wireless, but went instead to the spare room.

Denholm didn't wonder why.

In the back of a drawer, Agnes found a sewing workbag. She went through the scraps of fabric, and found the one she sought.

Rabbits on a sky-blue background.

The drawer was slammed, and Agnes scrubbed her face in the bathroom as if it was a dirty pot.

Then she gripped the edge of the sink and asked her reflection, 'What does this mean?'

AMBRIDGE WOMEN'S INSTITUTE
MEETING MINUTES

Date: 17th January 1945
At: The Cherries
Chairwoman: Pamela Pargetter
Present: Doris Archer, Agnes Kaye, Emmeline Endicott, Magsy Furneaux, Lorna Horrobin, Nance Seed, Ruby Bonnet,
Susan Grundy, Wanda Lafromboise,
Julia Pargetter
Minutes: Magsy Furneaux

1. Pamela opened by asking who would vollunteer for minutes and said 'thank you Magsy' although I had not vollunteered because of my teribile spelling and my mistrust of full stops

2. We said a silent prayer for poor dear Frances

3. Mrs E said 'Frances was Mother Molly's first victim!' and recited the prophecy 'A beest will gild the sky'

4. Pamela said we are not here to discuss folklore

5. Susan said 'Tell old Frances it is folklore'

6. Mrs E wondered if Mother Molly's beest is a lion that will escape from a circus and eat one of us

7. Agnes said that beests come in all sizes and maybe Pamela will trip over Minko

(Do I minute glances? If so, Pamela gave Agnes a definite look)

8. Pamela congratulated everyone on Winter Tonic and Julia took a bow

9. Lorna asked that the proffits be spent on books for the children at Arkwright Hall

10. Susan said 'No that is boring let's have a party'

11. Peggy said 'ow'

12. Agnes said Peggy should be at home she could have the baby at any minute and get blood on Mrs E's rug

13. Peggy thanked Agnes for her kind wishes but she was not due for a fortnight

14. Pamela asked about the quilt

15. Agnes took it out of her bag and said it is higgledy-piggledy and a waste of time

16. Doris said kindness is never a waste of time

17. Agnes advised Doris to keep her hair on and asked who is next to sew a skware

18 Pamela said 'according to the list it is Walter Gabriel'

19. I said that was nonsense as men cannot sew

20. Wanda said some women cannot sew

21. Doris said Walter was most insistent. She also said that the little rabbits on Agnes's fabric were delightful

22. Ruby took it (Aktually Ruby snatched it)

23. Agnes compained she had one of her heads and left, knocking over my cordial

24. Ruby stood up too but Pamela told her to sit down and said Agnes will be fine, we have a lot to get through

25. Mrs E said talk of headaches always gives her a headache

26. Pamela said please lets get on

27. Peggy said 'ow sorry ow'

28. Mrs E suggested the beest in the prophecy could be a hedgehog with rabies

29. Lorna voiced some skepticism that a hedgehog could gild the sky

30. Pamela said in a higher voice than usual that we are not here to discuss hedgehogs

31. Pamela reminded us we need to find a housekeeper for the vicar

32. Mrs E went to see what was taking the maid so long with the tea

33. I said Mrs E should sack that lazy maid

34. Pamela said 'never mind the maid'

35. While Mrs E was out of the room Nance showed us a picture in a magazine, she said 'this is Bathsheba and Donald Burton and they are still alive and they live nearby why don't we invite Donald to meet the young lady he once kissed! It would make our dear Mrs E so happy'

36. Susan said it might well kill our dear Mrs E stone dead

37. Ruby said it can be dangerous to rake over the past in a miserable voice

38. Peggy shouted 'no!'

39. Susan said 'calm down it is only a comment'

```
  40. Peggy fell off her chair and said 'no
I mean the baby the baby'
  41. Mrs E came back in and dropped
the tea tray
  42. Pamela said 'we may as well end there'
```

Wanda stuffed rosehips into her pocket as she left the meeting and made her way to Woodbine Cottage. The hips would find their destiny in the syrup the Boss cooked up in great vats.

Hope this jumper and skirt is fancy enough for taking tea with Grayson.

The invitation had surprised her, as did Doris's immediate consent when she begged the afternoon off. Removing her beret and gloves in Woodbine's hallway, she was even more surprised when she looked through to the drawing room, where a fire leapt up the chimney and Grayson's academic paperwork sat alongside china figurines.

'You!' she said to Max as he rose from a low chair.

'And, um, *you*.'

They both rounded on Grayson, who was impish with glee. 'Doris and I agree it's time you stopped behaving like magnets. You either cling together or spring apart, as if your electrons have a dipole moment, generated by the electrons' intrinsic . . .' He grimaced. 'Sorry, I forget not everybody lives their lives in textbooks. We thought you need a chance to get to know each other a little better in a civilised setting. Good idea?'

'Good idea.' Wanda smiled, but Max did not seem able to go that far just yet.

The rituals of tea were observed, a little clumsily. 'I'm no host,' said Grayson, neglecting to strain the Lapsang Souchong. 'No doubt your aunt threw spiffing tea parties here, Max. By rights you, as a Gilpin, should have this place. I'm a cuckoo in the nest.'

'I admire your ability to navigate Aunt Blanche.' Max took a fishpaste sandwich, and risked a glance at Wanda. 'She's a queer duck.'

'Quack-quack,' said Wanda.

'Grayson, how do you know Aunt Blanche?' Max asked.

'Our families shared a housekeeper for a time.'

'I rather dread her,' confessed Max. 'Makes the most fearful fuss of me. Only boy in the family, you see, carrying on the Gilpin name and all that. Forever winking at me, as if she has a secret to share.'

'You should ask what she's hiding,' said Wanda. Her foot was very close to Max's beneath the chenille tablecloth.

'I have no desire to know Aunt Blanche's secrets. She's the type to throw gasoline on a fire.'

Grayson was arch. 'Sounds like the family expect you to get on with making babies, Max, and perpetuate the noble Gilpin lineage.'

Max said it lightly, but there was no other way for his response to land other than with a dull thud. 'My wife was expecting when she died.'

Wanda put down her cup with a clatter. *No wonder he's*

susceptible to Mother Molly's visions of the other side. Compassion crowded her. The poor man needed to believe his family waited somewhere for him.

'I had no … I'm *so* sorry.' Grayson's horror turned his birthmark crimson.

'No, *I'm* sorry.' Max frowned. 'I should know better than to blurt it out like that.'

'I'm glad you told us,' said Wanda.

Max fiddled with the crust of his sandwich.

'Was that the door knocker?' Grayson jumped out.

When he left the room, Max said, 'Old Grayson's a lousy actor.'

'But a good pal.' Wanda folded her hands on her lap. Whatever happened now, whatever was said, it must come from Max. *I've made my position clear.* Very few women would be so bold about their attraction to a man; the ball was firmly in Max's court.

'I don't know your surname,' he said.

'Lafromboise.'

'Wanda Lafrombroise, come over here.'

She went over there. She stood in front of him and let him pull her down beside him on the small sofa. She bent like a paperclip into his side.

'I'm going to kiss you,' he said, and did just that.

Ammazza! thought Wanda. She had heard Italian POWs say it when they were thunderstruck.

He held her then, quite tightly. She moved her head into the space beneath his chin, which seemed to have been tailor-made to fit. Into his chest she said, 'Max, tell me about her.'

'You're sure?' he asked, looking concerned as she sat up. 'Very well. We lived in Queen Anne's Gate. We loved each other.'

'I should hope so too.'

Max did smile then. 'You are . . .'

'I am what?'

'Surprising,' he said. 'It was a good marriage, Wanda. Not perfect, but good. She was sensible, calm, reserved.'

Nothing like me, thought Wanda, and the thought pleased her.

'The bomb that ... *got* her, it was my fault. I made her late that morning, wrapped up in myself as per. She was impatient. I told her not to nag. She told me off. And then the building vapourised around us.'

Wanda kissed his hand, and for a second it seemed as if Max might cry at such tenderness. 'I woke up in hospital. They wouldn't tell me at first, but I knew. Because I could hear her.'

Wanda kept her features composed. 'You heard her?'

'In here.' Max tapped his teeming head. 'I knew she was gone. And the baby, our girl or our boy. All my fault. All because I couldn't get a ruddy move on. I am a man made entirely of regrets, Wanda.'

The war made men melancholic, Wanda had noticed. It held up a dirty mirror to their basic and forgivable faults. 'Why don't you see yourself the way the village sees you? As a hero.'

'Me?' Max pulled a face. 'Nothing heroic about me, Wanda Lafromboise.'

'They all know you lost your arm in France.'

'Yes, Petty France.' Max smiled. 'Silly as it sounds, that was our address: Queen Anne's Gate, Petty France, London SW1.'

'No!' Wanda sat up on her knees among the cushions. 'You lost your arm over Calais during the Battle of France, the whole village knows that.'

Max's mouth made a shape but he gave up on whatever he was going to say and pushed his hand through his thick fair thatch. 'I've never even flown in the war. I was a Whitehall chap. This . . .' He flicked his empty sleeve. 'This is no badge of courage. I lost it in my own bathroom, combing my damn hair.'

The realisation wrenched them apart. Max was agitated. Wanda said, 'Let's not disillusion everyone. It's just a silly misunderstanding. You're still the same man.'

'But it's not true!'

He spoke as if this was her fault. Wanda could be cold when she needed to be, and she was cold now. 'I should get back to the Boss. I won't speak of this. The rest is up to you.'

By the time Wanda trudged back to Brookfield and dumped the rosehips in the pantry, there was a whole new human in the house.

'Hello baby,' whispered Wanda to the swaddled child, purplish-pink and bawling in Peggy's arms. She sat carefully on the bed and asked, 'How was it?'

'It was ... challenging.' Peggy hadn't expected to give birth on Mrs Endicott's Persian rug. 'Morgan got there in the blink of an eye, and it was quick, but holy moly, Wands, I won't lie to you. It *hurt*.' She shifted in the bed with a wince.

The bedding was the best in the house, a fire roared in the grate, dried lavender sat in a bowl on the bedside table.

'Doris got me through,' said Peggy. 'Felt like I was hanging onto a rope for dear life and she was at the other end. I knew she wouldn't let go.'

'What're you going to call it, sorry, her?'

'Not sure.' Peggy regarded her daughter, still new, still strange to her. 'She has a look of Jack.' Peggy loved the girl in a simple, huge way. *You've changed everything,* she thought, gratefully.

Holding hands as instructed, Michele and Evie meandered home from Arkwright Hall.

The door of Turnpike opened. 'Yoohoo!' croaked a voice.

Brought up on English fairy tales, the girls knew that the wicked witch sometimes lived in a pretty cottage, all the better to lure unsuspecting – and tasty – children.

Evie pulled Michele up the path. 'Mother Molly lives at the grotto,' she hissed. 'No village has *two* witches!'

'Give this list to your mother at the shop,' said Agnes. 'I'm too poorly to go out.' She opened her purse with a click. 'This is the correct money, so don't try nothing.'

'*Madame*,' asked Michele with a frown, 'how could we try

nothing?' She scanned the list. 'English mustard! Are you sure?' English mustard was dynamite; Michele missed the fragrant Dijon mustard of home.

'No backchat.' Agnes shooed them away, and watched behind her curtains for their return.

A few minutes later, taking the bag from them, she asked if Frank had said anything.

With a creditable impression of the big, bluff man, Evie recited Frank's puzzled, 'What the 'eck's wrong with Agnes? She's avoiding the shop like the plague.'

'None of his beeswax!' Agnes's colloquial English again stumped the girls, but the halfpenny she gave them made perfect sense.

Sewing was trickier than Walter had expected.

He could patch trousers or secure a button, but adding a square to the village quilt needed a lady's light touch.

As do I.

Above his head, something fell on floorboards. Probably Nelson's *Beano* annual slithering off his bedclothes. Walter had packed him off to bed with the same warning his own mother had used: 'Straight to sleep or Mother Molly'll nip your toes!'

A branch tapped at the window like a bony finger and he jumped. Took a sip of wompo.

Biting off the thread, he considered his handiwork and was proud. Annie's apron was no more.

For a decade after her death, it had hung on the back door, bringing him up short when he saw it.

My wife did everything in that apron. Wiped her floury hands. Lashed him with it when he staggered home, pickled.

Adding it to the quilt paid homage to the apron's years of service. It would help someone.

And get it out from under my gaze.

He kissed it roughly, and took a long draught of wompo.

Hazel catkins opened up and flung their golden pollen at the coats of the faithful as they filed up the church path.

The colours in Wanda's dress reflected the crocuses pushing merrily up between the graves. She left Doris at the gate, dispensing bulletins on the progress of mother and baby.

The church was dim after the sharp January brightness of the day. Wanda felt Max's eye upon her as she went up the aisle. Before meeting him, she had assumed that no woman could think about any man all day long, but now she knew better. Whether she was spreading slurry in the cold, or passing nails to Dan as he repaired the calves' quarters, she thought about their romantic impasse. *It's stalemate, like the war.* The Germans had finally given up trying to encircle the Allies but both sides were now in a staring contest, not unlike the static pair in Ambridge.

A hymn. A prayer. A gospel reading. Ruby brought round the collection plate, and Wanda dropped in a coin. All the while thinking about Max, and knowing that the misunderstanding about his arm muddied the waters still further – she knew the truth about him; she had witnessed a dent to his pride.

Ruby stretched over the pews and Agnes dropped a twist of notepaper into the collection plate, along with half a bob.

Ruby was quick. The note was pocketed and the plate was taken to the next row.

Outside, Walter shook the vicar's hand and hurried over to Pamela, who wore a mink stole over her cashmere jacket. ''Ere,' he said.

Pamela praised the stitching on the quilt's new square.

'Bright fabric!' Mrs Endicott could always dig up a compliment, even for the florid froufrou of the apron.

'My Annie was a lady of great taste,' said Walter.

'Very much so.' Pamela remembered that lady's wellington boots and the safety pin that held her cardigan closed.

'You remind me of her,' said Walter gallantly.

There had been a shift in attitude towards Mother Molly since Frances's death.

Nance, helping in the shop on Ruby's day off, agreed with her father that it wasn't so easy to laugh off the fourth prediction. 'We should be working out which beast it refers to, and how it'll gild the sky!'

'You're all barmy.' Hildegard took her change. 'Frances Bissett's death was a red herring. Coincidence.'

'I hope so.' Nance clanged the till shut as Hildegard left.

She took an envelope from her pocket, and slit it open with a knife, grinning as she realised it was a reply from the great Donald Burton himself.

She didn't hear her father tutting at the till, as she read how Donald remembered the family well. 'Charming folk,' he wrote, 'with a strikingly pretty daughter.' He was adamant that he had never kissed her: 'I was a married man, and can only apologise if I gave the sweet young thing any sort of encouragement, but there was no flirtation and most certainly no kiss.'

Sensitive Nance was crushed; there would be no romantic reunion. Daft Mrs Endicott had exaggerated a dashing older man's courtesy.

'You gone deaf, Nance?' Frank held out a tuppence. 'I said chase after Hildegard. You gave her the wrong change.'

She caught up with Hildegard at the bus stop, and put matters right just as the bus trundled into view.

Agnes trotted over from Woodbine, avoiding Nance's eye.

'Feeling better?' called Nance. 'Off to Felpersham?'

'What's that got to do with you?' Agnes hopped up onto the bus.

'And a very good day to you, too,' said Nance under her breath.

'Want to hear the latest letter from hubby?' Julia found her mother-in-law in Lower Loxley's great hall.

'Edited version, please.' Pamela had a butler to berate.

'Bulawayo blah blah blah. Very hot ... Tiger Moth ...

says he scraped through the final exam.' Julia tossed some photographs at her mother-in-law. 'He enclosed some awful photographs of elephants.'

Watching the café from across the street, Agnes felt like a scarlet woman. If Denholm knew what she was up to, he would consider it infidelity. *He'll never know!* she told herself; that was the whole point of this hush-hush meeting.

She pushed at the glass door.

Deviating from the most direct route home, Nance passed The Cherries.

Inevitably, Mrs Endicott was at the window, and inevitably she invited Nance in. She fed Tudor biscuits dunked in warm milk, and wiped his mouth gently with a napkin. 'Never fear, Tudor, I have moved the budgie cage to the larder, just in case my Twinkle Toes turns out to be Mother Molly's "beast". The seventh of February will be upon us before long.'

'True.' Nance was distracted by the photograph of the Burtons on the piano; she was glad her hostess still had her delusions about Donald. Mrs Endicott followed her gaze. 'Ah, that heavenly day! I was never so bold again. I resisted temptation.'

Nance felt burdened by her knowledge, but all attempts at changing the subject failed.

'One wonders what might have been if I was as brave as my counterpart.'

Nance nodded mechanically, looking over at the Burtons

in their foppish finery. She put down her cup. She blinked. Donald wasn't wearing the famous chequered waistcoat; his was dark tartan It was his sister, Bathsheba, who wore black and white checks beneath her linen coat.

Wheeling to look at her cherubic friend, Nance realised she had approached the wrong Burton.

It was Bathsheba who kissed Mrs E.

'Are you mad?' seethed Agnes. 'Sitting right in the window like that! Follow me.'

Ruby followed her to an alcove.

'Tea!' barked Agnes at the waitress. She took off her gloves and folded them into her handbag. Put it on the table between them like a dam. 'Now, madam. What's what?'

'I think I'm your daughter,' said Ruby. A rehearsed line, much simplified from its first draft.

'Pssh.' Agnes made the noise she used for scaring cats out of her roses. 'You look nowt like me.'

'It's locked.' Magsy tried the key again, but the vicarage door remained stubbornly shut.

'Try the knocker.' Doris hated being away from the new baby, but the Women's Committee rota for 'doing' the vicar was implacable. 'We'll change the beds, whizz round the rugs and skedaddle.'

The door flew open. A woman asked them, 'Yes? Who are you?'

They knew who she was. Valerie Micklewood was a

hussy, whose lust for the pigman on her husband's farm had led to a shocking divorce. Spurned by the pigman – turned out there was a Mrs Pigman – she had fled the area. Now, she told them, as she led them over squeaky-clean floorboards to Henry's study, she was housekeeper at the vicarage.

Magsy was quick to deliver a potted biography of his new housekeeper to Henry, who listened, nodded and finally said, 'I know all about Mrs Micklewood, thank you. She's doing a marvellous job. Was there anything else?'

There was nothing else except a great deal of 'Well I never!' and 'What is the world coming to?' from Magsy, and joy at being able to get back to her granddaughter from Doris.

'I always wondered about my real mum and dad.' Ruby had ordered more tea.

'Hmm.' Agnes had no words. A box, long locked, was open and leaking all over her tidy life. Everything Ruby said made another mess.

'Not that my adoptive family were cruel. They're good people. They've never understood me, though. They said I was a free spirit, but they said it like it was a problem.'

She met Henri when he was teaching at Birmingham School of Art.

'My parents wouldn't allow me to attend, but I hung around the cafés, and listened to all the talk of art and, you know, *big* subjects.'

Agnes didn't know and said so.

'Henri and I . . . It was electric, immediate. I fell pregnant with Michele.'

A glance flickered between the women. History repeating itself.

'My mother wanted the child adopted but I followed Henri back to France, and we got by. We had Evie. We were happy.'

'No mention of marriage,' said Agnes.

'No need,' smiled Ruby. 'I simply took his name. We were in love.'

'Love! I was in love at seventeen and look where that got me.'

Ruby quickened, leant forward. 'Tell me about him.'

'Don't go romancing him. He was just some chancer.'

Ruby looked so hard at Agnes that the woman flinched. 'Watching war ruin the world convinced me I had to get a move on and finally find out where I'm from. Find out why I'm left-handed, why my teeth cross slightly at the front.' Ruby pointed. 'Like yours.'

Agnes clamped a hand over her mouth.

'Why I love dogs.'

'You certainly don't get that from me.'

'A soft-hearted nun at the adoption society took pity on me. Gave me ten minutes with my file.'

'You were never supposed to find me.' Agnes fidgeted. She hated this café. She hated the sugar bowl and the place mats and the spoons. 'Rules are rules.'

'Tell me about him.' Ruby was gentle and relentless.

'Will you shut up if I do?'

'I might.'

'He was handsome, I'll give him that. He's where you get all *this* from.' Agnes waved a hand at Ruby's comeliness, nothing like her own stick-insect physique. 'Ran for Borsetshire, he did. Had trophies. Should have seen him run when I told him I was in the family way. He's probably still flippin' running.'

'That must've been hard for you.'

Suspicious of sympathy, Agnes drew in her chin. 'You have his nose. He had a lisp. Soft hands. He was kind, until . . .' That seemed to exhaust her ability to praise her disappointing lover. 'My mother said she'd die of shame – she didn't – and my father stopped talking to me. You'd think I'd done a murder. Bundled me off to my aunt, who ignored me for seven months until I gave birth.'

'Did you . . .' Ruby's face apologised for the question. 'Did you hold me? I always hoped you'd held me.'

'No.' Agnes shrank, once again the naive teenager who must do as she was told; the last time she had ever done as she was told. 'They said it was for the best.' Her voice almost crept to a standstill and Ruby had to listen hard to hear. 'I spent my pregnancy making you a blanket, from scraps I found. The nuns promised you'd be wrapped in when you were given away.'

'They kept their promise.' Ruby reached into her bag and took out a small quilt, bright in the dim restaurant. She held the bunnies on a blue background to her cheek. 'All through everything, the escape from France, I held on to it.'

Decades worth of unshed tears filled Agnes up and made her nauseous. She battled the feeling, as she had always done.

Ruby put her hand over Agnes's on the tablecloth. 'You can hold me now,' she said.

Agnes stood up so quickly her chair fell back. Faces turned, but it was the face at the window, looking in, that had provoked her.

She stumbled out into the street.

The last patient of the day sneezed in the waiting room at Holmleigh.

Nance stole into the surgery the back way, from the kitchen, and surprised Morgan dotting his i's at the desk.

'Oof!' he said, as she plonked herself on his lap. 'My dear! There's someone waiting!'

'I need your medicine too.' Nance curled into him, enjoying the smell of him, the heft of him. Her older man. Her wise owl.

'Where have you been today?' Morgan whispered into her flossy hair. 'What have you got to tell me?' He adored her dispatches from Ambridge.

'I visited Mrs E.'

'Then I can't expect any scandal.'

'Well . . .'

As he and his wife waited for the bus, Denholm found himself on the wrong end of a ticking off.

'Staring into the café like a spy!' Agnes's hat was wonky

with rage. Too much, she knew, for her husband's transgression. 'What got into you? Following me! Have you gone mad?'

'I thought,' said Denholm, shoulders slumped, 'that you might be having an affair.'

She laughed. Ten minutes ago she had thought she'd never laugh again. 'You what?' Her accent slipped in a way she rarely allowed around Denholm. 'Me? An affair. Who with? Walter Gabriel?'

'You've been very up and down, Aggie. Neglected the house; me. A faraway look in your eye all the time.'

That was undeniable. Agnes took in Denholm's greatcoat that she brushed so carefully on Sundays. The remaining strands of hair he was so proud of. She had assumed he was incapable of thoughts beyond the Neanderthal 'Pork chop! Now!' variety.

He values me.

She valued him, too; she valued him for what he brought her: Turnpike's cupboards stacked with china and the full coal scuttle and the account at the store. 'I'm sorry,' she said, possibly for the first time in her life.

'Imagine my relief,' said Denholm, 'when I saw you taking tea with that French girl from the shop. No deception there, eh!'

The bus came. He got on first, without helping her on. Agnes watched the dreary January fields pass and wondered what he would say if she confessed all.

She knew what he'd say, and she saw the china and the coal and the account disappearing in a puff of smoke.

*

'Well . . .' The *dot dot dot* hung in the air between Nance and Morgan.

'Yes?' smiled Morgan, jiggling her on his knee.

'Mrs E is terrified of the seventh of February, in case her budgie is the beast Mother Molly refers to.'

Morgan howled with laughter.

The secret was not Nance's to tell. Mrs Endicott had been frank about the kiss in all but one detail. *Did Mrs E find her grooms lacking when she stood at the altar?* She had been unable to follow her heart; the furore would be too much for such a delicate little soul. *Ladies simply don't set up home with ladies in Mrs E's world.*

By contrast, Nance's story was simple. She had a wonderful man, and his wonderful baby. And this wonderful lap to perch on.

The sneezing beyond the door revved up.

'Up you get, my dear,' said Morgan. 'I'll keep an eye on Mrs E. February seventh is just around the corner, after all.'

Nance shivered, as if a ghost had walked over her grave.

FEBRUARY

The seventh of February had three hours left of its allotted twenty-four.

Grayson sat among Woodbine's cushions with only the wireless for company. The nine o'clock evening news was all of the conference at Yalta, in Crimea. No mention of the patina of dread that had subdued Ambridge all that chilly day. No beast had yet misbehaved. The sky was ungilded. Academics knew that reality never bent to superstition, but Grayson's fingers tapped out a Morse code of anxiety on the arm of the sofa. 'Distract me, Aunty Beeb,' he said.

Churchill, Roosevelt and Stalin were apparently working out a post-war world.

'Hitler hasn't surrendered yet,' Grayson reminded the smooth, patrician newscaster. 'Bit early to carve up the spoils.'

In one way, Ruby's mission was completed. She lay, wakeful, by her daughters, reluctant to snuff out the candle.

The date meant nothing to her; she cared little for the

prophecy. She pored, instead, over the nuggets Agnes had given her.

Her father had soft hands.

A lisp.

Same nose as Ruby.

She gave me precious little else. No touch, no open arms.

Stretching to kill the candle, Ruby reminded herself that she had been careful to expect nothing, which was more or less what Agnes offered. She closed her eyes in the dark.

Soft hands.

A lisp.

His nose.

Just back from a sick bed, Morgan wound the grandfather clock in Holmleigh's hall. Already after ten; a young man driven wild by head pains had kept him out late.

Morgan had smelled alcohol in the room, and suspected an ailment of the soul beyond his medications.

'Time for a cigar.' Morgan went, yawning, to the silver box. Read out, as he always did, 'One good friend is all I need.' The box conjured up his father and his best friend. Herbert and Aubrey, two fine gents, who seemed to exist in one long Edwardian summer afternoon.

Until that other dirty war, the one that was supposed to end all wars forever.

A memory pounced. He remembered the reason for the box's engraving.

A tennis match! That was it. It was an apology from

Magsy's late father, Aubrey, to his own dad. Herbert had won on a very close line call. Aubrey astonished the crowd by refusing to shake hands.

'The decent thing to do', he had said, 'is to declare a draw.'

Guffawing, Morgan's father had said, 'The decent thing to do, old chap, is admit I trounced you!'

Aubrey took great offence. There was no contact between the two households for an uncomfortable week. No jaunts on the Am in their punt. No late-night conflabs over whisky.

A week to the day, Aubrey turned up with the box Morgan now owned. He had gestured to the silver trophy on the sideboard and told Herbert, 'You won that fair and square, sir.'

With a last puff of his cigar, Morgan took himself to bed, wondering what those two patriarchs would make of the Mother Molly sideshow. Less than two hours to go, and then the village need never mention the silly old bat ever again.

The baby had a name.

Jennifer Archer more or less ran the farm; her whims were mandates. She asked for, and got, an 11pm feed.

'Shush, darling, shush.' Peggy cooed down at her daughter as they sat in the comfortable old chair Dan had heaved up to the bedroom. 'Who's my pretty one?'

Jennifer absorbed the devotion with *sang froid*. She was the only person on Earth who could tell Peggy what to do. The clock was ignored; Jennifer's schedule was all, and

Peggy thanked providence for the extra hands that reached out for the child when she was tired. *Christine's so excited to be an aunt!*

Downstairs, Dan and the Boss were up late.

Doris half listened to Dan's assessment of Yalta. He was impressed with 'our Winnie' but didn't trust 'that Stalin'. He wondered why his wife was so quiet. 'Cheer up, love. Adolf's licked! Just a question of when he surrenders.'

'Maybe.' Each minute of war cost lives. There was something *worse* about hope; what if Jack, new father of that little bundle upstairs, was to catch it right at the very end?

'When did Wanda say she'll be away?'

'Twenty seventh of this month to ninth of March.'

'Such fuss over weddings,' grumbled Dan, who relied on his land girl.

'Her younger sister, apparently.' Doris moved around, putting the kitchen to rights. 'She's leapfrogged Wanda; found herself a nice local barrister to marry.'

This barrister had a brother, and Wanda feared he was earmarked for her. Her mother had already let slip that he was wealthy. 'Nothing', Wanda had kvetched, 'about whether he's funny or kind or can darn a sock.'

'It'll be nice to see your family,' Doris had said, touched when Wanda corrected her.

'My *other* family, Boss. They'll stuff me into a frock and expect the old Wanda, the one who'd been nowhere and knew nothing.'

'And had never fallen in love.'

Wanda didn't bother disputing it. 'Fat lot of good that's done me. You know me, I don't waste time on something that's going nowhere.'

If Denholm awoke and saw her sitting in the low chair like a ghoul, Agnes planned to say she couldn't sleep because of Mother Molly's prediction.

He didn't wake up; he never woke up until prodded out of bed for his kipper.

She didn't give a fig about the beast that would gild the sky. *He'd better get on with it, he's only got twenty minutes!* It was the past that kept her up.

The hard fact of a baby in her stomach, all those years ago. Growing and growing, the engineer of her disgrace. The birth was long and difficult, and the midwives automatons who showed no gentleness, only distaste.

That was when Agnes closed off her body from her mind. Apart from appeasing Denholm with it once a month, Agnes paid her body no heed. Certainly, she expected no pleasure from it.

They were right, she thought. Her parents were unkind but correct when they told teenaged Agnes a baby would ruin her life.

They really were, she repeated. *They were right.*

Walter Gabriel looked sideways at his hens. 'Don't go gilding the sky, girls,' he said, shutting them in.

Accused by the Lower Loxley chaps of being 'the beast',

Minko licked her bottom and then jumped when they all howled with laughter.

In a dark pantry, Mrs Endicott begged Twinkle Toes not to 'do anything silly'.

Dan, climbing into bed, wondered at the mooing from the sheds. Did they sound . . . different? Evil? *Get to sleep, you fool,* he counselled himself.

In pyjamas, Grayson opened the curtains to peek out at the Green.

All was well. 'Better get your skates on, Mother Molly,' said the man of learning.

A scream sounded, so shrill and wild, it could only come from a child. Something gold hit the Green, bright as a comet. The grass was bright suddenly, golden.

Gilded.

As Grayson dashed out of Woodbine, the clock in the parlour struck midnight.

The Bull spat gold rain up into the night sky. Thatch burned ferociously and fast. The noise was unexpected; a dull roar. Grayson saw the painted sign catch and flame.

Nobody had guessed that the beast might be a building.

'Bob!' he yelled, kicking at the saloon door.

'The children!' Max turned up out of the darkness, his face lit like a pagan at a sacrifice.

'They're coming.' Grayson held the door and ushered out Ruby, sheltering her girls under a sodden blanket.

'Here, here.' Max picked up Evie as easily as if she was a shopping bag, and deposited her on the Green. She wailed and her sister wailed, and their mother coughed out, 'Bob?'

The pump, at the apex of the Green, croaked in protest when PC Jenkins jumped off his bike and worked the heavy handle. Frank brought out buckets, and Grayson filled them, and then the basin brought by the Vicar, who bowed his head in front of The Bull and prayed.

Mrs Micklewood worked as hard as the men, taking her place in the human chain. Their efforts seemed a mere spit in the eye to the inferno.

'We have to get Bob out!' Ruby was sooty and damp and wondered if in fact she had died up there in the attic, and this hot nightmare was hell.

Max plunged inside, shouting Bob's name.

Grayson watched. The buckets stilled.

'Please no,' said the vicar.

They both barrelled out, Bob leaning on Max, his head down.

There was a plan: PC Jenkins connected a hose to the pipe in the yard. A volunteer was needed to run the hose upstairs, and contain the fire before it ate The Bull whole.

They all looked at PC Jenkins, who looked back at them.

'I'll do it.' Grayson plunged in. Bob gasped and spluttered, but insisted he was 'fine, fine'. He kept his back to his pub. He couldn't watch his Bull die.

Evie clung to him, and he patted her back. 'There, there, we'll be all right,' he said, unconvincingly.

She hiccupped she was sorry.

'You got nowt to be sorry about,' he said, as shouts and exhortations continued over the crackle of his life burning.

'It was just a small candle,' said Evie. 'Mama said no but the attic is old and I get frightened.'

'Evie . . .' Ruby understood at the same moment as Bob.

Morning lit the scene.

Villagers gathered around the smouldering inn, wincing at its new damaged face.

The earth around was damp and dirty, debris pressed into the mud. The sore void of the thatch gave an improbable view into the filthy attic, like a doll's house belonging to a careless giant.

Hanky to her nose against the hellish smell, Mrs Endicott suggested that The Bull didn't look as bad as she had feared.

The vicar agreed, pointing to the black jagged thatch still breathing out brimstone. 'The flames didn't reach the ground floor. The stairs are intact, more or less. Everything's sooty, of course, but it's complete up until the rafters.'

'It's not a disaster.' Frank regretted saying this when he realised Bob was a few feet away, sitting in the dirt by his ruined begonia tubs.

'Easy for you to say – it's not your home.'

Reaction was brisk and efficient. An unseen hand seemed to organise the long ladders that arrived from Brookfield, the men sent from Lower Loxley, the tea that turned up from every point of the compass all day long.

The local thatcher cut away the blackened reeds, leaving The Bull looking sickly and bald.

Seeing the solid, sacrosanct inn so vulnerable dragged the February clouds even lower over the village.

'Ruby!' called Frank from the counter.

She was at an ad hoc desk among the shelves in the shop's back room, sunk deep in ledgers.

'Your girls are here,' continued Frank. 'They have something for you.'

Reluctantly, Ruby rose, sighing like an invalid. As she went through into the store, she saw the street door clang shut, and she caught sight of Agnes's plaid coat hurrying away.

Of course, she thought, wearied even further. *She can't even face me.* Her optimism had burned along with her belongings. She had been crazy to expect a welcome. 'What is it, girls?'

Evie did not look at her mother. She kept her eyes on the ground; shame had changed the little one. She took responsibility for the fire and no amount of consolation could change her conviction that Bob hated her.

'Look!' Michele beamed and held out a box. 'It's our things, Mama.'

Their world was in a cardboard box. Ruby fell on it, ransacking it. *Is it there?* she thought, too seasoned to trust fate. *Is it?*

'Mama,' said Evie, in a fairy voice. 'Are you looking for this?'

'Oh!'

The photograph of Ruby and Henri was framed in green-painted wood, now ashy black. They were younger. She rode on his back around an orchard. *Their* orchard. She wept, so noisily that Frank turned the sign to 'Closed' and left a disgruntled Magsy out on the step.

'To think,' she cried, 'that this is all I have left!'

'No, Mama,' said Michele. 'You have us.'

'I do, I do.' Ruby grabbed Michele and held her close. 'Evie, here, *mon ange*.'

Evie held back, then ran to her.

Ruby staggered, arms tight about her girls, grateful and desolate.

Dear Alec

So much to report! The Pargetters' very own sorceress has laid waste to The Bull. A coincidence of course; it requires a rather tortured reading of Mother Molly's silly riddle, but poor Bob Little's pride and joy went up in flames.

Thank heavens, the damage is chiefly cosmetic. The thatch is ruined. And the smell . . . the valley stank like a charnel house for days.

The stable lads are helping out. In due course I'll send whitewash.

You'd be so proud of your village. All are pitching in. Bob is lodging with Mrs Endicott – an odd pairing! Ruby Bonnet and her daughters have gone to the vicarage. Evidently the new housekeeper is more hospitable than Frances ever was.

The grand reopening is scheduled, despite tarpaulin flapping across the roof. Takes more than a black magic fireball to put Ambridge off its ale.

I would like to tell you that Hero is fine, but I can't. He pines for you more and more. That dog and I have something in common at last.

I must stop there. There is other post to attend to. Important correspondence which I can't share with you just yet. All in good time.

Come home, Alec, won't you? Come home.

'He's handy, if you'll pardon the pun.' Bob, devouring a doorstep of bread and cheese, gestured at Max, passing with a bucket. 'Comes straight here after a day's work.'

Doris, who did not pardon the pun, said, 'You look worn out, Bob.' The innkeeper had the blackened face of a miner. 'Sure you're up to opening at the weekend?'

'Beer', said Bob, with some hauteur, 'is in my veins.'

She understood. Chickens and calves and breadmaking were all in her own veins. 'You visited Ruby and the little 'uns yet?'

'Don't, Doris.' Finishing the sandwich with a gulp and blustering through the crumbs, Bob said, 'I made it clear! No unattended candles! One rule and that babby ignored it. Now look at the place.'

They did. They looked at the august old pub. It had withstood centuries of wind and weather, only to be brought to its knees by a seven-year old who was afraid of the dark.

'She's only a kiddie,' began Doris, but Bob was away, and up a ladder. She heard her name called. 'What is it, Max?' she said in the posh accent she attempted around him.

'Is Wanda about?'

Doris sighed. 'Am I my land girl's keeper?'

'Oh dear. I fear if you're quoting the bible at me, I must have irritated you.'

Softening, Doris said, 'You're a big boy now. Brookfield's not so far. If you want Wanda, you know where to go.'

'True.' Max was rueful.

Watching him help the men, a stylish flamingo among the rough sparrows from Lower Loxley's stable yard, Doris wondered if such a haunted fellow was good enough for 'my Wanda'. She smiled at that 'my', and chased away a tiny worry that Wanda would not return from her upcoming visit to Bath.

Homes are sticky places.

Magsy picked her way across the cluttered yard with a seed cake in a tin. After some desultory conversation about the progress on the thatch, she said, one eyebrow up under her stiffly curled fringe, 'Did you notice Mrs Micklewood's dressing gown on the night of the fire? Very *sheer*.'

'Goodness me,' said Doris.

* * *

In the February calm before the storm of March calving, Brookfield's fences were repaired, its outhouses washed down, the boundaries walked and checked.

In a shady patch carpeted with snowdrops, Wanda sat on a tree stump and took out a sheet of writing paper with cold hands. Licking her pencil, she wrote a note that had been infusing in her mind for a while.

Clearly, you need a deadline, so I hereby give you just that.

On the twenty-seventh of this month I go home for ten days. Decide, Max, and if you want me, tell me so before I leave. If you don't want me, simply stay away, and I will abide by your decision. When I return, I will be a different Wanda. No clandestine kisses. No complicated conversations. I will be rinsed clean of any affection for you. We all deserve to be happy, and I believe we can make each other happy, but if you don't agree that will be an end to it.

She was hungry. Wanda was always hungry. She retraced her steps out of the glade.

Come and get me, Max, she begged him as the farmhouse grew in the distance.

The leylines of Ambridge ran invisibly beneath the village.

Nothing like the rutted main thoroughfare, they were subtle, more like the foot-flattened grass paths across the Green.

Stan's path was crooked, avoiding PC Jenkins, his pockets bulging with bloody contraband.

Mrs Endicott's path was vague, made as she drifted across and back, to the store, to Magsy's house, to Holmleigh to talk of her 'bad leg' and her 'worse toe'.

Wanda made no impression on the Green. She avoided the village – and Max Gilpin – in order to bring him to her. There would be no more nudging him along.

Likewise, Agnes was nimble in order to avoid Ruby. Changing her route at the last second if she spotted her across the way, sending a bewildered Denholm to the shop with a list and coping with the peculiar items he brought home.

Ruby passed Turnpike every day, dawdling by Agnes's garden, and feeling a strange sensation in her heart when Evie or Michele exclaimed at the house's prettiness. Her hope that Agnes might come out and smile at them were dashed every time.

Ruby was no fool; she knew Agnes had manipulated Denholm into marrying her, jockeying him down the aisle of St Stephen's so as to provide her with a pension.

And I threaten all that.

Ruby accepted people as they were; she had little choice – her adoptive parents were strangers to her now, with no interest in the 'bohemian' life she had chosen, no matter how many photographs she sent them of their granddaughters.

This mission was never going to be straightforward, and so she tried to be patient.

Patience had been needed with Henri, with the invasion,

with the train ride out of Sceaux. Composed even in the chaos of evacuation, Ruby dug deep and found her reserves of resilience.

Hope I won't have to dig much deeper – not sure how much I have left.

What Ruby didn't know was that Agnes watched her every day from behind her thick lace curtains, and puzzled how she had made such a personable, lovely woman. Each morning Agnes's first thought was of Ruby, and that thought was *I hope she's left the village.*

Tending to Denholm, hiding her sleeplessness, Agnes was perturbed by the feelings Ruby aroused. She had never courted connection.

Sometimes, when she was up in the night stirring yet another hot milk, she could not avoid the question that lifted the corner of a curtain on a whole other life.

What if I had kept my baby?

The thatch was done, and in record time, too.

The thatcher had dragged his sons from other jobs, and the weather was kind. Insufferably cold, of course, but no rain.

'You've embarked on the whitewashing!' Pamela toured the site like a visiting royal, Hildegard by her side, dishing out sweet treats and tots of whisky to the 'marvellous, marvellous fellows' all pitching in to rehabilitate The Bull.

Picking her way around in kid boots, Julia kissed every workman, leaving a little lipstick on their cheeks.

Standing back to survey the progress, Pamela spotted Evie Bonnett standing awkwardly at a distance. 'Give that girl a biscuit,' she told Hildegard, who did as she was asked.

'I hear this is all your fault, you naughty girl,' said Hildegard, as Evie stretched out a hand to the tray.

Evie pulled her hand back, empty. 'Mother Molly woke me,' she whispered, 'when the candle fell.'

Hildegard scoffed the biscuit herself. 'How'd you mean?'

'She put her hand here.' Evie touched her shoulder. 'She woke me.'

Hildegard retreated. 'Weird little so and so,' she muttered to herself.

'Coming along fast, innit?' Whitey White jumped down from the scaffolding. 'Them tiles are all grouted, Bob.'

Bob didn't know where the tiles came from; the nation was divided into folk who could wiggle between the seams of rationing and those who could not. Luckily, the Home Guard was replete with men who could lay their hands on materials, no questions asked.

Number 9 Platoon had neglected manoeuvres to scramble all over the roof; a new bed was procured using coupons donated by Ambridgians who had sore need of new furniture themselves. Bob, never good at speechifying, had gruffly thanked more people in the last few days than in the rest of his life. Now he thanked Grayson, who turned up in borrowed overalls, ready to pitch in.

'Rather have you here than digging up them blasted prophecies!' shouted one of the men up in the thatch.

Whitey White sidled up to Grayson. 'Do us all a favour. Leave them predictions in the ground.'

'I intend to.' Grayson was sheepish. 'Don't get me wrong, I don't believe in Mother Molly, but clearly her riddles are bad for the village. First Frances, now The Bull. I'll stick to books for a while.'

'Good man.' Whitey White slapped Grayson on the back.

The rota for the vicarage had been replaced by a rota for The Bull. Press-ganged into washing glasses, Doris gave Bob a nudge when he came inside to warm his hands by the stove. 'Is little Evie still out there? Why not go and say hello?'

'She sent my home up in flames, Doris.' Bob had a surreptitious brandy. 'Am I supposed to thank her?'

'The whole world is scrapping over slights and grudges, Bob. Let's keep our corner clean, eh?'

He seemed unmoved.

'Must have been hard for you,' said Doris, taking up another glass and wiping it. 'Seeing your Jimmy's room on fire.' She recalled Jimmy Little setting off to fight, and she recalled the dreaded telegram that came soon after. 'But you saved most of it. They're just *things*, Bob. No flame can reach where Jimmy really lives.' She laid her palm flat on his shirt, above his heart, and the man flinched.

Does anybody ever touch poor Bob? Doris regretted her daring when he turned abruptly and stalked out.

Through the window carved into the deep solid wall, Doris saw him approach Evie.

'Look 'ere,' he said. 'Accidents happen. You're a good girl, Evie.'

Evie burst into tears.

'Hey now, what's this? We're chums, love!'

She cried even harder, and when he bent down to dry her tears, she clung to him and he was glad that, with her arms about his shoulders, she hid his own wet face from the men.

'As soon as the attic's ready,' he said, 'you hurry home, yeah?'

'*Oui*,' snotted Evie. '*Oui*, Bob, yes!'

Neither Dan nor Wanda were listening to Doris's description of the touching scene between man and child. 'What *are* you two whispering about like spies?' She threw a tea towel for punctuation and the pair sprang apart.

'Nothing,' they said together.

If Wanda thought her wink at Dan went unnoticed by Doris, she was very, very wrong.

'You finish that tea, Dan Archer, and get yourself over to Lower Loxley,' said Doris.

'What? But!' Dan sounded just like Christine and Phil when they were sent on errands. 'I've to finish patching that lean-to before the rain we've been promised.'

Ignoring this, Doris said, 'Pamela's donated a big carpet for The Bull. You can pick it up and deliver it to the pub, and at the same collect our ladders and bring them home.' She fixed her husband with a specific look. 'Got that?'

Muttering darkly, Dan said something that might or might not have been *Women!* and went out to the truck.

'You've put it away safe?' Wanda leaned in through the truck window.

Dan patted his breast pocket.

'You must give my note *directly* to Max. Directly.' Wanda hated to keep anything from the Boss, but they both knew Doris would disapprove of the Shakespearean fol-de-rol of secret notes. 'A lot depends on this, Dan.'

'I understand, love.' Dan put the truck into gear and sped away.

With a toot-toot, he drove past Walter's cottage, but Walter's 'Whoa there, Nelly!' made him back up.

'Thought we was going to finish that lean-to, Dan?'

'Change of plans. I'm off to Lower Loxley.'

'Gonna rain, you know. According to my arthur-ritis, it's coming tonight, not tomorrow.' Ambridge trusted Walter's dodgy knees more than the BBC weather forecast. 'I was going to borrow your vehicle and all.'

'Were you now?' smiled Dan.

'I've used up me petrol, and you get extra, like, being our War Ag man. There's this lady over Lakey Green way . . .'

'Hmm. Not very appropriate use of War Ag petrol.'

'You've never met this lady, Dan.'

A deal was struck. In return for use of the truck, Walter would finish the lean-to, pick up and deliver the carpet, and bring home the ladders.

There were two conditions. 'One, you do *not* tell my good lady wife about any of this, and two, you deliver this note into Max Gilpin's hand.'

Walter, who smelled strongly of what Dan assumed must be cologne, put the folded paper on the dashboard with great care.

'Remember!' called Dan as Walter chugged away. *'Into Max's hand!'*

Cycling home from the library, Lorna passed verges where the spring crocus looked down on the nettle; the nettle did not give a monkey's.

Free and fast on her bicycle, Lorna flew along, the closest she could ever get to her friend Wanda's insouciance. The plan to net Max was typical of Wanda's blithe confidence in the universe.

'Sending a note didn't work out well for Tess D'Urberville,' Lorna had warned.

'Who's she?' Wanda had wanted to know. 'Is she from Felpersham?'

A horn honked, and Walter saluted as they passed in opposite directions.

The carpet was gone from the back of the truck, the note was gone from the dashboard, ladders were stacked in the back, and Walter's vest was on back to front.

Chauffeuring Wanda to Hollerton Junction, Doris hummed to herself but said very little.

She knew – of course, she knew – about the note. Wanda's demeanour told her that the past eight days had brought no rejoinder from Max.

The high-risk strategy had backfired. Max had missed a clear deadline – his silence told Wanda everything she needed to know.

Almost home after a low-key leave-taking with Wanda, Doris stopped the truck to hop down and lock the tailgate. It had flapped loose over a bump by Nightingale Farm.

The truck was over the hill. Doris knew how it felt. She banged the tailgate shut again, dismayed by how patched and bodged it was, like everything in war. It felt like a lifetime ago that she had owned anything genuinely new.

Except for our Jennifer. The baby waited in her cot back at Brookfield, warm as a new loaf.

Just as the engine hacked into life, Walter sauntered around the corner.

'Any chance of a lift, missus?'

There was every chance. 'You gave me a fright, Walter. Thought it was Vic emerging from his hideout!' As he settled in beside her, Doris said, 'Good of you to do all those chores for my Dan last week, Walter. The ladders, the lean-to, the carpet.'

'Um. What? Well . . .' Walter looked as if he wished he'd walked. 'Now, so, yes . . .'

Doris knew Dan would have sworn his partner-in-crime to secrecy. 'Ta ra,' she said, arch, when they reached Walter's turn-off.

A muddy scrap of something dropped from the sole of his work boot as he jumped down. Doris's back tyres ground it further into the rut, and it almost disintegrated.

But not quite. The keen-eyed could still make out the handwritten words *we can make each other happy.*

SPRING

1945

Though a good deal is too strange to be believed, nothing is too strange to have happened.

THOMAS HARDY
Personal Notebooks

March

The hawthorn in Magsy's garden was always one of the first trees to wake up. Its frothy blossom was a flag of hope.

The clock in Magsy's parlour struck eleven. Time for a little something. She rang for Dolly, who had risen two hours before her mistress that morning to black grates, lay fires, scour basins and make soap.

Was she as tired as Magsy, though? Dispensing advice to one's neighbours is taxing work, and the lady of the house was glad to hear Dolly's feet in the hall.

'Your cordial and your bumbum-thingy,' said Dolly, backing in with a huge tray.

'It's a *bonbonnière,* Dolly.' Magsy corrected her every other day. It was one of a thousand inherited Edwardian gewgaws, remnants of an era of luxury and high spirits. Venetian masks. Ivory dice. A tennis trophy.

This eleven o'clock ritual was a link to a vanished past, but some days it only served to underline the difference between her parents' carefree lives and her own wartime existence. The bonbonniere contained not sugar-dusted Turkish Delight but dried figs.

'Had such a fright, Miss Magsy.' Dolly poured the cordial. 'A mouse jumped out of the kettle, bold as brass.'

'But we dealt with the mice problem!'

'Tell that to the mouse,' said Dolly, but under her breath because Miss Magsy was particular about cheek. She held out the glass urn and lifted the lid. 'Oh,' she said.

Magsy said it too. There was no wrinkly fig. There was instead a folded scrap of parchment. Then Magsy put her hand to her throat. 'Is that . . .'

Dolly dropped the bumbum-thingy and Mother Molly's fifth prophecy lay among the shattered glass.

Over at Arkwright Hall, Peggy brought lessons to a halt by bringing in baby Jennifer to show her students.

'Oh miss, look at her lickle nails!' gasped a girl.

Proud as punch, Peggy enjoyed the staff's swooning praise. *They're right,* she thought. *Jennifer is beautiful and good and clever!* It was hard to believe her own mother had ever felt this way about Peggy; she hadn't seen her moon over her younger brothers. It was a secret, maybe, this intense communion between mother and child.

Lorna, visiting with a basket of library books, took her turn holding the two-month-old. Something clicked within her, a key finding its bite.

This will never happen to me.

She knew it, like she knew her own name. Lorna handed Jennifer back and let the knowledge settle.

'Let me, let me!' Ruby, turning up to surprise her daughters by walking them home, held out her arms and took the baby, sniffing her head with tightly closed eyes. 'Susan Grundy was in the shop with her little Alf this morning. She wants a double christening with this one.'

'Over my dead body,' said Peggy, without thinking.

Ruby, discreet but understanding, laughed. 'Good to know this *bébé* won't have to worry about another one of those horrible predictions.'

The village was relieved that Grayson had seen sense and stopped digging.

'What'll happen to Arkwright Hall,' asked Ruby, 'after the war?'

This phrase could now be used without caveats. Ambridge glimpsed a future where they didn't wait on news of battles or queue for basics.

'Heaven knows,' said Peggy. 'I'm just glad there's going to be an end to the madness and my Jennifer will grow up in peace.'

'Amen to that,' said Ruby.

'You staying on?'

'In Ambridge?' Ruby felt the question smack her in the face. 'No.'

Agnes's repudiation was hard to accept, but Ruby darned over the pain the way she repaired the girls' socks. It hurt to know she made her birth mother's life more difficult; *that was never my aim*. It hurt to lose another mother.

'Don't do anything rash,' said Peggy.

France beckoned. Ruby would be part of her adoptive nation's renaissance. Taking her children back to a flattened town to live in the embers was a noble ambition – *Henri would be proud* – but the thought of it was an anvil around her neck. All the same it was more attractive than dawdling endlessly in Agnes's eyeline; the die was cast.

Watching Peggy bundle Jennifer up for the pram, Ruby felt a prick of envy. The young woman was in the foothills of her life, with a husband, a home, an identity. Ruby would once again have to build from the ground up, with nobody to offer unconditional understanding.

Kicking the brake on the pram, Peggy set off for Brookfield. She was thinking of dancing and nylons and gum, of kissing and singing. That was the road not taken, but Peggy preferred this, occasionally stony, road.

Even though Jack is ... He was small, not in stature but in outlook. Perhaps she could open up his horizons, spur him on to do, well, *something*.

And perhaps she couldn't.

Peggy bade farewell to Ruby, envying her freedom. Ruby said a cheerful *'Au revoir'* to Peggy, envying her security.

Max knocked, and stood with his back to Woodbine's door. He wondered at the village's quick costume change during the ten days Wanda had been away. Spring boasted everywhere, from the pale wood anenomes beneath his feet on his weekend constitutional to the twiggy forsythia by his gate that had stabbed him in the side all winter but was now in a showy yellow get-up.

He knew exactly how long Wanda had been absent because he had counted the days; that's how he knew she was due back today.

Grayson was unkempt when he joined Max on the step. 'Can't find my glasses ...'

'They're on your head.' Max took in Grayson's higher-than-usual levels of dishevelment, his troubled eyes. 'Well, I'm here. What was so urgent?'

Grayson handed him the parchment.

Severe, Max said, 'You promised no more excavating.'

'This turned up at Magsy's house.' Grayson hesitated. 'They also saw a mouse.'

'Mice are ten-a-penny in the country, don't even *suggest* to me that Mother Molly's familiar planted this.' He read the riddle. He swallowed. 'This can only refer to one person.'

'I know.' Grayson planted both hands in his hair, as if to tear it out. His birthmark burned. 'Do I tear this up, Max? Pretend it never happened?'

'It's out of your hands. If Magsy knows, Mrs E knows. If Mrs E knows, Agnes knows. And if Agnes knows ...' Max shrugged. 'You have to tell the family before the gossip network reaches them. I'll come with you and we'll do it right now.'

Grayson's 'thank you' was heartfelt.

A bus passed them, then slowed.

'Fetch your coat, I'll be right back.' Max sprinted to the bus stop.

Stepping down from the vehicle, Wanda took her case from the driver and thanked him.

'Allow me.' Max swooped to take the bag in his good hand. 'I missed you,' he said quietly.

'Yes, you did.' Wanda snatched back her bag. 'You missed your chance.'

In his ardour, Max hadn't noticed the welcome committee of Doris and Lorna.

'Congratulations!' Lorna threw her arms around Wanda, and Max stepped back to allow for embracing and cooing.

'Show us the ring, then,' said Doris.

Wanda held out her hand as if expecting it to be kissed.

'That,' said Doris with feeling, 'is a whopper of an emerald!'

The gem blinded Max and he took a step back, then another, until he was in the dim sanctuary of the bus shelter.

Out there, in the cold sun, Wanda glowed and said, 'Can't quite believe it myself! Two months from now I'll be Mrs Christopher Pinkerton-Wells.'

Spotting the scrum, Susan Grundy elbowed her way through to appraise the ring. 'Cor,' she said, and laughed. 'Does this one have both arms?'

She was roundly shushed as Max strode back to Woodbine.

There the one-legged Grayson took one look at the one-armed Max and prescribed them both a stiff malt.

*

The quilt was laid out on the flags of Lower Loxley's terrace.

Pamela poked at one square with her foot. Was it . . . ? It was. *Longjohns!*

'Pamela!' called Max.

Turning to see him and Grayson hurrying up the drive, Pamela said, 'Oh dear, have you two seen a ghost?' When they didn't laugh, she waited for them and led them indoors without a word.

Whitey White's bicycle turned into the gates at a hell of a clip. With his postbag on his back, he whipped unseen past the drawing-room windows as Pamela offered the men a seat.

When they remained standing, she asked what on earth could be so grave.

Seeing Grayson stuck for words, Max stepped in. He was curt, businesslike, pushing at memories of that blasted emerald. 'Another prophecy has turned up.'

'And?' Pamela was at her grandest. 'What is that to do with me?'

'I'll read it,' said Max. He took a breath; he was giving bad, eerie news to this woman, even if he knew her to be a sceptic. *'Beware my proud beloved house! The last damaged boy lifts gin to lip and falls. They glared at the end of the noble line and buried him in his own blood.'*

'That could be anyone,' laughed Pamela.

Grayson shook his head. 'Mother Molly refers to *her* proud beloved house. That suggests Lower Loxley, the patrons who took her in.'

Pamela lifted Minko into her arms, where the dog panted and tried to lick her mistress's careful maquillage.

'Mother Molly favoured anagrams. "Glared" can be rearranged to read . . .'

Max had to take over again. 'Gerald,' he said.

'These are children's ghost stories,' scoffed Pamela. 'Besides, if Gerald was *damaged*, I'd know. He's still training in Bulawayo, and doing splendidly.'

Hildegard entered, with no knock to announce her.

'We're busy,' said Pamela.

'But . . .' With none of her usual buoyance, Hildegard held out a salver. 'Whitey's been. This is for you, ma'am.'

Light-headed, Pamela couldn't feel the telegram as she took it from her maid. She had no sensation in her body except fear. The message was about one of her men. It was Alec or Gerald's name she would read.

'Sit, Pamela, please.'

She ignored Max, and turned her back when he approached her. She read the printed letters so fast they made no sense. She read them again, and her knees turned to water.

Hildegard slipped a chair beneath her as Pamela sat. 'It's Gerald. A bad landing. Shattered femur. But alive. And heading home.'

Minko complained at being held so tight.

Grayson sank to the sofa. 'No need to panic just yet. I decoded the words at the bottom – *Mr Sins*.' He closed his eyes, weary. 'Hard to know if Mother Molly is mocking us with these little phrases, but the date to worry about is the eighth of May.'

'What Grayson means to say,' said Max, appalled by such clumsiness, 'is you shouldn't worry at all, Pamela. The date is meaningless. We just wanted you to hear about the prophecy from us.'

The lady of the house didn't seem to be listening. Pamela said, 'Hildegard, remove every drop of gin from this house.'

'Eh? The chaps won't like it.'

'*Now*!'

Dan yawned, partly because he had had one long night up with his lambing ewes and another to look forward to, and partly because he was already bored of talk of the engagement. Privately, he thought Wanda's ring looked like something out of a cracker; if he had that sort of money to chuck around, he'd buy a new truck.

Mother Cat on her lap, Christine squealed, 'Hey! I'll be a bridesmaid!'

'Wait until you're asked, young lady,' said Doris.

'Of course Christine will be my bridesmaid!' Wanda was brought up short by a sudden realisation. 'Crikey, I'll have to organise a whole wedding. White dress and all that malarkey.'

'Why not have the reception at home, like your sister?' Peggy had been transported by tales of the marquee in a Somerset garden, dicky bow-ed waiters setting out gilt chairs.

Wanda crossed her eyes. 'So many decisions!'

She's slipping away from us, thought Doris, tying on her apron. Her precious land girl already had one foot back in a world where tea was served by a woman who's 'been in the family for simply *yonks*', and ponies were shown off at gymkhanas, not ridden bareback through rivers. Privilege, clean hands, double-barrelled surnames.

'Describe your fiancée again!' begged Christine, to Dan and Phil's chagrin.

'Christopher? He's a catch,' said Wanda. 'Ever so nice-looking. A stockbroker. Comes from a good family.'

Doris murmured that Wanda sounded just like her mother.

'Perhaps the moment one grows up,' said Wanda, 'is when you concede your mother is making sense.'

'But what's this Christopher *like*?' Doris needed detail.

'Lovely,' said Wanda. 'A lovely man. A lovely, lovely man.'

Peggy, one ear cocked for sounds of baby Jennifer, said, 'That Max was mooning about the whole time you were gone.'

Putting up one hand like a constable directing traffic, Wanda said, 'I don't want to hear one word about Max. Mooning about is all very well. Sometimes one has to *act*.'

'What if,' said Phil, devilry in his eyes, 'Mother Molly's next prophecy is about a wedding?'

'Shush you!' Christine was scandalised.

Their father said, 'We've heard the last of Mother Molly. I can feel it in me water.'

In the pantry, Doris scoffed to herself. Her Dan never had a feeling in his water. She could have told them there and then about the latest prophecy, retold to her by Mrs Endicott as they arranged flowers on St Stephen's altar. She could have told them of the poisonous cloud that hung over Lower Loxley.

Plating up the bakewell tart she had somehow bewitched into being, Doris felt that it could wait until tomorrow. Nothing must mar Wanda's homecoming.

It was like an Olympic sport – Competitive Silver Polishing.

Nance sat across from Magsy, both in smutty aprons, their cloths going nineteen to the dozen.

'You really don't have to help,' said Nance, for the hundredth time, unaware of the black smudge on her nose.

'I always helped my dear departed sister,' said Magsy, and that settled it.

They heard Morgan see out his first patient of the day.

Mrs Endicott's voice, tremulous, floated in from the porch. 'They do say that if you die in your dream, you actually *die*, Doctor.'

'If that's true then who survives to tell us? Take this sleeping draught and I foresee no reoccurrence of last night's unpleasantness.'

Morgan looked in on his wife and his one-time sister-in-law. 'Our Mrs E dreamt last night that a hammer came to life and smashed all the crockery in her dresser.'

'Sounds like what went on in Tokyo.' Nance covered the newspaper headlines with a duster. 'Decimated, they say. The most destructive night of the war.'

She rubbed harder at a shadow on an ugly tray.

'This war will soon be over, dear.' Morgan laid a hand on her shoulder.

Shaking it off, she said, 'But will it? What if Hitler has something up his sleeve? What if we end up like those poor Japanese people?'

'Is it talk of the prophecy that has you all a-jitter?' asked Magsy from across the table.

Thinking mutinously that maybe, just maybe, it was reading of constant violence and death that had her all a-jitter, Nance glanced at her husband's pink, moustachioed face and wondered why she was taking it out on her own family. She took his hand, the one she had refused, and said, 'Growing up over the shop I never had any silverware to clean!'

'At one time we had more than this,' said Morgan. 'We were burgled one summer, and lost many lovely pieces.'

'Remember,' said Magsy, 'how my dear papa stepped in?' She never lost a chance to eulogise her sainted father. 'Moved heaven and earth to find the culprits.'

'He did his best, but nothing was recovered. My mother was very distressed.'

Ever empathetic, Nance asked, 'Did she lose anything special?'

Feeling that the smudges on his wife's face made her question all the more charming, Morgan said, 'She mourned just one item among the sundry salt cellars and fish knives. A shawl from the old country, embroidered with a gamayun.'

The 'old country' for the late Irina Morgan was Russia, a fact which thrilled Nance whenever it came to mind;

her husband and her son had blood in common with the plucky Russkies currently fighting for possession of the Narva Isthmus.

'Whatever is a gamayun?' Magsy looked suspicious.

'A fabled creature, a bird with the head of a woman. It knows all, and can foretell the future.' Morgan remembered stroking the gamayun's silken feathers as he sat on his mother's lap as a child, the shawl around them both. 'Same powers as Mother Molly, but possessed of striking beauty. We assumed the rotters used the shawl to bundle up their loot. Let me think, when was it? Must've been, ooh, 1901. I would've been fifteen, and I . . .' He stopped. That was the summer, one of those peerless summers of youth, when he first noticed the younger Furneaux girl and decided that one day he would marry her.

No need to mention that.

He and Nance were beyond the tricky first stage of their marriage, when Nance had felt lacking in comparison to Magsy's *non pareil* sister. All the same, he hated to see any cloud in the blue of his wife's sky.

My father felt the same way about my mama.

Perhaps that was why his father had bought a replacement shawl, a pretty thing that Morgan's mother had tried to love, but both she and Morgan remembered the chilli shades of the original and the slithery caress of the Russian silk.

'We've all lost so much along the way,' said Morgan, and he tenderly wiped his wife's face clean with his handkerchief.

* * *

'How about this one, ma'am?'

Hildegard held up an organza dress on a padded hanger.

'To be godmother at a country christening? Hardly.' Pamela flicked through the hangers in her wardrobe. 'No. No. *God,* no.' She hadn't known how to politely decline the Grundy family's request, and so she must dangle Alf over the font. *They didn't ask me out of friendship!* The baby would receive the gift famously given to all the Pargetter godchildren, a solid silver rattle.

'This is perfect.'

'Ooh,' said Hildegard, taking out the plum silk gown. The sleeves belled out, and a plump bow hung at the back of the rustling skirt.

It represented a beauty the world lacked; Pamela was surprised by high emotion as she handled it. Realising Hildegard was watching, with those ferret-bright eyes, she collected herself, and laid the dress on the bed.

'Why was the doc here this morning, ma'am?'

'Checking up on our new RAF chap. He took bad in the night, imagined he was in a burning cockpit, and tried to jump out of the window. Once the others had calmed him down, it was warm milk all round. I sent for you, Hildegard.' Pamela folded her arms. 'But you weren't in your bed.'

'With all due respect, t'ain't part of my duties to heat milk in the middle of the night.'

'Nor mine, but it's all hands on deck during war, no?'

The atmosphere between the women, never balmy, cooled further.

'It's time I donated a square to the village quilt.' Pamela

dug out an old Norman Hartnell day dress, pistachio cotton and smart in its day. 'If you snip one out from the bottom of this, you can take the dress and re-hem it for yourself.'

'Thank you, ma'am.' The dress was laid on top of the burgundy gown while Hildegard looked out the shears from the sewing box. 'The portrait of Mother Molly's gone up to the attic, like you asked, ma'am.'

Pamela imagined the old bag lurking up there.

Hildegard set about the day dress. The shears flashed. Snip snip snip. 'The chaps are proper riled about having their gin taken off 'em. They miss their martinis.'

Not in the habit of explaining herself to the help – or to anyone – Pamela said nothing.

'Still, I can see why you did it.' Snip snip snip. Hildegard chanted the fifth prophecy like a prayer. *'Beware my proud beloved house! The last damaged boy lifts gin to lip and falls. They glared at the end of the noble line and buried him in his own blood.'* Snip snip snip. 'No wonder you're frightened, ma'am.' When Pamela didn't reply, Hildegard cut the last side of the pistachio-coloured square. Snip! 'Awful, innit, how the villagers have more or less killed off poor Mr Gerald and him not even home yet.' She stowed the fabric piece in the pocket of her apron. 'When does he get back from that place?' Hildegard couldn't pronounce Bulawayo, and didn't quite believe it existed.

'That's all. You can go.' Pamela loathed how her maid got under her skin.

'Very well, ma'am.' Hildegard hung up the silk gown and trotted off with the day dress.

Alone, Pamela faced her fears. Not just the horror of Mother Molly, but the trepidation about having an invalid Gerald about the house. He would need nursing, attention. Mother and son had not put in the necessary prep for such an eventuality.

Did she even know Gerald? The idea of losing him before she had the chance to see him as a person in his own right was too much to bear.

God, I could do with a martini right now.

Pamela smoothed her hair and became once again Pamela Pargetter of Lower Loxley, a woman with standards and expectations, who would not permit such a slipshod hold on her feelings.

Furthermore, a woman who would not allow her son and heir to be hurt by a dead witch.

AMBRIDGE WOMEN'S INSTITUTE MEETING MINUTES

Date: 26th March 1944

At: The Bull

Chairwoman: Pamela Pargetter

Present: Doris Archer, Agnes Kaye, Emmeline Endicott, Magsy Furneaux, Lorna Horrobin, Wanda Lafromboise, Susan Grundy, Nance Seed, Ruby Bonnet

Minutes: Magsy Furneaux

1. Pamela opened by thanking Ruby for hosting the committee in The Bull
2. Agnes said 'place stinks of beer'
3. Pamela congratalated Wanda on her engagement and Mrs Endicott said did she ever tell us about the time her husbands proposed
4. Pamela said 'yes you did' and confirmed that the vicar's new housekeeper Mrs Micklewood is settling in nicely
5. Agnes said 'getting her feet under the table more like'
6. Pamela asked for vollunteers to help keep order with St Stephen's altar boys as they have gone somewhat downhill since Frances's parsing
7. I said 'I caught one blowing his nose on his cassock'
8. Mrs Endicott apologised for her coughing fit when all could plainly see she was sniggering
9. Pamela said 'I vollunteer Agnes and Ruby you will soon wip the boys into shape'
10. Agnes said 'no'
11. Pamela said she was sorry but she did not quite make that out

12. Agnes said 'let me put it another way - not on your nelly'

13. Susan enquired if Agnes was all right and had something got her goat

14. I saved the day by volunteering in Agnes's place as everyone knows Ruby would let the boys get away with all manner of nortiness

15. Doris asked if anybody has seen Connie Horrobin and should one of us check up on her

16. Susan said 'what's the point, poor old thing is always the same'

17. Pamela gave me the qilt and I said 'I have found the perfect fabric for my skware it is very ~~eco exx ecks~~ exotic'

18. Mrs Endicott asked for donations of coupons towards the Grundy christening buffay

19. Susan kissed Mrs Endicott and said 'you next for a baby Lorna, about time Cliff got you in the family way'

20. When I recovered from such vulgarity I saw Lorna was also horified as she made no reply

21. Pamela said any suggestions for the next communal village event are welcome

22. Nance said it's hard to focus

on fripperies after reading about the massacre in Rome of Jewish foke and resistance fighters

23. Doris took Nance's hand which will only encourage her

24. Doris said 'why are we fighting this war Nance?'

25. Nance said 'for freedom'

26. Doris said 'exactly, love the freedom to have our village celebrations it's all part of the same thing'

27. I said I was glad nobody brought up the prophecy as it would surely cause our dear chairwoman great distress

28. Pamela said 'I assure you it would not'

29. Susan said 'Mother Molly's got it in for Gerald this time no doubt about it'

30. Pamela said she had given it no thought and that this was a good time to wind up the meeting

31. Pamela said 'Magsy please no personal comments in the minutes this time just facts'

32. If I was a different sort of woman I might take offence at that as I have no idea what she ment

* * *

Julia sat on the end of the bed, feet up beneath her. 'You're staring, darling,' she giggled.

'God, if it wasn't for this damn leg.' Gerald, in striped pyjamas as tailored as any suit, cursed the cast that ran from his hip to his toes. 'I'd chase you round this room.'

His wife smelled delicious, and wore a slippery chemise that just might – although never quite did – fall off.

'Glad to have me back?' he asked. Every atom of his body revolted at coming home from training but it did have its upsides.

'So so glad.' Julia pouted, knowing what this did to Gerald. 'Although it's a bore sharing my room.'

'*My* room, wifey!'

When Pamela entered, she hoped Gerald didn't notice how relieved Julia looked to be set free.

'Any gossip, Mother?'

'Lots.' Pamela spilled the latest titbits on the bedspread. She loved how he was all ears, not disapproving like Alec. In fact, Gerald was so surprisingly pleasant to have around that he had put a spring in her step.

'D'you think I'll get back to my regiment?' Gerald saw the neurotic tilt of his mother's head. 'Dash it, I don't mean will Mother Molly polish me off! I mean will my leg mend before all the fighting's done?'

The village was ticking off the days before the end of the war just as Pamela ticked off the days to the eighth of May. 'Hitler might have something gruesome planned. I daren't count my chickens before they're hatched.'

'No, no, Adolf's done for and good riddance.' Gerald was mild, even when discussing a genocidal dictator.

'I do hope you're right. Soon we'll all be together again. You, me, your father.' Pamela didn't note her son's surprise at such a sentiment, too busy gloating over the documents sitting in her bureau, ready to be shared with Alec. The success of her project would move him; *he'll see I'm worthy of his love, after all.*

Pamela fussed with the room, patted his pillow ineffectually, and said she must get on.

'Send Julia up, will you? Tell her I want her to read me some Shakespeare.'

'Some evenings she launches into a soliloquy at the dinner table. The chaps always cheer.' Pamela knew the chaps would cheer seductive, flirtatious Julia if she burped the alphabet. 'I never dreamed you would enjoy Shakespeare, Gerald! You've become so cultured since you married an actress.'

We've all changed, thought Pamela. The Pargetters were turning towards one another like blooms finding that the sun is not up in the sky but right there in Lower Loxley.

Conversation via letters involved long gaps, blurred words, and a great danger of misinterpretation.

Dear Jack,

We must make plans!!! What'll you do for a job when you're demobbed? And where will we live? DON'T say Brookfield. Me and baby need a house of our own.

Take care, won't you?

All best

Peggy

PS Jack, do you love me?

Dear Peg,

What a queer question. You're my missus. I'm cracked about you. That's love isn't it?

Don't you worry about after the war. My mates warned me babies make girls go all serious but you just look forward to your hero hubby coming home.

Something will turn up!!!

Your Jack

Pamela knew Alec's regiment had crossed the Rhine, and was speeding across the North German Plain towards Osnabruck, with the First Canadian Army wheeling on their left.

Pamela,

I'm high on excitement until I am cast down by the cost. Men scythed like dandelions. I long to sit and talk with you in our drawing room, your voice a cool drink of water after the incessant uproar of battle.

We do this bloody work for you, all of you.

I remain,

Your devoted husband,

Alec

Alec,

Our son is home and I must report the invalid does not like being an invalid.

He has matured. I rather enjoy my sojourns at his bedside. You and he will have much in common when you come home.

Gerald the man is a different creature to Gerald the boy!

Hildegard could see in the dark.

She didn't see him, though. The first she knew of him were the hands that reached out and pulled her against his chest.

It was expected, what they did next, but not mechanical. She loved him, and she believed he loved her, even though they never used that word.

The moment shimmers.

Ambridge lies drowsy on the cusp of something ending, something else beginning. They had almost forgotten hope, but can't resist it now.

A Common Quaker moth leaves the camouflage of tree bark to investigate a light.

The light goes out. Bob climbs into his bed. Above his head the new thatch settles, and he can almost hear his trio of lodgers breathing their gentle ins and outs. The Bull is its old self again, thanks to the efforts of the village.

Bob hopes they know how grateful he is. He hopes they don't expect free beer.

Some villagers' dreams involve Mother Molly.

Not Gerald's. He can't sleep. He sees Mother Molly without

closing his eyes. The terror humiliates him and must be kept from his wife and his mother. He appreciates the mater making an effort; *the old girl hates a sickroom.*

Mrs Endicott has a pink and pearlescent dream. She is with Bathsheba Burton. They are young. Their lips are soft. She will wake to Twinkle Toes' squawks at dawn, and wonder just what these dreams mean. She will wonder who – or what – she really is. Then she will rise and forget.

Hildegard and her beau sit against an oak that will outlive them both.

She tells him, 'Her ladyship had a right go at me about not being around to give out hot milk at all hours. Bleedin' cheek. Still, I got me own back. She'll find out, soon enough.'

April

One baby was much like another to the vicar.

'Very, um, nice,' he said, as Susan Grundy held up her Alf for his delectation.

'Grand sermon, Henry,' said Doris loyally, filing past. 'Very fortifying.'

The vicar beamed. He had talked of Jesus's stoic acceptance of his fate for quite some time; his parishioners had needed similar stoicism to stay awake. 'Mrs Micklewood is the perfect sounding board. I test all my sermon ideas on her.'

Doris attempted a non-committal, 'Oh really?' The housekeeper stood waiting by a weeping angel. She was – and Doris had to look twice to double-check – *smoking in the churchyard*.

There were some as said Mrs Micklewood was auditioning for the role of vicar's wife. Doris wondered what Frances would make of the new broom at the vicarage and sighed to herself. The year turned. Time passed. People and things changed.

'Move along now!' Walter, glad to have the churchy part of the day out of the way, elbowed past Doris and Susan. He had no interest in the baby, but behind him, Max stopped and tickled Alf's cheek.

'How old?' he asked.

'Four and a half months.' Susan jiggled the boy. 'They grow so fast.'

The banal comment lit a flare inside Max. His brain did some sudden and unwelcome maths: *our child would be three years old.*

He walked jerkily away, only stopping when he reached a tomb low enough to sit on and catch his breath.

The tomb was warm from the sunshine. Max looked around him. He could no longer hear his wife's voice, but he had heard Wanda and knew he must get to her. She was a lifeboat. She was the future. He saw her hat – a silly hat – and made for her.

'Wanda.' Max was stern as he caught her arm.

She half turned, her eyes not lifted as if seeing him might damage her vision. Her other arm was caught by Mrs Endicott, who was saying, 'Tell us *everything*, my dear. Where, when, how many bridesmaids!'

Wanda turned her back on Max, and was swallowed up by her neighbours.

The vicar's presence at the Lower Loxley Easter lunch table was an Ambridge tradition set in stone.

Surprised to see his housekeeper by his side, Pamela

nonetheless welcomed them both warmly, and discreetly despatched a dissenting Hildegard off to set another place.

'Damn pretty frock, Mrs Micklewood!' called Gerald, propped up with pillows on a chaise longue. The chaps had manhandled him downstairs, a farcical operation that would not be attempted again.

Lower than the guests as they took their seats, at a right angle to the beautifully set table in the glowing room, Gerald served as an allegory of war: rules no longer applying, familiar scenes somehow topsy-turvy.

As if to underline this, Mrs Micklewood asked Gerald, 'You 'appy over there on your own?' Her broad, local accent was rarely heard at this lunch table. Serving, certainly, but sitting down, no.

'I'll keep him company,' said Dodgy.

Kissing his forehead, Wanda told Dodgy he was 'an old softie,' and left him spluttering as she went to the table in a chic dress she had brought back from Bath. 'What's on the menu?' she asked greedily.

'Venison.' Pamela accepted the oohs and aahs. 'I have my sources,' she said, mysterious, as Hero slipped under the tablecloth. She knew the black Labrador would accept no smuggled morsel; *he won't be quite himself until Alec comes home.*

The vicar had loosened up sufficiently to bring his housekeeper to lunch but in other ways Henry was still Henry. He swallowed compliments like champagne, drooled as the meat was carved, and leapt in for seconds while the others were still picking up their cutlery.

Pamela despaired of him; *he brings Mrs Micklewood and then leaves her to fend for herself!* With exaggerated movements, Pamela took up the correct knife and fork from the cutlery radiating from the sides of her plate, so Mrs Micklewood could copy her.

Across the table, Wanda leaned over and asked the housekeeper about herself.

A well-brought up young woman. Pamela noticed how the Mayor of Borchester and his wife ignored the vicar's Plus One.

'*Adore* your hair,' said Wanda.

'It's a victory roll.' Mrs Micklewood patted the elaborate twist on her head.

'Oops,' muttered Dodgy from the chaise longue, and Pamela knew her satin cushions had been compromised with gravy.

A skinny whippet of a man, the mayor had that breed's long nose. 'I've been hearing about your Mother Milly, Pamela.'

'*Molly*,' snapped Pamela, recovering her manners to say, 'Just local poppycock.'

'I daresay.' The mayor's wife was as round as he was narrow. 'Still, when your own son's implicated it must be unsettling . . .'

'Not at all.' Pamela felt there must be a special circle of Hell reserved for people who devoured one's black-market venison while goading one for sport.

Gerald said, 'Julia and I have a secret plan to vanquish the old crow.'

'Shush, naughty boy.' Julia's suggestive smile could fell an RAF chap at ten paces. 'I'll read you some Shakespeare after lunch.'

'Jolly good!' He held out his glass for Dodgy to refill.

'Let's not mock Mother Molly.' Pamela spoke without thinking, and added quickly, 'It's rude to sneer at things others may believe.'

'Pamela.' The vicar was not taken in. 'It sounds as if you have given into superstition.' When he laced his fingers together, the table sighed silently as one; they were in for a lecture. 'Belief is a gift from God. My own beliefs were undermined by Frances's passing.'

Mrs Micklewood dabbed her lips with her napkin. She did not meet anyone's eye.

'I prayed and I found a way back. There is a celestial plan for each one of us, but it is *not* Mother Molly's plan. Promise me you won't get sucked into the dark whirlpools of fear.'

Shocked by sincerity from the vicar, Pamela didn't answer.

'Dark whirlpools sound rather fun.' Julia's remark lightened the mood, and talk turned to the upcoming christening at St Stephen's.

'The Grundys and the Archers at one font . . .' Henry seemed thoughtful. 'Young Alf Grundy is rather . . . lively.'

'It'll be fine, Henry.'

A jolt ran through the guests, not only at Mrs Micklewood's

use of her employer's first name, but for the hand she placed on his.

'Bakewell tart, anyone?' Pamela rang the little bell by her glass. 'Well, Bakewell-*ish*! Cook does wonders with our rations.'

A rap at the latticed window made them all turn.

Pamela frowned, then laughed, and crossed to yank open the latch. 'Max! You have *heard* of front doors I assume?'

Grave, Max didn't get the joke. 'May I steal one of your guests?'

Wanda was out of her chair before he finished his sentence.

She took the lead.

Max followed Wanda around the side of the house with no words spoken. He studied the back of her head.

I won't take no for an answer, he thought.

She kept walking. He kept following.

He no longer strained to hear his wife's voice. The past was ebbing. It would never disappear – Max would not allow that – but he felt the tug of the future.

The house was left behind. Trees closed in.

She plodded on, leaning into the small slope.

'Isn't our Wanda promised to another?' blinked Henry.

'That', said Pamela, 'is her affair.'

'An unfortunate choice of word!' said the mayor's wife, who was rapidly earning herself a lifelong place in Pamela's bad books.

Dodgy kindly brought over some Bakewell-ish tart for the marooned Gerald; Julia was midway through a theatrical anecdote and hadn't noticed he was left out.

In a whisper, Gerald said, 'I love her, you know, Dodgy.'

'Yes.' Dodgy was vague. He wasn't much cop at heart-to-hearts about the ladies.

'Properly. Really. It's love.'

'Nice,' said Dodgy.

'Does she love me, though?'

'Oh. Well. Hmm. I'm sure she does.'

'I want a family with her. I want *everything* with her. But . . .' He lowered his voice. 'Sometimes I suspect she's a little shallow.'

Dodgy knew Julia was deeply shallow but said nothing.

'She fell for the bells and whistles, the house, the grounds. I fell for *her*.'

Dodgy gently pointed out that if a fellow baits his hook with a mink coat, he can't complain if he lands a shallow fish.

They were in Mother Molly's grotto, each as surprised as the other. Wanda had simply walked where her feet took her.

The breeze dropped. The sun dared not peek in at them. The stones were cold, and made for a dull acoustic.

'So?' Wanda turned to face him.

'Wanda, I want to live with you. I want to marry you. I love you.'

'This is sudden.'

Expecting repudiation or surrender, Max was thrown by the coolness of her response.

'It must seem that way, but it's true and it always has been. Tell this Christopher what's-his-name he can't have you. He *can't* appreciate you like I do. You're the most exciting and the most comforting thing I've ever come across.'

'A word of advice.' Wanda almost smiled. 'Don't call a girl a thing when you're seducing her.'

'I'm not seducing you. I'm offering myself to you. Heart. Head. All of it. I have never met anyone so blazingly alive as you, Wanda.'

'Find somebody else to darn your socks, Max.'

'I can darn my own socks, thank you.'

'You *can't*.'

He took off his shoe to prove it. Waggled a darned toe. 'It's not women's work, just work.'

'And what do I get out of this, apart from your darning prowess? A man who had to be dragged here, who looks over his shoulder when he's with me. Why now?' Wanda folded her arms and studied him, as if trying to work out a difficult crossword clue. 'Because somebody took away your skipping rope? Seems like you only want women when you can't have them, when they're engaged to somebody else. Or dead.'

'I deserved that.'

'I know. That's why I said it.' Wanda thought of the impassioned note Max ignored, and could not feel generous. 'When *I* told you I wanted you, you didn't have the civility to reply.

Suddenly, because you've changed your mind, I must swoon at your feet.'

'You didn't say it in so many words.'

'I couldn't have been clearer! If someone tells you they believe you can make each other happy, what else could it mean?'

'But . . .' Max seemed confused.

The grotto darkened, as if a bat flew overheard. 'This place . . . nothing good comes out of here.' Wanda shivered.

When Max moved to put an arm around her, she jumped out of reach, out into the gentle spring sunshine, which caught the gleaming pearliness of her skin. 'You've twinned me with your wife, Max. I can't share. I want a man of my own. I don't want to be a replacement, or a cure. Love shouldn't wear black. When you're ready you'll find someone.'

'You know that someone is you.'

'I know nothing of the kind. I've been transparent, but you take one step forward and two steps back. This, you and I, it's a delicate mechanism. It can be spoiled, Max. And you spoiled it when you ignored my declaration.'

This was moving downhill fast, and not making perfect sense to Max. 'The truth is I found the woman before I was ready, and yes, I've had to catch up. But I feel the sun on my back now. I can lift my head and all I see – all I think about! – is Wanda.'

'It's too late, and you insult me by pretending it isn't, that you don't know what I mean. Another man came along, saw me, and said, *her*, I want her. There were no complications.'

'And you want him?'

'You have no right to question me about Christopher.'

'Love gives me the right.'

'Love? This relationship is too crowded for me. Me, you, your wife, your poor lost child.'

Max came closer. So close she could see the short eyelashes ringing his eyes. 'Tell me you don't love me.' He was confident; he was playing his ace.

'I don't love you,' said Wanda, and left him there.

'I hate being a crock.' Gerald had been bumped and bodged back up to his room.

'It's not forever.' Pamela tucked him in, set a glass of water within reach.

'Where's Julia?'

'Singing for the chaps.' Pamela brought him the *Sunday Times*. 'You'll have to make do with me for now.'

He snatched the newspaper, and batted her hand away as she tweaked his pillow. 'Get *off,* Ma. What's this about? You're not the nursey type. You really do think I'm going to die, don't you? You think Mother Molly will get me, like she got the vicar's snippy little wife! That's why you're getting all maternal. Bit late, eh?'

Pamela counted to ten. 'Just trying to make you comfortable.' She switched on the lamps, hung up his dressing gown.

Gerald opened the newspaper with a *huh*. Sometimes the old anger flooded back, along with the guilt. He had been a disappointment at school, a lout and a cheat and – to his eternal shame – a thief. A ringside seat at his parents' infidelities had made him both reject and need them, but they had never once asked him how he *felt*. The Pargetters were fettered by convention, and trapped together in a house under siege from a witch.

The last lamp went on.

'Ma,' he said, and she turned. This togetherness was exactly what the younger Gerald yearned for; perhaps they could time-travel together, and make things right? 'Fancy a game of rummy?'

'I do,' said Pamela, who did not. She did fancy stealing a quiet hour with her son, however.

The Archer christening gown was laundered. A small cake awaited modest decoration. Everything was ready for the next day's ceremony.

Chin on hand, Peggy looked out of the kitchen window. Not much of a horizon was offered to her. She wondered why Wanda was working the pump as if it had wronged her.

Passing with a pile of washing, Doris back-pedalled. 'Hey, you, Peg,' she said. 'Follow me.'

On the way out to the yard, Phil was strong-armed away from where he sat thinking about girls, and told to bring a wheelbarrow of soil around from the paddock.

'Tip it in here, there's a good lad.' Doris pointed to an old enamel sink she had tucked in against the fence, knowing it would come in handy. Brookfield was making do and mending long before the war.

'Can I go now?' asked Phil archly, as if his mother had called him away from important matters of state.

'Off you trot.' Doris took a handful of small brown dots out of her apron pocket and poured them into Peggy's palm.

'What are these?' Peggy poked at the flat, grooved ovals. 'Seeds or something?'

'Carrot seeds. Each one is a little world of its own, ready to burst into life.'

'Hmm.' Peggy was unimpressed.

Doris passed her a wooden dibber. 'You can plant them and grow them and these'll be *your* carrots.'

Don't I have enough to do, with the baby? thought Peggy, but she said nothing, and inexpertly introduced the seeds to the soil.

'My hands are filthy,' she said afterwards, and Doris raised her eyes to heaven.

Pamela prepared for the christening in the armour of her class.

Diamonds at her throat, a fur stole standing by, her face powdered and set. She laid the chosen plum silk dress on her bed and gasped.

'Hildegard!' Pamela rarely shouted but the occasion merited it.

The lady's maid also gasped at the dress. 'Oh Lord, I

must've cut through both dresses when I cut out the square for the quilt!'

Both women knew it was no accident.

One corner of Hildegard's mouth lifted.

Pamela shut her eyes. 'Out,' she said, then, shouting for the second time in as many minutes, '*Get out of my sight*!'

In a serviceable coral two-piece foraged from the back of the wardrobe, Pamela strode downstairs to find a huddle of officers around 'poor Hildegard', who was sobbing histrionically.

'I say,' said Cad, his face like thunder, 'don't turf the girl out for one little mistake!'

There was no time to educate him about the difference between real tears and these tears, so Pamela simply stalked out of the house.

There were more tears outside St Stephen's.

The Grundys were already assembled when the Archers turned up, Jennifer at the forefront in the family christening gown. It shone like a good deed in a naughty world, hand-smocked, passed down through the decades.

Alf's crochet pinafore suddenly struck his mother as 'rotten!' Susan Grundy was inconsolable. 'It's not fair!'

Speeding home, Magsy was soon back with the Seed christening dress. One quick change later and Alf was a young czar in Flemish lace and swansdown cap.

'That's more like it,' said Susan, tears dried, and a certain loftiness to her gait as she preceded the Archers to the font.

'The whole of creation is filled with your light,' intoned Henry, but way back in the shadows of the church there was little light and nobody noticed Agnes watching the ceremony.

The two young women bowed over their babies and Agnes felt a pain in her stomach so keen she could have doubled over.

Nobody had assumed that Agnes might love her baby.

Motherhood was depicted everywhere as something natural and all-powerful; love for babies was sacred. *But only those born in wedlock*, thought Agnes, bitterly feeling the apartheid.

Memories sat alongside her on the pew. How she was overridden, as if she was nothing, as if she was dirt.

They took her baby away and in its place gave Agnes a red-hot resolve never to be bullied again. That was why, even as a servant, she had never been humble; *I ran the place!* That was why she had elbowed her way into respectability.

That was why she didn't wait for the final blessing and instead went home to pick a fight with Denholm.

Afterwards, in the back room of The Bull, the jam tarts didn't last long.

'I should have made more,' said Mrs Endicott weakly, watching Stan Horrobin take three.

Bob felt a sneeze coming. Doris Archer had placed a posy of narcissi on each rickety table, and his sinuses had been tickled all morning. He groped for his handkerchief, but instead repressed the sneeze, and carefully folded the hanky into its original creases. The embroidered initial and the scallopped hem, although imperfect, were the work of Evie, and far too good for one of his trombone spectaculars. 'To say sorry,' she had said, '*Encore*', and Bob had immediately used it to dry his surprised tears.

New godmother Pamela presented the proud parents with the babies' gifts.

'That's too much!' said Doris, taking the silver rattle out of its pink box.

'Not at all. I know Alec wishes he were here to present it himself.'

Doris pressed Pamela's gloved hand. 'Not long now,' she said, daring to overstep the invisible boundary of class and temperament Pamela maintained around herself.

'One hopes,' said Pamela, touched and embarrassed. 'Shame your son couldn't be here.'

'Oh, he's here all right.' Doris swallowed hard. 'Been thinking about him all day. I just hope . . .'

'He will, Doris,' said Pamela, who was not at her best around sentiment but felt she must step up. 'Your Jack will see his little girl.'

Grayson's birthmark throbbed red. 'Been at Walter's hooch?' asked Max, pretty much the only thing he said all day, since learning that Wanda was holding the fort back at the farm.

Max wondered if Grayson's birthmark was semaphoring his guilt at overhearing the worried whispers about Mother Molly. Gerald's date with destiny was on everyone's lips.

One guest was not in her best clothes. Perhaps Connie had no 'best' clothes.

'Lovely to see you,' said Doris. 'Take a glass of summat and wet the baby's head!'

'Ain't 'ere to hobnob. Just wanted to see the babbies, like.'

Doris slipped a sandwich into Connie's pocket. 'For the way home.'

In a corner of the inn, Julia tucked one last hairclip into Pamela's hair. 'There. Perfect.'

'Had to fend for myself, after Hildegard's outburst. I'm hopeless with hair.' Pamela eyed herself in a mirror advertising ales. 'Thank you, Julia.' The rapport between mother and daughter-in-law was welcome, but Pamela couldn't shake the worry that Julia was too racy an addition to the Pargetter bloodline. 'How long, I wonder, before you and Gerald are bringing your own little one to St Stephen's to be baptised.'

Pamela was not privy to the couple's plan, devised by Gerald, to thwart Mother Molly's prophecy. The riddle depended on the 'poor damaged boy' being the last male Pargetter, and his death bringing about 'the end of the noble line'. If Julia were to fall pregnant before the eighth of May, the Pargetter line would carry on, and the prophecy would lose its power.

And so, they made love daily. Whenever they closed the bedroom door to discuss Shakespeare, it was for a marital game that did not include the bard; both enjoyed the frisson of discussing their lovemaking openly in front of others.

'Oh. Goodness.' Pamela staggered as the hefty young

Alf was propelled into her arms by the baby's father. 'How delightful.' Small, chubby hands reached for her necklace. 'I do hope he's not headed for a life of crime!'

Her joke went down badly with the Grundys.

As the last guest called out their farewell, Bob handed Dan a bill. 'Payable immediately,' he said; it had been a long afternoon.

'But . . .' Dan stared at the startling handwritten figure. 'Me and the Grundys are splitting it.'

'Joe said it was on you. So . . .' Bob held out his hand.

Denholm Kaye was a happy man.

He didn't look happy; he looked befuddled. But he was fed, watered, his house was warm and clean, and his shirts were perfectly ironed.

Agnes looked after him like a prize pooch, and carefully hid from him the Ruby-shaped comet that threatened their orderly domestic life. They did not share anxieties; they were not romantically minded. When Agnes made her enormous decision that Tuesday morning, she felt no need to tell her husband.

No skin off his nose, she thought.

Watching her set off, correct in buttoned coat and soft hat, a sympathetic narrator might tell you that the young Agnes, treated as if she had no feelings, shed them; that this late delivery of a lifetime's worth of emotion had changed her, so that a very altered Agnes waited by the back of the store to ambush Ruby.

'C'mere.' Agnes's hand on Ruby's elbow was proprietorial when Ruby stepped out to haul in a sack of potatoes. She spoke in a rush, her words hissed. 'Listen, girlie. You're mine, right? I'm yours, got that? Oh.' Agnes was not prepared when this child who had grown so much taller than its mother threw her arms around her.

Affection was easier than it looked; Agnes simply held Ruby. 'There, there,' she said, and – astonishingly – meant it.

'You're in charge.' Ruby pulled away, nose red, eyes likewise. 'Nobody need know.'

'I'm sick of shame,' spat Agnes.

'Please tread carefully.' Ruby hadn't come into her mother's life to ruin it. 'Nothing rash.'

'Can't promise,' said Agnes.

Birdsong isn't always lovely, but Max had a fondness for the cawing of the rooks who congregated in the ash tree behind his cottage.

He lay in bed listening to them long after his alarm clock danced on the bedside drawers, trying and failing to find a version of his current predicament that was not entirely his own fault.

Fair play, Wanda. He saluted her ability to fashion a fiancé out of thin air.

Turning, punching the pillow, he growled at how he had

behaved as if he, and only he, could call the shots in their . . . *affair?* There was no word for the limp non-starter of a liaison he had so adroitly ruined.

His wife had stepped away at precisely the right moment. *She always did know what was best for me.*

His foolish notions of gallantry – condemning himself to a lifelong widowerhood – would appal her. She was gone now, and so was Wanda. Max was alone with his bruises, and without his wife. Without his child.

Without his Wanda.

'*Who's* dead?' Dan was aghast.

'President Roosevelt.' Doris was solemn. 'God rest his soul.'

'So sudden.' Dan was chastened. 'Who's in charge now?'

'Truman,' said Peggy, who had brought the terrible news from the village. She didn't share with them Mrs Endicott's diagnosis: 'The war killed the poor man. Hitler's enough to give anyone the head staggers.'

'I'll put the kettle on.' In the face of something enormous, Doris did something small; tea would help the sorry tidings go down.

'Oh lordy!' Peggy jumped up and dashed out. She had forgotten to water her carrot seedlings. Again. It was only a matter of time before they gave up the ghost; Peggy had the opposite of green fingers.

*

Agnes cleaned the entire house from top to bottom.

She waxed the venerable old wood. She brought the parquet up to a warm gleam. Every stemmed glass was taken down and wiped and replaced, to sparkle in the April sunshine.

The will, locked up in the secretaire, named Agnes as Denholm's sole heir; she was safe here for the rest of her days. Fifty years of scrimping had brought her to a final act where she was doyenne of Turnpike.

It would hurt to let it go. A lifetime spent in cold back bedrooms meant she appreciated each chest, each mirror, each and every spoon in the scullery drawers.

Telling Denholm the truth about Ruby – *about my daughter* – would end her marriage.

She told him anyway. Curtly, with no curlicues. She stood back, hands together, and awaited his response.

'What would Mother say?' was Denholm's only comment. He looked her up and down with stark distaste.

The rug shifted beneath Agnes's feet as Denholm retreated beyond a slammed door.

One could hardly call it shopping; the windows in Borchester's high street were spartan, or sported fake displays of food and goods.

Pamela paused, basket over her arm, to look in at the jeweller's window. A pearl pin. A handsome watch, but too slight for Alec's tastes. The curtain behind the window moved and a disembodied hand propped up a new item on a velvet stand.

A silver rattle, of particularly fine quality.

Pamela bent at the waist to make out the engraved words:

To Alfred Grundy on the
occasion of his christening

from Alec and Pamela Pargetter

15th April 1945

'Thought I'd drop in on my way home,' said Morgan.

Cliff was wry. 'That might work with my mother, but not with me. Did Lorna call you?'

Morgan surrendered, his hands up. 'She did, Cliff. She's worried about this rash of yours.' He trained the lamp on Cliff's face. The small parlour was dark, warm, and insulated by rows and rows of books.

Nothing, thought Morgan, *could be farther from the house where Cliff grew up.* He made a noise in his throat his patients knew well as he examined the flaking skin around the tide-mark of Cliff's facial scars. 'Should've come to see me, young man. This looks unbearably itchy. No need to soldier on when you have a doctor in the village.'

'It's not so bad. Have you . . .'

Morgan knew what he wanted to ask. 'Yes, I've seen Connie. Had to put a stitch in a gash on her thigh. Dropped a knife, she said.' Morgan wrote a prescription. 'Still not on speaking terms, eh?'

Cliff didn't answer; he was as private as he was stoic.

Together, Lorna and Cliff saw the doctor out. They passed the Ambridge quilt, folded in the small hall. When she saw Morgan's double-take, Lorna said, 'I'm pressing it before it gets passed on to Mrs Micklewood. The other fabrics look a little drab beside Magsy's, don't they?' She picked it up and held out the red satin square.

'You say Magsy added that?' Morgan pointed to the red fabric, embroidered with brilliant silks.

'Well, yes . . .' Lorna wondered why unflappable Morgan was so agitated. 'It's some sort of bird.'

'A gamayun,' said Morgan and Cliff together.

Cliff went on. 'It's a creature from Russian folklore. It foretells the future.'

'Like Mother Molly,' said Lorna. 'I hope it doesn't have any bad news for the village.'

His mother's long-lost gamayun certainly had something to say to Morgan, and he pondered what that might be all the way back to Holmleigh.

Agnes lost her temper.

She had never shown Denholm anger; irritation, yes, over spilt cream or a forgotten glove, but her raised voice was new to him. He was not to know that his coolness reminded her of her parents' reaction to her pregnancy.

'You have to talk to me! I'm your wife.'

Nothing. Denholm was a dense slab of disapproval.

'Denholm! Say something!'

Eventually, he spoke, while he sat at the table with a fried fillet of cod in front of him and Agnes standing by, holding a fish slice like a pistol.

He repeated himself. 'What would Mother say about all this?'

'I can guess,' snapped Agnes. 'But we don't really know. Women know more about the nitty gritty of life than they let on to their menfolk. Even in this genteel house, your mother would know about pain and loss.' She pointed the fish slice at him. 'Your mother might surprise you. What if she praised me for my honesty?'

'Your honesty is rather late.' Denholm cut into the cod. 'Mother would turn you out.'

'She probably would, the miserable old bag.' Agnes tore off her apron with great energy. It felt good to finally insult Denholm's sainted mother. 'No need to turn me out, Denholm. I'll go.'

Another meal in another house.

Nance's sterling cottage pie went untouched.

'I barely had to ask Magsy.' She had undertaken some spying for her husband. 'She was excited, said she found the red satin shawl rammed in the back of a wardrobe. She called it "showy", and was surprised at her mother owning such a garment. Magsy said she'd never dare wear anything so exotic, but it seemed perfect for the quilt.'

Morgan was angry, but at who? Not Magsy, who had no idea of the shawl's history. 'What was a stolen shawl doing in the Furneaux house? The last time my mother saw it was the night of the burglary, when all the silver was taken. I can't work this out, my love.'

His love knew he didn't want to work it out, because of the one inescapable conclusion. 'Tell me,' asked Nance gently. 'Was the tennis trophy among the stolen silver? The one Magsy's father felt was rightfully his?'

'Good grief,' Morgan swam towards full realisation. 'Aubrey, my father's dearest friend, burgled our house in order to get his hands on the trophy!'

'All the other silver was taken to make it seem like a common-or-garden break-in. And he swiped up your mama's shawl to wrap it.'

'The gamayun was a casualty.'

'Exactly. Heaven knows where the rest of the silver went.'

'My mother', said Morgan, 'adored that shawl.'

'And you adore my cottage pie,' said Nance. 'Eat, love.'

And he did, but slowly, and with more knowledge of human nature than he had started the day with.

People with low expectations are rarely disappointed, but Agnes was disappointed in her husband.

She packed only what was indisputably hers; a small pile that fitted easily in a suitcase she had never thought to use again.

When she touched the mahogany bedstead she thought, *I'll*

miss this. She would miss the framed oil paintings. She would miss the heavy curtains she drew every evening. She would miss the man downstairs.

Why will I miss Denholm? She asked herself. He did as he was told, but gave little of himself. Their conversations were more like monologues, but she would miss his 'Yes, dear' and his 'No, dear' and even his 'What was that, dear?'

There was no sparkling wit to miss, no sweet nothings. But she would miss his bulk, his reliability, his ordinariness.

She folded a nightdress.

Downstairs, Denholm listened to her slippered feet going to and fro across the floorboards.

Who'll cook? panicked Denholm. His brain whirred as he sat slouched over his fish. *I tried to cook after Mother died and oh dear . . .*

He loathed disruption, was allergic to change.

And there was also a stirring of anticipated melancholy. To have no Agnes after having so much Agnes – how would that be? He was accustomed to being a husband; accustomed to Agnes.

He lumbered up the stairs and addressed her narrow quivering back as Agnes put her good shoes in the suitcase.

'Stay, Aggie,' he said.

She wheeled around. 'What?'

'But we must never talk of it again.'

'I beg your pardon.'

Denholm was nonplussed; he had expected feminine gratitude for his condescension.

'I've kept quiet long enough!' Agnes returned to her packing.

Denholm retreated downstairs to slump in his chair. Nothing would materially change when his wife left; he would still own this house and everything in it. He remembered the room around him as it had been between the two reigns, first of Queen Mother, then of Queen Agnes.

The dust, the gloom. The emptiness.

It was always Agnes who lit the lamps. Then she would sit in the chair next to his and knit and chatter. Who would fill the silence when she left?

They were suited to one another – this came as a revelation.

Agnes carried her case downstairs; the lumpy bed was all Denholm's once more. She hoped he'd remember to change his vest now and then.

There was a not a trace of self-pity as she took her coat down from the hook. She would start again from scratch, and find some new perch.

The taste of doing the 'right thing' was unexpectedly sweet in her mouth; Agnes generally did the wrong thing.

I'm standing up for my kin.

That Denholm would let her go without a word did not surprise Agnes, but it did hurt her. She said no goodbye either, just squared her shoulders and stepped out of Turnpike.

Grayson crossed the Green deep in thought as the day died.

His was a tiny rut in the old earth beneath his feet, but he felt himself at the centre of many designs. The war moved inexorably on, picking up pace, heading not for hellfire but for a decent peace. The year ignored the news, and Ambridge grew more green by the second. And Mother Molly? With the calendar counting down to the eighth of May, her grip on the imagination of the villagers tightened.

He had resurrected her. The fear that pulsed beneath the confident surface of Lower Loxley was all his doing.

I am her high priest, he thought, as he reached his gate.

'Aggie.'

She almost didn't hear her name called, quietly, from his armchair. She dithered, tutted, then went back indoors to stick her head around the drawing-room door.

'What's for pudding?'

He's crying. Her husband's face looked like a ruined cake.

'Can't we just have pudding?' he begged. 'Like always?'

Agnes did not put down her case. She did not remove her hat. She had played poker; she knew Denholm had never progressed beyond Old Maid. 'If I stay then Ruby is welcome here, Denholm. People don't need to know anything about it. Not their business. But Ruby and her daughters are my business.'

Denholm fidgeted, then said, 'Invite her to Sunday lunch.'

Agnes tilted her chin. 'And the kiddies?'

'And the kiddies, Aggie.'

Her coat went back on the hook. She patted his shoulder as she passed him. 'It's your favourite. Spotted Dick.'

May

As April turned the corner into May, even those immune to Mother Molly's fearmongering could not help but look at the calendar and wonder. They went about their business – the vicar in his vestry, the farmers notching lambs' ears, the children cheering the swallows on their return to Borsetshire – with the date hanging over them like the rusty scythe of Death himself.

Seven days to go, Bob caught himself thinking as he wiped the bar counter on the first of the month. He looked at his regulars and knew they'd be hard to shift tonight.

'Turn it up!' Whitey White gestured at the wireless on a shelf. 'Newsflash, Bob! Turn it up!'

The bar went quiet. Outside, the Green was still and silent, the dog daisies' petals closed for the night.

A cheer went up that almost raised The Bull's new roof.

Lower Loxley's French windows rattled with an RAF 'Hurrah!'

At Brookfield, Doris sat up in bed, her hands to her

face. She roused the children and sent Christine running for Wanda.

'He's dead!' Christine bounced on Wanda's ricketty bed. 'He's dead!'

'Who's dead?'

'*Him!* Hitler! He's a goner at last!'

The chaps embarked on an all-night session at Lower Loxley. Pamela left Gerald and Julia alone in their room, and tiptoed to her boudoir, avoiding the revelry.

'This must mean the end, mustn't it, Minko?' she asked the clueless dog. 'Alec will come back, won't he?' She thought of the correspondence in a locked drawer, of the news that awaited him. *What a homecoming that will be!*

Nance got Tudor up, so she could tell him later, when he was tall and grown, that he took part in this incredible night.

Grayson and Max hugged.

'Are we barbarians?' asked Max. 'To exult like this over a death?'

'We're humans,' said Grayson. 'The barbarian is the one who died.'

A jig broke out in The Bull. Somebody knocked over Stan's pint, and Stan punched him just the once, in deference to the historic event.

'Dear God, he's *gone*,' whispered Mrs Endicott to Twinkle Toes. 'He was a swine,' she said, horrified by her own bad language and horrified that she could not bring herself to pray for him.

Ruby brought the girls downstairs, where they goose-stepped

along the bar. Only Evie knew that she, as her alter-ego, had sought out and run Adolf through with her sabre.

'*Vive la France*!' she yelled, the imaginary weapon held high.

'*Vive* Ambridge!' yelled her mother.

Julia could not sit still. 'Is this it?' she said, again and again. 'Can this be it? Is it over?'

'Not just like that,' said Gerald. 'But yes, this is, in a way, my darling, *it*.'

She hadn't mentioned the countdown to the eighth, and Gerald was glad. *If I can get through the next seven days, I'll never be frightened of anything ever again.*

The crash had not scared Gerald. He was a simple soul, a blank pebble, bred to hunt foxes and overeat. Only Mother Molly had ever perturbed him like this and he loathed her for it.

'Don't, Dan, no!' Doris felt she should seem scandalised as her husband doled out thimbles of sherry to Phil and Christine.

'It's not every day we get news like this.' Dan took up Mother Cat and danced with her.

Christine joined in. 'Mum, they *swore* on the BBC.'

'No, love,' said Doris. 'They were quoting Shakespeare.'

The day is ours, the newsreader had said. *The bloody dog is dead.*

'Peace,' said Dan, spinning round with the disgruntled cat. 'Our Wanda can marry her Christopher in peace!'

'I can't wait,' said Christine, disappointed not to be drunk on her half inch of sherry.

Doris felt one of her curlers fall out. The kitchen was upside down. She would have to get up early and set it on its feet; Hitler or no Hitler, the Brookfield lambs needed castrating.

She ran a fingernail along the grain of the table. She thought of words she hadn't known until she read them recently in headlines.

Buchenwald. Bergen-Belsen.

Doris could not bring herself to celebrate, and crept back to bed.

'Steeped in murder,' said Magsy. 'That's what the *Daily Mail* called him.'

'Wasn't he just.' Frank wondered if any of the customers crammed into the shop would buy anything today. 'Can I help you, Grayson?' he asked hopefully as the bell over the door tinkled.

'Just popped in to say, well, I don't know what!' Grayson's hair was more electrified than usual. 'Isn't it all incredible?'

'Good riddance,' said Susan Grundy, 'to bad rubbish.'

'We shouldn't glory in death,' said the vicar, who had accompanied Mrs Micklewood to the store. On a slower news day that nugget would already be piped to various cottages. 'Although I can imagine St Peter slamming the pearly gates in that gentleman's face.'

'Berlin's surrendered,' said Magsy.

'Unofficially.' Grayson dared to correct an Ambridge elder.

Evie, in her favourite cubby hole beneath the counter, asked, 'So all the daddies will come home now?'

Grayson was cautious. 'Bit early to celebrate. The Japanese aren't the sort to back down.'

'You're overthinking, dear boy,' said Mrs Endicott indulgently. 'All you academics are too clever for your own good. The end is in sight.'

The third of May brought more headlines, both lurid and ecstatic.

Doris, pinning out washing and eyeing the chickweed taking over her borders, tried to lose herself in the flapping of the sheets and the giggling of the hens. She stood with her empty basket, and closed her eyes against the grainy images she had seen in the newspaper. A bread van giving out clods of bread in a Berlin reduced to rubble.

She thought of Ambridge being destroyed, of Brookfield burned to its cellar. She thought of competing with old Mrs Endicott for a lump of mouldy loaf.

She thought of her son and wished he was home, and getting on her nerves.

At Lower Loxley, Pamela thought of her own son, and wished the days would go slower. A rota ensured he was never alone; Pamela or Julia or Max or Grayson was always in the sickroom, playing cards, rolling dice, smoking.

Although what any of us are supposed to do if Mother Molly materialises through the floorboards, I don't know.

Croquet was on the cards. Max was expected; even with one arm he was a deadly shot. Pamela went to meet him on the gravel not because of his croquet prowess, but because she felt the need of his quintessential Englishness, his exquisite refusal to panic. The gaiety of the chaps was too much for Pamela; as the rest of the world dared to relax, Lower Loxley was in a stranglehold that tightened each day.

They would surely all pop with the pressure on the eighth.

Head down, Max did not notice his hostess waiting on the sun-warmed step.

His feet itched to turn, hunt down Wanda and tell her, 'You know you didn't mean what you said.' He ignored his feet, because above all else Wanda hated being told what she thought.

I must accept her decision.

And yet he couldn't. Max did not consider himself irresistible – quite the opposite. With his empty sleeve and his introspection, he knew himself to be a bad bargain. Even so, he had seen something in Wanda's eye, heard something in her pique, that told him she was in love with him.

'Max!'

Hearing his name, he looked up and saw Pamela wave in greeting.

He sped up, straightened up. *I'm a fool,* he thought. The vast America of Wanda had been there for the taking and he must accept he had failed her. Being a man entailed a great deal of acceptance. He had accepted his wife's death under the rubble of their home. He accepted that her voice had stopped.

I'm strong, I'll be all right, I'll play croquet as if nothing is wrong.

Or . . . he could just get drunk.

He turned, forgetting etiquette, forgetting Pamela, and went back the way he had come.

He was watched by two women, a nonplussed Pamela at the door, and cat-eyed Hildegard at an upper window.

'Ooh, madam won't like *that,*' smiled the maid. The gallant hero was one of her mistress's trophies, and one of Hildegard's favourites, too. She watched his behind as he marched away, and found it pleasing.

She held the kimono against her cheek for a moment, checking first that she wasn't being spied on; she had enemies among the staff. Julia's clothes were so sensual, so fine. *I deserve to wear stuff like this,* she thought, stepping into Julia's bathroom to replace the kimono on its hook.

Gotta hand it to Julia, she's getting away with it, thought Hildegard, expertly costing each bottle of scent and each glimmering ring; she noticed when Julia's accent slipped, even if the toffs did not.

Something by the arsenic-green sink caught her eye. A small, strange item very familiar to Hildegard. A plastic dimple, like a comical bowler hat.

Interesting, thought the maid.

*

When Grayson answered his knock, Max wasted no words. 'Fancy getting blotto?'

Peggy carried Jennifer across the yard to check up on her seedlings.

A tiny, frothy forest had struggled up out of the soil. The edges of some of the fragile leaves were dark, unhealthy.

It might be better if they just keeled over – *Haven't I enough to be getting on with?* – but Peggy called out Doris to diagnose the problem.

She gave Peggy an onion. 'Bury that beside 'em. I've always sworn by an onion alongside a blighted plant.'

Doing as she was bid, Peggy whispered to the baby, 'Your grandma's a bit of a Mother Molly, isn't she? This is nothing but an old wives' tale.'

The sun turned its face away from the farm, and Peggy bundled her baby up tight. With four days to go until the eighth of May, any mention of Ambridge's witch served as a reminder that, while the rest of the country anticipated glad tidings about the war, the village was braced for death.

Hildegard twisted around, doing up her brassiere.

Smoke coiled above him. She watched him, desiring him, loving the width of his shoulders and the curl of his hair. They were a match, Hildegard knew it.

But does he?

She said, 'Discovered summat today that'll earn me a decent few bob on the side.'

He didn't seem interested; he never did. Too busy thinking about himself. His life was complicated. He was trapped, he told her.

Tonight she had finally suggested her big plan. 'Let's just flee,' she had laughed. 'Leave this dump behind.' She had flicked his collar. 'Leave your uniform behind!'

She could tell he thought he was the one using her; Hildegard preferred it when people underestimated her.

'So, when are we off, lover boy? Nothing here for me anymore.'

He was laconic. 'It's not all about you.'

'It's about *us,* and we can do better than this dead-and-alive hole'.

Evie studied the man at the head of the table. 'Who *are* you?' she asked. She recalled him being very *very* harrumph-y the night she threw a grenade at the Home Guard.

'He's our new friend,' said Ruby. 'You can call him Mister Kay.'

'How'd you do, Misty Kay.'

Denholm laughed.

His funny bone had been located, and by Evie, of all people.

'Carve, dear.' Agnes handed her husband the knife, and he hacked away at the roast pork. She was twitchy, alert for problems, but even Agnes could find no fault with the exquisitely dressed little girls, who sat so straight at the table and said their grace with charm.

'Only two days to go,' said Agnes; the village's most hardened sceptic had joined the ranks of the superstitious. 'I'm on duty at Lower Loxley tonight.'

'You?' Denholm seemed surprised that Agnes was part of the relay team keeping watch over Gerald; he had often heard her rail against the 'stuck-up' Pargetters.

'Yes, me. I'm a villager, after all. An attack on one of us is an attack on all of us. I've put your name down for tomorrow.'

Denholm stopped carving and gaped.

'Cut a *huge* bit for me, Misty Kay,' said Evie.

The agony Agnes had felt at the prospect of leaving Ambridge left its mark; she would never be a model citizen, but she now acknowledged the bonds that bound her to the village. *Even if they are a bunch of twits.* 'Imagine poor Gerald being trapped with Mrs E listing every last one of her ailments,' she said, helping Michele to an extra roast potato. 'He'll be *praying* for Mother Molly to come and get him.'

'It's the last hour of the eighth of May that's crucial.' Ruby tried not to laugh at Agnes's disrespectful humour but it was hard – *we both have a dark side!* She loved finding similarities between them. 'That's when Gerald will do battle with old Mother Molly.'

'I do hope we're not on duty then?' ventured Denholm, giving himself by far the largest slice of pork.

'We'll be at the Seeds' party that night,' said Agnes.

'Max and Grayson are scheduled to be with Gerald for the last hour,' said Ruby. 'They might lack a leg and an arm between them, but I'd want them in my corner if I was in trouble.'

Uninterested – *grown-ups are boring* – Evie demolished her lunch. The strange knitting needle of a woman was a fabulous cook; perhaps England wasn't such a culinary wasteland after all.

Misty Kay though ... Evie studied him, covertly. *Probably a spy,* she thought.

The carrots had bucked up.

The onion worked.

They were still a pain in the you-know-what, but Peggy watered them, and evicted a slug.

The shop door was propped open.

Women milled in and out.

The occasional man wandered through.

They were all waiting for the news that would change the world, the news that would pop the war's grotty balloon.

'Any minute now,' Frank said as he wrapped butter for his daughter, 'the whole damn thing'll be over, pardon my French.'

Prone to 'what-ifs', Nance took nothing for granted, even though she and Morgan were throwing their home open to celebrate with friends and neighbours the next evening. She took the butter, and then took Tudor, who was being petted by Lorna and Wanda.

'He's a sweetheart,' said Lorna, with one last kiss on the boy's round cheek.

'Didn't allow me a wink of sleep last night! You'll see, when you have one of your own.' Nance's smile faded when Lorna didn't return it.

'Let's go,' said Lorna, and Wanda followed her out into the softness of an Ambridge afternoon.

'Oh, *perfect*,' hissed Wanda, spotting Max. She turned to Lorna, but her friend had taken a great – and sudden – interest in Mrs Endicott, who was ambling towards the shop.

Max caught up with Wanda, but found himself addressing the side of her head. 'Stop, please.'

The hand he laid on her arm scorched her skin, and she drew away from him.

'If you say one word, just one,' said Max, 'we can begin again. And this time—'

'I won't say any word at all. This "we" you talk about was never much in the first place.' Wanda darted a look at his expression, like an archer who regrets letting loose such a sharp arrow. She did not take it back; *I must cauterise this wound*. 'Excuse me. I have to post this.'

He could surely read the name on the envelope as she left him. The letter inside was long, chatty; it asked Christopher if he could darn a sock.

Cutting short Mrs Endicott's ode to her constipation, Lorna ran up to her friend at the postbox.

'What did he say? Did he–'

'It's *done*!' Wanda's unsinkable good humour was finally sunk.

It was cruel to arrange the assignation at the grotto.

The moonlight touched Julia's gold hair as she prowled in a tight circle, jumping at every tiny noise. With the hateful date drawing closer, she was infected with a fear of this place. Each day a ticked box, one less day of Gerald's allotted time.

Come on! Thought Julia, keen to get back to her husband. He was different, vulnerable, softened by his anxiety. He had changed her life – most stage-door johnnies want a roll in the hay, not marriage – and she knew he needed her close.

The money was in her hand. One mucky note.

'There you are, at last.'

The attempted imperiousness cut no ice with Hildegard; they both knew where the power lay. 'Yes, here I am.' She held out her hand and took the pound note. 'Nice doing business with you.' It disappeared into her purse with a click.

'That's it, you know.' The maid's chirpiness horrified Julia. 'This is a one-off.'

Hildegard was amused, kindly even. 'Don't you worry. I won't bleed you dry. But I'm one of them socialists now, like Clement Attlee. I like to see the wealth shared out. No, hold on, I'm a *capitalist,* aren't I? I got something you want and you're paying me for it.'

'What could you possibly have that I want?'

'Silence, love.' Hildegard seemed to draw energy from

Julia's disdain. 'Lower Loxley is very leaky. If I blabbed about that little diaphragm by your sink, word'd soon get to your darling hubby that you're only *pretending* to try for a baby to save him from Mother Molly.'

'It's complicated. Don't you dare judge me!'

'Judge you? I don't care enough to judge you. I'm grateful, if anything, for your contribution to my running away fund.' Hildegard bobbed a curtsey and blew a kiss. 'See you soon!'

Waiting until the maid disappeared into the dark, Julia dragged herself back to the house, head bowed, chafing at the trap she found herself in. Stepping into the golden rectangle painted on the terrace by the French windows – no blackout tonight! – she plastered on her best *ingénue* smile.

Even with every lamp lit and every glass full, Lower Loxley was in a vice, one that tightened and tightened until the family's bones cracked.

Two days to go.

The news ripped through the nation like wildfire.

'They've surrendered, Glen!' Doris told the sheepdog.

'It's over.' Peggy's legs went beneath her. 'It's really over.'

Connie Horrobin felt oddly removed from the jubilation. 'Does this mean our Vic can come out of hiding now?' she asked the back of Stan's head as he set off for The Bull.

The inn fairly shook. Singing, swinging, every customer lit up like a Christmas tree.

Only the landlord seemed solemn. Ruby nudged him. 'Tell me something about your Jimmy,' she said. 'I live in his house, yet I don't really know him.'

Bob's eyes questioned her, then understood. Like so many others, he and Ruby had lost their most important person, their most beloved. 'He was quiet,' said Bob, tipping his head back so the tears stayed put. 'Deep, like.' He couldn't go on.

'My shield is colour.' Ruby tweaked the fuchsia scarf around her neck. 'Your shield is this counter.' She tapped the bar. 'We'll get by, won't we?'

'We will, love,' said Bob. 'Now I'd better serve Stan before he gives me an earful.'

The next day – the eighth of May – was the official date of the surrender, the date that would go down in history books.

London, it was said, would be one huge shindig.

A stranger to sleep, Pamela watched the gilt clock on the mantelpiece. She had 'taken to her bed', as Dodgy called it. He was downstairs with the others, singing saucy RAF songs and being inappropriate with the parlour maids.

The eighth of May would be momentous. VE Day. A starting pistol for Alec's return; a day so yearned for, it seemed too good to be true.

But dread outweighed joy. By midnight tomorrow she would know if her son had survived the curse.

For now, Gerald was safe; he and Julia were enjoying one of their Shakespeare marathons.

*

The noise of stones hitting her bedroom window jolted Peggy out of bed. 'You loony!' she called down to Wanda, who stood in the yard in a pair of Dan's old pyjamas.

'Let's go to London tomorrow!'

The old adventurous Peggy, the one inside the altered, mature body, hollered 'Yes!' without a second thought.

The village hall sprouted Union Jacks, and sandwiches appeared on crepe-papered tables.

In a discreet corner, Walter's hooch claimed victims, and Mrs Endicott handed out small gifts wrapped in newspaper, raided from her knick-knack shelves, to any children who wandered in.

'We certainly picked the right night for our party.' Morgan reminded everyone of their invitation. 'We'll let our hair down.' He felt Magsy's eye upon him. 'In a decorous manner, of course.'

'Ooh, you've reminded me!' Agnes put down her tea cup. 'I'm on Gerald-duty in half an hour. Better dash.' She passed Michele and Evie, both of them wearing paste brooches from Mrs Endicott's collection. Evie opened her little mouth to speak, but Agnes frowned a 'No!' and was impressed at how the girl understood. *So smart,* she thought, congratulating herself on Evie's genes.

Ruby watched Agnes leave, hating the deceit being handed down to another generation.

Spotting her husband over the heads of their neighbours,

Doris called, 'Over here, love!' She handed him a sausage roll. 'The girls catch their train okay?' She had shed a patriotic tear waving off Peggy and Wanda to London in their frocks.

'Couldn't hear meself for giggling in the truck. Peggy made me promise to water her carrots.'

'The war isn't quite over, you know,' warned Joe Grundy, hovering by the buffet. 'Japan's holding out.'

'All this cheering and toasting, when so many husbands and sons are still in mortal danger.' Doris put down her sandwich, untouched.

Stan picked it up and finished it in two bites.

Walter put his face close to Stan's. 'No need to worry about your boy, eh? Unless he shoots his own foot wherever the coward's hiding!'

Stepping between the men, Grayson said, 'We all have our battles, Walter.'

'Yeah, well,' said Walter, while Stan said, 'Huh.' Neither men wanted to scrap today.

Grayson found Max by the open door. 'Given up on the fair Wanda, have we?'

'I'll never give up, but her heart is hers to give, not mine to smash and grab.'

'You posh boys,' sneered Stan. 'Women love a bit of rough handlin'.'

The men looked speakingly at Connie, who wore dark glasses to cover another black and purple eye.

Max tensed, only to feel Grayson's hand on his chest.

'A bit silly, Max, to start a fist fight on the day peace breaks out. Pamela's looking for us.'

When Pamela found them, she told them of the changes to that evening's sickroom rota. 'Doesn't seem fair to drag you both away from what will now be a victory party. Cad has volunteered for the, um, *final* hour, much to my surprise. Dodgy insists on being present. The old man's portly but turns out he's also a crack shot.'

'If you're sure . . .' Grayson seemed disappointed.

'I'm sure.' Pamela's smile betrayed neither her paralysing foreboding nor her resentment towards Grayson for bringing Mother Molly to their door. 'We need *soldiers* at midnight, not academics!' Whatever was coming their way was meaty, corporeal; Pamela was ready to swing a chair at it.

The air was sweet that day, the sunshine more vivid. England seemed ready to ripen and burst.

The outbuildings on the edge of the Sawyers' land would no longer be defended by the Home Guard. The old barn was just a barn again.

Except . . . what was that in the corner?

A camp bed, filched from Lower Loxley, was dressed as carefully as a four-poster, with a bedspread, blankets and soft pillows.

'See how nice I've made it for you?' Hildegard was proud of her handiwork. 'You'll be snug as a bug in a rug. I'll keep you fed and watered.'

Her swain shrugged.

'Aren't you pleased, Vic?' Hildegard put her arms around him. 'You were going to get caught, or worse. The barn's a much better hiding place than where you were.'

This was a different Vic Horrobin to the boy who skinned rabbits on Connie's table. Older, morose, less swagger.

'We won't be here long,' wheedled Hildegard. 'Now that I'm milking Julia we'll soon have enough to get away.'

'Brought any smokes?'

It was the nicest thing he'd said to her in ages.

The packed train lurched suddenly to a stop, flinging Peggy into the arms of a corporal.

'Throwing yourself at me, ducks?' he laughed.

'You should be so lucky!'

Nothing could perturb the high spirits of that packed train as it hurtled giddy men and women towards London. They sang 'Roll Out The Barrel', and passed around buns, and bottoms were pinched and faces were slapped.

Accepting a sip of a boy's beer, Wanda tucked herself into a corner, bracing herself against the train's swaying as it started up again. Beneath her pretty dress she had muscles; she was unchaperoned; she was nothing like the gentlewomen she was descended from.

What will Christopher say about this jaunt? No need to wonder – she knew.

'We're here!' Peggy hung out of the window, greeting her home city like a long-lost love. 'Next stop, St Paul's!'

*

Pamela oversaw a changing of the guard at 5pm.

Devilled eggs were laid out for Magsy and Ruby; an odd pairing. Gerald braced himself for his fourth game of draughts that day.

Only seven hours to go before Pamela would either laugh at her own gullibility or weep over Gerald's body.

They knelt in the scented hush of the cathedral.

A hundred prayers drifted upwards with the candle smoke.

Wanda prayed for the dead of Ambridge, for the dead of Borsetshire, of England, of Europe. For the Asians and the Russians and the Americans and the Japanese. For the Germans. For the bonfire of bodies the war burned to ash.

Peggy prayed for Gerald, waiting for his deadly gamayun at Lower Loxley, and she gave fervent thanks that her brothers – just a bus ride away from the cathedral! – would never have to carry a gun.

'Bring Jack home safe,' she murmured, and then added some extra entreaties. 'And get him to buckle down, would you?' Her nagging about their future had provoked a deluge of ideas from her husband: 'We could run a shop or a public house, or keep turkeys, I could buy a taxicab!'

All of them based on nothing at all.

The women stood, as if on cue, and made their way down the grand aisle, heads respectfully down, peeking sideways at each other.

Time for fun.

*

The noise!

Jeeps and vans honked all along Ludgate Hill. People hung off the vehicles like monkeys, Tommies and GIs and sailors berserk with feeling, one huge family coming together.

The red, white and blue of the Union Jack was everywhere, with a smattering of stars and stripes, and the odd pool of vomit.

Two girls linked them on The Strand.

'We're meeting our fellas in the Chandos!' the redhead said, as if she'd known Wanda and Peggy all her life. 'Come with us!'

Buoyed by the crowd that turned and boiled, they were dragged happily down William IV Street.

'Go and enjoy yourself at Morgan's, Ma!'

No amount of pleading from Gerald would move Pamela. At seven o'clock she took up her position in the easy chair by the window. Because the Pargetters had stiff upper lips that reached all the way to their hairlines, she did not say, 'How on earth could I *enjoy myself* knowing you are in danger?' Instead she just said, 'I've seen enough parties to last me a lifetime.'

A handbell sat on the bedside cabinet. If anybody – or anything – got into the room it would be rung. The chaps downstairs would be drunk as skunks, but all had been told to listen for the bell, and charge.

She glanced at the rota, and her heart sank. Next up was the vicar.

*

The stained glass might be church-like, but the behaviour in the Chandos's wood-panelled bar was anything but. Crammed in like sardines, Wanda and Peggy gave up hope of clean glasses, and grabbed a departing man's beaker and held it up to be filled.

A GI, corn-fed and all of eighteen, told Wanda she was the prettiest girl in the world and kissed her on surprised lips.

'That's what the Yanks are like!' grinned Peggy.

The pub, the street, the city was a dreamscape, floating outside of time, with no rules.

Magicked out of the pub, Wanda and Peggy were two motes of dust, caught up in a conga around Trafalgar Square.

Breathless, Peggy swung away from the conga line and looked up at the impassive face of a stone lion, who had witnessed many such celebrations. Peggy had lost her purse, but couldn't seem to care. Nobody let them pay for anything anyway.

Hang on! I've lost Wanda as well.

'Thought I'd be the first!' Grayson rang the doctor's doorbell at just gone eight.

'Heavens, no!' shouted Nance over the blaring gramophone. There were people on the stairs, people in the hallway, people in the back garden. 'Take a glass of this dreadful punch.' She steered him towards Max, with instructions that they were both to talk to the pretty girls who dotted the house like pot plants.

The front door blew open and Nance went to close it,

staring briefly out at the village. Tudor slept in his cot above their heads, and Nance imagined for a stark moment what Pamela must be going through at Lower Loxley. *Tomorrow,* she thought, being firm with herself, *the prophecy will be revealed as a silly trick.*

She closed the door with a steady hand. No malevolent breeze would sneak through Holmleigh on this special night.

The sun had gone down, and Wanda and Peggy were reunited, the gods moving them like chess pieces across the heaving board of Central London. Sharing a bag of chips on a bomb-damaged wall, they saw curtains defiantly left open in flats and houses.

'I've never eaten chips out of a newspaper before,' said Wanda, cheeks bulging like a hamster. 'It does something extraordinary to the taste!'

'Not enough vinegar.' Peggy was a chip connoisseur. She crumpled the greasy paper into a ball and threw it on the bonfire, one of many on street corners. 'My folks live that-a-way. I could walk home from here!'

'Home?' Wanda and Peggy shared a thought as they warmed their hands.

Where was home these days?

The sun went down in Ambridge, too, reminding the giddy partygoers that it was still May, that the evening could not be trusted to carry on the good work of the sunny day, and that cardigans must be pulled on.

'Brrr!' Morgan pulled the glass doors shut on the garden as guests retreated into the house. The rug had been pulled up; Susan and Joe Grundy were jitterbugging to Glenn Miller.

Cliff and Lorna sat out the dancing; Lorna knew better than to try and coax her self-conscious husband onto the floor.

'You all right?' Cliff nudged her arm. 'You're a bit . . .' He smiled. 'You're faraway, love.'

'Just thinking,' said Lorna.

Cliff understood. Yet he could not have guessed what she was thinking about.

She thought about Tudor. About Alf. Jennifer. All the babies blooming like flowers in the village.

Will I ever be a mother?

Lorna had assumed she would never be loved.

Cliff had disproved that; she turned to face a different conviction. She neither truly wanted nor could have children. It hadn't mattered when it was theoretical, but now she was a wife. The next logical step, according to Ambridge, was motherhood. Yet they had never had so much as a false alarm.

Morgan pulled the curtains, but not before he saw the delphiniums outside shiver.

A breeze nipped through the village like an imp. It rattled a flowerpot outside Woodbine Cottage, and kissed the side of Ruby's face as she left The Bull. She put a hand to the spot, repulsed, as if something malignant had firmed up and reached out of the night.

The imp would not rest until its work was done. Until midnight. Activated long ago, it would find revenge on this historic night. Sprightly, it leapt over garden walls, and sprinted across the Green, north-east to Lower Loxley.

There was a changing of the guard in Gerald's room.

Frank, cap in hand, cowed by the grand surroundings, brought up a bright-eyed flier.

Pamela welcomed them with good cheese and stilted conversation. Gerald dozed.

The breeze rattled the windowpane; a sudden memory of the portrait in the attic assailed Pamela. She imagined Mother Molly's eyes, bright and sour in the gloom.

'Aw, no *stay*, girls!' pleaded the GI, but Wanda and Peggy had already jumped down from the jeep.

They were back in Trafalgar Square, back at the party that just might go on forever.

'My feet hurt.' Peggy took off a shoe and rubbed her sole.

'Let's cool them down.' Wanda went first, dangling her feet in the water of the fountains.

A soldier said, 'Bet you daren't go in up to your knees!'

Wanda had never met a dare she didn't like; tucking her skirt into her knickers she waded in, pulling Peggy by the hand.

'Not that cold when you get used to it!' Peggy tugged the soldier in after them and he fell full length.

They laughed until they thought they would be sick.

This was freedom.

This was that longed-for 'after the war' and it was good.

'Can't stop thinking about Frances Bissett.' Gerald shut his eyes at the ache in his busted leg.

'Oh now, well, I daresay yes um . . .' Frank wished Pamela would come back from the bathroom; he was not engineered for such conversation.

The young flier hiccupped.

'Keep thinking of something my old instructor said. What if Frances was on the earlier train and I'm headed to the same destination?'

'Such thoughts', said Pamela, returning, 'are unhelpful, darling.'

'I wish Father was here.'

'Do you?' The surprise in Pamela's voice could not be contained.

Gerald turned, laying face down in his pillows. He was slowly drowning, his life passing in front of him. There was so little of it, and much of it reflected badly on him. All that Shakespeare and still Julia was not pregnant; nothing stood between him and Mother Molly.

His voice muffled, he said, 'If I get through this, I'll be steady and reliable and I won't drink and I'll go to church every Sunday.'

I don't care if you massacre half of Borsetshire, thought Pamela, *so long as you're here to see tomorrow morning.*

*

Vic Horrobin woke from a bad dream; all his dreams were bad these days. He had crossed a line and would pay for the rest of his life. He would always be separate from other people. It was why he slept in the damp corner of a roofless barn.

The breeze pushed at his hair and he burrowed down into the sleeping bag. He knew what that imp was capable of; Ambridge had no idea what was coming for it.

Hildy's so naive.

His outcast status was catnip to his girlfriend; she was too dim or too excited to notice how constrained and ugly his life was.

How bloody scared I am!

Vic pulled the sleeping bag over his head, as if such a pathetic gesture could thwart the imp.

With enough pain to startle a tear out of him, Vic missed his mother.

At Broom Corner the breeze travelled up Connie's spine as she emptied the fireplace ashes. She jumped, turning, thinking for a moment her Vic was back.

'Don't you dare!'

The soldier did dare. Peggy was dunked in the fountain, and so was Wanda, the pair of them rising up like seals.

Cheers from the crowd redoubled when Peggy kicked her Tommy in the behind. He was gallant enough to help them out, and the girls stood, dripping, half hysterical.

*

Two sherries were Mrs Endicott's limit; she'd had four.

'Won't it be relaxing just to think about Ambridge again?' she said, wet-eyed, to Nance as her hostess shepherded her to a quiet corner, away from the dancing and away from the decanter. 'Because Ambridge *is* the whole world to me.'

Nance settled her down with a blanket over her knees, and imagined a different Mrs E, sharing The Cherries with a glittering star of the stage.

The coat the American gave them was so huge both Wanda and Peggy could fit in it. He waved away their thanks – 'Couldn't see you freeze, gals!' – and wandered tipsily away down Charing Cross Road.

Blown with the crowd into Bloomsbury, teeth chattering and hair dripping, the women pushed their way to a bonfire.

'Let's dry off.' Wanda sat far too close to the fire, just as Mother Cat did by Brookfield's stove. 'And then we'll get home.'

'How?' Peggy bared her wet legs.

Wanda had no answer, and they laughed again.

They would be all right. The good guys had won and anything was possible.

With only one hour left of the eighth of May, the breeze eddied over the bridge.

Hate had built for decades; the imp could wait and relish the fear that leaked from Lower Loxley for sixty more minutes.

Then, as the grandfather clock in the great hall struck midnight, its life's work would be done.

Gerald missed the last change of sentry; tension could be dull, and he had given in to sleep.

A bird was caged in Pamela's chest, threatening to burst through her ribs as she walked the room like a duchess visiting the stalls of a county fair. She wondered if Cad was sober enough to be any use, and felt grateful for doughty Dodgy, who sat in a gilt chair in the middle of the room, pistol out, whisky in hand, emanating derring-do determination.

If Pamela was any other woman, she would have kissed the back of his balding head as she passed, but she was Pamela, and she carried on with her leisurely, frantic circuit.

Like sirens, Wanda and Peggy fanned out their hair to dry by the bonfire.

'We're on the forecourt of the British Museum!' realised Wanda, as the Greek revival colonnade grew and shrank in the flicker of the flames.

'You are indeed.' A man leaned down with a tray of scones and tea. He was a parody of academia, with massive eyes behind his glasses and a book stuffed in the pocket of his jacket. He was Freddy, he told them, a curator. 'But tonight I'm curating scones.'

Peggy's breasts were heavy with milk. It was time to get back to the farm, to her daughter's hungry mouth. She was in her beloved London, but her tired feet yearned for the uneven terrain of the lane that led to Brookfield.

But first she would finish her scone.

'Here,' she said to their bookish benefactor. 'You probably know our pal, Grayson Lemmon. He's one of your lot at the museum.'

Minko nosed through the bedroom door.

Gerald woke up and scrabbled for the bell.

They all laughed. It had a ghoulish quality.

'Half eleven,' said Cad. He was drinking from a brandy bottle.

'Thirty minutes to go,' said Dodgy. His revolver was cocked.

'Grayson? You mean the cleaner?'

'No, silly.' Wanda pushed Freddy playfully. 'Grayson Lemmon, he researches folklore. Oversaw the relocation of the museum treasures to Aberystwyth.'

'I don't think he did,' scoffed Freddy. He drew a little nearer. Perhaps, on this momentous night, he might get to kiss a member of the opposite sex at last. 'Only Grayson I know is a cleaner who didn't turn up for his shift one day, and then we discovered a packet of priceless old parchment was missing. Terrible stink, there was.'

Wanda frowned, trying to square this with her friend back in Ambridge. 'He has . . .' She tapped her forehead.

'Big birthmark, yes, that's the chap!'

Wanda was jostled by yet another conga line. She almost didn't hear Freddy say, 'He's not Grayson *Lemmon*, though. His surname was Gilpin.'

'Let's make a move, eh?' Peggy got to her feet. She hadn't been listening, and didn't notice Wanda's abrupt change of mood.

'Gilpin?' Wanda stood too, and dragged Freddy up with her. 'Take me inside. Now.'

'Golly.' Freddy's glasses fell off. He ran across the forecourt with his new ladyfriend.

'Hurry,' she chided as they crossed the stone floor. They scurried upstairs, along corridors, into the innards of the stately establishment.

'What, if you don't mind me asking, is happening?' Freddy had heard that women could be mercurial, but this one was positively frightening.

'And he has both legs, this Grayson Gilpin?' Wanda badgered Freddy as he fumbled with the keys to his office.

'That's the sort of detail one notices, yes, he has two legs!' They fell through the door and Freddy pointed to the phone on his desk. 'There, use that.'

Wanda grabbed his wrist so hard he exclaimed. His watch told her it was eleven forty-five.

Collecting herself for a moment – *Where would he be right now?* – she picked up the weighty Bakelite receiver and asked the operator for Morgan Seed, GP, Ambridge, Borsetshire.

When Morgan answered, Wanda could hear 'Moonlight

Serenade' and the bird-like babble of her neighbours, all of them up far too late and skittish.

'You want Max, my dear? You've just missed him! Pamela called to say Dodgy had shot a hole in the floorboards, so Max went to Lower Loxley to take over. Oh Lord, it's almost midnight. I do hope everything's all right.'

'I'll call him there.'

As the receiver went down, Wanda heard a name that made her put it back to her ear. 'What? Grayson what?'

'I said, Grayson trotted after him, to back him up. A true chum!'

Wanda slammed down the phone and glared at it.

Freddy began, 'May I just ask—'

'No!' snapped Wanda, and grabbed the receiver again, asking this time for Lower Loxley.

The breeze played about Grayson's unkempt hair as he moved through the dark, sure, certain, at one with the imp he had nurtured since childhood. He thought with pleasure of the score he was about to settle, once and for all.

'I can't find anywhere by that name.' The operator was cool. 'Are you sure of the address, caller?'

'For pity's sake yes!' Wanda wanted to throw the small desk clock out through the window. Six minutes, it told her, pitilessly. Six minutes to go. 'Lower Loxley, Borsetshire.'

'Ah! I misheard. I looked for Lower Boxley. Bear with, caller.'

*

The telephone in the great hall rang, its tinny report competing with the sing-song in the drawing room.

Pamela, her ears acute, heard it. *Let someone else answer it*, she thought. She forced herself to take a seat, envying Julia's composure. Her daughter-in-law watched the door with the focus of a sniper. They both knew a gun would not stop whatever might come through that door.

Cad's forehead had begun to sweat. His left leg, Pamela noticed, shook. The brandy bottle lay empty on the rug.

Shamefaced, Dodgy had retired to a small stool by the wardrobe. He opened his mouth to speak, but said nothing. All were beyond small talk, and the ticking of the clock sounded like anvils being struck.

The massive main door beneath them slammed shut.

'That'll be Max,' said Gerald, with relief.

Pamela felt only a chill. As if the evil she had not allowed herself to quite believe in had entered the house.

The phone stopped ringing.

In the office, far away, Wanda gabbled, 'Oh, it's you, Max, it's you!'

'Wanda?' said the small voice in her ear.

She heard the delight, the inappropriate joy. 'Max, concentrate! The prophecy's not about Gerald, it's about *you*. *Lifts gin to lip*, it's an anagram, he's crazy, he has the same last name as you!'

Clearly just glad to hear her voice, Max laughed. 'Slow down. Are you near? Can I come and get you?'

'For pity's sake, listen. Grayson is Mother Molly!' It was the best précis she could summon up. 'He's a Gilpin!'

'What?' He was still laughing. 'Grayson is a Gilpin? Have you been on the wompo? He's just walked in, in fact. Hey, Grayson, are you a secret Gilpin, old man?'

Wanda heard Max's voice recede as he turned away to say, 'Good Lord, are you quite well?'

A crack then, the sound of the phone falling and the receiver swinging against wainscoting.

'Max, I love you!' Wanda strained to hear. A scuffle, the flat bland sound of a smack. A clatter then, like furniture breaking. And a cry of triumph.

But whose?

'Max!' She screamed it now. 'Please,' she begged him, or God, or whoever might be listening.

The great old bell of St Stephen's Church tolled, loud and unashamed, for the first time in six years.

Tears streaming down his face, the vicar pulled hard on the rope. He was happy, and he did not know why, or how. Since Frances went, he had blundered along, constantly catching his strange reflection in a fairground mirror, but now he trusted his saviour to rifle through the ragbag of his soul and bring him back to life.

'Midnight!' shrieked the bell. 'Midnight!'

*

'Midnight!' Julia sagged, her bones turned to liquid. 'It's over!' She kissed a stupefied Gerald as the bells spoke to them across the fields.

Light-headed, Pamela shook herself, like Minko after a bath. Dashing out, she had no notion of where she was headed. It was enough to be free of that prison, and already relishing how they would tell Alec of their folly.

She halted on the landing.

That prickle again. That certainty of wrongness. She peered over the balustrade at the disturbance in the great hall.

It was dark down there. She saw a shape, or was it two? It merged and came apart, like lovers, but this was not love. One man was throttling another.

'Hey! You there!' Thought was deed with Pamela; no time to summon the chaps. Fleet of foot down the stairs, she almost tripped over a strange metal tube on the checkerboard floor of the great hall.

She picked it up. She swung it.

The shape toppled, and revealed itself as Grayson, eyes wide, his hands to his bleeding head and no longer around Max's neck.

Max got to his feet, coughing, and other bodies appeared, in RAF blue, to tackle Grayson to the floor.

Pamela held the heavy tube out in front of her. 'What the hell did I hit him with?'

'His leg,' managed Max.

*

Wanda couldn't interpret the uproar. She cried and did not move and she regretted the last few months with a fervour that made her tremble.

Freddy watched and wondered and was about to suggest a glass of water – he had seen this done in movies – when her name floated out of the receiver.

'Wanda! You there?'

'You're alive!' The universe tilted again. 'Did he . . .'

'Yes, he did. Heaven knows what this is about but Grayson's tied to a chair now and Gerald's safe and I have a sore throat but never mind all that.'

'Rather a lot of "all that"!'

'I heard you, you know. I love you too. Come back, darling.'

'I'm on my way.'

Freddy got his kiss, albeit on the forehead, and Wanda found Peggy among the crowds, delirious with emotion at the sound of Big Ben chiming the end of the war.

PC Jenkins had an aunt.

This aunt loved to gossip.

This aunt was a customer at the store, and this aunt found herself in great demand when she popped in for some Trex two days after Grayson's arrest. Happy to share what she knew, her rapt audience disseminated her police station snippets far and wide.

'Grayson has both legs, the full set!' Susan Grundy told Frank.

Meanwhile, Magsy described to Mrs Endicott how 'the bounder fashioned a tin sleeve to wear over his leg, to explain why he wasn't called up to fight'.

Mrs Endicott passed this onto Nance, adding, 'He's a deserter, my dear, to add to his other crimes.'

One of these crimes was murder. It was Valerie Micklewood who sat the vicar down and said levelly, 'There was a phone call while you were out. The police. Seems that Grayson's implicated in Frances's death. They're still working out the whys and wherefores but . . .'

The vicar's homily was short that Sunday, giving his flock all the more time to discuss the only real topic on everyone's lips as they lingered in the churchyard. Grayson had usurped even the new peace as Ambridge's latest preoccupation.

Anger and incredulity powered every conversation. The village had taken Grayson to their hearts. They had welcomed a dotty fellow with a naive zeal, but had harboured a callous murderer who trampled over them to gain . . . what? There were so many pieces of the puzzle missing. The villain was no longer Mother Molly – it was one they had adopted as their own.

'He's a *Gilpin*? Related to Max?' Frank pulled in his chin. 'But we know all the Gilpins. They're a big Borsetshire family. They're quality.'

'His intention', drawled Pamela, 'was to kill *Max*, not my Gerald. Mother Molly was a smokescreen. He's no more an academic than my Minko.'

Minko, investigating a dirty handkerchief on the gravel path, was not insulted.

'What's he got against Max?' Phillip, on the edge of the conversation, was ignored, as was the rule with children.

Pamela went on. 'Max was in the great hall, on his way to Gerald's room. The telephone rang, he heard Wanda on the other end, and turned from his conversation to see Grayson creeping in. Max greeted him cheerfully, then saw the knife. Well, if a chap has only one arm, you can bet that arm is *strong*! Max lifted the phone receiver and struck the man we knew as Grayson Lemmon, and the two struggled. No doubt about who was the stronger – Grayson didn't stand a chance.'

Nobody could shed light on Grayson's motives – PC Jenkins' aunt had been gagged by her embarrassed nephew – but all knew that another man was implicated in the plot.

Cliff stood, dumbstruck, as Dan Archer broke the news. 'They're saying your Vic's involved.'

'Not with . . . Frances?' Cliff felt dizzy.

'Wish I could say, lad.' Dan wished Doris was at his side, to say the right thing, to comfort this suffering boy. 'Let's hope not, eh?'

Whitey White sauntered up, enjoying himself, as if Frances was a character in a *film noir* and not a real person. 'Your brother's all over this, matey! No place for him to hide now – they'll find him soon enough and then it's a date with the gallows.'

'Shush, you fool,' said Dan, and turned back to Cliff, but he had gone.

*

Still in her Sunday best, Peggy watered her carrots. Out of the corner of her eye she saw a couple turn into the farmyard, so closely entwined as to look like one person, and she scurried indoors.

Joining Christine at the kitchen window, Peggy gawked with her at Wanda and Max, taking a turn about the pump as if they were in a Parisian park.

'D'you suppose Wanda'll marry him instead of Christopher?' Christine was yanked away by her mother before Peggy could answer.

'None of your business!' said Doris. 'Give them some privacy, you nosey pair.'

She took a moment to watch them, however, and knew old double-barrelled Christopher didn't stand a chance now that Max had finally stepped up. *Never liked him,* thought Doris about the blameless young man miles away in Bath who was about to receive his returned diamond ring by registered mail.

Max and Wanda had much to say, but they said hardly anything. She touched the bruise on his face, and pouted at the healing cut on his brow. He was strong again, this shredded man, and she knew she could rely on him.

They did not need to say they loved each other. They did need to talk about his wife. But they did need to talk about Walter Gabriel.

'Let me get this right.' Max pieced the tale together. 'You gave Dan a written ultimatum to hand to *me,* but he gave it to Walter Gabriel who somehow lost it? Bloody Walter!'

Christine had sneaked back to the window. 'Ooh, *kissing*,' she swooned.

'Not now, Valerie.'

The vicar closed his study door to his housekeeper, and tore off his dog collar – sometimes it felt like a noose – battling his hate for Grayson whatever-his-name.

Vicars' wives should die genteel deaths. They should not be violently despatched.

It's as if she died twice, thought Henry. Once on the riverbank and now, again, when she was revealed as a victim of madness.

He put his head in his hands and wished he felt more grief for his waspish wife.

A detective from Birmingham was expected.

PC Jenkins' instructions were clear. He could engage the prisoner in conversation while they awaited the Brummie big shot, but he must not, under any circumstances, attempt an interrogation.

There was no need; Grayson was primed to go off like that grenade Evie unwittingly threw at 15th Battalion.

'Nice cell,' he said.

'Well, we're not used to accommodating, like, *proper* criminals,' said Jenkins. They sat in the police station back parlour, a comfortable wallpapered room. No hard benches here; a needlepoint cushion supported Grayson's back. 'Can't get used to you having two legs!'

Grayson attempted to cover his birthmark with his fringe, but the handcuffs made that tricky. His mannerisms, his speech patterns, even the look in his eye were all subtly different. This was the real Grayson, and he was an unsettling man. 'You might want to take notes,' he said.

'Eh?' Jenkins put down his Horlicks.

'One simple fact explains everything. Max Gilpin is my brother.'

Gerald shook the bell by his bed; now that he was out of danger, the staff had come to dread its silvery sound. 'I want more port!'

'You've had enough,' said Julia, from the window.

'Golly, someone's in a mood.' His tearful promises to the Almighty forgotten, Gerald was his old, gluttonous self again. 'You're not . . . are you?' He pointed at his wife's flat stomach.

'No, silly.' Thanks to her trusty diaphragm, Julia's figure was safe for a while, but it was the cause of a new problem. *That wretched Hildegard thinks I'm made of money.* She had already pawned one of the Pargetter brooches to feed the maid's demands.

'No Shakespeare today?' Pamela entered, wheezing dog at her heels.

'Maybe later,' said Gerald, sly.

'I'm not in the mood', said Julia tartly, 'for the bard,' and left them to one another.

Pamela lit a cigarette. She would never tell Gerald how fearful she had been; she may not even share it with Alec.

Her heart was a bank vault; although full, it was locked and alarmed.

'Mother.' Gerald sounded shy. 'You've ... I've ... dash it, you've been a brick!'

'Foolish boy,' she said.

'Max and I are twins,' Grayson went on.

Jenkins' Horlicks grew cold on its doily.

'My – *our* – mother was Imelda Pickering, housekeeper to the Gilpins, the Dorset faction, just outside Stalbridge. My father died before we came along, and Mother couldn't cope.' Grayson's lip pulled up at one corner. 'Which is another way of saying she was a slatternly baggage.'

'Ooh here now.' Murder was one thing, insulting one's mum quite another.

'Her employers, the Gilpins, they'd given up on having children. Mother offered them one of hers, like we were slices of pie. Obviously, they chose the *unmarked* one, the *perfect* one, the one with no stain on its forehead. Money changed hands, the Gilpins had an heir, and Mother was guaranteed a job for life.'

Jenkins knew he should put a cork in Grayson, tell him to save it for the detective, but he was loathe to relinquish a front row seat to such a confession.

'She drank, Mother. Neglected the house. And *me,* but that didn't matter so much. The Gilpins let her go. Her wages still arrived every month, but they kept their distance from the disaster of our daily life.' Grayson grinned at a sudden memory. 'Old Blanche Gilpin, your neighbour, she was ... sympathetic isn't quite the word. She acknowledged me, put it that way. Used to give me a wink. It was Blanche who told me lurid tales about Mother Molly.'

Growing up twisted, like a poisoned shrub, Grayson knew his imperfection had cheated him out of a golden life. Instead of the doting Gilpins, who sent his brother to Eton and bought him a pony, Grayson was dragged up in two squalid rooms by a bitter woman who took little notice of him, preferring to spend her afternoons with 'gentleman callers'.

'Made me laugh,' said Grayson, 'watching you villagers hero-worship my twin brother as the quintessential English gent. He's made of the same raw material as me! Wait 'til you hear how he lost his arm, Jenkins.'

'Don't you go slandering Max Gilpin.' Jenkins was severe.

'Heaven forbid!' Grayson drew up his cuffed hands as if holding a handbag. 'Max may be an accomplished horseman, a brave pilot, etcetera etcetera, but I have skills too: I'm an accomplished liar.' The young Grayson slid from scam to scam, living a liminal life; the war proved to be a jamboree. 'I've been French, I've been Italian, I've left various ladies' hearts broken and their purses empty. I receive not one but two pensions from the War Office. You should see my collection of ID papers.'

Jenkins snorted. 'Nothing to be proud of. You should be defending your country.'

'From what? I'd scam the Nazis too, if they took over. I made those prophecies with parchment I nicked from the

British Museum. One of the toffs at the museum knew Max – they're all connected, these swells, now *that's* a scam, Jenkins! – and he gave me the push I needed to take revenge. I heard him say how glad he was that "good old Gilpin" was going to convalesce in Ambridge. Amazing the stuff you hear when you clean rooms; they take no notice of you. When I told Blanche Gilpin I had an inclination to see Ambridge, she offered me her cottage.'

'Miss Blanche'll be horrified when she hears what you've done.'

'Will she? Your Miss Blanche told me to shake the village up a bit.'

'Where does Vic fit into all this?'

'Ah, the fragrant Master Horrobin. He simply fell into my lap.'

Pamela read the letter twice. Stood up. Sat down.

Why am I so excited?

She had kicked against this for months; now it was happening and it was all her doing. Alec would be jubilant. He would be proud of her. Pamela squealed, girlish, quite unlike herself. From the door, Hildegard said, 'You feeling all right, ma'am?'

That girl is always in the wrong place at the wrong time. 'Go and rouse Miss Julia, would you? She missed breakfast.'

'She's probably feeling a bit off.' Hildegard smiled at this, as if she knew why.

'Once again, Hildegard, you don't need to give an

opinion – you simply need to do as you're asked.' In the mirror, Pamela saw the little pink tongue Hildegard poked at her as she left, but she was too happy to reprimand her.

'Vic's plan for evading the military police was predictably stupid.' Grayson leaned back and recalled his protegé.

'Them Horrobins is all bent,' said Jenkins.

'He doubled back off the bus, and made for the woods. Stan was bringing him food there. No doubt he'd have frozen to death if I hadn't discovered him while I was searching for the grotto. I know a useful idiot when I see one, so I brought him back to Woodbine Cottage as soon as darkness fell.'

'You never hid him in your house all this time?' The bravado astounded Jenkins.

'The fool'd get pissed on Blanche's booze, and stumble about. Jumped me once, marked my face. Had to explain that away to Ruby, she's a sharp one. Said I slipped in the bathroom. Having Vic around was like keeping a half-witted dangerous animal in the house. He'd leave the curtains open and get me into trouble with the vicar for breaking blackout. I let slip to Vic that the army executes deserters.'

'That's not true!'

'True. Not true. Does it matter? It meant Vic was trapped in Woodbine with me. It meant I made the difference between life and death.'

'So he did whatever you told him,' said Jenkins.

'Exactly.'

*

The end stool at The Bull's bar welcomed Walter's bottom with its usual creak.

'So all them prophecies', Walter said as he eyed his tankard filling, 'was made up?'

'Nowt to do with Mother Molly. All poppycock,' said Bob.

'So how come your thatch caught fire on the right date?'

'God knows.'

Not only God knew; Jenkins knew, with Grayson still boasting about his deeds.

'The first prophecy, about the Pargetters' dog dying, was real, a historical fact. Clever little Lorna thought *she* found the letter saying the dog died on Christmas Day, but I found it first, and put it back where she was sure to come across it. Odd . . .' Grayson came to a stop.

'What's odd?'

'When we worked out the date from the codeword Mother Molly put on the prophecy, it was real. She truly foresaw the dog's death.'

Jenkins looked around him, as if Mother Molly might be in the corner of the warm room.

'It was a jape working out the riddles. I used my own blood to write them on the stolen parchment.'

'Yuk,' said Jenkins. 'What about the little leather pouches the prophecies were found in?'

'It was the same pouch every time, the one kept under glass in Lower Loxley's library. Nobody thought to check on it.' Grayson leaned forward, as if imparting vital information, and the handcuffs jangled. 'People *want* to believe what you tell 'em, PC Jenkins. You all sleepwalk through life. I'm wide awake at all times.'

He trotted helpfully through the prophecies.

'The lamb? I sent Vic out to steal it. He did all my dirty work, shimmying up Max's drainpipe to pop the creature into Max's bed. Of course, Vic thought he and I were colleagues, that I was shielding him in return for his . . . let's call them skills. Like I say, another sleepwalker.'

Jenkins never thought he would feel sorry for Vic Horrobin.

'Everything changed when the third prophecy went wrong. Frances – *awful* woman – wasn't supposed to die. The plan was perfect. Vic kidnapped that dog, Hannibal, the night before. We muzzled it and kept it indoors at Woodbine. Then, at twilight, Vic crept back to the vicarage garden, and put the dog in the vicar's rowing boat. Had to tether him to the seat. Vic took off the muzzle and swam to the opposite shore, hanging onto the rope so the yappy little swine wouldn't float off. Frances hears the yapping, dashes out, as planned. She was supposed to leap into the water – a champion swimmer, allegedly – and rescue the stupid hound. The prophecy would be fulfilled just by luring her into the water. But no, the silly woman had to slip in the mud and career into the vicar's beehives. Vic's face must've been a picture watching her get stung over and over, flailing about. When he saw her slip, unconscious, into the water, he panicked and came crying to me.'

'I knew Mrs Bissett,' said Jenkins. 'She didn't deserve the end you gave her.'

'Wasn't my doing, Mr Plod, it was the lovely Vic. I made sure to sound horrified, told him he was now a murderer. He was more in my thrall than ever.'

'It was more like manslaughter.'

'Vic wasn't to know that. Probably thought he'd be shot for deserting *and* hanged for murder. It was easy to cajole him into creeping into The Bull for prophecy number four. It's next door to Woodbine; he just jumped the fence and scuttled through the yard. He set a small fire in the roof, then buggered off. The little French girl's confession made me snigger – the fire was nothing to do with her candle. She told people Mother Molly woke her up, but of course that was Vic, acting against my orders. Even a goon like him has his limits, it would seem, and he didn't want the girls to burn. Couldn't save the thatch though!'

'That pub means a lot to this village.'

'This village, Jenkins, isn't the centre of the universe.'

'Oh yes, it is,' said Jenkins. He leaned forward. He was intrigued. 'Why'd you run in with the hose when we was all fighting the fire at The Bull? That was heroic. You risked your life.'

With a smile, Grayson said, 'Do you still expect human beings to make *sense*?'

On days like this, Doris could almost feel the earth working beneath her feet. She swayed, apron on, Jennifer in her arms, a breeze tickling her hair, and looked out over the farm.

It was alive, and it was *good*.

'And it's free,' she whispered to the baby. 'This is what peace feels like, little one.'

Jenkins said, 'All of those prophecies, all that death and destruction, it was all leading up to the last one, wasn't it?'

Grayson nodded like a proud schoolteacher congratulating his student.

Emboldened, Jenkins said, 'You misdirected us, like a magician with a card trick. The prophecy talked about "the end of the noble line", but it was the Gilpin line, not the Pargetters. Max is the last male, in't he? And him being "damaged" was about Max's depressions, or whatever you call them.'

'Correct. You really are coming along nicely.'

'But we all thought you meant Gerald, 'cos his leg was busted. How the hell did you know that was going to happen?'

'I didn't! I meant damaged in a metaphorical sense; all these aristos are more or less messed up. Mother Molly stepped in with the plane crash, and all of a sudden Gerald was literally *damaged*. History co-operated as well; I wasn't to know May eighth would be VE Day, but that was a delicious detail. Typical of Vic to ruin it all!'

The plan was straightforward enough.

'Max and I were scheduled to guard Gerald for the last hour of the day. I would sneak Vic in through the back way, and secrete him in a cabinet just outside Gerald's bedroom. Then, just before the witching hour, I'd claim to hear a noise outside, and leave the room. I'd let Vic out of the cupboard, fall as if I'd been struck, and Vic would race into the room like a Rottweiler. Max, being a gallant Englishman, would of course spring to Gerald's defence.'

'And?' Jenkins pulled a face.

'And Vic would stab him. Once, twice, whatever. Enough to end my brother once and for all.'

'Dear God.' Jenkins wished the detective would turn up and take over.

'Vic would rush out to the landing and black my eye, so it would look as if I tried to stop him, when actually I'd escort him safely off the premises. Who'd expect a bookworm prof like me to overpower a bullyboy like Vic Horrobin?'

'I bet you can hold your own.' This was not a compliment.

'I've been street-fighting since I was in my nappy, copper. Once Vic had got away, I'd give a fake description of the assailant to, well, you lot.' Grayson's smile was inward, insular. 'Or that's what I told Vic. Of course, I planned to kill him with the knife.'

'So Vic couldn't squeal and you'd be the hero who fought Max's murderer.'

'They really are hiring brighter young men in the police force these days.'

'So what went wrong?'

'The Lower Loxley rota was changed, meaning I wouldn't be there to let in my trusty henchman. Furthermore, my trusty henchman went AWOL for the second time. He'd been creeping out some evenings, coming back reeking of perfume; some woman had her hooks in him. So I had to think quickly. I decided I'd suggest to Max that we pop over at midnight to check up on Gerald. As luck would have it, Max was summoned and all I had to do was follow him.'

'And kill him. How were you going to explain that?'

'Very easily. I'd say there was an odd glint in Max's eye. He'd been unstable since that fool of a girl, Wanda, turned him down. I worried he'd flip. Luckily, there's evidence of mental fragility in his RAF record. I'd say I opened the door to find he'd buckled under pressure and slit poor dear Gerald's throat. Oh, don't look at me like that, Jenkins! You're hurting my feelings. I planned to weep as I explained how I grabbed the knife and fought him and – oopsadaisy! – stabbed him to death.'

'We'd never believe that.'

'Maybe not, but would you have enough to charge me? Lord, how sweet the anticipation felt. Even that dull party at the doctor's couldn't spoil it. I was a bird, a spirit, flying above you all. Huge. Fearless. Hate is excellent fuel; just ask Herr Hitler.'

'I would, but he's dead.' Pleased with his retort, Jenkins made a mental note to tell his auntie later.

'When I broke into Lower Loxley and heard Max on the phone, I knew the game was up. All that mattered then was snuffing him out, getting my revenge, even if I ended up in prison. So I threw off my tin leg and pounced.'

'And Max whupped you good and proper.'

'My one mistake was underestimating my twin. The RAF got him all wrong: he's made of iron. So here I am, a giant held down by your Liliputian ropes.'

Jenkins didn't know where Liliput was – a suburb of Birmingham, perhaps? – but he didn't ask about it, as an outbreak of back-slapping in the hall announced his superior. He leapt up. 'You'll have to say this all over again.'

'Happy to.' Grayson sat back, relaxed, as if welcoming a curate to afternoon tea. 'When you cluck about this to your village chums, do be sure to include one last detail. Their precious Max Gilpin, the archetypal Englishman with an upper lip so stiff you can balance your Pimms on it, is half German. Our dear father was *not* Mr Lemmon, our mother's husband. We are the result of one steamy night with a certain Gerd Jäger, from Bonn.'

SUMMER

1945

A resolution to avoid an evil is seldom
framed till the evil is so far advanced
as to make avoidance impossible.

THOMAS HARDY
Far from the Madding Crowd

June

Summer, lush and scented, rewarded the village for making it through an endless winter and a drawn-out war. Just as the fat, blowsy roses and the wild chamomile and fat hen returned, so did the chores. Calves were de-horned, sheep were shorn, and horses dragged tedding machines up and down drowsy fields.

A Bentley, glossy green with a camel-coloured roof, sped over the bridge. Alec's pride and joy, it had spent the war in a stable, but now it was buffed up and hitting its stride on the road to London.

I used to make this drive a few times a month. Putting her foot down, Pamela ignored the tedious, goody-goody speedometer.

'Someone's in a hurry,' commented Agnes, as the green blur passed the shop.

'Might be Vic,' laughed Ruby, loading Agnes's string bag with extra-special care, the care one gives to a family member, although the other customers simply saw Ruby doing her job, and knew nothing of their connection.

'He's long gone.' Hildegard slapped down coins to pay for her cigarettes.

'Hmm,' said Agnes. 'What would you know about it?'

'Me?' Hildegard's eyes opened wide and innocent. 'Nothing, missus. Just saying.'

'Well, *don't*.'

By Euston Station, Pamela parked the car and rolled down the window to take in the forgotten perfume of the filthy capital. It was noisy and noisome and she adored it. No horses and carts here; she had been cut up by a black taxi and thoroughly enjoyed the experience.

Adjusting her hat in the rear-view mirrow, Pamela wondered where Alec would be when he read the letter she posted a week ago.

Alec,

I know we prefer to be ironic and to understate, but for once let me tell you plainly how desperately proud I am of you, and how passionately I long to see your face, and how very very lucky I am to be married to Major Alec Pargetter. I don't know where you are, but something tells me you are already on your way back to me.

'Sir!'

Alec, about to open the envelope from home, turned. 'Are you for me?'

The blunt-faced squib of a lieutenant said 'Yessir!' and held the door of a jeep idling outside the half-a-house that served as post office.

Alec tucked the letter into his pocket, to read on the way home.

Her business done, Pamela popped into Maison Bertaux on Greek Street, emerging with a cake box tied in ribbon. She was jittery, drunk on her own daring. This must be how it felt to leap from a trapeze. *I've done the right thing,* she reassured herself, heels flying over cracked paving slabs to Charing Cross Road where she had parked the car.

There it was, in the distance. Her own words, written to Alec, came back to her, and she imagined his dark eyebrows riding up his forehead when he read them.

After all, what is reputation if not people seeing one do the decent thing? We have the privilege and the means to do good, and maybe society's perception of respectability will evolve if we lead the way.

Truth matters, my darling, and the truth is that Caroline is your daughter. And here is another truth; I have found her. After extensive correspondence, her Irish relatives have consented to send her to England. I promised an affectionate home where her mother's name will be respected. I promised not just status but love. The remorse I feel about my initial reaction is a deep scar. Scales have fallen from my eyes.

Caroline is yours, Alec, and I will be the fondest stepmama a girl ever had.

Pamela placed the cake box reverently on the Bentley's back seat, then climbed in and turned the ignition key. 'All set?' she asked the big-eyed child in the passenger seat.

'Yes.' Caroline held her small suitcase possessively on her lap. She had said little since Pamela met her at Euston. She had been through a lot for a seven-year-old.

July

'You keep me like a pet.'

'Nah, a dog'd be less trouble.' Hildegard lay in her slip, smoking. 'Here, lover.' She handed the cigarette to Vic, hoping it might sedate him.

When he prowled like this, he could get handy; Hildegard hit back but she never won.

'We've got to be sensible,' she said, as he passed her back and forth, in the corner of the barn she had made habitable. 'We've got to *plan*. Look where being impulsive got you.'

'We gotta go. They'll hang me, Hild.' Vic knelt in front of her. 'You know I didn't mean it, don't you? You know I would never kill a woman.'

The answer felt important. 'Of course.' Hildegard kissed him and tasted tobacco.

She didn't believe him, but Vic's obvious inclination for violence did not rule him out as a choice of mate. She said, 'I've saved and pilfered and soon I'll have enough. *Then* we run, got that?'

'What if I just up and leave?'

She pushed him to the blankets. Straddled him. 'You won't.'

That Caroline was not fond of frills and cared nothing for ribbons did not deter Julia from dressing her up and curling her hair and making a doll of the child.

'She's bored, aren't you, duck?' Gerald's nickname for his half-sister always made her laugh. He grabbed her hand and rescued her from Julia. 'Let's visit the horses.'

'And off they go,' said Julia. 'She likes him best, doesn't she?'

'Two children together,' said Pamela wryly. The closeness between Gerald and Caroline was all the sweeter for coming after his blow-up on first meeting the girl.

'Father's bastard, Mother?' he had fumed. 'Under our roof? Have you gone quite mad?'

'She's a Pargetter.' Pamela had stood her ground, chin up. 'I recall someone around here making vows to be a better, nicer person if his life was spared.'

'Huh. Well,' grumbled Gerald.

They never spoke of Mother Molly; her reign was over and communal amnesia set in. No villager admitted to memories of sleepless nights or how they once jumped at noises in the dark.

A week was all it took to cement Gerald and Caroline as a duo. She was quiet, which he liked, but she was not studious, which he liked even more. They walked the dogs, they rode the horses, they tripped the servants and put a field mouse in Julia's lingerie drawer.

For now, the servants were told Caroline was a niece.

The servants knew exactly who she was.

Morgan saw Lorna to the door. 'I wish', he said, 'I had better news for you.'

Lorna was grateful for his empathy, but keen to get away from it.

'I could be wrong. We doctors often are. Ladies are a mystery!'

'You're not wrong,' said Lorna. 'I've always known.'

She left him, and rehearsed the conversation she must have with Cliff. She would not use Morgan's gynaecological terms; she would simply ask, *What if it will always be just the two of us? Is that enough for you?*

'Smell 'em.' Walter would not take no for an answer, and Ruby bent to smell the basket of chanterelle mushrooms he had picked.

'Oh!' She lifted her head, surprised. 'They smell of apricots.'

'Come on, *Maman*.' Evie was impatient to get to Misty Kay's house, where the kitchen always smelled of good, edible food. She dragged her mother away from the table outside The Bull, leaving Walter to turn back to his fellow philosophers.

'Wish they'd hurry up and count the votes,' said Dan. The general election of a fortnight ago was not yet decided, but Dan had, again, a feeling in his water. 'I reckon it's looking bad for Churchill.'

'Crying shame, if we boot him out after all he's done for us.' Bob mopped his brow with a tea towel – it was hot; his customers noted it was the same towel he used to dry glasses but didn't much care.

'See that picture of Winnie sitting outside Hitler's bunker?' Walter was close to tears at the thought of losing Churchill from the national stage. 'He's a card.'

'Max!' Dan hollered at the figure crossing the Green. 'Come and have a pint!'

A hero twice over after his valiant capture of Grayson, Max shook his head in polite refusal. He was headed for the bridge, and for Wanda.

Will we, Max wondered, *ever get weary of planning our future?*

'Will you be Mrs Gilpin?' he asked her, now. 'Or Mrs Lemmon? Maybe you should be Mrs Jäger.'

'I'm just Wanda, and you're just Max,' said Wanda, as she took his hand and they headed for the shade. They preferred the shade, where they could kiss and breathe against each other, and hear each other's hearts.

'My parents seem relieved it's all come out. Mother asked if it changes anything between them and me.'

'And does it?'

'Why would it? My feelings for them are elemental. That won't change.'

'And me?' Wanda enjoyed asking him questions she knew the answer to. 'Will you stop loving me one day, find me dull, hate the way I sneeze?'

'You?' Max pulled her close. 'You're the sun and the moon

and the stars and you're a warm beer at The Bull and the cool side of the pillowcase and the future Mrs Me.'

'The infuriating thing is', said Wanda, tucking herself into his side and setting them both walking beside the Am, 'that Mother simply adores you. Without meaning to, I've "done well", just like my sister.'

'We're not inviting Christopher to the wedding.'

'He wouldn't come!'

They both knew Max's wife would be at the ceremony. Wanda had understood when he'd said he would never stop loving and missing his first partner; she had smiled when he added, 'I'm not a tiny apartment, I'm a mansion! There's room for both of you.'

It would be rotten to envy a woman who died in rubble, her child inside her. Confident, generous Wanda was glad of Max's loyalty to her predecessor. *If I dropped dead,* she thought, *I'd adore to be remembered like that.*

Drinking glorious coffee in a terrible chair, Alec tried out his French on the waiter. The man rolled his eyes; even the girls plying their trade on the scrappy strip of dock laughed at Alec's accent when he respectfully declined their business.

Scanning the jostling boats, he ordered himself not to hope. He'd been promised passage many times. Yet, when a burly man in a sooty vest waved from a tug, he stood and broke into a run.

The skipper wasted no time in setting off. Deposited in the

hold, the lively bitterness of the coffee still on his tongue, Alec patted his pockets, remembering the weeks-old letter from Pamela. It would be something to read on the way, while the crew sniggered at the Brit with seasickness.

AUGUST

The land wheel was a dark shape out on the field. Doris knew Dan was out there, sweating, as the binder drove a knife into the crop and snaked string around each sheaf.

She would have liked him to be at her side. The village felt small and vulnerable in the shadow of the headlines. Doris was certain she was mispronouncing 'Hiroshima', wished she could forget the phrases from the newspaper. *A mass of boiling dust.* She called for Glen, and he came, of course. *The rain of ruin.* She told the dog, 'Japan's been threatened with annihilation, so they say,' and Doris knew Glen would agree with her that this was unholy, and that Japanese people were made of the same bits and pieces as Ambridgians.

Across the fields, another woman, in a better-cut dress, oversaw the liberation of Mother Molly's portrait from the attic.

'Who's she?' asked Caroline. She and Minko were chums; the duo tailed Pamela on her daily round.

'Another misunderstood woman, my pet,' said Pamela. She

had never called her own son 'my pet' or anything similar, and was rather enjoying this new way of mothering.

No, not mothering, she reminded herself. The girl called her Pammy; from anyone else it would make her shudder, but she loved to hear it called along the hallways.

The sermon was subdued that Sunday after VJ Day.

The vicar seemed to have no taste for crowing about Japan's surrender.

'Someone should remind Henry Bissett that we *won*!' scoffed Denholm *sotto voce* to his wife in the third pew.

AMBRIDGE WOMEN'S INSTITUTE
MEETING MINUTES

Date: 20th August 1945
At: Lower Loxley
Chairwoman: Pamela Pargetter
Present: Doris Archer, Agnes Kaye, Emmeline Endicott, Magsy Furneaux, Lorna Horrobin, Nance Seed, Ruby Bonnet,
Susan Grundy, Valerie Micklewood
Minutes: Magsy Furneaux

1. Pamela opened by asking us not to try and stroke Hero under the table as

he is still pining for Alec and tends to disappear if anyone shows him kindness

2. Pamela said 'where are my manners welcome Mrs Valerie Micklewood' and thanked her for doing such a grand job as Rev Bissett's 'housekeeper' and asked us all to stick to the agenda

3. I asked if the blouse Mrs Valerie Micklewood was wearing was one belonging to the late Mrs Henry Bissett, our friend Frances

4. Mrs Micklewood was prevented from ansering by Pamela saying in quite a sharp tone 'that is not on our agenda' but I want the minutes to reflect that it most certainly was Frances's blouse (and furthermore was tight about the bust)

5. Mrs Endicott asked if there was any news on Vic Horrobin's wereabouts as she cannot sleep knowing such a broot is on the loose

6. Susan coffed and nodded at Lorna and Mrs Endicott went red and said 'oh dear, I mean no offence about your brother-in-law dear Lorna' and Lorna said 'I cannot sleep either Mrs E'

7. Pamela asked could we all please get on and asked Doris to show us the finished qilt

8. Doris laid the qilt on the table

9. Agnes said 'the skwares are all different sizes'

10. Pamela said 'the stitches are haphazard'

11. I ventured to say 'it is a trifle lumpy'

12. Nance said 'I think it is beautiful'

13. Doris said 'you have got me worried now ladies it seemed like a good idea but it has come out a right dog's dinner what if the qilt is more about giving us all something to do and less about helping foke?'

14. Pamela suggested that Doris stop holding up meetings with philozophical questions

14. or is it 15. I have lost track Alec's 'niece' shouted 'Pammy!' very loudly even though children should be seen and not heard and Pamela said 'I think that concludes today's bizness'

'You can call them Grandma and Grandpa but only indoors,' Ruby told her daughters. 'Got that?'

Evie shrugged. Her own double life – schoolgirl/adventurer – involved a great deal of subterfuge, and she blithely accepted Misty Kay's promotion to grandfather.

Older, more thoughtful, Michele was harder to convince. 'But why, *Maman*?'

Ruby heard the hurt. The suspicion that they were second-class citizens at Turnpike. 'Just because,' she said.

Wednesdays found them, without fail, at Agnes's table.

I love how greedy the little beasts are, thought Agnes, ladling stew into bowls. She kept a beady eye on Denholm.

There had been a fuss, earlier, about Evie cutting up the newspaper to make paper dolls. Denholm still gave the occasional wince when the chatter got too animated.

But he's come a long way, thought Agnes approvingly. She rarely approved of her husband, and misdiagnosed the glow it gave her as indigestion. He sat beneath a new painting of Turnpike's garden in full summer pomp. It was a little too modern for Denholm's tastes, but it hung in pride of place.

'My grandma', said Evie, 'makes the best slop in the world.'

Denholm snorted, amused.

'Stew,' corrected Ruby. 'Not slop.'

'When do we go back to France?' asked Michele, taking a slice of bread. The stew might be excellent but she would never get used to the English loaf.

Agnes twitched. Denholm's spoon paused on the way to his lips.

'I'm not sure,' said Ruby. She pre-empted Michele's next comment by saying, in French, 'Some subjects are for grown-ups to discuss.'

'Hoh-hee-hoh.' Denholm's impression came out every time French was spoken.

Evie loved it. 'Hoh-hee-hoh!' she yelled.

'Hoh-hee-hoh!' said a different voice, and they all turned to see Whitey White's face sticking through the window, like a horse over a stable door. 'Forgot to deliver this package earlier, thought I'd drop it off on my way for a pint.' He looked up and down the table, taking in the diners.

Agnes stiffened, and Ruby looked into her dinner as if keen to climb into it.

''ello, 'ello, 'ello! You got visitors?' Whitey seemed puzzled by the juxtaposition of two very different Ambridge families.

'My granddaughters?' said Denholm. 'Oh yes, they're often here.' He went back to his stew, and Whitey jumped on his bike, almost toppling it in his haste to tell the world this news.

'Are you quite sure?' Alec resisted the impulse to tear the clipboard out of the young lieutenant's grasp.

'Sorry, sir, no can do. Not a driver available on the entire barracks until tomorrow.'

'Damn. I want to get home to my wife.' Alec's wounded hand was stiff. He massaged it with an irritated sigh that clearly provoked the other soldier.

'There *is* a war on, you know, sir.'

Both men laughed together.

'You can't use that excuse any more, lieutenant,' said Alec.

'Hold on.' The lieutenant glanced again at his clipboard. 'Pargetter? Operation Market Garden?' He stood a little straighter. 'I heard about you, sir, you—'

'I don't talk about that.' Alec was severe. 'More than ten thousand men fell during that operation, and that's ten thousand reasons to keep bloody quiet about it.'

'Yessir. Apologies sir.' Chastened, the young soldier said, more quietly, 'I'll see what I can do about a driver, sir.'

'These are Peggy's carrots!' Doris put down a dish of orange medallions, slaked with farm butter.

'Give us some!' Phil leaned over the table.

'They're sweet,' said Dan, crunching one between his teeth.

I grew them. Peggy was astonished that the dull little seeds she pushed into the mud with such bad grace were now part of dinner.

Doris winked at her over her glass of dandelion and burdock. 'Here's to Peggy's carrots!'

A wail began in another room. Peggy pushed her chair back. 'And to the other little seed I planted in Ambridge soil!'

'Only ten for dinner tonight,' said Julia, as she and Pamela left the men to their port, and settled down amongst the cushions of the drawing room. 'An end-of-term feeling, isn't it?'

'So much is changing, but this time things are changing *back*.'

'I wouldn't be so sure of that,' murmured Julia, nodding a *yes* to the offer Pamela made by holding up the whisky decanter. 'Do you mind me asking . . . the girl . . . Caroline . . . is she here for good?'

'Yes.' Pamela knew that, despite their affection for Caroline,

Gerald and Julia did fret about the possible damage to Alec's standing in the village.

'Are you—'

'Am I sure? Julia, I hope nobody in this house is under the impression it's a democracy.' Pamela handed her a glass. '*Fait accompli*, my dear.'

'When I grow up,' said Julia, 'I want to be just like my mama-in-law.'

'Caroline looks like her.' *Don't be a goose, say the woman's name*. 'Like Kitty.'

'Does that bother you?'

'I thought it might.' Pamela twisted a pearl earring. 'But no.'

Yes, Kitty had given Alec things he couldn't find at home. Affection. Sex. Playfulness. *But that was then*, thought Pamela, as she rose to greet the remaining chaps. Alec was on his way home to their backwater. They would find the right words from now on, build something that made them both happy. The confidence that carried Pamela on a headwind all her life had returned; destabilised by the fear that Mother Molly would swoop on Gerald, she had felt destiny toy with her like any other mortal. Now the old witch was back to her proper place in children's tales and the war was over. Her husband would soon be home, and his battered hand would be merely an emblem of all they had escaped. The future was bright.

Hurry, darling, she thought, and caught Hero's eye as the black Labrador slunk beneath the grand piano.

*

'That wedding wasn't just small,' said Dan, watching his wife clear away the dishes. 'It was invisible to the naked eye.'

'It was perfect,' said Doris.

Wanda and Max said their vows in front of Doris, Dan, Christine, Phil, Peggy and baby Jennifer. Pamela had joined them for the ceremony, having lent Wanda a peach-coloured silk suit that did its best with the bride's rather different figure. Henry waffled through the marriage service. Wanda and Max held hands so tightly their fingers were white.

Pamela drove back to Lower Loxley, leaving the others to return to Brookfield where Max produced real champagne – Dan pronounced it 'hiccups in a glass' – and Doris cooked a rib of beef that would make an atheist believe.

The newlyweds would live in London; they would keep a dog – they agreed on everything.

'Where's that bugger, Grayson, now?' asked Dan, lighting his pipe, and glad to be alone with his Doris.

'Language,' said Doris, as she must. 'He's in Winston Green prison. No bail; he's stuck there until the trial. Let's not talk about him today of all days, love, eh?'

'The new kiddie at Lower Loxley . . .'

Doris knew what those dots meant. 'Yes, you're right,' she said darkly, 'she's Kitty Dibden-Rawles' daughter.'

Neither went any further. Both were tired of mysteries.

'I wish our Jack'd come home,' said Doris. 'And Alec. All our missing men.'

'Bet you a pound to a penny Alec'll be back first. Toffs always get first dibs.'

'You a revolutionary now, Dan Archer?' laughed Doris, leaving the kitchen to hunt for her slippers. Her good shoes pinched her bunion.

Almost colliding with Max in the dim hallway, Doris said, 'You two off to the hotel, are you?'

'Yes. Our one-night honeymoon. Wanda's just fetching her things.'

'We'll miss her,' said Doris.

Max heard the understatement. 'I'll look after her, Mrs Archer.'

'You'll look after each other.' Doris settled his tie. 'That girl finds it easy to be happy. It's a gift.'

It was dark. Alec's hand ached. It was the last leg of an epic journey, just two hours' drive from Ambridge.

Yet here I sit like a lemon and wait.

The unattended jeep caught his eye. He ignored every instinct, every rule, and leapt in.

Bugger the consequences!

The jeep was nippy, nothing like his beloved Bentley. It flew along, and Alec felt every stone in the road. Changing gears was a challenge with busted fingers.

The moon lit his way. He remembered the unread letter in his kitbag. No need to read it now; he would soon have all the news from the horse's mouth. It would be fun to surprise his wife; she was a more or less un-surpriseable woman.

If only she'd changed her mind about Caroline.

He imagined the child, spinning out there, somewhere in space, and put his foot down.

At Lower Loxley, Hero lifted his heavy, dark head, and pulled himself to his feet. He was alert for the first time in a long time.

'You gave me a fright!' Hildy scolded the Labrador as it passed her in the dark back passage. She eased open the back door, and lugged her duffel bag up onto her shoulders. It contained little, just feminine essentials and a stolen suit for her unkempt beau.

The long tramp to Sawyers Farm lay ahead, then she and Vic would take the back roads to Felpersham. Catching a train from a busier station meant less chance of his fugitive face being recognised.

'What's the matter?' She bent and scratched Hero's ear.

The dog ignored her attentions. Eyes bright, he was twitchy, excited, turning on his paws and sniffing the air.

That's when Hildegard saw it. The Bentley, parked sideways, keys in the ignition, where Pamela had left them after rushing home from the wedding. It awaited some lackey to put it away in the garage, but this lackey sprang into the driver's seat.

Why not add car theft to my crimes?

Hildegard had a Pargetter pearl necklace in her drawers, and would soon be on the run with a suspected murderer; she may as well depart decent society in some style.

The car lurched. She laughed. She had only ever driven her pa's jalopy, but cars were like men: basically much the same.

The Bentley crept around the side of Lower Loxley, and its throaty snarl as it sped up took Hildegard aback.

'Bye, Hero!' she called, but the dog ignored her.

'Doris, you're pacing like a tiger in a zoo, love.' Dan sent smoke signals up from behind the newspaper.

'She's missing Wanda already,' said Peggy.

'Me too,' said Christine, still in her wedding glad rags beneath her dressing gown.

'They've only gone to Felpersham,' said Dan. 'They'll be back tomorrow, and living in Woodbine Cottage for the foreseeable.'

Ambridge can't hang on to a young couple like Wanda and Max, thought Doris. The girl's life would be one of luxury; the hotel suite was just the beginning.

Desperate for distraction, she tidied the last stray threads of the quilt. A specially made crate awaited it at Lower Loxley; it would be sent to the Red Cross the next day. Doris still had doubts about who might want the thing. She wrapped it in brown paper, stroking the square made from her mother's scarf, and smiling at the dark patch of the vicar's cassock. All village life was there: Mrs E's waistcoat, Lorna's embroidered swatch, the yellow and green square contributed by Connie.

'I won't be long.' All at once decisive, Doris grabbed up her handbag and swiped the truck key from the table. 'Just nipping out to deliver this.'

'Eh?' Dan emerged from behind the headlines. 'Doris? It's late!'

She was gone.

By the truck she stood a while, wondering at her mood. She was not unhappy or worried; she was . . . *I'm peculiar,* was all she could come up with.

Glen padded over and waited expectantly, his eyes on the door handle.

'In, boy,' she said, and up he leapt.

Peggy waved from the farmhouse door. She waited until the rear lights disappeared down the track. Before closing the door, she took a deep lungful of scented night air, and swayed at the richness of it.

Vic had not smiled since Frances died, but he hooted with laughter at the sight of the green Bentley bumping over the field towards his barn.

He threw his rucksack in the back. 'Slide over, girl!' He took the wheel. 'I love you, Hildy!' he shouted as they sped towards the five-barred gate.

That's a first, thought Hildegard.

It was much darker than Doris had envisaged. Pulling out onto the back road, she realised the drive was a bad idea. Not much moon that night; the landscape looked different, as if she journeyed through a dream, a not-quite-Ambridge.

Night amplified sound; she could hear the roar of a powerful car on some nearby road. Doris feared for them, going at such speed, as the truck limped along. Ironically, now that there were no regulations about fitting blinkers to vehicles, one of the truck's headlights was broken, and Doris had to squint at the road ahead.

'Where you off to at such a clip, fella?' an RAF chap asked Hero as they passed on the gravel.

The Labrador took no notice, and headed for Lower Loxley's high gates.

The loving couple's new rapport didn't last long.

'Stop yelling,' cried Hildegard, as the map flapped in her grasp. 'I'm trying to work out where the hell we are.'

'You didn't bring enough cash.'

'You didn't bring any!'

Vic raised his hand and the car swerved.

'Keep your hands on the wheel, fool,' said Hildegard.

'I've never driven anything this powerful. It's like riding a dragon.'

'Go slower, then.' Hildegard was, she realised, tired of pointing out the obvious to him.

Vic jammed the pedal to the floor and they shot over a crossroads. His whoop made a mockery of their discreet escape.

'We could be going the wrong way very fast!' Hildegard's complaints were lost in the engine noise.

Glen sat up and watched the night pass the passenger window.

His mistress hummed the hymn she had sung earlier at the wedding, then stopped to cock an ear.

'Hey, Glen,' she asked the sheepdog. 'Is that car getting closer?'

Hero reached the end of the long drive. The swishing of the trees overhead played a melody over the bass of his thumping tail, as he watched the road, eyes shining.

'Left here, *left*, you idiot!' said Hildegard.

'Shut up,' said Vic.

The Bentley flew.

'Left!' shrieked Hildegard. She had seen the other vehicle.

Blinded, Doris spun the wheel. She hit the brakes. Glen shot off the seat beside her. She had no time to think or speak.

The noise, heard for miles, was abnormal. The cymbal clash of metal hitting metal.

'Don't Fence Me In' sang Bing Crosby on the big brown wireless.

Short of a dance partner, Christine wrapped her arms around herself, and mouthed 'I do' in the mirror.

Dan's pipe went out and he sent Phillip to the drawer for tobacco.

'House feels odd,' said Dan, taking the pouch, 'without your mother in it.'

Hero barked. There was only the moon to hear him, the same moon that silvered the village as it settled down for the night.

It slid over the new thatch of The Bull, the imposing respectability of the vicarage. It glanced at Woodbine Cottage, nodded respectfully at St Stephen's and shone in on Connie, listening for Stan's footfall at Broom Corner. Arkwright Hall stood empty and ready for the next day, and Holmleigh was lit up; Morgan was just back from a visit to Mrs Endicott, whose suspected heart attack had turned out to be the effect of a new corset.

Felpersham, Penny Hassett, Lakey Hill.

A cloud dawdled in front of the moon, and it felt like a farewell.

The one headlight that still worked on the Brookfield truck spotlit the wreck of a jeep, its snout jammed into a tree.

Doris, her heart pounding, heard the car she had swerved to avoid thundering away. The jeep was not so lucky; it had met the car and come off worse.

'Glen, come.' She was glad of his doggy bulk beside her as she crept to the jeep.

'Alec,' she said.

Doris saw his eyes were closed, and she saw how closely he and the wheel were entwined. Was he breathing? That, she couldn't say.

'Don't cry,' she upbraided herself. 'That's not useful.'

Grabbing the quilt, she tore at the brown paper with hands that did not shake.

'There you go,' she said softly. Inserting herself awkwardly into the mangled jeep, she wrapped the quilt around Alec. 'There you go, my boy.'

The quilt was, she realised, perfect. It had been made for this moment. It had been made for Alec.

She wrapped herself around him, too. Alec needed kindness as he left this life, and Doris laid her cheek on his back and cried. She cried for him and for all of us who must die and leave, or lose and be left.

A part of Ambridge would go with Alec; he was embedded in the village like the squares all joined together with terrible stitches.

'We'll miss you,' she told him, and promised she would go to Pamela, daubed in his blood, and tell her what had happened.

Hero stood stock-still by the gates of Lower Loxley. The dog sniffed the air, and turned for the house, his noble head down.

The moment shimmers.

Ambridge slides into another night, another turn of nature's wheel. It will wake up to terrible news.

Hero lies beneath the poisonous umbrella of a great yew, and barely notices the truck pass him. He would recognise the lady who gets down and stands and stares at the house with a sort of hopelessness, but he is not interested enough to glance her way.

Agnes mumbles in her sleep at Turnpike; probably ticking off an imaginary shop assistant. Beside her, Denholm is awake, thinking about Christmas on this soft August night. He has never anticipated Christmas before – *all that fuss and bother* – but this year he will dress up as Santa Claus for his girls.

Valerie Micklewood is bored in her bed. She was never bored before she came to keep house at the vicarage, but she is profoundly grateful for the monotony. After ricocheting from neglectful husband to libertine lover, she needs the rest. If she's reading the signs right – and she *is* reading the signs right – she'll be a vicar's wife this time next year. Let the Women's Institute put that in their pipe and smoke it!

In a room across the landing, the vicar thinks of Valerie. And Frances. And then of Valerie again.

It's clear to Grayson which prison guard he should befriend. Incarceration is just another test of his ingenuity. There is no guilt as he lies on his hard bed. Shame is for others.

The baby sneezes at Grange Farm. Alf is unaware the war is over, or that it ever happened. He will not understand the solemn talk above his head tomorrow, when the bereaved village comes to terms with its loss. He is happy.

A different baby grumbles and fidgets at Brookfield. Peggy walks the floorboards with Jennifer, the old wood creaking beneath her bare feet. 'Everything's all right,' she tells the baby, believing it. She can almost feel the countryside growing around her. The weeds. The flowers. The good food in the earth. She is where she is meant to be; Peggy is not at Brookfield to wait for feckless Jack – she is there to make a life for herself.

Miles away, a mild young man called Christopher cries himself to sleep. In the fireplace is a letter, burned to ash.

'Shush, love.' Nance's whisper soothes her husband back to sleep. She tiptoes downstairs, to Morgan's desk. She writes, 'Dear Bathsheba, you don't know me but my great friend is an old acquaintance of yours.'

With Wanda's head against his chest, Max is almost asleep, almost there, when a voice in his ear says, 'Well done, darling!' He blinks. He recognises the farewell. He takes a deep breath, and Wanda stirs but stays close. He is married. He is in love. And, apparently, he is part-German. 'Which part, I wonder?' his new wife had asked, as she undressed him.

The portrait of Mother Molly cannot sleep, of course. She is awake in her new room. A rapping at Lower Loxley's huge front door brings a servant flying past her. It may be a trick of the light, but it could be argued that Mother Molly's thin lips curve into a smile.

Lying flat, like a noblewoman on a tomb, Magsy feels, as she always does, rather pleased with herself. The last Furneaux, she has done nothing to sully the family name. She owes that much to her father, still there on the pedestal she built in her childhood, a beacon of integrity. Drowsily, she repeats the motto on his cigar box. *One good friend is all I need.*

The clock is meaningless in a sickroom. The tingling in his leg keeps Gerald awake most nights. How he envies Julia, fast asleep, in photogenic fashion, beside him. The resolutions he made lie in tatters around the four-poster. *I'm weak,* he thinks; the night is made for introspection, one of Gerald's pet hates. He was a bit of a brute to his parents, he knows that. *I'll make it up to Father when he comes home.*

Badboy patters around Broom Corner. He hops up onto the rusting car in the yard, and terrorises a hedgehog. He can't go back indoors until the shouting stops. Connie will be crying again; Badboy loathes the noise she makes, and might nip her to shut her up.

Tomorrow, thinks Walter, turning like a whale in his soft bed, *I'll take my Nelson fishing.*

The room is still unfamiliar to Caroline. The dressing gown on the back of the door looks like a ghoul in the dark. She does not miss her mother; it is more than that. She feels her lack in every cell. These new people are kind, though, if a bit stiff. She will make the best of it. She will have a new Daddy soon. She hopes he will love her, and resolves to be good.

Mrs Endicott smells like the flower garden that surrounds The Cherries. She fiddles with her lace nightcap, and worries about the peculiar noises coming from her tummy. Idly, she wonders if they could be related to the eight macaroons she ate at Magsy's, and decides *No.*

Evicted from a lady's rumpled bed before her night-shift husband returns, Whitey White trudges home. Whistling, he passes Arthur Sweet's cottage, and the whistling stops. The old fellow's confusion is growing worse. *We covered for him in the Home Guard, but how much longer can Arthur live alone in his little palace?*

The wheel turns beneath Whitey's boots and Arthur's slippers, and beneath Brookfield, a robust place that is nevertheless vulnerable to change like everywhere else.

Phillip is not built to fret; he is fast asleep. In the next room,

Christine cuddles Mother Cat and wonders where her mother can be. *Mum's never out at bedtime!* The farmhouse feels off, wonky; she smells the pipe smoke that curls up the stairs and under her door.

Dan knocks his pipe against the big solid ashtray. No doubt there's a logical explanation for Doris's absence. She'll waltz in, coat askew, with a story of a flat tyre or a wrong turn. He will commiserate, brew a healing pot of tea, but he will not tell her that he has sat in their kitchen and imagined a life without her in it.

At that moment, Doris stands in a fine hall, looking up to the top of the carved stairs. A woman stands there, her chic thinness suddenly starved-looking. Her face is a mask. She is about to know something she does not care to know.

Curved around each other like commas in the books that have slipped to the bedside rug, Cliff and Lorna snore in unison. Lorna has finally been courageous enough to ask her question of him. He had sat back, staring at her. 'Are we enough? You and me? You really have to ask, love?'

Sleep might be fine for the villagers, and for the likes of Ruby and Michele, but is Evie asleep? Not she! She stands on the bed in valiant pose; there are villains to defeat, wrongs to right, and Papa to rescue.

A wing chair is a terrible place to doze off. Dodgy will wake with a stiff neck. For now, he is anaesthesised by Lower Loxley claret, with Minko a warm cushion on his lap.

Hero puts his head on his paws beneath the yew, and decides never to eat again.

There is blood on Doris's face.
Pamela puts out her finger and touches it.
'I must be brave,' says Pamela. 'I've done it before.'
'Be brave tomorrow,' says Doris, and takes her in her arms.

Epilogue

1st January, 1951

The moment shimmers.

Doris is up first, shoulders squared for the new year.

She sniffs the air and smells rain, and romance. All those looks between Phil and his boss's daughter, young Grace Fairbrother, did not go unnoticed at the New Year's Eve get-together in the Archer kitchen.

Glen limps to her side. 'Breakfast time, eh?' The ageing dog is in retirement – less work, but just as many ear scratches.

Doris recalls his arrival, a pup bundled inside Dan's jacket. Glen has never, as Dan likes to say, 'put a paw wrong'.

'Stop the car!'

'But, Nance,' protests Morgan, 'the shop's bound to be shut.'

To his eyes, bright-eyed Nance is unchanged since their wedding day. He knows he has less hair and more tum since they married, but he does not realise the small change taking place within his cells. The tumour that will steal him from his sunny wife and his bonny child before the next turn of the year is merely a rumour in his body, but it will grow.

'Just want to see what they've done with the old place.'

Frank refused to come on this trip down Memory Lane. He was busy, so he said, in his Welwyn Garden City flat, just a few doors down from Morgan's new GP practice.

'New sign,' says Nance approvingly. 'And they've painted the woodwork.' Her father, she knows, would find the shade too gaudy.

Her childhood bedroom was directly above the side door. She squints up at the window, pulls her coat collar against her cheek. She remembers her mother calling her for school.

'Mummy!' Tudor, seven now, and a larky boy, shouts from the back seat.

'Coming!' Nance jumps back into the warm fug of the motor. 'Let's not go past Holmleigh. Let's hurry home and get this young man fed.'

'Yesss!' Tudor punches the air.

The ferrets keep Stan company, and nibble his nose to wake him.

He sleeps where he falls. There is no stagger back from The Bull anymore; a permanent ban means he buys bottles and empties them at home. They stack up around him, taking the place of people.

Connie left. They say it was his fault. Stan never listens;

they all hate him and want to bring him down. He is doing just as he pleases these days and it suits him fine.

His lip seems to be cut. Nausea swells and fades in his stomach.

Badboy, though ... Stan misses Badboy.

The Reverend Henry Bissett is confused.

He does not know where to find his favourite tea cup in the endless white cabinets of the new kitchen. He gives up – it saves time.

Ironically, this modernised rectory in Surrey is exactly the setting his late wife envisaged for herself. 'How Frances would love the new vacuum cleaner,' he says to himself as he heads upstairs to work on his sermon. The new congregation are appreciative, attentive; most of them even stay awake.

Perhaps, he thinks, it's easier to believe in God during peacetime.

He hears movement in the kitchen he just left. He smiles. This can only mean that Valerie will soon follow him upstairs with a tray of the sugary somethings she knows he cannot resist. He suspects his new wife is part-pagan; *I'll pull strings with St Peter when she reaches the Pearly Gates.*

And what if Frances is there to greet them on the other side? Henry chooses not to think about that.

The prefab bungalow is dark, poky even, but Cliff is snug, like a creature in its burrow.

He is now a 'real' teacher; Lorna pushed him through the

doors of the oversubscribed Emergency Training Scheme, and took over as breadwinner while he studied. The qualification matters, but Cliff knows it was at Arkwright Hall that he became a teacher, and in Lorna's arms that he became a man.

He glances at her, bent over *Jude the Obscure,* and she senses it and looks up. She meets his good eye, and there is a change in the room. That furry tension that is prelude to a kiss.

The rattle of the letterbox changes the mood.

Sitting up in bed, fingers freezing as she writes, Christine vows to have a fire in the bedroom when she has her own house.

The correspondence cards are embossed – embossed! – with her name. A Christmas present from Wanda, she is using them for the first time to thank her friend.

She tells Wanda all about Phil's interview for a new farm management position, and the latest on her own early starts for the National Milk Testing Service. 'Us Archers!' she writes. 'You can't keep us away from cows!!'

Wanda will hoot at that.

Another rattle of the letterbox. A shout of 'Only us!'

'In you come.' Lorna lets in Bert and Maisie Horrobin, and embraces their mother. Connie will never be well rounded, but the starved look is gone. She keeps herself to herself in the Birmingham back-to-back she shares with another family, still suspicious of the world.

In the bungalow, she is more relaxed. 'Off to visit my Vic later,' she tells them over a bun.

'Want me to give Bert and Maisie their dinner?' Lorna worries about Bert; the boy is sullen and secretive, a cadger of cigarettes with a tendency to get pie-eyed on cider when he should be at school.

'That's a long old journey on New Year's Day, Ma.' Cliff stokes the fire. 'Why not go tomorrow?'

'Vic relies on my visits,' says Connie. 'I won't let him down.'

It is more than a year since any of them breathed Stan's name.

'Get down them stairs, girl!' calls Doris. 'Else you'll be late.'

Doris likes these first new moments of the day, when it's just her and the kitchen. She pours a cuppa for Dan; Christine will dance back up the stairs with it. The noise of the spoon in the cup is pleasing.

Doris is a storehouse of all that has happened in Ambridge. She forgets nothing about the war, how it tested them, what it took.

She recalls, too, how life felt afterwards. How new it was. Oh, not just the clothes and the food – so much is still rationed – but the sudden onslaught of modernity.

She glances out of the back door. There is rain in that sky. The wet washing will have to hang like spooks in the scullery.

Joe Grundy takes the coal scuttle from his wife.

Not accustomed to such gallantry, Susan supposes there are upsides to being seven months preggers.

He asks, 'Is that your steak and kidney pie I can smell?'

She nods. Then she says 'Gordon!'

'Nah.'

They have been auditioning baby names for days, but can't agree.

A ball flies from upstairs and bangs against the hall door.

'Watch out, Alf!' barks Joe.

Their boy is in disgrace, confined to his room. PC Jenkins gave him a talking-to, illustrating the path to hell that begins with nicking a chocolate bar from Woolworths.

It has not done the trick.

'Edward!' says Susan.

'Ooh,' says Joe, considering. 'Ed?'

'Eddie!'

It is decided.

Vic likes the monotony.

No decisions. Plenty of food; prison grub is better than Broom Corner's cuisine. Like-minded gents to consort with. He is amassing a little black book of contacts that will ensure him a career when he gets out.

Girls, though. He misses girls. Sometimes he thinks about Hildegard, and curses her for dropping him. No letters, no nothing. He might look her up when he's a free man; pay her a visit she won't forget.

For now, though, Vic has stuffed his conscience into the back of the one drawer he is allowed in this place, and smokes and argues and kips.

Then he remembers. Lordy. Visiting Day. His dull old mother will subject him to another lecture and have another ugly weep.

I'll get the screws to tell her I'm not well.

Dan savours his once-in-a-blue-moon lie-in.

Phil is clattering about; some business about Jack not returning the car so he can't get to his all-important interview. Dan stays out of it when his sons lock horns.

The century flies past. Rather like this lie-in. Dan feels Mother Cat enter the room and reaches down to help her up onto the counterpane before realising no, it's not her, it's the new kitten, and it's perfectly capable of hopping up without assistance.

It purrs on his chest and it's a good cat, a very good cat, but it's not dear old Mother Cat.

Dan is not keen on change, but so long as he has Doris, his north star, he can't complain.

Walter Gabriel expects little change from the new year as he splashes his face at the basin.

His fences will remain half mended. His arthritis will give him jip. There will be beer and ladies and animal friends.

Perhaps my Nelson will move out, away. The lad is eighteen, and he is busy busy busy with this scheme and that scheme. Already a . . . what's the word? Onter-summat?

Walter yawns. January already. Possibly time to change the bedclothes.

'Entrepreneur!' he shouts, triumphant.

*

Bob Little has no curiosity about who will take over his inn.

He has the keys to a pleasant cottage a few miles to the north-east, and will no longer have to tolerate drunkards, nor be a slave to a timetable, nor wake to the stench of ale and tobacco.

Bob will have a little garden. He is considering a spaniel.

Why, then, is he weeping into the sink as he shaves?

If his life is a jigsaw, Bob cannot click the pieces together. They are all separate, and rough-edged. The wife he never cherished; the son who went to war and never came home; the Frenchified lady who roused his heart.

One piece, though, clicks into place as he wipes his face.

I love this place.

Silly Bob. He never knew until now.

He loves the timbers, the smells, the ricketty tables in the bar. He loves the new roof, just as he loved the old thatch it replaced.

All those odd feelings down the years. They were love.

Finding fault is Agnes's favourite hobby, but she is speechless at the perfection of her bedroom. Mattress just right, and the linens crisply laundered.

Neither can she find fault with the town square they are exploring. In fact, she tells Ruby, 'France isn't half as barbaric as I feared.'

'They even celebrate new year.' Denholm is delighted by each proof of Sceaux's similarity to Ambridge.

Waiting by the patisserie, Evie and Michele's outfits no

longer match. The older girl is in a hurry to get to church, where the boys congregate, but Evie looks forward to her grandmother's attempts to pronounce *madeleine* or *chouquette* as they choose their treats.

There are no Nazis in the patisserie. Evie's hope that Papa will come home has been shed, along with other childish fancies. Evie knows she will leave this town, just as she knows Michele will marry and settle here. Evie is built of salty stuff; her mama catches her eye and winks, and Evie experiences the thrill of being perfectly understood.

'But why?' Ruby badgers Agnes with the same energy Agnes badgers others. 'Why is it such an absurd idea?'

'Me and Denholm? Live in France?'

They turn to let Denholm catch up; his top speed is slow. Perhaps it is too late to transplant an English oak, especially one all covered over with ivy.

Agnes slips her arm through Ruby's. They are family. They don't have to live next door. The ties that bind them are so elastic they could girdle the moon.

'Be honest, Pamela, you married me for my money, didn't you?'

A moment's pause, and then gales of laughter. Everyone at the mile-long breakfast table knows Douglas hasn't a penny to his name. Looks, yes. Breeding, ditto. But an empty wallet.

'I married you', says Pamela, 'for the way you make a Bloody Mary.'

Not quite true. Douglas is a disguise. He normalises

Pamela as just another married lady. She does not wish to stick out in any way. She wants to conform and do her duty and be asked no questions.

Pamela does not love Douglas. He is scintillating company, and his weekends away with the handsome scion of a noble family do not bother her.

I am tiring of paying off footmen, though.

Pamela loves Alec; Alec is not here.

Each evening, Douglas toasts his predecessor's portrait before dinner. Pamela is warmed to see the eyes in the painting replicated in Caroline.

'Yuk,' that girl is saying now, as Dodgy allows her a sip of his Bloody Mary. Twelve years old, she is a handful.

'Pammy, when do Gerald and Jules arrive?' she asks. 'They're taking me to a revue.'

'Is it suitable? And it's Julia, dear, never Jules.'

'Oh Pammy, it's fun.'

Pamela finds it hard to say 'no' to Caroline. Odd, when for so many years it was her favourite word.

Competitive nursery rhyme singing brings Peggy to the foot of her daughters' bed.

Lilian loves to sing, and Jennifer loves to correct her sister. Lilian is, allegedly, reciting 'Ding Dong Dell, Pussy's in the Well' all wrong.

Peggy referees, hoping the baby inside her will be a boy. Sometimes her girls remind her of those two French poppets. Must write to Ruby, she thinks, knowing she won't have time. The smallholding and the children gobble up every available hour.

The small of her back aches. The baby factory of her body sometimes complains. She repeats the new year resolution she made as the bells rang in midnight.

This is the year Jack will make good.

Lilian twirls in her nightdress as Peggy removes the rag rollers from Jennifer's hair. Her midnight optimism feels misplaced; she cannot control her husband. I couldn't even control how much beer he downed last night. Yet facts must be faced. The smallholding can't support them – not the way Jack goes about it.

She laid down the law, Doris-style. 'You need something steady, with more cash coming in, and you need to stay away from the booze.'

'Ducks,' says Jennifer. She loves ducks. 'May we visit them?'

A trudge over frosted grass is not what the doctor would order.

'Super idea!' says Peggy.

They encounter Jack in the passage. Hair on end, pyjamas buttoned up wrong.

'I've got it, Peg! I'm going to be landlord of The Bull!'

Grayson is an adaptable man.

The grey walls don't bother him. He has eaten worse than the terrible slop they serve at mealtimes. The punishing routine is a cakewalk.

In fact, public school is very like prison.

The new history master, Mr Grayson D'Urbeville, has fitted right in since he took up his position at the start of the scholastic year.

The headmaster swooned over his references. 'Miss Gilpin describes you in glowing terms, and your five years out of the country seem to have almost entirely been devoted to charitable works.'

Grayson agrees with the head's assessment.

He was right, I am a great favourite with the boys.

Twinkle Toes is a little bald but still perky.

Mrs Endicott wishes her budgie a happy new year. She knows he believes, as does she, that Ambridge is the centre of the known universe, so it is a joyful surprise that he has taken to Eastbourne with the same enthusiasm as his mistress.

Opposite them both, Magsy is finishing a hearty breakfast. 'I propose a constitutional to your splendid pier!'

A voice from the conservatory concurs. 'Topping notion.'

Bathsheba Burton puts down her watering can and joins them at the table, where the three ladies make a fine tableau of outmoded and faintly dusty elegance. Her foot finds Mrs E's beneath the lace cloth.

'Such a sensible idea,' says Magsy, popping in one last piece of buttered toast. 'You two gals moving in together to save on electricity bills.'

'Crikey,' had been Gerald's stunned reply when Pamela told him Lower Loxley was all his.

It was, she said, his birthright, and she was now 'shuffling offstage, as your wife might put it.'

'Crikey,' he says again most mornings when confronted with the piles of estate paperwork and the myriad questions from the staff and the earnest conversations with the head gardener about weevils on the hollyhocks.

'Crikey,' he says now, at the sight of Julia in Dior at the breakfast table.

'Buck's fizz, darling?' She holds up a bottle of Moët. 'Rude not to!'

Julia and he agree: the only riposte to the hellish bills generated by Gerald's birthright is the pop of a champagne cork.

They say it's better to be an old man's plaything than a young man's slave.

Hildy toasts her toes at the bars of a gas fire, relishing her few hours off-duty.

Not from her job – Hildegard doesn't have one of those – but from the aforementioned old man. Her swain is a bigwig around Cardiff.

On high days and holidays, he must be with his family. He calls, though, on the telephone he installed in her apartment. Hildegard wears a ring from him, but she will never have his name.

Thank God, she thinks.

The doorbell rings. It can't be him; he's busy pretending to get along with his wife.

She presses the intercom, listens. 'Oh, it's you,' she purrs.

A slash of lipstick while she hears feet on the stairs. Bigwig knows nothing about her afternoon boys. This one has a look of Vic.

They all do, come to think of it.

Octavia Gilpin is well named; she makes as much noise as eight children. She is everywhere all at once, and now she is marauding in the satin dimness of her mother's bedroom.

'Ow!' Wanda's eye mask is yanked off by small fingers, and catches in her hair.

'Let poor Mummy snooze.' Max, already dapper at dawn, hauls the girl off with his good arm. 'She had one too many grown-up lemonades last night.'

'Thank you, you angel,' murmurs Wanda.

Later she will make it up to Octavia, take her to their favourite spot – the Peter Pan statue in Kensington Gardens.

'Wish I could fly, Mummy,' the child always says.

If she could fly, Wanda would tuck her husband and their daughter under her wings and whizz to Ambridge. How the little Knightsbridge girl's eyes would widen at the glorified shed where Mummy spent four years of her life. She wants Octavia to smell the very specific smell of Doris's kitchen, and learn to wipe her bottom with a dock leaf.

Wanda may look just like the other women at the party the Gilpins threw last night, but there are stripes of Ambridge through her, like 'Brighton' through a stick of rock. She was not born in the village, but she was forged there.

And I found you there, she thinks, dozing off again to the gentle soundtrack of Max talking to – and listening to – his little girl.

Doris Archer is wise.

As wise as Mother Molly, with none of her dark undertones. Doris is fresh, like the sheets flapping on the line, and gentle, like the kitten Dan's holding up at the window. She is strong, too, and she is seasoned.

She knows better than to assume that everything will be fine and dandy in the coming year. And yet she has hope for Ambridge, and all its souls.

After all, she thinks, *I was wrong about the rain.*

ACKNOWLEDGEMENTS

Authors always thank their editors, and with good reason. Clare Hey held my hand throughout; I am grateful for her understanding and advice. I hope I've done justice to the memory of Clare's Uncle David, whose story was similar to that of Tudor Morgan, one of my favourite characters in this novel.

Also available for hand-holding, plus conversations about bovine disease, were the sainted BBC folk who bring us *The Archers* twice a day, Sunday to Friday. They protect and love the show, and gave generously of their time and expertise. So, thank you, Jeremy Howe, Sarah Swadling, Mel Ward and Hannah Ratcliffe. And, yes, Jeremy, I've named a tortoise after you in one of the chapters and there's nothing you can do about it.

Nursing a final draft through its metamorphosis requires skill, tact and patience. Luckily Judith Long has all these in abundance, and I'm grateful to her.

My agent, Charlotte Robinson, is the best agent in the world, and I will hear no arguments on that front.

Coincidentally, I also have the best daughter in the world; what are the odds? Thank you, Niamh Strachan, for letting me close the study door and get on with it, and also for winkling me out of the study for ice cream on a regular basis.

Thank you, always, to Sara-Jade Virtue, who stands in my peripheral vision at all times, a font of encouragement and a pusher of lychee martinis.

Thank you Janet Cosier – your cheerleading means so much – and thank you Kate Haldane, my wise and precious chum, and thank you Gwen Modder, for the giggles and the support.

Researching the big battles of the Second World War is straightforward. There are dates, data. Mining the internet for personal stories is more engrossing and rewarding. Discovering how so-called 'ordinary' people survived the intense practical and psychological pressures of war never failed to move me. I have borrowed some of their personal histories for this book.

Private Joe E Mann, mentioned in one of Alec Pargetter's letters home, was a real person and a real hero. He served in the United States army, Company H, 502nd Parachute Infantry regiment, 101st Airborne Division.

If you have the time, do look up the exploits of Cynthia Covello and Joyce Digney. Their giddy day out in London on VE Day inspired the frolics of Peggy Archer and Wanda Lafromboise within these pages. https://www.iwm.org.uk/history/who-were-the-women-in-the-trafalgar-square-fountains-on-ve-day

Finally, allow me to thank *you*. What is a writer without readers?

Catherine Miller
Kingston upon Thames
2023